BEST KEPT SECRETS

Also by Gwen Florio

The Nora Best mysteries

BEST LAID PLANS *

The Lola Wicks series

MONTANA
DAKOTA
DISGRACED
RESERVATUINS
UNDER THE SHADOWS

Novels

SILENT HEARTS

* *available from Severn House*

BEST KEPT SECRETS

Gwen Florio

First world edition published in Great Britain and the USA in 2021
by Severn House, an imprint of Canongate Books Ltd,
14 High Street, Edinburgh EH1 1TE.

Trade paperback edition first published in Great Britain and the USA in 2022
by Severn House, an imprint of Canongate Books Ltd.

severnhouse.com

British Library Cataloguing-in-Publication Data
A CIP catalogue record for this title is available from the British Library.

ISBN-13: 978-0-7278-9026-9 (cased)
ISBN-13: 978-1-78029-807-8 (trade paper)
ISBN-13: 978-1-4483-0545-2 (e-book)

All Severn House titles are printed on acid-free paper.

Typeset by Palimpsest Book Production Ltd.,
Falkirk, Stirlingshire, Scotland.
Printed and bound in Great Britain by
TJ Books, Padstow, Cornwall.

To my parents, Tony and Pat Florio, who – unusual in that time and place – raised us with a deep awareness of the corrosive effects of racism.

ONE

Nora Best is done running.

Almost.

She's put two thousand miles and change on the odometer in the last two and a half days, the numbers ticking along in a caffeinated blur, twelve hours and more on the road each day, the mountains of Wyoming long ago giving way to lonely rolling prairie, tamed in turn into the endless cultivated fields of the Midwest and, finally, the crowded and claustrophobic East, skyscrapers replacing grain elevators, Priuses outnumbering pickups.

Home, just ten miles ahead.

Because that's where she's going, to claim the great American privilege of starting over. Not in the way she'd thought just a few weeks earlier, tossing aside an unexpectedly broken marriage in an escape that initially felt freeing but almost ended in her own death. And not in the way, decades ago, she'd fled Chateau, the hometown to which she was now returning; that earlier trip a blend of teenage heartbreak and pique, a fuck-you cross-country move in a metamorphosis from lovestruck country girl to urban careerist.

All those determined redefinitions, and not a goddamned thing to show for it except for the truck she's driving and the Airstream trailer she hauls behind it. Heading into her latest transformation, one that given her age – fifty – she supposed would be termed a midlife crisis.

'Not a crisis.' She started talking to herself halfway through the endless second day, an attempt to stay awake through the monotony of miles. 'Opportunity.'

Until she'd blown up her life just a few weeks earlier, Nora had worked in public relations, paid well to put distracting hues of lipstick on various pigs, though never a boar quite as tusked and bristly as the last few weeks of her life. She'll spend a few days, maybe a couple of weeks, on this long-overdue visit with her mother and use the time for – what are they calling it now? Self-care. The physical wounds of her recent ordeal nearly healed, she'll tend to the wounds of the soul.

Take to bed, draw the curtains, shut down the phone and get a good night's sleep for the first time in ages. She lifts a hand from the wheel and knuckles her eyes.

It's going on eight o'clock, the August sun dipping a little lower each night as it releases a final blast of pulsating heat. Its dying light haloes the pale tassels topping the man-high cornstalks in the flat fields that flow past her truck, unspooling like a reel of her childhood, memory assailing her so hard and fast that for a brief moment she wonders at her decision to return, moving backward instead of forward.

The soaring grandeur of the Chesapeake Bay Bridge briefly revives her, sailboats bobbing cheerfully on the startling blue of the bay, marshland stretching golden in the foreground, a watery counterpoint to the prairies she'd left behind. But the monotonous straightaway of Route 50 nearly undoes her. She reaches for her Thermos, only to find it empty but for a single swallow of coffee gone cold and ineffective. Sleep tugs at her eyelids, teasing them down, down . . .

'Christ!'

Nora jerks at the wheel, the three-and-a-half-ton Airstream swaying dangerously with her involuntary swerve at the blast of a horn. A kid in a Kia, music vibrating so loud she can hear it through her rolled-tight windows, cuts so close in front of her their bumpers nearly kiss.

She catches a glimpse of his face, the apologetic smile and the shrug, and he's gone, leaving her heart skittering and bumping in her chest, sweat-slick hands slipping on the wheel as she wrestles pickup and trailer back into her lane, the Kia disappearing around a curve, its driver seemingly even more in a hurry than she is.

Then, a sight that makes her nearly forget the Kia. Nora blinks, and blinks again, sure her eyes deceive her. As she pulls off the bypass skirting Chateau, a coffee kiosk appears, enticing as a church promising salvation to a sinner. A sign says *Open*, in warm, welcoming letters. A red fox darts across the road, so quickly that Nora's foot barely has time to tap the brake before it's gone. She looks longingly toward the kiosk. But the encounter with the Kia and the surprise of the fox have jolted her into wakefulness, just enough adrenaline for these last few miles.

She draws a breath. Her heart resumes its metronome lub-dub, her hands stop shaking. She'd driven the pickup-and-trailer combo for the first time only a month earlier, steering it in a rage away from a marriage in ruins. But now, despite the assholes who seemed to regard Baltimore's Beltway as the sole province of harried commuters and *would she please get the hell out of their way*, she's confident of her ability to maneuver it on to the narrow back road that will take her to Quail House, where her mother will be waiting up to reassure herself that her daughter, despite the disasters that have befallen her, is truly alive and well.

'Just a few more minutes,' Nora reminds herself. She's got this.

Lights flash – not the reassuring red blink of a driver slowing for a potentially suicidal roadside deer but the red and blue spelling trouble for someone who, for a change, isn't her. She slows to steer around the poor sucker who got caught in the speed trap that has existed outside Chateau since speed limits were invented.

Nora slows nearly to a crawl, edging truck and trailer a little over the center line – no oncoming traffic at this hour – and sees it in slow motion: the blue-and-white cop car with the annoying lights, a green Kia idling in front of it and, sure enough, that same kid at the wheel, shaking his head in response to something the cop has asked.

Nora checks the road ahead – still nobody – swings truck and trailer wide and drives on past, mouthing 'Karma's a bitch' at the kid. The music still blasts its driving beat, her own head inadvertently bobbing along, shoulders shimmying. A rueful laugh escapes. When's the last time she danced?

TWO

Nora rolled the window down, thinking to revive herself with fresh air. And laughed.

She'd been so long in the West – two decades in Denver when she'd thought herself happy, the brief time in Wyoming after she'd realized she wasn't – that she'd forgotten about East Coast heat and humidity. She touched a hand to her forehead, confirming the dampness there. Sweat? Or just a layer of steamy air, clinging to her skin like plastic wrap?

Something bumped against her – something else she'd forgotten about. By the time she'd ineffectually slapped her hand to her neck, it had helped itself to a chunk of her flesh and buzzed safely away, leaving a wound that would swell red and lumpy by morning. A greenhead fly, the bane of her childhood, the insect version of a vampire, except that there were more of them – by a factor of millions – and they attacked in daylight and were harder to kill. Old farmers told tales of plow horses being driven mad by their relentless assault; watermen, of jumping overboard to escape the scissoring bites.

She raised the window against more intruders, shutting out the skunky aroma that rode the air. She was well past town now, the cornfields giving way to marshland that crept a little closer to the road every year, a warning that human intrusion would ultimately prove temporary. The scent let her know it was low tide, black mud exposed and glistening, miasma nearly visible in the gloaming.

Just as the window closed, she caught a clean, sharp whiff of the Lenape River, flowing through the marsh, spreading out, relaxing in its final miles before its fresh water was vanquished by the salt of the Chesapeake.

Nora turned truck and trailer on to a winding lane lined by leaning cedars, falling away only at the last minute to reveal the rambling brick farmhouse, the river beyond, gone pewter in the sun's last light. A sign announced Quail House, built in 1720 by Thomas Smythe off the proceeds of market hunting and in the same family ever since, named for the bobwhites whose two- and three-note calls arose from the surrounding fields every fall. Chateau had gone crazy with historical markers in recent years, and the house she'd grown up in, even though it was on nobody's idea of a beaten path, was no exception.

Quail House was one of the earliest of the grand old homes that staked out the prime riverbank land. Its owner was one of the few who turned his back on the loamy earth that enriched his neighbors, who planted tobacco and later corn and soybeans, and instead turned to the river and the bay beyond, making his fortune from shooting geese from the sky by the thousands, and pulling rockfish and blue crabs from the bay. Generations of black women trooped into the series of Quonset huts at one end of town, where they sat at long metal tables extracting sweet meat from the crab shells and packing it into tins stamped with the colonial-style lettering of Smythe's Best Backfin Crab.

The house was miles from the grubby reminders of what funded it, a stairstep brick edifice added on as the Smythe fortune increased, anchored by the original single-story, two-room house at one end that contained the kitchen, with a two-story addition in the middle and a final, three-story ell that held the sitting rooms and library necessary to people of consequence.

On either side, mossy brick paths wandered among tall boxwood hedges shaded by spreading oaks, while, to the rear, a clipped green lawn ran down to the river, where a rowboat clunked gently against a dock.

The first time Nora brought Joe, the husband she'd met in Colorado, home for a visit, he'd turned to her in awe. 'You just said the house you grew up in was old.'

'Because it is.'

'You never told me it was a mansion.'

She'd never thought of it that way. It was just home, its quixotic arrangement of rooms providing the sorts of corners and cubbyholes that sheltered a solitary child. The river was her personal playground, and on midsummer days when the sun ricocheted off the water in a punishing glare, she tied the rowboat up at the dock and sought shade in the neighbors' cornfields, running barefoot between the tall rows of rustling stalks, searching for the chipped flint arrowheads left by the land's earliest inhabitants.

The dying light coppered the tall windows of Quail House, its chimneys silhouetted black against a fiery sky. Her mother stood on the stoop, a hand raised in eager greeting. Michael Murphy, the Chesapeake Bay retriever long retired from his hunting days, slanted down the steps on legs stiff as stilts. Nora cut the engine and climbed from the truck on knees nearly as creaky as the dog's from too many days on the road. He jammed his graying muzzle against her thigh, tail lashing the air in furious delight.

She bent to wrap her arms around him, clutching the dog the way she wanted, childlike, to cling to her mother. 'Murph, you old man. You must be nearly a hundred.'

She rubbed her face dry against the dog's kinked fur and straightened. Her mother remained on the stoop, one hand braced against the wall behind her for balance, the other clutching a silvery metal walker, a heavy black boot encompassing her leg. Nora forgot her own need.

'Mother! What happened?'

Penelope looked past her. 'So this is the famous Electra.'

In the innocence of anticipated adventure, Nora had named the trailer Electra after Amelia Earhart's airplane and paid for a decal of the Lockheed Electra on its side. More than one person had reminded her of Earhart's fate – comments that had come back to haunt her during her own travails. But now her mother was the one with the problem.

She tried again. 'What happened?'

Sound drowned out Penelope Best's response. She, Nora and the dog turned as one toward the rising whine. Nora first took it for the mosquitoes that arose in great clouds from the marsh at dawn and dusk, bookending the daytime misery inflicted by the greenheads. But it grew in intensity and volume, finally resolving as the wail of sirens.

Kids came down to the river this time of year, congregating beside its inlets, building bonfires, drinking beer and smoking weed, just as Nora herself had done decades ago. Sometimes the fires got away from them, leaping to the marsh grass and racing merrily through it. She scanned the sky for smoke as she helped her mother into the house. Saw none. Shrugged.

She closed the door against the wail that went on and on into the night.

They sat in the kitchen, the oldest part of Quail House, its white-washed brick walls three feet thick keeping the heat at bay, the room cool even without the air conditioning that Nora's mother refused to install.

A six-foot-wide fireplace stretched across one wall, once the room's sole source of heat, its shining brass andirons these days purely decorative; the chimney capped with tin against the incursion of winter's rainy downdrafts, spring's nesting birds and summer's voracious insects. A handyman replaced the chimney caps every few years, carefully tightening shiny new sheets around the bricks and removing ragged squares pockmarked with the physical evidence of the flickers' futile yet relentless assault, the early-morning machine-gun burst of their beaks against it serving as Nora's alarm clock as long as she could remember.

Copper pots hung from ceiling hooks. Pewter plates, flanked by candlesticks, stood along the mantel. A long table, scarred from two centuries and more of use, vied with the fireplace for domination of the room.

'Can you imagine,' Penelope often asked, running her fingers over the gouges in the wood, their rough edges long ago sanded smooth and nearly filled with layers of furniture wax assiduously applied over the decades, 'what it meant to turn this old table that they made by hand over to the kitchen help? To replace it with one shipped from Europe? How much that must have cost, how long they must have waited?'

The good table sat largely unused in the dining room, its reddish cherry surface dusted and polished weekly, its slender curved legs balanced on an Aubusson rug whose fringes brushed the baseboards, awaiting the events – holidays, luncheons – that demanded the formality highlighted by Penelope's oft-repeated recitation of Quail House's original wonders. 'Real glass in the windows instead of oiled parchment! Silver instead of everyday pewter!'

A tea service gleamed from a sideboard, its teapot and the taller coffeepot arrogant as dancers, one arm akimbo, the other curving high and graceful. Unlike the dining-room table, Penelope used it on occasions both special and everyday, smiling in satisfaction as she tilted the teapot over Spode cups, proclaiming as though it weren't obvious, 'I like pretty things. Just like those early Smythes who built this place.' Her tinkling laugh echoed in the clink of spoon against china.

And the room, indeed the whole house, *was* pretty, albeit in a chilly, formal way, as though preserved in some sort of colonial amber.

Can you imagine, teenage Nora often thought rebelliously, *the work it took to keep this house so pretty? To polish the silver by candlelight after a day of hauling water from a well, chopping wood for the fire, hoisting heavy rugs over a cord and whacking at them with woven rattan beaters until one's arms went rubbery? Chasing a squawking chicken across the yard, grabbing its scaly legs, twirling it once, twice to leave it too limp and dazed to flap away from the descending ax? To plunge one's hands into the still-warm cavity and claw out the steaming guts, sink on to a bench for the brief respite afforded by plucking, feathers sticking to fingers slick with blood? Not so pretty now.*

Still, Penelope's vision was compelling, and in her more charitable moments, Nora indulged her mother's evocation of a woman in a long dress and ruched bonnet gliding into the room in predawn darkness, striking a flint against the kindling laid the night before, hanging a cast-iron pot from the hook that extended over the flaring sticks and stirring its contents with a long-handled spoon. Over the years, Nora had imagined this ghostly occupant as one of the unsmiling ancestors whose portraits hung in dark hallways, filmed with dust despite Penelope's weekly circuits with a feathered brush, staring disdainfully down imperiously arched noses – which, unfortunately, she'd inherited.

A fond smile played across Penelope's face as she watched Nora's survey of the room that had remained unchanged for decades, but for the occasional replacement of appliances hiding behind colonial-style cabinetry painted a slate blue.

'Good to be home?'

'So good.' Nora sank on to one of the Shaker chairs surrounding the table, mentally shedding the burdens of the past few weeks, the collapse of her marriage, her husband's subsequent murder and her own near-death at the hands of the people who'd killed him, not to mention the perilous days that had nearly seen her charged with homicide and earned her national notoriety.

'I'll make us some tea.' Penelope's response to every occasion, willfully oblivious to the fact that most of her friends and especially her daughter were committed coffee-holics.

Nora jumped up. 'Let me. You shouldn't be moving around.' She gestured to the booted contraption that went nearly to her mother's knee. 'Why didn't you tell me?'

She knew, even before the answer came in a voice nearly as insubstantial as the steam wafting from the pot Penelope must have put on the stove as soon as she heard Nora's approach. Her mother hadn't wanted to bother her.

'A hairline ankle fracture. I was carrying laundry downstairs and – you won't believe this – a mouse ran right across my foot. I tumbled the rest of the way down. I suppose I'm lucky it wasn't worse.'

'A mouse!'

'Sometimes they come in from the fields.'

Nora stepped away from the stove to hear. She'd always suspected her mother's voice was a trick, a way to make everyone around pay close attention for fear of missing something. It wasn't just the hushed tones, but the urgency with which Penelope Best infused every sentence, as though even an innocuous account of a clumsy slip and fall bore a thrilling secret. She opened her green eyes wide as she spoke, a smile hovering on her lips, and when she finished, it was as though her listener had been given a gift, although later, out of her presence, a question nagged: Of what, exactly?

Penelope – never Penny – waved a hand, a broken bone regally dismissed. And yet the boot, the walker standing ominous in a corner. 'Truly, it's nothing. Not compared to what you've been through.'

Nora had fled the searingly public wreckage of her marriage, only to run straight into the clutches of a kidnapper. The stab wound he'd inflicted upon her, the deep scrapes and a Rorschach array of bruises she'd suffered in her escape, counted as good fortune, given his ultimate lethal intent.

'But how are you managing? Can you drive? Of course not.' Nora deflected her mother's comment with her own question. The boot enclosed her mother's right leg from knee to toes. Impossible to press an accelerator with that contraption.

Penelope surprised her with a small, transgressive smile. 'I'm not supposed to. But I can. I take the boot off once I'm in the car.'

'But if you had to brake suddenly . . .'

Penelope nodded. 'Inadvisable, according to the doctor. Anyway, Miss Grace comes by on occasion.'

Another wash of memory, so strong the teacup rattled in its saucer as Nora set it before her mother. The casual courtesies of the South, Maryland the northernmost state on the wrong side (depending on which side you were on) of the Mason–Dixon Line, infused with attitudes and traditions in equal parts charming and lethal.

People were Mister or Miss First Name, and although a married woman still proudly adopted the title of Mrs along with her husband's last name, in direct conversation she remained Miss So-and-So, morphing into ma'am as she aged. Or, for men, sir.

Unless the person in question was black and the speaker was white. Then it was first name only, except in Penelope Best's house, where the honorific applied to all concerned. Nora had never known otherwise until a friend's mother had pulled her aside and quietly imparted a message underscored by centuries of this-is-the-way-things-are: 'You don't ma'am the help.'

'Miss Grace? She's still alive?' She'd been old when Nora was young.

'Of course she is, dear. We're very nearly contemporaries. She was only a few years older than me when she came to work for my parents.'

THREE

1963

In point of fact, Grace was a gangly thing of eighteen, three years older than Penelope, just out of high school and needing a job, preferably not one in the cannery where her own mother sat for ten hours a day running a rubber-gloved fingernail under the crown in a blue crab's shell, snapping the carapace up and away, peeling off the gray rubbery lungs – aptly nicknamed Dead Man's Fingers – and flinging them aside before digging deep to prize free the sweet meat within; and finally, a single swift blow with a wooden mallet to crack each hooked claw and extract its treasure in an unbroken chunk. Work that left Davita Evans's hands swollen and crosshatched with a thousand tiny cuts, perennially sore despite her daughter's dutiful nightly massage with the clear, gelid applications of Corn Huskers Lotion.

'Spoiled girl,' she said, when her daughter showed her the ad under the Domestic Work heading in the *Chateau Crier* classifieds. 'Thought you were all about that Black Power business, and now you want to go work for white people.'

Grace did not want to work for white people, especially not now, with change gusting through the country, the occasional breeze stirring even in Chateau, where segregation had reigned long after its legal end. Grace had just graduated from the Smythe Grove school, which remained all black because, as Chateau's town fathers explained to the federal education types who persisted in sniffing around, schools in Chateau served neighborhoods, and Smythe Grove was in a black neighborhood. Never mind that the black kids who rode buses from the district's rural reaches could just as easily have been dropped off at the white school.

Grace had paid close attention to the actions in other towns – the sit-ins, the demonstrations and even riots – and had heard rumblings of groups from those cities planning to stage similar events in Chateau. When they came, she planned to make herself useful, so useful that maybe she could enlist their help in getting her out of Chateau and into someplace better, a plan she had no intention of sharing with her mother.

The ad she showed her mother wasn't just for work in any white person's house, not even just any rich white person's house. It was the home of Chateau's Police Chief, and the more she could learn about him and how he operated, the better.

Her mother sniffed and rubbed her oversize knuckles. 'Go on, then. Apply. But they won't take you. They'll want some big-legged mammy-looking woman.'

Davita Evans knew the denizens of Quail House, of course. Everyone in town knew who the Smythes were. But she didn't know Philippa Smythe personally, didn't know she had the same love of elegance and pretty things that she passed on to her daughter. And so when Philippa beheld the tall, slender young woman on the back steps – Grace knew better than to knock at the front door – in her starched shirtwaist, her snowy white cotton socks edged with lace and matching white gloves, she clapped her hands in delight. 'Oh, aren't you just perfect!'

She led Grace into the kitchen and seated her at the table, offering her a cup of tea – although it arrived in a heavy crockery mug, not the delicate, near-translucent china cup rimmed in gold from which Philippa herself sipped. Belatedly remembering why Grace was there, Philippa asked, 'But do you know how to clean?'

A snort sounded in an adjoining room. Grace cut her eyes sideways and saw a teenage girl lounging on a flowered loveseat, auburn hair pulled back into a messy ponytail as she bent over a bare foot, applying nail polish to her toenails with minute brushstrokes, the sharp scent cutting through the aroma of whatever was baking in the oven. She wore pale-green babydoll pajamas, even though it was nearly noon. And Davita thought Grace was spoiled.

Grace wondered why this family was advertising for household help when they clearly had a child at home more than capable of performing routine chores, as Grace herself had done as long as she could remember.

Grace assured Philippa she was equal to the tasks that Philippa outlined, cleaning the floors and dusting, wiping down the bathrooms daily with a deep-clean once a week, polishing the silver . . .

'I don't polish silver.' The words were in the air before Grace could stop them. They hung there, nearly visible, shimmering with resentment. Her hand rose as though to snatch them back.

Her mother had been consigned to a lifetime of work in the crab processing plant after her job in Johanna Hampton's house came to an end when Mrs Hampton accused her of boosting a Gorham teaspoon, its floral Versailles pattern making polishing a nightmare, the tarnish sinking deep into the grooves and whorls.

Davita had been offended on multiple levels, the outrage to her integrity first and foremost, but her intelligence insulted as well. 'If I was gonna take anything, it wouldn't be a damn pain-in-the-ass piece like that Versailles. Useless.' Before the Hamptons, she'd worked for the Eberlines, who'd left Chateau for Washington when he got a wartime job in the Office of Civilian Defense, and Mrs Eberline had used Reed and Barton's Hepplewhite, elegant in its simplicity and polished to a blinding gleam in half the time.

'Ma'am,' Grace added, far too late. She'd seen the change flash across Philippa Smythe's face. She dropped her hand to her lap, lowered her eyes and awaited her dismissal. Her head snapped up at Philippa's chiming laugh.

'I suppose Penelope is capable of doing the silver,' and Grace chanced a glance, catching the look of pure hatred shot her way from the girl in the next room. Penelope's hands were in the air in front of her, the nail polish drying, all her fingers but the middle one curled inward.

'I don't imagine you do windows, either.'

'Oh, no, ma'am, I'll wash your windows,' Grace hurried to reassure Philippa. Did she still have a chance?

Philippa shook her head and bit her lip. 'No. They're so tall. We might need to find someone to help with those. Carry the ladders and such. We had a boy who used to do the heavier work – cut the grass, things like that – but he left along with his wife; up and moved to Philadelphia. Which is why we're looking for household help now. Philadelphia! Can you imagine?'

Grace could imagine, oh, yes, she could, because if she were in Philly, no way would she be working for some skinny-ass white woman and her lazy-ass daughter, but she twisted the cloth of her skirt tight between her palms, wrinkling it unattractively, and forcing herself to say to Philippa Smythe in her mildest, most flattened tone, 'Maybe my brother could help. He's a little younger than I am, just sixteen. But he's strong. He plays football.' Her chin lifted and a smile lit her face before she remembered herself. She lowered her eyes. Rounded her shoulders in submission. 'Ma'am.'

Which was how Bobby Evans came to work at Quail House.

FOUR

Nora Best loved her mother fiercely, and so was inclined to overlook Penelope's unapologetic snobbery, the way she clung to long-outdated notions of femininity and propriety, an insistence upon closed-toe pumps and sheer hose even on summer's sultriest days, her refusal to acknowledge anything deemed unpleasant, but the one thing she could not excuse was Penelope's belief in the superiority of tea.

Which meant that there was likely no coffee to be had in Quail House unless one counted whatever was left in a folded-over brown paper bag tucked in the back of the freezer. Or, worse yet, the crusted remains in the bottom of a canister of instant on a pantry shelf with other little-used items – the tins of sardines, envelopes of fossilized bouillon, jars of olives floating in oil gone cloudy, and Maraschino cherries, their neon-red hue distracting attention from the long-gone expiration date stamped into the jar's metal lid.

If she was going to spend any amount of time in Quail House, she needed the good stuff and she needed it fast.

'I'll probably do some work on the book later at the library,' she told her mother on her first morning home, ostentatiously packing her laptop and a file folder into a bookbag, counting on the fact that Penelope wouldn't realize she could just as easily look up what she needed while googling like mad at the kitchen table. 'Do you need anything in town? I thought I'd bring us home one of those rotisserie chickens. We can eat it cold with a salad on the side. It's too hot to cook.'

Penelope turned wide pleading eyes upon her.

'Nora, do you have to write that book? What good does it do to air all of that unpleasantness?' It wasn't the first time she'd asked.

'I'll tell you what good it does.' Nora pushed her hair away from a forehead already moist, even within the relative cool of Quail House. 'If I don't write it, I have to pay back my advance, which is all I've got to live on for the foreseeable future. If I'm lucky, I'll make a little extra on it once it's published. Not like that first book.'

'Oh!' Penelope's hands flew to her cheeks. 'Don't remind me. I couldn't leave the house for weeks after that one.'

Nora's first book, *Do It Daily*, a treatise on the benefits of sex nearly every day for a whole year, hadn't sold as well as expected, probably because she'd made the mistake of placing it within the context of monogamy, a variation on the old how-to-keep-your-marriage-hot theme. 'In hindsight, a tactical error,' Lilith, her agent, had grumbled. 'If you'd written about sex with a different person every day, we both could have retired on the proceeds.'

'Having sex with a different person every day sounds just as awful as having sex with the same person day after day,' Nora had pointed out, alluding to the problem she herself had had with carrying out the book's recommendations – an issue not discovered until she'd already signed the contract.

'But it would have been controversial. Wonderfully scandalous. The religious right would have had a cow. You can't buy publicity like that.'

An observation Lilith trotted out again after Nora's near-demise in the mountains, which she'd persuaded Nora should be the focus of her next book – a substitute for the cross-country travelogue in the Airstream that been her original topic.

'Sex and death,' Lilith said with satisfaction. 'The two eternal subjects. But you've got to turn this one around fast, before everybody forgets about you.'

Which, frankly, Nora wished everyone would do, almost as fervently as Penelope wished it.

Penelope sighed theatrically, lifted her cheek for a kiss and said that if Nora was going to stop at the store on the way home anyway, she might as well pick up some buttermilk.

'I can make us some biscuits for breakfast tomorrow morning before it gets too hot. You'd like that, wouldn't you?'

Nora allowed that she'd like that very much and made her escape.

Nora remembered the coffee kiosk she'd passed the night before and gave the truck a little gas. It had been open late into the evening. She hoped its morning hours were correspondingly early. But when she pulled close, she saw that it was shuttered, its drive-through lane empty. She continued on into town, telling herself that convenience-store coffee was better than no coffee at all, her craving so strong her hands were beginning to shake.

The road from Quail House led into Chateau from the poor side of town, although no one would so openly call it that. For starters, its appearance spoke for itself, the narrow frame houses set so close in their dirt yards that if their occupants chose to extend their arms from the side windows, they could pass neighborly cups of coffee between them. Paint dangled in faded curls from the clapboard. Porches sagged. Screen doors flapped an arrhythmic backbeat in the hot, desultory breeze.

No railroad ran through Chateau, but if it had, this would be the other side of the tracks. Commerce Street formed the dividing line, businesses shielding the tidy middle-class homes to the north, while the homes of the poor crowded to the curb of the busy street's south side, much to the chagrin of town fathers who in public spoke in vague and hopeful terms of beautification, while in private they decried the eyesores in Jimtown, as Chateau's black neighborhood had been known before such terms became politically incorrect.

Commerce Street divided white from black as surely as a wall, the races mingling by day in schools and workplaces and retreating to their own neighborhoods at night, and woe betide the real estate agent who tried to sell a house in one side of town to someone from the other. As Penelope might have said, *it just wasn't done.*

Little in that regard appeared to have changed during the decades of Nora's absence, although the years she'd been gone had brought differences aplenty to the center of town. New shops proliferated, clearly aimed at the tourists taking detours to and from the beaches of Maryland and Delaware, as well as the old standbys from her childhood. Hard by the gift-shop windows displaying the region's waterfowl winging their way across T-shirts, mugs and kitchen towels were outdoors stores already showing stacks of decoys designed to lure those same waterfowl to legions of hunters who in a few short weeks would flock to the area as surely as the migrating geese.

Betty's Beauty Parlor now styled itself a salon, with a new name, Waves, in allusion to the beaches not an hour away. Nora wondered what had happened to Betty. Then forgot all about her when, like a mirage, a sign rose before her eyes, a single word – *espresso* – promising the only thing she demanded of life at this moment.

She pulled the truck to the curb and jogged up the sidewalk, trying to temper her expectations. Chateau was still a small town. She feared espresso of the variety that spewed from the automated machines in convenience stores. But once inside, she contemplated her choice with hopeful surprise. Lattes, cortados, shots in the dark. Whole milk, two percent, skim. Soy, oat, coconut. Options long grown familiar in Denver, but astonishing here in Chateau where, throughout her childhood, coffee – offered at friends' houses, never her own – meant a cup of Nescafé pale with powdered creamer and sludgy with sugar.

Inside, the shop was nearly full, and a line waited at the counter, another reason for optimism. The man in front of her turned to inspect the offerings in a pastry case. Something about him – the slightly stooped stance of a tall man who'd spent his life trying to fit himself to those around him, the nose whose bump and sideways swerve bore testimony to an old break – seemed familiar.

As if sensing her gaze, he turned and caught her eye. His brow wrinkled and she saw him making the same calculation she'd just made. She took a guess.

'Em?'

'Nora?'

A grin cracked his face. They'd been high school classmates, where they'd always hovered on the edges of each other's orbit. Emerson Crothers played basketball – given his height of six feet and three inches, he'd had no choice – and Nora had been a clarinetist in the band, so they'd ridden the same yellow school buses to games and tournaments. Afterward, there'd been parties at the Beach, the grand name given to a patch of sandy earth along the river where in the spring of their senior year they'd found themselves seated together on a piece of driftwood and, during a beery conversation about something that had seemed profound at the time – whatever had it been? – he'd tried to kiss her. She'd ducked away and they'd spent the brief remainder of their time in high school avoiding one another.

He placed his order – black coffee and a slice of Smith Island cake – and asked the cashier to put Nora's oat milk latte on his bill.

They stepped aside to await their orders and went through the obligatory it's-been-years and how-have-you-been conversation.

'What are you doing these days, Em?' She figured he'd been teaching somewhere, a few classes to justify a full-time salary in exchange for coaching a team a few months a year. She had a vague recollection of hearing something to that effect, probably from her mother.

He laughed. 'Brace yourself. Real estate.'

'You're kidding. Here?' Chateau had always been considered a backwater when they were growing up, so much so that kids from larger schools made fun of them at games: 'Hey, farmer. Where's your overalls? Be sure and scrape the cowshit off your sneakers before you set foot on the floor.'

'I still can't believe it myself. I quit teaching years ago. People from Washington are snapping up places here like mad. Call something a country estate, and they can't throw money at me fast enough. You ever want to sell Quail House, you'll be set for life. People ask me about it all the time. It's the best place on the river.'

Sell Quail House? Unthinkable. Although she'd never given much thought to what would happen to it when Penelope died.

'Not a chance. Penelope wouldn't hear of it.'

He gave her a funny look. 'She hasn't . . .?' He stopped. 'Never mind.'

'Besides,' she said, when he didn't explain further. 'It's got mice.'

'They all do,' he said. 'Along with basements that flood whenever it rains, no closets whatsoever, and plumbing that's like something out of the Dark Ages. But the people who buy them can swan around like lord and lady of the manor. They only live in them a few months out of the year anyway.' Their coffee arrived. Em's was in a paper to-go cup, while the towering slice of cake, its ten thin layers of yellow cake and chocolate icing too tall for a standard container, balanced on a paper plate within a covering of cling wrap. 'Gotta run. I've got five showings today. This' – he nodded at the cake – 'should give me enough of a sugar fix to power me through. Good seeing you. How long are you staying?'

'Not sure yet.'

'Hope to see you around.'

She knew the local paper had run the wire stories about what had happened in Wyoming – 'Chateau native in lurid kidnapping, murder case' – but he hadn't asked about it, a bit of tact that left her weak with gratitude.

She took her latte, regarding it with suspicion. The barista was, after all, closer to her own age than the hipsters she was used to, in their T-shirts sporting the names of bands she'd never heard of, and their full-sleeve tattoos in tropical colors. This woman wore a Peter Pan blouse printed with small sprigged flowers and lemon-yellow shorts that went to her knees. Nora tugged at the hem of her own Lycra shorts. She was proud of her thighs, lithe and corded from years of running, and in Denver – where physical fitness was practically mandated – people wandered in and out of stores and restaurants in athletic gear without a second thought. But she was starkly underdressed compared to nearly everyone else in the shop.

Still, the latte, when she steeled herself for a sip, was just right, the caffeine hitting her veins with a welcome jolt after twenty-four hours' deprivation. She drained it embarrassingly quickly and went back for another, selecting as well a bag of ground beans, a plastic cone and filters thoughtfully stocked on a shelf beside Italian espresso machines that Nora could not imagine, no matter how hard she tried, in a single house in Chateau.

'Nora Best!'

Nora's heart slammed so hard against her ribs she put her hand to her chest, as though to contain a panicked bird fluttering to escape the bars of its cage. She'd been listening for that voice from the moment she'd driven into Chateau, the town so small, everybody congregating in the same places.

She'd figured the diner. The supermarket. Maybe even the hardware store. But the coffee shop was unfamiliar territory and she'd let her guard down, so when she turned, she wasn't quite prepared, her smile still a little shaky, her gaze roaming hither and yon until she forced herself to look Alden Tydings directly in the eye.

* * *

Of course, she knew he still lived in Chateau; that and much more.

Who didn't cyberstalk their first love?

He'd married that simpering twit Kyra Dexter, and the fact that Kyra stood beside him now, her hand possessively on his arm, did much to shore up Nora's composure.

'Hey, Nora Best.'

'Hey, yourself, Kyra Dexter.'

'It's Kyra Tydings now.' Show of teeth.

Oh, for Chrissakes. As if she didn't know. But Kyra wasn't done, smiling even more broadly as she rattled on.

'It's been Kyra Tydings for – oh, honey, how many years has it been? Twenty-five and change? It seems like yesterday.'

Yesterday apparently a reference to the year she swooped in and scooped up Alden in what seemed like moments after Nora's tearful departure for college, leaving Alden behind to work his family farm with an understanding they'd marry the day after her graduation.

The iPad on the counter beeped. Nora swiped her card, wishing she'd ordered her coffee to go. The barista frothed the milk, the machine's shriek giving her a precious few moments to collect herself and pose the usual haven't-seen-you-in-forever questions. 'How have you been? And your kids? They must be nearly grown by now. What are you both doing these days?'

She already knew those answers, too. Kyra was one of those aggressive stay-at-home moms, posting photo after photo of herself at soccer games or birthday parties with their three daughters, the one they'd had in the first year of marriage and, years later, twins. In each photo, Kyra's smile testified both to expensive orthodontia and the excellence of her choices in life. Now, flush with recently acquired insight, Nora noted the clenched jaw and narrowed gaze of dissatisfaction and wondered if that's how she herself had looked the last few years with Joe, subtly broadcasting her unhappiness to the world before she'd even admitted it to herself.

Compared to his wife, Alden's presence on social media was rare unto vanishing. But Nora knew that, like every other area farmer, he'd taken a town job – in this case, on the police force – something that had allowed him to keep the farm going. But the farm, in his family for nearly two centuries, apparently remained his first priority. His own photos showed him perched high in the air-conditioned cab of a futuristic vehicle that bore zero resemblance to the tractor a third its size, where teenage Nora had bounced on his lap as he'd driven her up and down the rows, teaching her to steer in a precursor to driving a car. Teaching her other things, too. She remembered the way she'd traced the vee on his bare chest, where skin browned by the sun in those hours in the fields met the white that had been covered by his shirt, oddly erotic when revealed, then had let her fingers trail lower . . .

'Oat milk latte for Nora!'

Saved by a latte. Nora reached for her coffee with relief, buying time by thanking the barista, who barely looked at Nora but stared at Kyra with a stricken expression.

'Oh, Kyra,' she said.

Kyra's lips thinned in a grimace that maybe, viewed with a determined squint, could have been called a smile, though far short of the wattage she'd determinedly aimed at Nora.

'Sandy, you and Nora remember each other, don't you? Sandy was a couple of years behind us.'

Nora had no memory of Sandy. And she'd never have pegged her as younger. Maybe it was the demure clothing, or the blank defensive curtain of her expression. Whatever Sandy had expected of life these decades after graduation, it hadn't included working a part-time, minimum-wage job in a coffee shop, every day serving her more successful schoolmates.

Now, though, her expression sharpened. 'Of course I remember you.' The avid light in her eyes told Nora the memory was recent. Sandy might not have remembered brushing past Nora in the halls of Chateau High, but for sure she'd seen the more recent stories, heard the talk.

Her husband, shot dead. Probably wishes she'd been the one who did it. And that business with the ax! Fingers flying through texts, voices lowered to whispers, savoring the piquancy of scandal.

'Nice to see you again, Sandy. You make a mean latte.' Nora took it and turned away, pointedly eyeing a counter across the room. Several of the seats were occupied by people working on their laptops – that dynamic, too, had caught up with Chateau – although nearly all of them had, in the way of small-town eateries and watering holes everywhere, abandoned the tasks at hand and turned to see the most recent arrivals. A single seat remained among a row of stools at a high counter. 'I'm just going to grab that,' she began, edging toward it.

But Alden and Kyra followed, hovering as she settled herself. Nora launched a new series of questions, hoping to forestall their own. 'Tell me about your kids. The younger ones must be in high school now. Please tell me Mrs Prince isn't still teaching home ec. That woman terrorized me with her white sauce. Mine always had lumps.'

'Oh, it's not home ec anymore. It's domestic arts, and even the boys have to take it.' Kyra, the authority on all things on the home and school front, took charge, exactly as Nora had hoped, although her eyes retained that strained look, as though focused on some separate, inner dialogue.

Nora sipped her latte, studying Alden over the rim of the bowl-size cup. He'd aged well, lean in jeans and a T-shirt conspicuously unadorned with brand name or any other message. Just a plain blue shirt, a color she'd always loved on him because it was the shade of his eyes. When she'd told him that, he'd started wearing blue more often, and she fought the crazy notion that he'd donned the shirt on this morning because he'd heard she was back in town and might run into her. His hair was shorter than when they'd been in high school, wavy dark strands shot through with gray, but still long enough to run her fingers through it, clutch it and pull him to her . . .

'Are you all right?' Alden made as though to pound her on the back as Nora choked on her latte.

She leaned away from the gesture. 'Fine. Just swallowed wrong. So, the girls are about to graduate?'

Kyra's eyes went big with overdone sympathy. 'You never had kids? I'm so sorry.' The light was back in her eyes now, an unsettling gleam, as though she'd put aside whatever thoughts had been distracting her and had squared herself to renew a battle against a foe she'd long ago vanquished.

Nora set down her coffee cup. It clattered against the saucer. Bullies came in all forms, she reminded herself, even lip-glossed and hair-sprayed, and the only way to deal with them was to push back, hard.

'I'm not sorry. I suppose I think of my books as my children.' Nora nearly gagged on the cliché, but subtlety had never been the way to go with Kyra. 'I'm working on my second one now.

The first sold so well they wanted more of the same.' Which wasn't even close to true, but two could play the stealth snark game, and Nora enjoyed the change in Kyra's face as she remembered the title of that first book and its subject matter. Kyra didn't know that after the first few weeks, daily sex had been anything but enjoyable, and neither did any of Nora's friends back in Denver, who'd kept a much closer eye on their husbands whenever she was around, not realizing that after that exhausting year, sex was the last thing on Nora's mind.

But with Alden, she'd never gotten tired of it. They'd been each other's first and now, watching the play of emotion across Kyra's face, Nora knew she knew it.

So Nora wondered at her drawn expression, the circles under her eyes. Still, Kyra may have dealt with her unwashed hair by pulling it back into a ponytail, but highlights hid any gray, and the arm she raised to brush a stray strand away from her face had more than a passing acquaintance with free weights. Kyra looked, Nora thought, as she herself had not a month earlier, before the events in Wyoming. Now Nora's gray roots showed more prominent by the day, and her muscles felt rubbery after weeks out of their routine. She would, she vowed, go for a run as soon as she got home. Then, looking at the windows of the coffee shop, fogged where the humidity outside met glass cooled by the air conditioning within, readjusted her timeline. Evening, maybe. Or very early in the morning, given the way sunset calmed without really cooling the throbbing intensity of the day's heat.

The coffee shop wasn't just chilly; it was downright cold, something that had more to do with the atmosphere than the actual temperature. People had not turned back to their laptops and conversations but continued to stare openly as Nora and Kyra's conversation rang out into a hard silence.

Jesus, thought Nora. How many years – decades – did it take to erase the dramas of high school? Because while the Alden–Nora break-up and subsequent Alden–Kyra pairing had briefly set tongues wagging, it was nothing compared to the too-soon pregnancies, arrests, drug overdoses and other strands in the warp and woof of faded small-town tapestry whose pattern repeated endlessly.

The bells hanging on the coffee shop door jingled as someone new entered, and Nora sighed in exasperated relief as attention swiveled his way. But the man walked directly to them. She braced herself for another introduction to someone she should have remembered. But he ignored her and laid a hand on Alden's shoulder.

'Hey, man.' His face was lined, its expression funereal. 'Thinking of you.'

Alden nodded and the man turned away. A woman at a nearby table rose and took his place.

'Oh, honey,' she said, wrapping Alden in a hug and a cloud of perfume. 'You, too.' She pulled Kyra into the circle they made. Tears welled in Kyra's eyes. 'Thank you,' she whispered.

Nora hovered to one side, not knowing what to say or do. The woman finally released Alden and Kyra, who turned back for a final hug before taking Alden's hand. 'Come on, sweetheart,' she said. 'It's best we go home.'

They left without saying goodbye to Nora, who forced her expression into immobility, equal parts astonished and annoyed at the way high school rivalries held sway decades later. She perched on the stool she'd chosen and turned her attention to her latte, sipping it slowly, trying to see how much she could drink without replacing the floral pattern the barista swirled into the foam, relaxing only when the hum of conversation resumed around her. The person on the stool next to her got up to leave, tossing a folded copy of the morning newspaper on to the counter as he did.

Nora reached for it. 'May I?'

'All yours.'

She nodded her thanks without looking directly at him. She wasn't sure if she could handle another unexpectedly fraught encounter with yet one more person who might be from her past.

She shook open the newspaper. There, in slightly off-register color, was a photo of the green Kia that had nearly clipped her truck's bumper the night before, with the police car beside it, a knot of officers standing nearby, and off to one side, nearly out of the frame, a white cover concealing what was obviously a body.

A headline in outsize type stretched across the front page:

Officer-Involved Shooting Claims Teen's Life.

Nora skimmed the story once, twice, three times, without success. The officer was unnamed.

It didn't matter. The stricken looks on the faces of those who'd greeted Alden suddenly made sense.

Nora had come home – the endless hours of hard driving, oblivious to everything but the dashed white highway lines by day, the stream of oncoming headlights by night – seeking the balm of the familiar, a respite from the multiple traumas of the past weeks, only to realize the one person in town she'd really hoped to see was the white cop accused of killing a black youth.

FIVE

Two other photos accompanied the story, one likely from a yearbook, showing a soft-faced youth with close-cut hair and a smile that seemed to be trying to break free of the disciplined expression befitting a high school senior; the other, similar, but years – decades – older, in black and white.

Nora read the story a fourth time. Words jumped out at her. Robert Evans – the youth's name. And a curious detail.

The motorist, Robert Evans, 19, of Baltimore, is the nephew of Bobby Evans, shot to death during a time of civil unrest in Chateau in 1967. That would explain the older photo.

Nora puzzled over the mention of civil unrest – it had occurred before she was born, but she couldn't remember hearing about it – and especially the name: Evans.

The woman who'd been helping her mother and who'd worked for the family since Penelope was a teenager was called Grace Evans. A common name in Chateau and up and down the Eastern Shore. Still . . .

'I'd know that face anywhere. You look just like your mother.'

They stood four strong by her stool, blocking any escape, faces alight with scandalized curiosity. 'The biddy brigade,' Penelope called certain of her acquaintances in a rare exception to the unspoken rule against unpleasantness of any sort, including verbal. But these women had pushed her past courtesy when they appointed themselves the most caring of Penelope's friends after Nora's troubles in Wyoming became newsworthy.

Penelope told her daughter they'd showed up at the house along the river with baked goods in their hands and newspaper clippings in their purses, all folded carefully so as not to obscure the photo of Nora in handcuffs, or Nora's mugshot or, in the less reputable publications, headlines such as *Ax-Wielding Socialite Fends Off Attacker.*

Nora wondered when she'd become a socialite. Her mother was the one with the boarding-school background.

Now they jostled for position, twittering in delight at an encounter in the flesh. Penelope had wielded accuracy along with irritation when she'd applied the biddy moniker, the women like so many hens with their puffed-out bosoms, their clucking voices, their heads bobbing as they scratched about for scraps of information. Nora wondered how they'd ask what they really wanted to know.

'When did you get into town, dear?' *And did you really come across your husband in an intimate encounter with his best friend's wife?*

'How long are you staying? Such a delightful surprise to see you.' *Almost as much of a surprise as it must have been to all your friends when you flashed a photo of said encounter on a big screen at your own party.*

'And how is Penelope? We miss her at church. She must be so happy to have you here to help her. A terrible thing, a broken ankle. So debilitating.' *Not nearly so debilitating as an ax sunk deep into a man's shoulder . . .*

They pushed close, resting shiny faux-leather purses (no casual shoulder bags for these women) on the counter. Daubs of pink on their cheeks, blue on their eyelids, but never eyeliner. Lipstick applied with increasingly unsteady hands, red creeping into the cruel vertical lines between lip and nostril. And, even on a muggy August morning, when the heat had wrapped Nora in a second skin of sweat in the block-long walk to the coffee shop, pantyhose – an abomination Nora had abandoned with relief a decade earlier. Despite husbands long dead, children fled to jobs in Baltimore and homes in its suburbs, Social Security checks buying a little less every year, and the world changing so fast – tattoos and piercings apparently no passing fad, girls turned boy and the other way around, and now the occasional father staying home with the baby instead of supporting his family – they still *took care. Kept up.*

Her turn. They waited. But Nora had learned a few things in her five decades as the daughter of Penelope Best.

She scanned faces, retrieved names. 'Miss Jayne. Miss Alice. Miss Anne. Miss Mary Ellen. It is so wonderful to see you again.' Was she gushing? Or at least competently imitating a gush? 'How have you all been? How are things in Chateau these days? It's been so long.' Turning it back on them, inviting their expertise about all matters Chateau.

Right move.

Chins dipped. Lips pursed. Heads shook. Agreement all around.

'Oh, honey, it's bad.'

'It's not that bad,' she said, choosing to misunderstand. 'It's just a hairline fracture. It could have been worse. A hip.'

They nodded agreement, but exchanged worried glances, whispering among themselves.

'Maybe she doesn't know. She just got into town, after all.'

Alice leaned in close to Mary Ellen. 'She knows. She's got the paper right there.'

Nora sipped at coffee grown cold, tilting the mug so it nearly obscured her face. She held it there until Mary Ellen acknowledged defeat. A lengthier probing of Nora's past would have to wait. 'You take care, dear. We'll have to come visit. Give you a rest from taking care of your mother. Such a lovely thing you're doing.'

And for just a moment, she saw the flash of fear behind the unearned credit accorded her involuntary caretaking. Would their own daughters drop everything, rush across the country to tend to the women who'd raised them? Or would there be a hurried visit, just long enough to shuffle them off into the living coffin the rest of the world had come to call a care facility but here in Chateau remained a nursing home?

Nora lowered her mug. The women repositioned purses on arms, clucked their goodbyes and began to move off. But Jayne Townsend lingered, leaning so close Nora could smell the coffee on her breath and the Jean Nate dusting powder tracing spiderweb lines along the creases of her throat. 'You'll want to explore town. See how things have changed. But be careful, especially now. Make sure you get home before dark. You're too young to remember how things were here for a while, but your mother could tell you. Not everyone here was like your Grace Evans. Look how Baltimore went crazy, riots and all, after they said police killed that Freddie Gray. No telling what might happen here now that *they* are all stirred up again.'

Except she didn't say *they*, instead dropping a word that Nora hadn't heard used by an acquaintance since she'd left Chateau for good all those decades earlier.

SIX

1963

The Corner Boys hurled the same word at Grace Evans when she walked by, saying it just loud enough to guarantee she'd hear.

They'd halt their endless game on the baseball diamond at the corner of Commerce and Oak, next to the construction site where the new bank was going up, and watch, bats and gloves dangling. Sometimes Todd Burris, the one who always talked the loudest, would hold his bat in front of his crotch and thrust it back and forth, and they'd all laugh like a bunch of motherfucking hyenas.

Words that would have brought Davita Evans's hand crashing across her daughter's mouth had Grace ever spoken them aloud. She aimed them silently as she walked past, shoulders stiff with resentment, head held high, because no way was she going to duck and hunch and scurry away, giving them the satisfaction of knowing they'd gotten to her.

The corner was on her route to work and, given that Quail House lay three miles out of town, Grace was not inclined to take a detour just because of some damn fool boys. The thing about the Corner Boys was, four days out of five, they'd leave her alone, intent upon their game, hollering encouragement to one another after the crack of bat against ball, and she passed blessedly unremarked.

But other days – she never knew why; maybe she came upon them between innings, or in the midst of some dispute that had paused the game – they turned as one to watch her pass and to speculate aloud as to what they'd like to do to her.

'Make her holler, yes, I would.' Todd, of course, was answered by a chorus of moans and yelps she supposed was meant to imply sexual ecstasy.

Assholes. Pencil-dick crackers. Pea-brained, ball-scratching bastards. She'd like to grab that bat out of Todd Burris's hand and go right upside his head with it. Smash it across the no-lip mouth that spewed those ugly words. Shove it up his . . .

But on this day the abuse unaccountably stopped.

At the sudden silence, Grace cut her eyes sideways. Todd dropped his bat, a smile spreading across the face, not the eyetooth-showing leer he directed her way, but wide and guileless. She looked past him and saw why. Penelope Smythe had shucked the babydoll pajamas that she wore well into every afternoon at Quail House and donned a yellow sundress and red Keds for a trip into town. She raised an arm high in greeting. The sun flamed her auburn hair. 'Todd, hey! Gonna hit a home run for me?'

Grace listened for the double entendre that would surely follow something served up on the most obvious of silver platters – Lord knows he'd made enough remarks about rounding the bases with her – but he merely bowed low in the girl's direction and called, 'Your wish is my command, Penelope.'

Grace wanted to run to the white girl, grab her by her freckled shoulders, shake her. Shout, 'What's your wish, Penelope? Would you like it up the ass, the way he says he wants to do me? Wanna suck his dick? Want him and his friends to pull a train?'

A sour taste filled her mouth at the memory of the way the Corner Boys had hollered 'choo-choo' after Todd had called to them to 'Fall in line for your turn, boys. Here comes that gal with the fine black ass, right on time.'

Federal education officials had come to Chateau that year, brought in by surreptitious reports that *Brown vs Board of Education* had had zero effect in their town. Chateau Elementary, Middle and High Schools remained all white; while all the black students attended the Smythe Grove school across town, first through twelfth grades crammed into a single low building, its brick walls crumbling with age, its wooden floorboards warped and worn. The officials had come before and been sent away with promises and stacks of paper that showed a bullshit integration plan, but now they were back and more insistent than ever that a century-old system be undone in a single school year.

Grace knew it never would. The powers that be in Chateau had perfected the art of solemn agreement to plans they had no intention of ever putting into effect. And although she knew she should wish it, that she and every other student in Smythe Grove deserved the just-off-the-presses textbooks and gleaming chemistry labs and sports fields of clipped green grass rather than pounded dirt, she thought she'd kill Todd Burris with her own bare hands before she'd endure sitting next to him for even two minutes in school.

SEVEN

Nora Best locked eyes with Jayne Townsend.

'What did you just say?'

The other biddies took a step or two toward the door, edging away, looking anxiously for Jayne to follow.

Jayne repositioned her purse on her arm. A pinprick of dread flared in her eyes. Nora wouldn't. Would she? She made as though to follow them.

But Nora would. 'Watch out for whom?'

'You know . . .' Jayne had enough self-awareness to blush, not a pretty pink tint but an angry, patchy scarlet that crept up the wattles of her throat. 'People.'

'What kind of people, Jayne?' Nora's voice went low and dangerous, the omission of the standard honorific, Miss, as deliberate as a slap. Daring her to drop the word again into the renewed hush around them.

'I think you must have misheard something.' Giving Nora an out from the scene she was about to create.

'You said . . .' Nora's voice refused her. She swallowed and tried again. 'The n-word. I think you owe me, and everyone here, an apology.'

She didn't get one. Because she never said one goddamn word of that.

Instead, Jayne issued her warning, saw Nora stiffen. The defensiveness in Jayne's eyes – that was real. She'd made an assumption, forgetting that Nora had been gone for years, decades. No telling what notions she'd picked up in her time far away.

But the apprehension died, replaced by mingled relief and

approval. Yes, Nora was still one of them, could be counted on to follow the old norms. Some things never changed. She actually gave Nora's arm a solicitous pat as she left.

Nora's forearm burned as she drove toward home, the do-the-right-thing scene – the thing that didn't get done – playing out in her head, persistent and painful as a throbbing molar, everything she should have said. Could have said. Wished she'd said.

But the words caught in her throat, snagged there on generations of unspoken rules. Don't talk back. Don't make a scene. Don't embarrass someone in public – the minor offense of causing discomfort somehow judged far more harshly than the oozing, festering sore of racism. Always better, in the case of the latter, to look away. Pretend not to hear. To, as Nora did, stammer her way through a goodbye and flee the coffee shop a few minutes later, the aroma of fresh-ground coffee in the bag on the passenger seat beside her suddenly nauseating as it permeated the truck's cab, mingling with the stench of her guilt.

In her gauzy expectations of slipping into the warm, healing bath of *home*, how had she forgotten the casual racism that had permeated her childhood, simmering just below the surface courtesies? The jokes featuring watermelons, hos, welfare moms, at which she'd laughed uncomfortably, or at best looked away, but to which she'd never verbally objected? The rowdy kids on her school bus shouting 'spook' out the window at a black man walking along the side of the road? The n-word dropped into what otherwise passed for polite conversation, reserved, to be sure, for black people deemed unsavory in some way. Not, for instance, Miss Grace or any other of the legions of domestic workers and yard men deemed, in the queasy-making phrase, 'almost a member of the family.'

Every place has some version of the same, she told herself. How often in Denver had she heard references to Mexican time? And during her brief time in Wyoming, while she heard passing references to the state's lone Indian reservation, no one had ever mentioned the people who lived there, as though once relegated to a place safely away from the state's few cities, they no longer existed.

But *that* word, issued through the primly pursed lips of a matron with a careful perm, a purse and pantyhose, somehow fell with extra weight, a blow that left a bruise of guilt, one carrying the weight of generations, increasing rather than dissipating over the years.

* * *

The crawling sense of shame persisted until she walked into the kitchen at Quail House, where she found Penelope seated stiffly at the table, Murph by her side, both of them facing an orange kitten on the tabletop, back arched, ears flat against its head, hissing, holding them both at bay despite its diminutive size.

'What the hell?'

'Language,' Penelope said automatically, never taking her eyes off the kitten. It turned when it saw Nora. Its back relaxed. Its ears perked up. It sauntered the length of the table, rubbing up against the hand she'd automatically extended.

'What is this?'

Penelope, now that the thing was no longer inches from her face, strove to impose her characteristic ironic dignity. 'It appears to be a cat.'

'Where did it come from? Is it a stray? How did it get into the house?'

'Your friend Emerson brought it. He said you told him we have mice. Which we don't. When did you see Emerson?'

Nora ignored the questions about Em and scooped the kitten into her arms. It nestled under her chin and kneaded its paws against her collarbone, its entire body vibrating contentment. 'We do have them. You yourself said so.'

'I said no such thing. I said one came in from the fields. I'm sure it's gone back to its home.'

Penelope's green eyes went hard as sea glass. She brooked no criticism of Quail House: not of the windows that admitted winter drafts that set the heavy draperies billowing, nor of the way the floorboards had warped over the centuries, slanting at odd angles as the house settled, nor of the centipedes that emerged each spring to skitter along the windowsills, the crickets that somehow found their way indoors and chirped maddeningly in hidden crannies, the silverfish that chewed slowly and methodically through the books in the library, leaving their pages lacy with holes.

Those things had always been part of Quail House, the inevitable toll of centuries and the home's location in a humid climate, but Nora had noticed more in her first hours back – the Aubusson worn through to its backing in some spots, the wooden sashes in the twelve-over-twelve windows gone soft and splintery, paint peeling on the doors and trim. Not to mention the seed-like mouse droppings that scattered from the cupboard during her futile search for coffee that morning.

She'd always assumed that the proceeds of the sale of the cannery had been wisely invested, affording Penelope the twice-yearly trips to Baltimore and Washington to update her wardrobe in Hutzler's and Woodward & Lothrop, the new Lincoln every few years, the month-long rental of a cottage in Bethany Beach – never Rehoboth, even then beginning to be overrun by those fleeing Washington's swampy summer heat – and, of course, Nora's college tuition.

Now she wondered if the recession in the 1980s and the more recent one had dealt the sort of body blow to her mother's finances that so many other people had suffered. She calculated the cost of the most basic repairs to Quail House – the trim scraped and painted, the windows caulked, the brickwork repointed, the floors sanded and varnished to their original shine – and shuddered. She didn't even want to think what it might cost to replace the slate roof.

The mice, though. At least they were easily and inexpensively dealt with, if the creature in her arms lived up to its promise.

'When was Em here? I saw him in town not an hour ago. How'd he find a cat so fast?'

'I guess one of his neighbors has a cat with a new litter. It was either us or the pound. He was in and out of here in a flash; said he was on his way to a showing.'

She glared her disapproval at the kitten in Nora's arms, as though investing it with the same lack of manners as its benefactor. 'Whatever was Emerson thinking? What are we supposed to do with a cat?'

Nora gently lowered the kitten to the floor. She retrieved a saucer from the cupboard, sat it on the floor next to the kitten, and poured in a few teaspoons of milk.

Penelope gestured urgently from the table. 'Stop! Don't feed it.'

'Too late.' The kitten polished the saucer with its pink tongue and looked to her for more. 'Why not?'

'Emerson said if we feed it, it'll never catch mice. Of course, given that there are no mice to catch, maybe you should pick up some cat food the next time you're in town.'

Nora put the milk away. The kitten's eyes followed her every move.

'Does it have a name?'

'Not that I know of.'

The kitten patted the refrigerator with a tiny paw and meowed.

'It wants more. What a mooch. There. That's its name. I'll call it Mooch.'

Penelope made a face. 'It's dreadfully undignified.'

'No more undignified than having mice. It was nice of Em.'

'Em should be nice to us.' Penelope's tone was arch. She lifted a packet from the chair beside her and pushed it across the table. 'Read it.'

Nora eyed it warily. The envelope was large, manila, pedestrian, not the cream-colored stock of her mother's stationery, with the embossed return address in roundhand font. The only thing that gave away Penelope's provenance was Nora's name in the slanting even script she'd perfected during her time at boarding school.

Nora unfastened the envelope's metal prongs and withdrew a sheaf of papers, a legal document of some sort.

Declaration of Trust, it read across the top, and then: *Witnesseth.*

'Witnesseth?' Nora smiled at the formality of the word.

She skimmed the document. Phrases jumped out at her – 'the property known as Quail House.' Her own name. A lot of *wherefores* and *thereases*. She flipped pages. Came to the end, no more enlightened than when she began.

She looked up. Penelope beamed at her from across the table. 'Well?'

'What is this?'

'It's yours.'

'What's mine?'

Penelope gave her most regal wave. 'All of it.'

'All of what?'

'The house, the outbuildings, the one hundred and fifty acres, the three-quarters of a mile of riverfront. I lease the fields to the Hudsons and the Kinseys. They bring in a little income – not a lot, but you'll never starve. Of course, you have to wait until I'm dead. But as soon as I've drawn my last breath, all of this is yours, and without any significant tax penalty. Emerson helped me figure it out, and, of course, Mr Hathaway.' That would be George Hathaway of Hathaway & Valentine, who'd represented the Smythes from both families' earliest days in Chateau.

'Quail House is yours.'

That night, instead of returning to Electra as planned, Nora slept in the room that for the first time, despite all the years she'd spent in it, was really, truly her own. She didn't have to go anywhere. The impulse that had propelled her the last several weeks – to move, keep moving, get ahead of the desperation dragging her down – drained away.

She didn't have to think about any of it anymore.

EIGHT

Nights were noisy on the Eastern Shore.

The tall windows, whose panes of thick wavy glass distorted the view, stood open to the night breeze. Moths, drawn to the nightlight, bumped softly against the screens, leaving powdery blotches in a futile attempt to reach it.

Nora sat on the edge of the bed, listening, remembering. Her home in Denver had been insulated against the city's increasingly invasive traffic cacophony; in her brief time in the Wyoming mountains, the wind soughing through the pines had soothed her to sleep. Denver was, of course, famous for its mile-high altitude; the Wyoming campground had been higher still, something that discouraged insects and limited the more fragile birds and wildlife.

But Chateau was at sea level, with bountiful rainfall throughout the year and moist breezes off the river even on sunny days, and every living thing – flora, fauna and creeping, stinging insect – thrived. Especially insect. The night thrummed with their racket, the needling whine of mosquitoes, the rhythmic rattle of cicadas. Somehow she'd arrived on a seventeenth year, when the cicadas emerged from their years-long underground sojourn, and their vibrating call rose and fell in an echo of the sirens she'd heard the previous night.

From the river came the drowsy gabble of Canada geese settling in for the night, tucking their heads beneath their wings. They still arrived by the tens of thousands in the fall, but a certain number – Nora had always thought of them as the most Darwinian of their species – had abandoned the arduous spring flights to their nesting grounds in Newfoundland and elected to stay year-round in Chateau, whose surrounding fields of corn and soybeans provided a plentiful food supply. From one of the cedars, an owl hooted, perhaps frustrated by some small scurrying creature that had managed to elude it.

As though in echo of her thoughts, a *skritch-skritch* sounded close at hand, maybe even within the room. A mouse, Nora thought with a start, drawing her feet up from a thick new rug that had replaced the one she remembered. Possibly the same mouse that had sent Penelope toppling. Mooch, who'd followed her up the stairs and on to the bed, leapt into action, bounding across the floor in search of unseen prey, despite the fact that Nora had slipped him a bit of her chicken during dinner.

'Maybe you'll earn your keep, after all. Better luck next time,' she said when he returned unsuccessful, tail twitching in frustration.

She drifted toward sleep, lulled by the kitten's purring and, barely audible, the thunk of rowboat bumping against dock where it had been tied as long as Nora could remember. Something splashed in the river – a fish, maybe, or even a muskrat, leaving its home of reeds and mud and setting out for a swim. A puff of breeze, the barest exhale, stirred the sheer curtains. Despite the darkness, the temperature had barely dropped at all, another difference from the crisp air of the West, where the sunset heralded an automatic reach for a sweater, even in midsummer.

She vowed to sleep the following night in the Airstream, which she'd parked under the spreading elms to one side of the house. At least it had air conditioning. She dozed off, soothed by the thought of cool relief.

The demons crept back in sometime around three in the morning, when night burrowed deepest and darkest into an underworld impenetrable by a merciful sun. They jabbed her awake, these memories of staggering naked beside a mountain stream with a knife wound in her side, of the skepticism on the part of the law enforcement she'd assumed would protect her, of Joe's death, unmourned but undeserved. And now, her mother's infirmity, the accusations against Alden, the ugly word in the diner, all of it vanquishing sleep with ruthless efficiency. She put her hand to her side, fingering the ridge of scar tissue, the tiny bumps that marked the recently removed stitches, counting them over and over in a futile attempt to dull her racing thoughts.

She gave up after an hour and dressed quickly, forsaking shoes in the interest of silence, and left the house. The kitten slumbered on, but loyal Michael Murphy groaned to his feet and padded along beside her as she made her way across the lawn, her bare feet leaving a darkened trail across the dew-drenched grass. Mist twined above the river. A few mallards paddled away as Nora walked out on to the dock. She sat down at the end and swished her toes across the water's surface, not yet warmed to a near-simmer by the sun. Michael Murphy lowered himself to warped boards with a sigh and laid his graying muzzle on her thigh. It was light, just, the reeds in the marshes across the river standing in black relief against a sky shading to deepest azure. A lingering star blinked sleepily overhead. The air was damp but cool, and Nora luxuriated in the sensation of actually enjoying the outdoors, instead of seeking an air-conditioned refuge.

The river flowed past, wide and languid, in no hurry at all to join the salty waters of the bay. Nora closed her eyes and lost herself in the sounds of the awakening day: the ducks chuckling among themselves, the creaking honk of geese overhead, flying so low she heard the whistle of the air through their pinions, the lap of wavelets against the dock. The clunk and splash of oars.

She sat up straight and opened her eyes. Michael Murphy lifted his head. His hackles rose under her hand and then subsided. His tail thumped on the dock as the boat approached.

'Hey, Nora,' said Alden Tydings.

NINE

Alden pulled the oars into the boat and grabbed one of the pilings. The boat bumped against the dock. Nora looked into the boat for a fishing pole, a tackle box, something that would explain his presence on the river at this hour. Binoculars, even. Maybe Alden had become a birdwatcher in her decades away.

But the boat was empty. She looked at the hand wrapped around the piling. Imagined it wrapped instead around a service weapon, the forefinger flexing against a trigger. A young man slumping – against the wheel or to the ground? The youth had been sitting in the car when Nora passed them. Had Alden ordered him out of the car? Had there been some sort of scuffle? Had there been – please God, what was the bloodless phrase the cops always trotted out – probable cause?

Because, while she'd always rolled her eyes at those words when she'd heard them in news accounts of a white cop shooting a black kid, in this case she fervently willed them to be true.

'What are you doing out here, Alden?'

He mock-flexed an arm, although there was nothing mock about the bicep that leapt into prominence. 'Keeping in shape. Cops aren't allowed to get old and fat anymore like the ones we grew up with. Remember Officer Purvis?'

'Purvis the Perv?' She followed his lead into safe territory. 'How could I forget?'

Purvis, small and squat as a fireplug, knew all of the party spots in the woods and marshes surrounding Chateau and delighted in breaking up parties and even more in interrupting couples in or nearly in the act. 'Pull up those panties! Tuck that thing back in your jeans!' he'd been known to holler, the glare of his flashlight sweeping befogged car windows, not having the decency to turn away as the unfortunates scrambled back into their clothing.

'Please tell me you're not like Officer Perv.'

'Ouch, Nora.' He fell backward, clutching his chest, miming a mortal wound. 'Not even a little bit.'

Nora laughed. No, he wasn't at all like Purvis, who'd limited himself to embarrassing teenagers. Alden had shot one. Her laugh died in her throat. She wondered if he'd tell her.

He held out his other hand, inviting her in with another reassuring reference to their shared history. 'How many hours did we spend on this river when we were kids?'

Don't, she thought, even as she stepped into the boat and took the seat across from him. She found her balance within its gentle rocking and loosened her grip on the gunwales.

'We've got bigger things to worry about these days than kids getting frisky in the woods,' he said as he dropped the oars into the water and pulled the boat back into the current.

'Like what?'

Now, she thought. *He's going to tell me now*. She fought an urge to close her eyes and inhale. This close, Alden smelled exactly the way she remembered from high school.

'Drugs, for starters. They bring them in from Baltimore, D.C., Philly, New York. And not just weed like when we were kids. We're talking Oxy, heroin, shit that kills people. These guys, they're pros. Gangs, cartels. They think we're a bunch of hick cops who won't figure out what's going on. We deal with some really scary characters.'

Nora thought of her old life, the one with her husband, back when she'd thought part of the secret to a long and reasonably happy marriage was Letting Shit Slide – a tactic that had only sent it sliding right down on to her. She turned to face him squarely.

'Like the guy you shot?'

He didn't even blink. Or sling some crap explanation about not being able to talk about it.

'Had to. He came at me with a gun. I tell you what, Nora . . .' He shook his head in slow, sad turns. 'I walked up to the car, the door flew open and there was a gun, right in my face. First thing I thought was, "I knew it." It's been so damn hot I didn't wear my vest, even though we're supposed to, no matter what. I even thought, when I left the house without it, "Just watch. This'll be the day you get shot." And then all of a sudden, there I was with a gun in my face, and I thought, "Alden, you dumb sonofabitch, you deserve this."'

He passed a hand across his face.

'Everything happened so fast. I even didn't realize I'd shot him at first.' Another shake of the head. 'So fast, and so slow at the same time. All that stuff about things happening in slow motion, your life flashing before your eyes? It's true. In the time it took between that door opening and him stepping out of it, I grew up, got my heart broken, became a cop, ended up with teenage kids, all in the blink of an eye. Then – bang!' He slapped his hand against the side of the boat. Nora jumped.

'Once I realized I'd actually pulled the trigger, I was afraid I'd missed. That he'd come at me again. But I hadn't. He threw his gun away and went down.'

Nora blew a long breath. It was OK. Alden wasn't an asshole cop, pumped up on testosterone and adrenaline, throwing his weight around, assuming the worst of anyone with skin a shade darker than his.

'Thank God,' she breathed.

'That's what I said.'

She returned his smile with a shaky one of her own. Let him think her thanks were solely because she was glad he'd survived. Which she was, and gladder by the minute as they sat across from one another in the boat exactly as they had when they were sixteen, in the carefree years before he'd killed someone and she herself had nearly been killed.

She wondered if he'd noted the Airstream that night as she steered truck and trailer around him as he stood beside the Kia? Now the trailer sat beside Quail House, clearly visible from the dock, its airplane decal making it impossible to confuse with any other Airstream.

The boat rounded a bend and approached a narrow bridge. This close to the bay, the tides affected the river, and Nora and Alden both slid into the bottom of the boat as they approached the bridge, its dripping underside just inches above the gunwales. Later in the day, the water surface would drop considerably as saltier waters of the bay retreated during low tide. The rising sun silhouetted a solitary woman fishing off one end of the bridge, two buckets by her feet, a small one for bait and a bigger one to hold her catch.

Her gaze passed over Nora and fastened on Alden, and Nora saw him stiffen at her recognition. He scrambled back on to his seat and dug the oars hard in the water, swinging the boat in a wide turn, rowing back the way they'd come, his jaw rigid, knuckles white on the tanned hands clutching the oars, patches of sweat mapping continents across his shirt. Nora looked back and saw the woman lowering her hand, as though she'd started to hail them, then changed her mind.

The polite thing to do would have been to ignore the moment, to pretend that with his explanation of the shooting, the subject was closed, sealed in a box, no need to reopen it and risk the escape of further unpleasantness. But she'd been polite with the biddies, resulting in a lingering remorse. She reminded herself of the vow she'd made as she'd driven into Chateau: that she was done running away, even from something as minor as her own momentary involvement.

'I saw it, you know.'

He jerked. The boat veered. 'Saw what?'

'Not *it*. But I saw you stopping that guy. I didn't know it was you. The car – I recognized it. He almost cut me off a few miles earlier. You try slamming on the brakes when you're towing a few tons of trailer. He's lucky I didn't roll right over him.'

He kept at the oars, the dip-pull rhythm unchanging. But she sensed a quivering sort of attentiveness, one that made her think of Murph's predecessor in the duck blind on gray fall mornings when the first faraway honks of approaching geese sounded, the dog on full alert even before her father rose with his shotgun.

'What do you mean?'

Had he really not seen her? She watched him closely as she spoke.

'Just what I said. He cut me off. Just a few miles before I saw you stopping him. I just didn't know it was you.'

'Nora.' He dropped one of the oars. It clanked in its lock as his hand shot out, grasping her forearm with the sort of intensity she remembered from far different situations. 'Think. Tell me exactly what happened.'

She thought back, but what she remembered more than anything was how tired she'd been. She said as much. 'I was probably driving slower than I should have been. Then out of nowhere, this kid in a car came around me and almost sideswiped me going by.'

'A kid. So you saw enough to recognize his age.'

Had she? Or had she just assumed youth, because of the music? No, she remembered his face, eyes gone wide and white when she slowed to pass the traffic stop.

'Yes. Teenager, maybe. Of course, now everybody looks young to me.' She dragged up a laugh, trying to lighten the mood.

He dropped her arm and picked up the oar, guiding the boat back on course.

'What kind of car? Could you tell?'

'Please.' Didn't he remember? He'd taken it upon himself, all those years ago, to teach her how to recognize makes and models of cars and trucks, and though she'd protested the sexism of his assumption, she'd reluctantly gone along, taking unaccountable pleasure in nailing, say, a low-slung '68 Chevy Impala.

'A green Kia. That bright, neon green. A few years old.'

'You catch a license number?'

He'd gone full interrogatory cop, and although his face was a studied blank, a chill ran through her.

'You've got to be kidding me. No. I wasn't looking for that. Mostly, I just remember the music.'

'Yeah, that was him. That music. I'll hear it the rest of my life.' He ran a hand through his hair. 'Thanks, Nora. Maybe this will help with the investigation. They're going to put me through the wringer. Which they should. It's the only way to keep any credibility.' He squared his shoulders, as though adjusting to a weighty, if necessary, burden.

She let out a breath. If the shooting had been anything but self-defense, would he so readily welcome an investigation?

The dock at Quail House hove into view, Murph pacing its length. The boat glided alongside as the dog performed ungainly arabesques of relief at their return.

'I've got to go. It's going to be a tough week,' Alden said. He rested the oars and grabbed a piling. He lingered, though, backlit by the gentle shimmer of the rising sun, gazing at her so long that she dropped her eyes and began running her fingers through Murph's fur in old familiar patterns as though searching for ticks.

He reached over to stroke the dog, his fingers tangling with hers, tightening around them for a moment before releasing them.

'I'm glad you're back. Even under the circumstances, it's good to see you. You out here every morning?'

'Depends when I wake up. Maybe. I like it this time of day. It's the only time it's cool.'

'Same. This rowing – it's about more than staying in shape or distracting myself until they finish this investigation. I live in a houseful of women. It was open warfare when I left this morning, somebody already in hysterics. This is the only peace I get. Teenage girls. You can't even imagine.'

She laughed, remembering epic battles with Penelope. Over what, exactly? Penelope's horror at her choice of college, abruptly transferring from the nearby University of Delaware to Colorado after her break-up with Alden.

'It's so far,' her mother pleaded. 'You can't leave. You're all I've got.' The sense of suffocation, propelling the westward escape that ended up with Nora gaining her freedom but acknowledging that Alden was forever gone. Her laughter faded, but she tried to keep her tone light.

'Yes, I can. I used to be one.'

He let go of the piling and took up the oars. The boat drifted backward into the current. 'I remember.' He raised an oar in acknowledgment and then wielded it to set the boat back on its course. 'I remember very well.'

Nora tiptoed back across the lawn, her caution unnecessary as the thick clipped grass would have silenced all but the loudest footsteps. She veered away from the house and toward Electra instead, beset by an adolescent certainty that Penelope would be able to read in her expression the moment Alden rowed hard back to the dock, beckoning Nora, clutching the piling with one hand while pulling her to him and brushing her cheek with his lips, a chaste bittersweet bestowal of sweetness and regret and apology and promise.

'Old times' sake,' he'd whispered, and although she should have pulled away, she didn't.

TEN

1963

As jobs went, cleaning Quail House was a lot more work than Grace had expected.

Her mother had warned her. 'You think it's going to be like what you do here.' She laughed, short and bitter. The home's rooms gleamed spotless, all four of them – the kitchen, parlor and two bedrooms, one for Davita and Gerald, and one that Grace had shared with Bobby until she turned twelve and Davita declared that growing children needed privacy, after which Bobby slept on the parlor davenport. The outhouse stood at the far end of the packed-earth back yard, regular applications of quicklime and ashes keeping odors to a minimum. Once a week Grace cleaned the house to Davita's exacting standards, while Bobby tended the vegetable garden, those chores turned over to them by their exhausted parents as soon as Grace and Bobby were old enough to wield a broom or hoe.

'Six bedrooms,' Grace said at the end of her first week there. 'A kitchen bigger than this whole house, almost, and a dining room, too. Bathrooms with flush toilets upstairs and down. Two parlors – two! And a library, with shelves so high I've got to climb a ladder to dust the books. Bobby'll have it easy just doing windows and the lawn.'

'Poor baby,' Davita crooned, so solicitous that Grace stiffened. 'You just forget about that stupid old job and come pick crabs with your mama.'

'Yeah,' Bobby chimed in. 'You do that and I'll take over the housecleaning. I'll take that library ladder any day over one outside in the sun, washing all those windows with all those windowpanes. That house has got more windows than a fly's got eyes. But that's still better than pushing a mower back and forth about two acres of lawn and then getting down on hands and knees with the clippers around all those flowerbeds.'

Gerald looked at his wife. 'We have raised a couple of spoiled children for sure. You try following a tractor on foot, picking up the corn the harvester missed. You're crying about two acres, walking across green grass cool and soft as carpet. Try sixty acres, mosquitoes and greenhead flies dogging you every step of the way.'

The conversation echoed in Grace's brain the next time she found herself atop a ladder in the library, a tall-ceilinged room darkened by brocade draperies, smelling of dust and neglect, the former rising in great clouds as Grace attacked the stacks with a feather duster.

Philippa gave away her presence just outside the door with a sneeze.

Grace nearly fell. She grabbed a shelf for support and tried to recover her dignity along with her equilibrium. 'Wasn't expecting company. Doesn't anybody ever come in here?'

Philippa withdrew a lace-edged handkerchief from the cuff of her cardigan and held it to her face. 'Apparently not. Not any of us, and – from the looks of it – certainly not the last girl. I appreciate your attentiveness to detail. I appreciate it very much.'

She'd been doing that, showing up on some pretext wherever Grace happened to be working. Checking her out. Seeing how she compared to the last 'girl.'

She drifted away, and Grace, once she was sure Philippa was gone, chanced pulling a book from its place among the other leather-bound volumes, but found it yet another dry examination of the Roman Empire. Whoever had amassed the collection had a penchant for history, most of it about places and people that interested Grace not at all. She'd found a slender volume that purported to be a history of the Eastern Shore, but she set it aside after finding only brief mentions of Indians and none at all of black people, unless passing references to various tobacco plantations counted.

The lower shelves held art books of the kind appreciated in the region: glossy pages of Audubon's birds, protected by translucent sheets of onionskin, or drawings and photographs of skipjacks and other Chesapeake Bay watercraft. She was grateful to stumble across a Wyeth collection she enjoyed, preferring N.C. Wyeth's dramatic illustrations of *Treasure Island*'s glowering pirates, and especially a breathtaking one of Launcelot and Guenevere astride a galloping horse, Guenevere's hair streaming behind her, to the muted barns and fields favored by Andrew Wyeth.

Grace spent extra time in the library each week, dragging its upholstered chairs outdoors and pounding them free of dust, rubbing oil into their mahogany legs, to justify the reward she gave herself of leafing through the books when she'd completed her task.

She sometimes felt as though she spent most of her days polishing wood – the tables and chairs, sideboards and dressers, the finials on the Queen Anne beds, whose grooves collected stubborn lines of dust. So much polishing that after the first few weeks she felt as though the scent of lemon had permeated her pores, surrounding her with a citrus haze even after she'd gone home, although she quickly learned better than to say as much to Davita.

'Better than smelling like crab all the time,' her mother reminded her, and she hung her head in silent acknowledgment that, compared to a day in the steaming Quonset huts where the crabs were processed, she had an easy time of it indeed. Philippa, for all her early attentiveness, gradually drifted back into doing whatever it was she did all day – luncheons, mostly, Grace learned.

As for her husband, the Police Chief, Grace rarely saw him unless Philippa asked her to work a weekend when one of the endless luncheons involved husbands. Grace listened hard on those days, doing her best to busy herself with some task wherever the Chief happened to be, but as far as she could tell, the men's discussions centered on golf and duck-hunting, the conversational equivalents of the boring books in the library.

She was making beaten biscuits for one of those gatherings, spreading the dough across the kitchen's thickest cutting board, then alternately folding it and whacking the hell out of it with a rolling pin when, as she drew her arm back for a renewed assault, she heard a tap at the window.

It was Bobby, clambering down a ladder with his bucket and squeegee. He hopped to the ground as she hauled the heavy window sash up. 'You're not hitting them hard enough,' he said.

Grace's arm already felt like macaroni boiled too long, the way the Smythes liked it.

'I've been at it for half an hour. Still got fifteen minutes to go. You think it needs to be hit harder, get in here and hit it yourself.'

'Gladly! I'm burning up out here.'

Grace filled a glass with ice and dipped her brother some lemonade from the two-gallon Mason jar that sat on the counter. Kathleen Mavourneen, Chief Smythe's hunting dog, rose as Bobby came into the kitchen, hackles half-raised, tail stirring the air in a slow, uncertain wag. She knew Bobby by now, was used to seeing him shoving the lawn mower in diagonal lines across the endless expanse of grass, or on his ladder, rubbing newspapers dipped in a mixture of water and vinegar across the windows, and then flicking away the surface moisture with his squeegee. But she'd never seen him in the house before.

Bobby drained the glass in a single long draft and held it out for more.

'Must be ninety out there,' he said. 'Usually, I try to finish up a set of windows before noon. I don't know which is worse, being up on that ladder or behind that mower.'

'This is worse.' Grace brandished the rolling pin, gambling on the chance he'd fall for it.

She bet right.

'Girl, please. No harder than swatting a mosquito. Give me that thing.'

He snatched it from her hand and went at the dough with a crashing vengeance. The counter shook. Dishes rattled in the cupboards. The dog took cover under the table.

And Penelope Smythe appeared in the doorway in her frilly little pajamas, rubbing sleep out of her eyes and demanding to know what in the world was going on.

Grace froze.

There'd been no explicit instructions against Bobby being allowed in the house, but on the other hand, all of the Smythes' interactions with him had taken place out of doors – Chief Smythe instructing him how to use the lawn mower (as if he didn't know); Philippa on the back step handing him an envelope with his pay. He'd come inside a few other times, hanging around in the kitchen while Grace cooked, or positioning himself behind the big desk in the Chief's study, pretending to order Grace around, but always when Philippa had set off somewhere in her long black Lincoln and the Chief, of course, was at work. They'd forgotten about Penelope, who they hardly ever saw anyway. Sometimes Grace heard her, chatting away on the pink princess phone on her nightstand, the one that Grace regularly wiped clean of the residue of biscuit-colored pancake makeup it acquired after spending so much time tucked against Penelope's cheek.

Penelope rarely rose before noon and then spent her afternoons stretched out on a chaise lounge in the sun, reddening skin gleaming with a noxious combination of baby oil and mosquito repellant in hopes of a tan to fill in the spaces between her freckles. On the most oppressively hot days, she frittered away afternoons in her room. When her door was ajar, Grace would see her sprawled on her unmade bed, paging through fashion magazines, or sitting in front of her vanity, experimenting with various shades of lipstick or piling her auburn hair atop her head in some new style, and Grace wondered what such a summer would be like, free of school, no need for a job, and no expectation of doing anything so strenuous as picking her clothes up off the floor and placing them in the hamper across the room.

They stood motionless, Bobby's arm still raised, the rolling pin lofted high. Grace tried to read Penelope's expression. Shock? Outrage? Could she fire them herself? Or would she leave it to her mother or, worse, the Chief?

Bobby broke into an easy grin. 'Just showing my sister how to really beat these biscuits. Sorry if we woke you up. But the way she was playing pattycake with 'em, they'd never rise. Be like chewing on stones. To get it right, you've really got to wallop them. Here. Give it a try.'

He stepped forward and held the rolling pin out to Penelope.

'Lord,' Grace breathed almost audibly. How great an offense would Bobby's presence be? Especially in proximity to a barely clad white girl.

She closed her eyes and envisioned a life spent picking crabs.

She heard a tap. Opened her eyes. Penelope stood above the dough, rolling pin in hand. 'Like this?' *Tip-tap*.

'That's even worse than my sister. Both of you, you're an embarrassment. Give it some gas.'

The pin came down again, this time with a thud.

'Better.' Bobby gave a solemn nod, and a command. 'Again. Try it with both hands.'

Bam.

'Again.'

Bam. *Bam. BAM!*

Bobby took a step back. 'You see, Grace? That's how it's done.'

He held out his hand and Penelope, flushed, handed the rolling pin back to him with a breathy laugh.

He accepted it with a bow, then straightened and raised his eyes to hers. 'Remind me,' he said, 'never to make you mad.'

ELEVEN

'Old times' sake.'

Nora turned the phrase over and over in her mind as she showered and dressed, the memory of Alden's brotherly kiss and the decidedly unbrotherly kisses of their teenage years bringing a smile to her face that vanished only when she descended to the kitchen and found Penelope insisting that the cop at the table join them for tea.

He stood when Nora came in. The room dwarfed most people, the length of it, the fireplace dominating the far wall, but the cop was a big man, his body settling comfortably into middle age, softening without being fat, the sort of heft that denotes respect rather than sloppiness.

Nora took a step back.

Penelope, regal in a high-necked dressing gown with a demure trim of eyelet lace, remained seated. 'Here she is now. She can make the tea. I would, but . . .' A nod to the walker, accompanied by a self-deprecating laugh. Yet she must have struggled her way to the door to answer the knock Nora hadn't heard because she'd been daydreaming her way through a too-long shower.

Nora pushed her hair away from her face. It dripped slowly on to her T-shirt, the damp spreading across her shoulders. She'd forgone the blow dryer, hoping to preserve the illusion of coolness as long as possible.

She studied his face, as she did with anyone close to her own age in Chateau, assessing the chance that he might be another former schoolmate. But Penelope's next words disabused her of the possibility.

'This is Sergeant Brittingham. He grew up in Easton.'

So they'd already played that game, sussing out each other's *people*. Brittingham hailed from the tony town to the north, with a name that went back generations. Penelope, of course, had her own generational bragging rights, made manifest by Quail House, and the added fillip of a Police Chief father, leaving no doubt as to who held the social upper hand. Which explained Brittingham's deferential manner when he turned to Nora.

'We just need a few minutes of your time down at the station.'

Nora took another step back. The last time she'd gone voluntarily with a law enforcement officer – it had been a Wyoming sheriff – she'd ended up spending the night in a county jail on suspicion of kidnapping and possible murder.

'We understood you might be a witness to the, ah, unfortunate event of Saturday night,' he added.

That hadn't taken long. Nora wondered if Alden had called him from the boat as soon as he'd rowed out of sight.

'I didn't really see anything. I told Alden that.'

Penelope stiffened, and Nora cursed inwardly as she realized she'd just brought a raft of eventual questions down upon herself.

'You can help us with a timeline,' he said easily. 'It'll only take a few minutes. I'll drive you right downtown and get you back in time to make lunch for your mother.'

Penelope bestowed a smile upon the cop as she wielded a verbal stiletto on her daughter. 'I'm so glad to hear you and Alden got a chance to catch up.' As though it had been a few weeks, rather than decades. 'I can't wait to hear all about it.'

Nora considered her options – her mother's questions, or those of the police – and made the easy choice.

'I'll follow you,' she told Brittingham. After her recent experience in Wyoming, an infuriating and frightening unfairness that still rankled, no way was she getting in a car again with a cop if she could help it.

She caught the flicker across his face, so fleeting she might have imagined it, a quick tensing of the small muscles along his jaw. He knew, then. Had read the stories, seen photos of her in handcuffs. Which meant he also knew the real perpetrators had been found, her own name cleared. But that image must have lingered, and a shade of doubt along with it.

'Or,' she said, knowing he'd understand she'd glimpsed his suspicion, 'you can follow me.'

Without waiting for his answer, she grabbed her keys from the kitchen counter and made her best attempt at a confident saunter as she headed for the door.

The police station was a surprise.

It was where it had always been, in the rear of the courthouse, although in the decades she'd been away the building had acquired an addition. All sleek metal and glass, bespeaking a modern office full of computers and cubicles – a change from the rabbit warren of small dark offices and scarred wooden desks of her grandfather's time. William Smythe had taken great pride in leading the annual school trips through the station, pointing out to Nora and her thrilled classmates the holding cell that invariably held a fierce-looking, filthy-faced man apt to rattle the bars and scare the bejesus out of them, even at their cowed distance. Only later would Nora realize that her grandfather must have pressed one of the younger officers into service, ordered him to forgo shaving for a few days and wear the clothing usually reserved for barn chores.

The bigger surprise on this day was the name over the door: *The William Smythe Police Station*. When had that happened?

She must have heard about it. Penelope would have made sure the whole world knew. And she remembered, vaguely, something about a ceremony. Years ago, when she and Joe had been in full mid-career madness, each of them scrambling ever higher up the ladder, their perfect image perfectly maintained. Except she hadn't been perfect enough to take even a long weekend to fly back to her hometown to see her late grandfather honored.

She sat in her truck, staring at the sign, lost in memories until a car door slammed and Brittingham materialized beside her window, waiting for her to follow him into the building.

Inside, a cop sat in a booth behind a plexiglass window, a solitaire game open on the computer screen beside him. Nora tried to remember if she'd ever seen a black cop in Chateau. *No public admittance beyond this point*, a sign proclaimed.

'Nelson,' Brittingham nodded to him. A buzzer sounded and a steel door swung open.

'After you,' Brittingham gestured as Nelson turned back to his game without a word of acknowledgment.

Another officer joined them in a too-small room that harkened back to the old days despite the addition's newness. Maybe tiny interview rooms were intentional – some sort of police tactic developed with an eye to intimidation. Or maybe she would have felt intimidated no matter what, even though the two cops lounged in their chairs, relaxed, barely taking notes as she brought them through the brief sequences of events.

'It was a little before eight. It was getting dark.' She was sure of it. 'I was really tired. I'd been driving since Toledo.' She bit her lip. Would they consider her too fatigued to be reliable? 'But I was almost home,' she hurried on. 'Just after I pulled off the bypass, this green car passed me so close it nearly hit me. It shook me up, so much that even though I'd been wishing for coffee, I didn't stop at the little coffee place along the road.'

She blurted a sudden memory. 'Oh, and I saw a fox.' Then blushed, afraid she sounded foolish. What could a fox possibly have to do with anything?

The other cop, who'd introduced himself as Officer Lewis, nodded acknowledgment. 'We used to have a few proggers, those old-timers who worked the marsh, trapping muskrat and sometimes foxes, too. But they're a dying breed, and now we've got fox dens all around the edges of town. They come in at night, feast like kings on our trash and vanish by morning. They're a real pest on the golf course. They like to steal the balls.'

He rattled on, probably trying to put her at ease. Nora drew a breath and took up her narrative.

'And then, just around the bend, I saw that same car, only this time it had been stopped by one of you guys. I didn't know at the time it was Alden. I just figured the kid had been caught in a speed trap. I laughed because I thought it served him right.'

'Kid,' Brittingham said. 'So you could tell his age.'

'Just that he was young. But maybe I thought that because of his music.'

'What music? How could you hear it? Were your windows down? In this heat?'

This much, at least, she remembered. 'Yes. I'd opened mine to get some air, thinking it would help keep me awake. I'd forgotten how hot it was. And his were open, too. What kind of music was it? I don't know. Bouncy. Some kind of hip-hop.'

She remembered the energy of it, her own inadvertent dip and sway to the rhythm, the way she'd laughed at herself despite her irritation.

'You remember what song?'

'Are you kidding me?'

'Yeah, you don't look like the hip-hop type.' Lewis again, smiling now, maybe in an effort to belie the tinge of racism. Maybe that's not even how he meant it. Maybe it was just an age thing. Still, it rattled her, and she was more unnerved still at his next remark.

'So, road rage, then.'

'I don't think so. He just seemed like he was in a hurry, not mad or anything.'

'But you said he nearly hit you. Scared the shit out of you.'

She hadn't said that at all. 'I said it jolted me wide awake. Startled, more than scared me.'

'Car comes out of nowhere, almost hits me, I'm scared.' He looked at Brittingham, who nodded.

'Same. That's some aggressive shit right there.'

They weren't talking to her anymore, batting the words between them, a new and more ominous scenario taking place with each sentence.

'Almost dark, you're just driving along, minding your own business. No other traffic on the road, no need for him to do that. Could have put on his blinker and passed, just like a solid citizen.'

'Yeah. You gotta wonder why somebody would do something like that. Road rage, sure, that's possible.'

'Drunk, maybe. Or high. Even scarier, in its own way.'

They turned to her in unison, eyes flashing like high beams.

'You're lucky. You could've been forced off the road. Rig like the one you were driving, all that weight, could've ended up rolling over. You could've been killed.'

She tried to feel it, the menace they had invoked. But all she could remember of that night was her exhaustion, the flash of fear followed by annoyance, and her own amused satisfaction – now tinged by guilt, given the outcome – at seeing the driver stopped for what she thought was a simple traffic ticket a few minutes later.

'I guess,' she said. 'But I wasn't killed.' *He was.* A reality that lay heavy and unspoken in the room.

'Did you recognize him?'

'Of course not.' What an odd question.

'I thought you might,' Brittingham said. 'Given his connection to your family.'

He stared at her, waiting.

She stared back. 'What are you talking about?'

Lewis started to say something, but Brittingham held up his hand. 'She probably doesn't remember. She's been gone a long time. Grace Evans,' he said to Nora.

So Grace *was* related. Nora remembered her initial curiosity when she'd read the youth's name in the paper.

'She used to work for you, right?'

Nora almost laughed. God knows Grace had worked, and worked hard, whipping through Quail House three days a week in a frenzy of mopping and scrubbing and dusting, but somehow managing to convey the great favor she was doing them as she performed tasks of which they themselves were perfectly capable.

'This boy's her nephew.'

The incipient laughter dissolved in Nora's throat, the shock of the information pushing past the initial jolt at the word *boy*. 'I never knew her to have a nephew.'

'Had,' Lewis said quietly.

In the way of all children, Nora had never considered that Grace had a life outside her time at Quail House, let alone a sibling who'd produced this nephew – both of them now dead, if she remembered the newspaper story correctly.

'I didn't know,' she said.

Didn't she?

She thought hard, conjured a chubby child. Gurgling laughter during a game of hide-and-seek, ducking among the high-backed chairs and enfolded in the floor-length drapes in the library. Her grandfather looming in the doorway, the sudden bad feeling in the room like the queasy plunge in air pressure that heralds worst storms. She never saw the child again – if, indeed, she'd ever seen him at all, her memory so vague and unreliable she thought it best not to say anything.

'That'll make things easier,' Lewis said. He left the room and she relaxed, thinking they must be done with her.

But he returned and laid something before her. Five faces stared up from a computer printout.

'What's this?'

'Just wanted to see if you could identify him.'

Help with a timeline, Brittingham had said. Things had gone way beyond that. She pushed the piece of paper away.

'But I barely saw him. It's the car I recognized. A green Kia. Older model. You didn't even ask me about that.'

'Didn't need to. You just told us.' Brittingham put his fingertips to the paper. His nails were cut short and square, and they were very clean. The paper came back across the table toward her.

She glanced at the array of five young black men and wrenched her gaze away.

'I don't know. Like I said, I barely saw him. And besides' – she clutched at a just-recalled fact, her way out of this – 'I saw his picture in the paper. So I've been influenced, prejudiced, whatever you call it.'

'That was an old picture.' Brittingham pitched his voice low and comforting. 'Just take some time with them all. You'd be surprised what you remember. And if you don't recognize anyone, that's fine, too. We just want to make sure we've covered all the bases. Don't overthink it. Just go with your first impression, the split-second thought, just like when you saw him on the road.'

Thus reassured, she let her glance skim over the faces before her, this one's hair a little longer than the others, this one's eyes open a little wider, as though surprised to find himself facing the camera in such a situation. This one with a small scar that tugged at one corner of his mouth.

'Let's leave her alone with them.' Brittingham gestured to Lewis, and they moved across the room, standing in a corner, backs to her, chatting.

'What are you doing this weekend?'

'Fishing. Trying to get as much time on the boat with the kids before school starts. You?'

'Golf.' Brittingham raised his arms, mimicking a swing. 'Fore! How many kids do you have again? Seems like there's a new one every year.'

'Four.'

'For God's sake, man. Give your poor wife a break. We're heading over to Smokey's for crabs after work. What time you get off today?'

'Unless something comes up, same as usual. Four.' Nora jumped at the vehemence of that last word.

She scanned the photos again. The guy with the scar: probably not. A scar hadn't made an impression during that nanosecond encounter. Number Two's hair was too long. Number Five, too heavyset, dewlaps worthy of a bulldog. Number Three, maybe. Or Four. She studied the latter, forgetting the admonition about a quick look. Short hair, high forehead, stunned expression. So young, just a teenager.

She closed her eyes and tried to remember the kid; saw only the green flash of the Kia just off her bumper, the apologetic shrug – goddammit, she was sure of that, way more sure than she was of this photo. Did Number Four look like the youth in the newspaper? Maybe.

'It might be Number Four,' she said, and they stopped talking and sauntered back to the table.

'But I can't be sure.'

'Noted,' Brittingham said. He pulled a pen from his pocket and circled Number Four. 'Just initial here.'

'This doesn't mean I've positively identified him, does it? Because I'm not really sure. I just said it might be.' She wanted to be clear on that, almost as much as she wanted out of this airless room and away from these men who seemed determined to push her into something she hadn't said.

'You made that very clear,' Brittingham said. He held out the pen. 'We really appreciate the time you've taken today. It's a big help.'

'With the timeline, right?' It seemed they'd gotten way off track from the timeline.

'Exactly. It's pretty much what we already knew. Here.' The pen hung between them. 'You're free to go.'

But Brittingham stood blocking the door and he didn't move aside until she'd inked her initials in a jagged scrawl next to the photo of a youth whose stare suddenly seemed one of accusation.

It didn't hit her until the click of the closing door.

All those hints. Fore!

The four kids, beers after work at four.

And it had worked.

'Bastards!'

She whirled and reached for the door.

Stopped with her fingers folded around the handle.

Imagined returning to that claustrophobic room, facing Brittingham's avuncular superiority, Lewis's chatty condescension. Explaining herself. But how?

She'd have to accuse them. Piss them off. At the very least, they'd say she'd misunderstood. She'd come across as flighty. Unreliable. All the usual labels applied to women.

Besides, what did it matter if they'd steered her to the right guy? He'd been driving the Kia and now he was dead.

Her fingers released the door and she hurried away from the police station, feeling as guilty as the miscreants its inhabitants were meant to pursue.

TWELVE

Heat bent in waves above the hood of Nora's truck parked in the sun outside the police department, its black surface soaking up the sunshine and radiating it back.

Someone had tucked a piece of paper beneath the windshield wiper. It curled as though trying to avoid contact with the scorching metal. Nora reached for it, expecting a come-on for a pizza place or maybe a car wash, but instead found a flyer advertising a march along Commerce Street to the courthouse.

She stepped into the pool of shade beneath a tree, activated the truck's remote start, and studied the leaflet as she waited for the air conditioning to cool the truck's interior.

It showed the same photo of Robert Evans that had run in the newspaper, with large red block letters below.

March for Truth.

Demand Answers.

History must not repeat itself.

That last line was above the black-and-white photo of Robert's uncle, who must have been just about his nephew's age in the photo, although the corona of Afro and embroidered dashiki proclaimed a different era. Nora thought she saw a family resemblance in the high forehead, the set of jaw.

'How'd they get this together so fast?'

Nora looked up.

An older white woman removed the leaflet from her own car, pinching the folded paper between thumb and forefinger, holding it away from her body.

'The internet,' said Nora. She didn't recognize the woman. Maybe she was one of the Washingtonians who'd increasingly colonized Chateau, either with second homes or in their retirement. No one would ever mistake her for old wealth – diamond jewelry a little too ostentatious, clothing a little too bright – or even the yearning-to-be-old-wealth people snapping up the historic homes along the river. But at least an address in Chateau gave her proximity. Nora imagined her buying a one-level duplex in the new 'planned living' community outside town, or a condo in the multi-story monstrosity that loomed beside the river, marveling at how cheap everything was not two hours beyond the Beltway. The woman's next words disabused her of that notion.

'Coming down here from Baltimore, just like they did before, stirring up trouble, just when this has finally gotten to be a nice place again.'

She opened her fingers. The leaflet fluttered to the sidewalk.

'If I were you, I'd find someplace else to be that day. How many times can one town burn?'

Nora stood rooted on the sidewalk, watching the woman drive away. The hands on the courthouse clock pointed straight up toward the sun that hung directly overhead, pressing heat upon the town with baleful efficiency. It emanated from the sidewalk through the soles of Nora's running shoes. Her pores sprang a collective leak.

She spindled the flyer in her hand and, in a combination of impulse and muscle memory, clicked off the truck's starter and walked next door to the library, one of the first places in Chateau to be air-conditioned, and a reliable summer refuge in her childhood. She pushed through the door and into welcome cool darkness.

A voice as familiar as it was improbable greeted her. 'May I help you?'

'Miss Emily?'

A woman crept uncertainly from behind the desk, her head thrust forward from the indignity of a hunch that resulted from childhood polio. 'I'm sorry. I turn the lights off when I'm alone here. It keeps it cooler.' She clawed at the wall and found a switch. Light struck like a blow.

'Oh, my soul. Nora Best, is that you?'

Her head came only to Nora's chest, which is where it rested when she wrapped her arms around the younger woman, holding her for a long moment before pushing her away.

'Let me look at you.'

She stared up at Nora with the tilt-headed scrutiny mandated by her inability to straighten.

Emily Beattie's white hair was wound into a bun, the way she'd worn it as long as Nora could remember. The fierce attentiveness in her hazel eyes was likewise unchanged, belying her body's bird-like fragility. 'Come sit with me back behind the desk. If anyone comes in, I'll let you check out their books. Just like old times.'

Nora had worked in the library throughout her high school years, and the onslaught of memory – the smell of paper and ink and glue, the wall of polished wooden drawers that still held the old card catalogue, even she could see the row of screens to one side that had doubtless replaced it – left her dizzy. She perched gratefully on the same high stool behind the counter where she'd twirled back and forth as a teenager, winding a strand of hair around one finger, while Alden Tydings leaned across the desk, pretending an interest in books.

'I can't believe you're still working here.'

'I'm sure the board would love to get rid of me. Turn this whole place into a computer lab. But they don't dare. I know all the dirty books they checked out on the sly. Every time somebody none-too-tactfully suggests I retire, I go into full dotty-old-lady mode and remind them.'

She pitched her voice high, exaggerated her hunch, and held out a hand, suddenly shaking with a feigned palsy. 'Oh, Davey Leonard. How could I retire? There's nothing like seeing bright young children come through these doors, alive with the light of reading. They remind me so much of you. Imagine, a boy like you, in love with the classics! What was it, dear – *Fanny Hill*? You know, I tried to read that book myself, but I never did understand it. All that talk about some man and his giant machine – something about the Industrial Revolution, I imagine. What's that? Oh, you want me to stay? That's nice, dear.'

Nora threw back her head in laughter and nearly fell off her stool. 'I read all those books, too. But because I worked here, I never checked them out. I just read them in the stacks on my break.'

'Oh, I know, dear. I know. I think this library is the only way most people of a certain age in Chateau got any information at all about sex. At least, until they started doing their research firsthand.'

Another sly smile. More than once, she'd shooed Nora from the library some twenty minutes before closing time – 'It's so quiet tonight. Why don't I just finish things up so you can run along home?' – and watched Nora sprint from the library and leap into Alden's father's station wagon, knowing full well Nora's mother had calculated the length of the drive from the library to Quail House to the minute and there'd be hell to pay if Nora arrived any later than a quarter past. But, oh, the things that could be accomplished in those twenty stolen minutes, Alden pulling off the road into one of the gravel lanes that led into the marsh, the car shielded by waving reeds!

Miss Emily reached up and took Nora's face in her hands, studying it for a long moment. She dropped her hands. 'No, it doesn't show. At least, not so most people would notice. Well done.'

'What doesn't show?'

'Child. You were never stupid. Don't start now.'

Nora had forgotten the unvarnished intelligence so at odds with the vapid mask worn by nearly all the women of a certain age in Chateau.

'You've been through a terrible ordeal. How are you holding up, my dear?'

Nora swallowed, unable to speak. She could handle the imperfectly disguised curiosity of the biddies, the judgment in the barista's eyes, the malice in Kyra's, but genuine empathy nearly undid her. She lifted a shoulder, the shrug the only response she could manage.

Miss Emily laid an age-splotched hand, fingers cruelly knotted by arthritis, atop hers. 'You'll be fine. You were always strong. You take after your mother that way. You got out of this place.'

Nora started. 'But Mother never left Chateau. Except for boarding school, anyway, and then she came right back.'

Penelope Best had taken herself off – or her parents had sent her; Nora had never been clear on that – to New England for her final two years of high school. The move mightily offended the biddies of the day, bypassing as it did the local private school hastily created when it became clear the feds weren't kidding about desegregation, or even pedigreed Southern institutions like Madeira or St Anne's. She'd further offended everyone by marrying upon graduation a boy she'd met at a function with a neighboring school – a guileless Vermonter who never understood that the honeyed politeness of the South masked a chill deeper than the harshest New England winter – dragging him back to Chateau, where her father installed him in a manager's job at the crab-packing plant, leaving himself free to devote his full attention to the police force.

Miss Emily lifted an eyebrow. 'There's more than one way to escape this place. How is your mother? Is she recovering? So good of you to rush back to her aid.'

Her wry tone told Nora that Miss Emily knew good and well that Nora's appearance in Chateau represented a running away from the intolerable circumstances in which she'd found herself, the same way she'd fled the unbearable news of Alden's liaison with Kyra just a few weeks after Nora left for college.

'I didn't even know she'd been hurt until I got here.'

Miss Emily's chortle was deep and appreciative. 'That doesn't surprise me a bit. If you hadn't come home, chances are you'd never have heard about it at all.'

'I know.' Nora laughed again, relieved that they'd moved on to the subject of her mother.

But Miss Emily's mirth ceased abruptly. 'You've come back at such an awful time. That poor boy.'

No mention of Alden. Nora decided to leave it that way. 'Is it true that Grace Evans is his aunt? Do you know his people?'

The phrase slipped unthinking from her lips. One's *people* were everything in Chateau, firmly denoting place in the endless gradations of social strata, so much so that whenever Nora spoke of a new friend, her mother would inquire sharply, 'But who are her people?'

'Everybody knows his people. This town is full of Evanses.'

'I went to school with some.' All the Evanses were black, just as all the Brittinghams were white. 'And, of course, there's Grace. But how can he be her nephew? He was only, what, nineteen, twenty? Miss Grace is ancient. Great-nephew, maybe.'

Nora had done some imprecise math in her head. No matter how she worked it, the numbers seemed wrong.

'Apparently, his father was one of those late-in-life surprises,' Miss Emily said drily. 'I understand it happens.' She herself had never married, due to the disease that had so cruelly pretzeled her spine, even though most people now took it for a normal, if unfortunate, dowager's hump.

Nora smoothed the flyer on the counter, pointing to the black-and-white photo under *History Must Not Repeat Itself*.

Emily blinked rapidly and turned her head away. 'Yes, that's Grace's brother. A tragedy. And now this.'

Nora's hand crept to her mouth at the belated comprehension of the double weight of sorrow affecting Grace. She made a mental note to send flowers, then corrected herself. Such a gesture, while acceptable in her former world of acquaintances in Denver, would seem almost insultingly distant, given her family's long relationship with Grace. 'To lose them both . . .' she murmured.

'She didn't lose them,' Emily reminded her, with the precision for which Nora simultaneously had always admired and feared her. 'They were murdered.'

The word hung between them like an open door. Nora knew she

could turn and walk away, get in her truck and drive back to Quail House, tend to her mother and ignore whatever troubling history was bubbling up anew, roiling Chateau's placid surface. Curiosity kept her planted. An investigation would exonerate Alden. But . . .

She put her finger on the photo again.

'What happened to Bobby Evans?'

Miss Emily climbed down from her stool with some difficulty and made her way to the front door. She flipped the *Open* sign to *Closed*, then turned the lights off again for good measure. Then, as she and Nora sat in the dark, she told the story of Robert Evans's uncle.

THIRTEEN

'It happened a little before you were born. Maybe a year or two earlier. Chateau was different then. Segregated.'

'Wait a minute.' Nora hated to stop her as soon as she'd started, but she was doing more math in her head, harkening back to a dimly remembered college course in contemporary American studies. '*Brown v Board of Education* had to be a decade earlier.'

When Miss Emily shook her head, her entire torso swiveled with it, setting the stool in motion. 'In Topeka. A city in the middle of the country. Not a nowhere place like this, sticking out into the ocean and cut off by the bay from the rest of the country. You can't imagine how isolated the Eastern Shore was then. The Bay Bridge was only about ten years old, and just a single span, not the two bridges it is today. People from Washington drove over to Ocean City and Rehoboth in the summer, but not nearly as many as today, and they certainly didn't detour to a little place like Chateau. There really wasn't anybody to notice that *Brown* didn't change a thing in Chateau. Not anybody who mattered, anyway.'

Not anybody white, she meant. Minute by minute, Nora felt herself slipping back into the old codes, all the things that didn't need to be spelled out, just simply accepted as the way they were and always had been.

'Every so often, somebody from the federal government would

come poking around, and the school administrators would talk them blue in the face about our neighborhood schools. What that meant was, black kids – *colored* was the polite word back then – went to school with black, and white kids with white. The *Brown* case might have struck down separate but equal elsewhere in the world, but it was alive and well in Chateau.'

Nora thought back. For as long as she could remember, there'd been black kids in her classes. She said as much.

'It's because of what happened that year. You could say it got its start when Bobby Evans came back.'

'What do you mean, came back? I thought he was from here.'

'He was, but he left Chateau. The whole family – Miss Davita, Mister Gerald, Bobby and Grace – all packed up and went to Baltimore. They didn't go farther north like a lot of people, but even Baltimore was a big improvement over Chateau back in those days.'

'But he came back.'

Her white head bobbed. 'Yes.'

'For a visit?'

'No. He was in college by then. Morgan State. Some sort of sports scholarship, if I remember correctly. He came with a group of young people from the school. They were going to spend their summer trying to desegregate Chateau. Sit at the tables in the Wagon Wheel, come down from the balcony in the movie theater, just like in the South all those years earlier. Funny how progress, such as it was, came to Alabama before it got to the Eastern Shore. Chateau didn't have any buses, but if it had, I'm sure he and the others would have sat up front.'

She paused, and Nora remembered those pauses, the way Miss Emily had always forced her to figure out things for herself.

'What about Grace?'

'She came down, too, but not with the group. She was working for a newspaper in Baltimore by then, the *Afro-American*. They sent a columnist to write about what was happening here, and Grace came along with him. They left their parents and their baby brother back in Baltimore.'

She paused and appeared to be working out something. 'More than a baby by then. A toddler, he must have been. After her brother was killed, Grace never went back to Baltimore. Said she wanted people here to see her face every day so they'd never forget that they'd killed her brother.'

'Who killed him?'

The hump shifted in a shrug. Nora looked away.

'Nobody knows. They never arrested anyone. He'd been back a couple of weeks by then. They'd staged a few actions – took a table in the Wagon Wheel, marched along Commerce Street with signs. Some reporters came over from Baltimore and up from Washington and down from Philadelphia, expecting a big story. Selma in our own backyard – that sort of thing.'

'What happened?'

'Nothing.'

'What do you mean, nothing?' The woman she'd encountered outside had said something about the town burning.

Miss Emily sniffed.

'Nothing – at least not at first. You know this place. Everybody just looked the other way. There was barely a white soul to be seen on the streets during the marches. And at the Wagon Wheel – well, all the white people just up and left their meals right on the tables, and the owners sent the help home, turned off the lights and put up the closed sign. I guess Bobby and his friends sat there in the dark a while, and finally went home. So did those big-city reporters. No police dogs, no fire hoses, no stories.'

Nora could just imagine. Her own mother practically had a PhD in that particular Southern skill of looking the other way. 'Pretty effective tactic. But you said, "at first."'

'It must have been so frustrating for those kids. Coming over here all fired up, full of idealism, ready to be heroes – or martyrs. Because, given the things going on elsewhere, that was a real possibility.'

Even Nora, who'd been born after the worst of it, knew the names Goodman, Schwerner and Chaney, who'd ended up buried in an earthen dam. Emmett Till lynched. Medgar Evers, Malcolm X and then, of course, King, who was shot dead the year she was born. Just like she knew the more recent ones – Michael Brown, Freddie Gray, Tamir Rice – names to evoke a sad shake of the head and maybe a quick comment about rogue cops, before something more pressing claimed her attention. As if there could be anything more pressing, she told herself. Not if you were the mother of a black son. Or, thinking now of Grace, the sister. And the aunt.

'If everyone was ignoring them, what happened to Bobby Evans?'

'His group decided to bring in someone new, someone with a national profile. A radical, a lot of people called him. Maybe even a Black Panther. Someone nobody could ignore, the way they could a bunch of college kids. Except the night before he was supposed to speak, somebody killed Bobby. Shot him dead.'

The words dropped the temperature in the library a couple of degrees. Nora rubbed at her arms, surprised not to feel goosebumps.

'Who shot him?'

'Nobody knows, not to this day. Black people think white people killed him. White people think his own took him out. Black-on-black crime, I suppose they'd call it now.'

'Who's they?'

But she knew without asking, and Miss Emily's silence told her she knew Nora had realized it, too. 'They' would have been the police. And the Police Chief who signed off on that final determination?

Her grandfather.

Miss Emily watched it come to her and nodded slow confirmation.

'Grace Evans is still waiting for someone to be held accountable for her brother's murder. And now, her nephew's. And everybody in town – at least everybody who remembers that time – is holding their breath, hoping half the town doesn't go up in flames again. Which is what happened after they found Bobby's body. The governor even called in the National Guard.'

'How have I never heard about this?'

Emily didn't dignify the stupidity of the question with a response. Nora tried again.

'But this is different. There'll be an investigation. They've got all those cameras now – dash cams, body cams.'

'Not here. The referendum that would have paid for them got turned down last year.'

Nora issued a final, weak protest. 'Things have changed.'

'Change? In Chateau? Oh, child.'

FOURTEEN

1963

'You're wrong.'

Penelope's pronouncements carried the certainty of innocence – Bobby's interpretation – or straight-up ignorance, which was Grace's take on them. These days, Penelope dressed when she came downstairs, sometimes even before noon, hovering in the kitchen when Grace was working there, or out on the patio when she and Bobby took a break, showing up so frequently that Grace now routinely prepared three glasses of iced tea or lemonade.

'Change *is* coming,' Penelope insisted during one of those breaks. 'Chateau High will be integrated before Bobby and I graduate. You watch.'

Bobby and Grace exchanged glances.

'Sure,' Bobby said, one of those words that sounded like assent.

'Won't hold my breath,' Grace muttered. Bobby routinely teased Penelope, mock arguing with her until her pale cheeks turned pink and the tip of her nose, always peeling from her unsuccessful attempts at tanning, went bright red.

'You're going to get yourself in trouble,' Grace often warned him. 'Messing with a white girl's head like that. All you need to say is one thing wrong – or even just one thing she takes wrong – and' – she snapped her fingers and nodded toward his crotch – 'kiss Mama and Daddy's grandkids goodbye.'

Now he lifted his iced tea in a toast. 'Here's to integration.' Penelope raised her own glass in return. They both looked at Grace, who pretended to be fiddling with a hangnail.

The dog, Kathleen Mavourneen, heard the car first. She raised her head and trotted around the side of the house issuing a few warning barks. A door slammed a few seconds later. Penelope jumped up. 'That'll be Todd. We're going to Ocean City today.' The straps of her bikini peeked coyly from her sundress. It would return home wet and full of sand and sticky with salt, and it would be

Grace's job to pick it up off her bedroom floor, vacuum away the sand and wash the suit.

'What do you see in him? Boy couldn't hit a baseball if you hung it in front of him on a string.'

Grace hissed at her brother. *Knock it off*, her eyes signaled.

But Penelope just laughed. 'I'm going to run upstairs and get my towel. Tell him I'll be right down.'

Say please, Grace mouthed after her. 'What?' she said in response to Bobby's look. 'Would it kill her just once to ask instead of throwing orders right and left?'

'Yeah, Grace. You tell her.' Bobby fished an ice cube out of his glass and flicked it at her, dancing out of her reach as she lunged at him. She thought to give chase but wanted to escape to the safety of the house before Todd – even now calling for Penelope – rounded the corner.

'I'm gone.' Bobby hurried around the other side of the house, back to his endless windows. Grace headed for the back door, slowed by the necessity of balancing the discarded glasses on a tray. Too late.

'What do we have here?'

Todd moved quickly to the door, blocking her way.

'Where's Penelope?'

'Getting her things. Said she'd be right down.' It was, as far as Grace could remember, the first time she'd ever spoken to him.

'Knowing Penelope, that means fifteen minutes. Gives us time for a quickie. Come on. Whaddaya say?'

Grace's forearms flexed. The glasses rattled on the tray. She imagined them crashing against his face, the glass shattering against his forehead, the tepid tea mingling with hot blood.

He took a step toward her. Reached for the tray. 'Let's get this out of the way.' She jerked away and watched it fly from her hands, the only barrier between them, a potential weapon gone, the glasses catching the sunlight as they fell, shattering into sparkling shards on the patio's bricks,

Todd stood so close she could smell him, soap and aftershave and something musky, feral. His breathing quickened. A flush climbed his face.

'Leave me alone.' Her voice rose.

His hand shot out, his fingers pinching her nipple through the thin fabric of her housedress and bra, squeezing, twisting.

She cried out.

He dropped his hand, laughing, and fumbled at the front of his jeans. Then he was gone, falling away from her so fast that she staggered back into the wall and slid down to the patio's sun-warmed bricks. Todd, too, was on the ground, writhing backward to escape an assailant of his own.

Bobby stood over him, fists raised. 'Get up. Get up. What did you do to my sister?'

'No, Bobby!' Grace gasped. Somehow she was on her feet again, grabbing her brother's upraised arms, trying to pull him away. But he stood still as granite, and just as immovable.

'Get up.'

Todd scrambled to his feet, backing out of reach.

Grace let go of Bobby and stood between them on shaking legs. 'I'm fine, Bobby. Everything's fine.'

Todd's thin lips wormed into a semblance of their characteristic smirk. 'You heard her. She's fine.'

'You did something to her. Look at her. She's not fine.'

Todd edged farther away.

'She liked it. Soon as you left out of here, she was all over me.'

Bobby crouched, ready to leap on him. A voice floated from the house.

'Todd? Where'd you go?'

Bobby straightened. Grace watched the fear and false bravado drain from Todd's face. The door banged open. Penelope stood within it, hands on hips, looking to each of them in turn.

'What's going on here?'

Grace turned away, afraid of what Penelope might see in her face.

Todd recovered first, with the same practiced ease with which he'd left off tormenting Grace during his ballgames.

'Grace dropped the tray.'

'Then clean it up. And be glad it's not the Waterford.'

Early on, Grace had poured drinks into the pretty cut-glass tumblers that had a cabinet all to themselves, only to elicit a horrified shriek from Penelope. 'Not the Waterford! Mom'll kill us if she finds out we've used it.'

Penelope issued another order – 'Come on, Todd. We're going to miss the best part of the day' – and disappeared back into the house.

'You heard her,' Todd said to Grace. 'Clean it up.'

And, with the security of knowing his girlfriend remained within earshot of any raised voices, any sounds of a further scuffle, muttered to Bobby as he passed, 'Better watch your back from here on out, boy.'

That night, Grace undressed carefully, averting her eyes from her body until the last possible moment. Bruises bloomed across the swollen flesh. She cupped her breast gently in her palm, thinking of the question she'd posed Bobby as they walked home together that evening, the fury wafting off him in waves; a question he deigned not to answer.

'Still think things are changing?'

FIFTEEN

Nora stepped out of the library into the sun, its warmth welcome even as it blinded her.

Emily's story had left her chilled. Images flashed like an old-fashioned newsreel through her head. People marching, staging sit-ins. A confrontation. A shot. Bobby Evans slumping to the ground, much as his nephew had a half-century later. Alden had shot Robert. But who took aim at Bobby, pulled the trigger?

The door to the hardware store opened as she passed. Cool air rushed out, along with a man who moved in front of her, so similar in height and build to her grandfather that she gasped. She stepped back and shaded her eyes, unaccountably relieved as a stranger came into focus.

'Nora Best. Heard you were back in town. Happy to see you.'

He was one of those men who'd likely been almost too pretty as a boy and then watched those good looks fade into grotesquery as he aged: dark pouches under the eyes, the once-chiseled cheekbones sliding into wobbly jowls framing thin colorless lips, the neck gone soft and shapeless even as the belly protruded high and hard, preceding him like an announcement. Only the hair hinted at what it had once been, silver now instead of a likely blond, still thick and styled in a vain backsweep.

He held out his hand. 'Todd Burris. Your mother and I went to school together.'

'Of course.' She couldn't place him, not exactly. There were almost as many white Burrises in Chateau as there were black Evanses.

He helped her out. 'I own the car dealership and body shop.'

'Of course.' That explained the blazer and tie, the practiced smile, all teeth, stopping just before the eyes.

'Saw you walking past and hustled outside to thank you.' He was still holding her hand.

She pulled away. 'For?'

'For stepping up to help out Alden. Quicker we can get him out of this mess, the better.'

We? And how did he know . . . but this was Chateau. Nora fumbled for her keys and hit the unlock button on the fob. Her truck's headlights blinked, signaling her intention to leave. 'Nice to have met you,' she began.

But Todd wasn't done with her yet. 'I found myself in the same sort of situation back in the day. That boy Alden shot? They thought I killed his uncle.'

Nora forgot about leaving.

'Miss Grace's brother? Bobby Evans?'

'The one and the same. That boy who came back here stirring up all the trouble.'

There it was again. Boy.

'Did you?'

He blinked. She'd gone off script.

'Hell, no. Whoever shot him did it with some little popgun, nothing I'd ever own. Besides, I was down at the Beach that night. Half a dozen people vouched for me fifty ways to Sunday.'

She bet they had. But even as she fitted Todd Burris's bulk into the shadowy outline of the killer in the story Emily Beattie had just told her, his next words dissolved her suspicions, even as they cemented her instinctive dislike of the man.

'Tell you what, though. If I'd had the chance, I'd have shot him twice over.'

He grinned at the expression on her face, the meanness in it reaching his eyes this time. 'He worked for your grandparents; used to hassle your mother something fierce. Wouldn't leave her alone. This one time, if I hadn't been around, Lord knows what might have happened. Smartest thing your parents ever did was send her off to New England. Of course, that didn't work out too well for me. I sparked her, you know.'

Nora put a hand to her head. Too much information, too fast. Penelope – her delicate, wide-eyed mother who treasured fine things – used to date this goon? She tried to recapture her first fleeting impression of the young man he must have been, but saw instead her quiet, gentle father, a man who maintained his dignity even through the final agonizing months of ravaging disease.

'Anyway.' He took a step closer, well into her personal space, that old tactic men liked to use on women. Nora planted her feet and waited.

'Just wanted to let you know how much we all appreciate the way you're helping Alden avoid the same B.S. I went through. You take care.'

He laid a meaty hand on her shoulder. Nora held herself very still until he'd disappeared back into the hardware store.

SIXTEEN

1963

By the time Chief Smythe fired Bobby, so many weeks had passed that Grace had almost started to think things would be all right.

One day, though, the Chief came home for lunch, as he sometimes did, but instead of heading into the kitchen where Grace, upon hearing the crunch of his squad car's tires on the gravel driveway, had prepared a chicken salad sandwich and poured a glass of sweet tea, he instead strode around the corner of the house and into the backyard where Bobby was up on his ladder. Bobby was busy washing windowpane Number Five Hundred and Thirty-Eight, or at least that's what he'd told Grace that morning. 'I did the math,' he said. 'Time I finish, I'll have to start all over again. I could be washing windows the rest of my life, seems like. If that isn't incentive to get my ass to college, I don't know what is.'

The Chief's voice floated through the open kitchen window. 'Bobby Evans, you get down off that ladder right now. I want to speak to you.'

Grace caught her breath. Philippa was in town. Penelope was still asleep. The Chief stood outside the library, looking up at the ladder. She wiped her hands on her apron and ran to the library and eased behind the drapes, careful not to disturb them, and lifted the window an inch, thankful it wasn't one of the ones whose frame had warped over the years, leaving it impossible to raise. She pressed her back against the wall and listened.

'Hey, Chief Smythe,' Bobby said easily. Either he hadn't caught the tone in the Chief's voice or, more likely, he'd detected trouble and was trying to head it off.

The ladder creaked as Bobby descended.

'What can I do for you, Chief Smythe?'

'You can stay the hell away from my daughter.'

Grace clamped her hands over her mouth to keep a whimper from escaping. Of all the things that could have riled the Chief, this was the worst. Nothing – not guns or copperheads or a rusty nail to a bare foot – was more dangerous to a black man than a white woman; more deadly still when that woman was but a girl and the daughter of one of the most powerful men in town. Oh, Bobby. Tears dripped on to her fingers.

'Sir. With all due respect, sir.'

'Don't you "sir" me. And don't act like you don't know what I'm talking about.' The Chief's rage crashed through the open window like a thunderclap, pinning Grace in place.

'Sir, please. If you just talk to Penelope. Miss Penelope.'

Oh, God. He'd slipped and slipped hard, and the Chief had caught it. His voice dropped a register and quieted, far more terrifying than if he'd raised it.

'Don't. You. Dare. Presume to address my child by her name. I don't need to talk to her. Todd Burris told me all about what you've been up to. He said she's been scared to death, locking herself in her room day and night, afraid of what you might do to her.'

Rage flooded Grace, replacing fear. Penelope Smythe stayed in her room all day because she was the laziest person on the face of the earth. And she didn't lock her door, although Grace often wished she had, so that she wouldn't be able to see the mess within – one more chore to deal with on her endless list.

Her hand went to her breast. Had Penelope really said that to Todd? Or had he fabricated it, making good on his promise to get back at Bobby? It didn't matter. The Chief believed it. She thought of the service weapon that rode on the Chief's hip, its polished walnut stock within ready reach. Fury, so energizing, ebbed as terror rushed back in. Would the Chief shoot Bobby on the spot? How would he explain it? Would he even have to?

'Chief Smythe, I swear.' The panic in Bobby's voice mirrored her own.

'Not another word out of you. Get the hell out of my sight and don't let me ever see you again. Not around here, not around town, not on the road, not in the fields. You see me, you run like hell before I so much as catch a glimpse of you. You understand?'

The pounding of Bobby's feet echoed the jackhammer in Grace's heart. She didn't wait for the Chief to fire her, too, but fled the library and down the long hall to the front door – the one she'd never used except to clean – untying her apron as she ran, dropping it in the driveway and sprinting after Bobby as fast as she could, trying to outrun the evil reaching for them both.

SEVENTEEN

The phone shrilled at eight in the morning, so startling Nora that she nearly upended her coffee. She couldn't remember the last time she'd heard a landline, so much more insistent and demanding than the various chimes and chirrups of ringtones.

She dove for it, grabbing it on the third ring, glancing toward the phone's blank surface, reflexively checking to see who was calling even though the ancient phone had no such function.

'Quail House.'

'I'm trying to reach Nora Best.' A man's voice.

'Speaking.'

'This is Stephen Abrams from the *Baltimore Sun*. I'm writing a story about the Robert Evans shooting.'

Nora froze. The man spoke into the silence. 'I was hoping to talk with you about your account of the road-rage incident before the shooting.'

'Excuse me?' Nora held the phone away from her ear and glared at it. 'How did you get my name?'

'It was in the newspaper.'

'It most certainly was not. I read the *Chateau Crier* myself and my name was not in that story.'

The paper lay on the table beside her with a damning banner headline:

Police: Road-Rage Incident Preceded Shooting

She'd gone cold at the sight of it, relaxing only when she'd realized the story hadn't named her. But someone had.

'I repeat my question: How did you get my name?'

A stalling tactic, useless. Because did it really matter how? They had it now. Stephen Abrams told her, anyway.

'I'm sorry,' he said, his tone so perfunctory as to negate any real apology. 'I should have said. It was in the *Afro*. The, ah, *Afro-American*. It covers the black community in Baltimore.'

'I know what the *Afro* is.' But only because Emily Beattie had mentioned it the day before.

Abrams forged on. 'So, as I said, I was hoping to talk with you about your account, as well as your relationship with Alden Tydings—'

Nora cut him off. 'Sorry to disappoint you.' She hung up without saying goodbye, fingers flying over her cellphone even as the old tabletop phone beside her vibrated from the force of the slammed-down receiver.

The *Afro*'s story largely mirrored the *Crier*'s account – the pro-forma statements from Brittingham that, as far as Nora was concerned, far exaggerated her own version of events – with two important differences.

One, a sentence whose impact landed like a fist, leaving her gasping: *Brittingham did not identify the witness, but a source gave her name as Nora Best, once romantically involved with the officer who shot Robert Evans.*

Along with a photo she hadn't seen in years: herself in an off-the-shoulder dress with a poofy skirt, bracelets halfway up her forearm, hair teased and tousled and moussed – it had been her Madonna phase – beside Alden in a tux with a shiny teal bow tie that matched her dress. Their senior prom picture. Someone must have found a yearbook. Could anything be more embarrassing?

Then, a damning paragraph.

> Best is the author of *Do It Daily*, a book promoting daily sex, and more recently was involved in a notorious kidnapping and murder case in Wyoming that left her husband dead. One suspect remains at large in that case. She could not be reached for comment, despite numerous attempts.

Nora thought of the repeated calls to her cell the previous day from an unrecognized number. The source who'd provided her name to the *Afro* must have had her phone number, too. Her mind went to the lone black cop assigned to door duty in the Chateau Police Department. She shied away from the thought. But the *Sun* reporter hadn't had her cell number. Abrams must have found Penelope's number online somewhere and called it as a Hail Mary. And Nora had played right into it, instead of putting him off with some innocuous response. 'Wrong number,' would have sufficed.

She read the paragraph again, the coy 'involved in' the Wyoming case, suggesting her involvement was somehow voluntary rather than the terror-filled event that had sent her fleeing to Chateau for solace.

She read on.

> 'What's that saying? Déjà vu all over again,' said the Rev. James Warren, now retired, who was pastor of the AME Zion Church when Evans's uncle was killed in Chateau. 'They're trying to make out like the victim is the one at fault, just like they did back then. And they got away with it then. But not now. Once was too much. Twice – no, we're not having it.'

Along with a follow-up quote from Grace Evans, echoing the reverend's words in far more poignant terms:

> 'You think that once your heart is broken, the worst has happened. That the only good thing is nothing will ever be that bad again. Then you find out you're wrong.'

Nora sank into her chair.

Grace *was* wrong.

Nora didn't know what had happened in the past, but Alden's account of shooting Robert Evans had been so heartfelt she had to believe it. The investigation would bear that out, she was sure of it. But no matter how Brittingham had spun it, her narrative shouldn't be part of the story. Even though she knew better. How many years had she spent schooling clients that perception was reality?

Somehow, she was going to have to change the perception being formed of her in Chateau.

EIGHTEEN

Penelope found Nora not in her trailer where she should have been working on her book but in the kitchen with a streak of flour across her face stirring up batter for a cake. Michael Murphy, already the recipient of a flake of butter after she'd greased and floured the shallow rectangular pan, lay practically across her feet, positioned for more opportunity.

Nora heard the thump of Penelope's walker before her mother appeared. She grabbed the kettle, simmering on the stove, and poured the water over the leaves in the pot.

'Good heavens. What's happening? Are you baking something? You aren't seriously thinking of turning on the oven, are you? It's supposed to be ninety-eight degrees today.'

Nora set pot and cup on the table. 'It's more bearable now than it will be later. I'm baking a cake to bring to Miss Grace. Any other time of year I'd have done a casserole, but that's the last thing anyone wants to eat in this heat.'

She'd come up with the idea of the cake minutes after hanging up on the *Sun* reporter. Combine the twinned speed of the internet with small-town gossip and everyone in town would know what she'd seen the night Robert was shot – even though she hadn't really seen anything – and attribute all manner of motives.

Nora needed to put a stop to it but could hardly stand in the middle of Commerce Street shouting, 'It's not what you think!' She needed an ally, someone in the black community who could vouch for her character, and who better than Grace, who'd known her since childhood, and had the unassailable credentials as the dead youth's aunt?

Hence, the cake: the perfect excuse to approach Grace. After all, it's what one did after a death.

Penelope unfolded her napkin, flapped it in front of her face in a forlorn attempt to rearrange the air's molecules into a semblance of coolness, and poured tea. She looked better than she had in the last few days, Nora thought. Some color in her cheeks. Or maybe it was just the heat.

'What kind of cake?'

'Peach. They had just-ripe ones in town. I got extra so we could have some on ice cream tonight.'

The peaches were piled high in a basket on the counter, next to the cutting board and a paring knife, the fuzz aglow in the shaft of sunlight through the window over the sink.

'I should have known. I could smell them as soon as I walked in. Lovely. Nothing says summer like a ripe peach.'

'End of summer,' Nora reminded her. To her, peaches had always embodied both sadness and promise, ripening as they did midway through summer, reaching their peak in August, when the days were already growing almost imperceptibly shorter, and mornings – no matter how oppressive the heat of the coming day – teased with hints of cool. They held within them the knowledge of the end of the carefree indolence of childhood as well as the guarantee of the approaching autumn, the crisp air stirring somnolent senses alive again.

'A peach cake to Grace. Talk about coals to Newcastle.'

'She taught me how to make it. I used to make one every so often in Denver. They had peaches from the West Slope in Colorado. Not as good as ours, but you didn't dare say that there. And it goes without saying my cake was never as good as hers, especially out there, where the altitude played hell – sorry – with my baking. But I like to think it came close. We'll see how this one comes out.'

Grace hadn't exactly taught her. As a girl, Nora had hovered so insistently whenever Grace was baking that she'd finally barked at Nora to sit on a chair without moving, and then had narrated, as though to herself, the steps to a perfect peach cake. She addressed

Nora directly only once, turning to face her to import the seriousness of her message: 'Don't even think about putting cinnamon on this. Perfect peaches are their own glory.'

'She would have picked the recipe up when she lived in Baltimore,' Penelope said. 'Those old German bakeries used to sell them.'

Nora stirred sugar into warm milk in a small bowl and sprinkled yeast on to it, then whisked together flour, salt and more sugar while she waited for the yeast mixture to prove. 'I never knew she'd lived there.'

Leaving it open-ended, wondering if her mother would add to Emily Beattie's sparse account. Besides, it was true. To her, Grace was as much a part of Chateau as the Colonial-era homes, the meandering river, the ever-closer creeping marshes and, yes, the peach trees that lingered in people's yards, remnants of orchards that once supplied Baltimore with the makings of its famous cake.

Penelope stirred her tea, the spoon tink-tinking against the china.

'She was there for a few years.'

Tink-tink.

'Her brother went to college there. The whole family went with him.'

Tink.

'She came back here after he . . . died. Oh! Oh, no!' She shoved away from the table, nearly toppling her chair in her haste to escape the shards of china, the splash of lukewarm tea.

Nora rushed to her side with a towel. 'It's OK, Mother. I've got it. Look, there's hardly any mess. You'd already drunk most of the tea.'

Penelope pointed to the floor with a shaking finger. 'But . . . Michael Murphy. He'll cut his feet.'

Nora stooped and ran the towel across the floor. 'There's only a couple of pieces. Most of them are on the table. It's fine. Really.'

'No.' Penelope shook her head so hard that wisps of hair escaped her loose chignon. 'It's not all right. That was my great-grandmother's china. Now the set is incomplete. It's just one more thing gone wrong this summer. My leg. A mouse. This heat that just refuses to break. That child being shot. Alden Tydings the one who shot him. It feels like things are falling apart all over again.'

Nora balled the towel around the bits of china and stared at her mother. It wasn't like Penelope to complain.

'It's the heat, Mother. It makes everything worse. You sit back. I'll make you more tea. I know you don't like iced, but today it'll help. I'll put in lemon, a little sugar. Or better yet, I'll crush up some mint.' It grew wild amid the flower beds, escaping from a long-ago herb garden and insinuating itself among the showier blooms.

'No, thank you.' Penelope reached for her walker, pulled it close and hoisted herself from the table. 'It's too hot in here. I'm going to sit out on the patio while there's still some shade. Once the sun hits those bricks, it turns into an oven. Of course, you might not remember. You're only out there in the mornings these days.'

Message delivered, she thumped her way back down the hall, leaving her daughter to contemplate the fact that she'd been seen tiptoeing across the patio and over the grass at dawn, down to the dock, a view perfectly framed by Penelope's bedroom window, as was the river and anybody who might happen to be rowing a boat along it.

'Hell.' Nora looked at the yeast mixture, frothing higher than she'd ever remembered, bubbles swelling and popping on its surface. She wondered if she'd let it prove too long, and decided, given Grace's exacting standards, it wasn't worth taking a chance. She threw it away, washed the bowl, and started again.

She selected a peach from the basket while she waited, slitting the skin with her thumbnail. Juice ran in sweet rivulets across her hand and down her wrist. She chased it with her tongue and bit into the fruit, trying to suck what sweetness she could from a day that held every indication of going sour.

Grace Evans lived in Chateau's black neighborhood, not in the ramshackle rental houses hard by the street that even in Nora's childhood had largely been the only places available to black people, but farther back in a small, tree-shaded neighborhood of neat bungalows built when a lawsuit finally forced banks to change their mortgage policies.

Nora wondered whether she might find a crowd, but the street was quiet when she arrived, and Grace herself sat alone and unmoving on a green porch glider. Nora waited for her to pat the place beside her, or even nod to one of the wicker chairs, but Grace did neither, so Nora stood on the porch step in full sun, the cake pan balanced on her palms.

'It's a peach cake. I made it like you taught me,' she said by way of greeting. 'No cinnamon, no glaze.'

'Cinnamon,' Miss Grace murmured. 'The color of that boy's skin. Oh, he was beautiful.'

Nora tried to remember the photos of Robert that had run with the most recent stories; blurry, most of them, taken from social media postings, precise skin shade indeterminate. She'd glimpsed him twice in passing on the road, once when he'd tossed the unspoken apology her way and again when she passed the traffic stop, his head angled down in the universal posture of frustration and unhappiness naturally part of any such encounter.

'I couldn't tell,' she murmured.

'Excuse me?' The sharp tone Nora remembered, demanding a straight answer.

'I saw him that night.' Which Grace knew. There had, after all, been that story in the *Afro*. It had quoted Grace. But the *Afro* was only delivered in Baltimore and Washington. Maybe Grace hadn't yet read the online version; was no more adept with a smartphone than Nora's mother.

'He drove by me on Route Fifty. Almost cut me off – to be fair, I was going too slowly. And then, just outside town, I saw him pulled over by—' A cop, she started to say. But Grace knew it was Alden. 'I didn't know who it was when I drove by.'

She feared Grace's anger at even the choked-off mention of Alden, but her face had gone soft, almost tearful.

'How did he seem?'

Nora thought back to those two quick-as-a-flash glances – the first as he passed her, the second as he sat in his idling car by the side of the road, lights flashing red and blue across his green car. The rigidity in his shoulders and jaw.

'Pissed,' she said. 'He looked pissed.' Then remembered where she was, to whom she was speaking. 'Excuse me, ma'am. Upset.'

Grace almost smiled. 'He would be. Should be. Everybody knows about that speed trap. Robert grew up in Baltimore, but he used to spend summers down here with me.'

She shifted an inch, toward the glider's arm. Nora took it as an invitation and joined her on the glider, resting the still-warm cake pan on her lap.

'What was that like, those summers?'

Once she'd gotten over the worst of her heartbreak, she'd luxuriated in the move to Colorado, the escape from Chateau's stultifying slow rhythms, the impossibility of going anywhere without recognizing nearly every single face and the nods of recognition in return; every remark freighted with history-laden judgment.

Only more recently had she felt a different sort of tug, urging her back instead of forward, into the solace of familiarity. The reflexive Southern politeness, no matter its often-surface quality, that eased initial encounters. The careless scattering of 'honeys' and 'dears' and 'childs.' Anonymity was freeing, but it was also cold as hell. But Robert had never had time to figure that out and now he never would.

'He'd been coming down here so many years he had friends. So that helped. And, of course, as he got older, there was that phone. Face always in it, just like every other child, and adult, too. But he was such a help to me. Mowed my grass, pruned my trees, cleaned my windows, drove me places.'

Heat rose in Nora's face, defeating the porch's deep shade. For all the work Grace did around Quail House, it had never occurred to Nora that she might need help caring for her own home.

'I'm so sorry,' Nora said. 'I didn't know what else to do. So I made a cake.' Then blushed still harder at the clumsiness of the statement.

But Grace nodded. 'We none of us know what to do. You want to think things have changed, even though you know better. But it's human nature. Life goes along and you think, well, maybe. Maybe things truly are getting better. Maybe you can relax. And then this happens and you realize that what you knew all along is true. That nothing has changed. Not one blessed thing.'

'But surely some things are better?'

The glider lurched with the violence of Grace's rising. Nora grabbed the arm for balance. Grace took the cake from her lap and carried it into the kitchen. Nora followed, wondering how to bring up Alden.

Bouquets of flowers covered Grace's kitchen counter, nearly obscuring a sweating pitcher of lemonade, a puddle of water spreading slowly from its base. Mint leaves sailed on its surface between bobbing floes of ice cubes. A kitchen fan revolved lazily overhead, creaking with each revolution.

Nora looked longingly toward the lemonade, but Grace gestured toward the table without offering any.

Nora took a seat. The flowers drooped on their stems, their petals going brown and crisp about the edges. A vase of lilies sat in the center of the table. Nora particularly detested lilies, their petals like waxen scythes, their cloying scent. Her eyes watered. She hoped she wouldn't sneeze. Grace positioned herself across from Nora, her face hidden by the bouquet.

'I never knew about your brother,' Nora blurted. 'No one ever told me.'

Grace was quiet for a long time. Every revolution of the fan pushed the scent of the lilies into Nora's face.

'What happened back then?' The same question she'd posed to Emily Beattie in the library. But the longer she could sit and talk with Grace, re-establish some sort of rapport, the better. She remembered her manners, something that always counted with Grace. 'That is, if you don't mind talking about it.'

'You don't even know. And you, growing up right here in town. That's a crime.'

'Yes. Which is why I'm asking.'

The silence went on so long that she stirred in her chair, preparing to go. Grace wasn't going to tell her anything, and she was too cowardly to bring up the subject of Alden. But maybe when the *Sun* got hold of the same ancient prom photo that the *Afro* had unearthed and called Grace for comment, she would mention that Nora had brought her a cake. Grace's musing voice, speaking almost as though to herself, interrupted her self-serving fantasy.

'Some people came down here from Baltimore to help organize for civil rights. You'd have thought Chateau was Mississippi then. You didn't have those "Colored Only" signs here, but that's only because nobody needed them. Everybody knew the way things were. Still are,' she muttered, almost as an afterthought.

Nora wanted to protest – the black cop! Black and white people together in the coffee shop! – but thought better of it.

'My brother was one of the organizers. But the night before a big march, he got shot. Things got out of hand. Same thing happened here as happened everywhere else. Windows broken, fires set. Except the fires on the white side of town got put out. The fire at our church didn't. They said it was too *dangerous*' –

sarcasm sliced through her words – 'to come over to this side of town because of the shooting. But there was only one shooting and it didn't even happen over here. They blamed it on us anyway, same as the church fire. Why would we burn our own church? Or shoot our own? But that's exactly what your grandfather did. You really want to know what happened back then? You should talk with your mother.'

She rose, finally, to pour lemonade. Nora swallowed, imagining the cool tartness hitting the back of her throat. Somewhere on the counter, amid the forest of bouquets, a ding sounded. Grace moved a couple of the bouquets aside and found a phone, holding it close to her face to read the message. Nora's stomach lurched. So much for hoping that Grace and her mother were the last two people on earth not spending their days online.

Grace whirled to face Nora, her face contorted.

'Why'd you come here? You've got some nerve. Acting like you want to know. Trying to get something on us when there's nothing to get. What are you trying to do? Help them blame things on us all over again?'

'What are you talking about?'

'Running around with him again, just like when you were a girl. But he's married now. Is that how you people do? Go after men you can't have? Just like . . . just . . . just . . .' She doubled over, sucking in air.

'First Bobby. Now Robert.' She straightened. 'Who else are you trying to take from me? My parents died a long time ago. My little brother Kwame – Robert's father – is all I got left. You gonna take him next? I told him it's like he's walking around with a big target on his back, but he didn't believe me. He will once he sees this.'

She thrust her phone in Nora's face.

Nora stood and backed away, suppressing an urge to run. Whatever was on that phone, she didn't need to see it.

But Grace advanced upon her, holding up the phone insistently. 'Bad enough what I read in the *Afro*. That road-rage bullshit you told the police. Can't believe you had the nerve to show up here after spewing that stinking sewage about my grandbaby. I let you in because I wanted to hear what you were about. See if you would own it. Well, now I know. You think you could sneak around, help him out, and nobody know what you were up to. The whole world's going to know now. You are radioactive. Look. Look.'

Nora blinked and focused on the screen, the tiny montage of images, taken from a distance, but still unmistakably recognizable as her and Alden in the boat. She puzzled over it, then remembered the woman on the bridge, the way she'd raised her hand. Nora had thought she was waving. Now she realized the woman must have been holding a phone.

The photo she'd taken that day, now enlarged and blurry, was displayed prominently on a site named *Justice for Robert Evans*. It bore a damning caption: *Killer Cop Has a Side Piece.*

'Go home, Nora.' No *Miss Nora* as in days of old. 'Go home and look yourself in the eye. Ask your mother. Talk with her about what happened back in the day. Ask her who killed my brother. Because if anyone knows, she does. Being her daddy's daughter and all. Then come back and tell me how things have changed.'

The door slammed behind her, followed by a metallic clink and then a dull thump – the unmistakable sound of a firm foot on the pedal of a metal trash can just before a peach cake landed hard in its depths.

NINETEEN

1967

'Nothing has changed in that godforsaken place. Nothing. Never has, never will. And you think you're the one to do it? Lord help me for raising a goddamn fool.'

Grace's father was as angry as she'd ever seen him, so angry he cursed in the presence of her mother, who herself was so upset she let it go by.

'Bobby, what are you thinking?'

They were in the kitchen, her father and brother on their feet facing one another, radiating intensity, Grace and her mother at the tiny table that barely fit within the rowhouse kitchen's confines. Three years after leaving Chateau, Grace's mother still mourned the house that at the time had seemed so cramped, wistfully recalling its deep porch, the narrow back yard where she grew squash and pole beans. But the house, she always hastened to add, was the only thing she missed.

Kwame toddled about in the living room, blissfully oblivious to the seething conflict just a couple of yards away. Grace and Bobby had bought him a set of blocks, and he delighted in stacking them high and then knocking them down, interrupting their conversation every few minutes with a crash.

'Did you even' – his mother inclined her head toward the living room – 'think about him?'

'He's why I'm doing this!'

Grace fully shared their parents' concern, but still she thrilled to the conviction in Bobby's voice, the purposeful set to his shoulders, the shine in his eyes.

'Things have got to change. Not just here, but in places like that. We were lucky. We got out. But think of everybody back there, the plant the only place to work, unless you want to be a yard boy like me or do day work like Grace.' He put some extra spin on the word *boy*. Grace's father winced.

'And now look at us. Daddy at the shipyard, Mama working in Hutzler's. Look at her hands.' He grabbed Davita's hands and held them up like trophies. Faint white scars crisscrossed them like threads, the legacy of years in the canning plant, nicked daily with her knife or broken bits of crab shell. But they were no longer red and swollen, the cuts inevitably festering, as they had been every day she'd worked there. Now she sat before a sewing machine in a back room at Hutzler's department store, altering pretty dresses for rich white women, and when the other seamstresses complained about the occasional finger-prick from the needles, she laughed and laughed and laughed.

'Me in college,' he continued. 'And Grace a regular career woman, working for the *Afro*. The *Afro*! Can you imagine such a thing as a black people's newspaper in Chateau?'

Grace straightened despite herself. Her job was very nearly the *Afro*'s lowliest, one step up from the copy boys, answering phones, opening mail, running various errands for the reporters and editors – but still, she was part of the *Afro*. No matter what her bosses had in mind, she'd promised herself she would not be a clerk forever.

Bobby reached for his mother's hand. She snatched it away and folded her arms across her chest as he spoke.

'Chateau, the whole Eastern Shore, it's like it never came out of the Civil War. They freed people, but nothing really changed. Well, it's time for a change, and who better to give it a push than someone like me, who grew up there?'

Gerald and Davita Evans lowered their eyes. Impossible to argue with him. Maryland had never seceded, but it was an unrepentant slave state, and in rural areas Confederate flags still flew proudly from homes and the Stars and Bars were ubiquitous on T-shirts, caps and bumper stickers.

'You can't go. You were lucky to get out once. You, of all people, cannot go back.' Davita spoke barely above a whisper, but it was as though she'd shouted. It was the thing of which they never spoke, none of them, as though when they'd left Chateau, they'd closed a heavy iron door behind them, turned the oversize key in the lock and dropped it into the river on their way out of town, shedding memories as it sank through the dark waters and buried itself deep in the muck below.

'I'll go.'

Grace looked around the room as though someone else had spoken, letting her eyes fall on the familiar objects from their home in Chateau: the rag rug – made anew by Davita every few years from scraps of worn-out clothing – in front of the sink; the pair of snarling black-glass panthers on the mantel; the framed baby pictures on the sideboard, herself and Bobby in black and white, Kwame in color. And the unfamiliar, too: the view through the kitchen window of the back 'yard,' a patch of concrete softened only by the border of geraniums that Davita planted in empty five-pound Folgers cans.

She liked Baltimore, liked its energy, and the ease that came from living and working among black people, able to let down her guard for hours and even days at a time, and she loved her job at the *Afro*. But, much as her mother missed their old house, she missed the damp cool of grass under her bare feet, the ceaseless hum of insects, the chatter of birds and, above it all, the high, lonely honk of geese. The family hadn't been back since they'd left.

She stopped her survey of the room and focused on her parents' faces, looking each in the eye in turn.

'I'll go. I'll stick with him every minute. He won't be able to get up to any trouble.'

That single word – trouble – perhaps comprising the biggest understatement Grace had made in her twenty-two years.

TWENTY

Nora drove home from Grace's in a haze of regret that fell away only when she saw the red and blue lights flashing in front of Quail House as her truck emerged from the cedars and rounded the last bend in the lane.

'Mother!' she gasped.

She floored it the final hundred yards, slewing into a skid behind the police car, jumping out just as it came to a stop, rushing up the stoop to her mother, who stood clinging to her walker as she spoke with the officers on the steps below her. Brittingham again, along with Nelson, the black cop, released from his door duties.

Nora pushed past them and put an arm around her mother. Penelope trembled within her embrace. Michael Murphy, who'd pressed himself against her walker, pushed his nose into Nora's hand, then lay down, seemingly content to let her take over his self-appointed task of guarding Penelope.

'Are you all right? I was afraid—' She stopped herself. She'd been afraid that Penelope had fallen and lay unconscious or maybe worse.

Penelope lifted her chin and squared her thin shoulders. The shaking stopped. That was the mother Nora remembered. 'I'm fine. But you're not.'

'What do you mean?'

Brittingham cleared his throat. 'We're here because of that.' He pointed to Electra. Sun glinted off its shimmering surface. Nora shaded her eyes and details leapt into view – the ragged red letters splashed across the trailer's flank, stretching from step to roof, zigzagging across windows and the door.

RACIST GO HOME!

'I only noticed it just before you got home,' Penelope said. 'You'd been gone so very long, and, of course, I worry.'

A none-too-subtle reminder to Nora about how she'd avoided her mother's calls and emails during the worst of the time after her break-up with Joe, leaving Penelope to read in the newspapers (although she'd likely heard from tech-savvy neighbors first) of Nora's kidnapping and near-demise, not to mention her arrest, lurid tidbits that set Chateau abuzz despite the fact that Nora had been gone for decades.

Nelson stepped forward. 'Did you know about this?'

'Of course not,' she snapped. 'I'm seeing it for the first time. I've been in town all morning.'

He pulled a slim notebook from his back pocket and removed a mechanical pencil from the slot in his shirt pocket. He twisted the top of the pencil and poised it over the notebook. 'What time did you leave the house?'

About a thousand years ago. 'An hour, give or take.'

The pencil scratched on paper. 'Where'd you go?'

To Robert Evans's aunt's home. 'I was running errands.'

'What kind of errands?'

The kind that made me wish I'd never gone. 'I was delivering a cake to a friend.'

He waited for her to elaborate.

Careful, Nora. She, too, could wait.

Nelson tapped his pencil against his notebook. 'And the friend?'

Nora glanced skyward, as though waiting for a different name to tumble providentially from a cloud. 'Grace Evans.'

'Who?' Nelson's visible annoyance gave way to shock.

'Grace Evans. She used to work . . .' *For us*, she started to say. 'Here.'

Brittingham stepped forward, cellphone in hand. He tapped the screen and held it up. 'Is this you?'

For the second time in an hour, the words caught her eye first, the font bold and black – *Justice for Robert Evans.*

And below them, the photo. Two people in a rowboat emerging sideways from beneath a bridge, faces in profile but still identifiable. The mortifying smaller type below it:

Killer Cop Has a Side Piece.

Nora looked everywhere but at her mother.

'Yes. That's me.'

* * *

Her mother never saw the photo.

Brittingham tucked his phone away, seemingly as reluctant as Nora to spend any more time on that aspect of her morning.

'That's all we need. It's clear you didn't do this yourself.'

Brittingham's words seemed directed as much to Nelson as to her.

'I'm sorry you got caught up in this. It's not fair. Not to you, not to Alden, not to any of us. Come on. Let's go.' He looked at his colleague and jerked his head toward their car.

'But what are you going to do about it?' Penelope inched forward with her walker, to the very edge of the stoop.

'Looks like we'll file a report,' Nelson said. Was Nora imagining the sarcasm in his voice, the weary assumption of motions made, the minimum done?

'A report. When some stranger came into my yard, even as I was in the house. Anything could have happened.'

'Anything didn't, Mother,' Nora murmured.

Brittingham's face went stern, Nelson's blank. 'No, your mother's right,' Brittingham said. 'When you're dealing with this bunch, anything could happen. I see you've got a dog.' Michael Murphy, sensing the glances turned his way, lifted his head and wagged his tail. 'What about a gun?'

'My father had shotguns. He hunted, of course. He taught me how to shoot. Nora here, he taught her, too.'

Nora harkened back to predawn mornings with men in waxed jackets and pants milling about the kitchen, filling Thermoses with coffee as Penelope sliced Grace's beaten biscuits in two, buttered them with quick slashes, and filled them with thick-cut ham. It was Nora's job to enfold them in foil packets – and to keep them out of the mouth of Kathleen Mavourneen, one of Murph's predecessors, who bounded among the men in paroxysms of excitement as soon as they pulled guns from cases and rubbed them a final time with soft, oiled cloths.

The dog would return with the men late in the morning, when the geese had ceased to fly and settled for the day amid the stubble in cornfields, pecking about for stray kernels. But all morning long, she'd have done the job she was bred to do, leaping from the blind at the crack of shots – sometimes having seen the goose tumbling from the sky before Nora's father could give the command – landing with a reverberating splash, legs pumping through the frigid water with mighty strokes, returning with a ten-pound Canada goose held so gently in her massive jaws that the soft down beneath the water-shedding outer feathers was barely disturbed.

'You might want to dig out those shotguns, keep them handy, the two of you living out here alone the way you do,' Brittingham said, the subtext – *without a man* – so clear that even Penelope winced.

She shook her head. 'Long gone, I'm afraid. I gave them away to one of my husband's hunting partners after he died. They were beautiful old pieces. He wanted to pay me, but I told him to donate the money to the church.'

Penelope had always loved playing Lady Bountiful. Nora wondered if the money from the guns might have covered the repair of the threadbare patches in the rugs, or maybe repointing the bricks in the chimney.

'Think about getting new ones,' Brittingham said bluntly. 'You can call nine-one-one until you're blue in the face, but even if we drive a hundred miles an hour, we won't get here in time if you have a true emergency. You're lucky this is all you're dealing with.'

They all looked at Electra, the red slashes like wounds across her flanks. Nora didn't feel lucky.

'You'll want to get that taken care of,' Brittingham said. 'Nice unit like that, you don't want to do it yourself, risk messing up that finish. Try Burris's dealership. Their body shop does good work.'

He nodded his goodbyes and left.

Penelope turned to her daughter.

'Nora, I'm worried about you. Clearly, you've upset people. The kind of people who have no compunction about sneaking up to our house and vandalizing your trailer.'

'Mother, I'm fine.' All evidence to the contrary.

Penelope spoke past the obligatory demurral, clutching her daughter's arm to underscore the urgency of her appeal.

'I love having you here. It means the world to me. But maybe, just for a little while, it would be better if you leave Chateau.'

TWENTY-ONE

Penelope was already at the table the next morning, teacup in hand, distressingly bright-eyed in comparison to her daughter's pre-caffeinated fog. They'd stayed up late, in a running verbal push-pull that ended when Nora slammed her hand on the table, saying, 'I'm not leaving you until your leg is healed, and that's final,' and stomped up to bed.

True to form, Penelope greeted the day as though nothing had happened, chattering about a fox she'd seen running across the lawn with a half-grown duckling in its mouth, a mallard hen in frantic pursuit. 'That poor mother. I felt so sorry for her. It's a terrible thing when a mother can't protect her young.' Said with a sly glance at Nora.

Nora made her way to the stove, added water to the still-warm pot and turned on the flame beneath it. She retrieved the plastic cone, fitted in the paper filter and shoveled in a tablespoon of ground coffee, then added a second tablespoon. She decided to ignore her mother's gibe. She poured the water, and the bright arabica scent hit her, almost as good as the first sip.

Penelope, having made her point, changed the subject. 'Have you read the *Baltimore Sun* today?'

'We don't get the *Sun*.'

'I thought maybe you'd read it on that phone of yours.' Penelope continued to resist her daughter's blandishments to get a smartphone. She had a cellphone, of sorts – a little flip phone that nestled in her handbag, which she kept charged only so she could play the solitaire game Nora had shown her. As far as Nora knew, she'd never once used it to call anyone.

'We got it today,' Penelope said. She lifted the newspaper from its concealment on the chair beside her and smoothed it out on the table, pushing it toward Nora's place. 'Someone was' – she paused, seeking the right word – 'gracious enough to leave it on our doorstep. Perhaps the same person who decorated your trailer.'

Nora took a swallow of coffee and ran to the window. Electra was there and, but for the painted message slowly darkening to a scablike color, did not seem to have suffered further injury.

She returned to the table, gulped the rest of her coffee and, thus fortified, turned to the newspaper lying in wait for her.

Prime front-page real estate went to a banner story about the government's feeble attempts to track down the children it had forcibly removed from their undocumented immigrant parents, some as young as infants disappearing into the foster care system. But a one-column story below the fold bore a stacked headline:

Shooting
Victim's
Violent
History

Nora drew the paper closer.

A year earlier, according to the story, Robert Evans had pulled a knife on a classmate in his Baltimore high school, sliding it from temple to jaw, parting flesh to the bone beneath. The reporter – Stephen Abrams, the same one who'd called Nora – had interviewed Evans's victim, one Henry Little, who'd obligingly tilted his face toward the photographer's lens to show off the raised keloid scar running the length of his face.

'Another inch or so, he'd have cut my throat. I'd have bled out right there in the cafeteria in the middle of Taco Tuesday.'

Because Evans was a juvenile at the time, his record – including the charges filed against him and the penalty levied – was closed to the public, the story continued. Nora wondered how the reporter had found Little, who helpfully filled in the blanks.

'He never did no time in juvie. Got off on, what do you call it? A technicality.'

She read on. There'd been another brush with the law, a misdemeanor involving marijuana. The paper had somehow obtained the photo from that arrest – one she recognized as Number Four in the photo lineup the Chateau police had shown her. She rolled her eyes. Evans was lucky to have been arrested while still a juvenile, given the wave of laws sponsored by tough-on-crime politicians eager to advance their careers at the expense of the tens of thousands of people, disproportionately young black men, who did hard time for crimes as innocuous as possession of a joint. The story continued:

> Those youthful incidents set a troubling pattern, police said. Chateau police are investigating Evans's possible ties to Baltimore drug gangs. 'We can't rule it out,' said Detective Sgt Thomas Brittingham. 'The road-rage incident just before he assaulted our officer speaks to a certain state of mind.'

A certain state of mind?

> Brittingham would not identify the motorist involved in the road-rage incident, but a source named her as Nora Best, an author and Chateau native recently returned to her hometown following her husband's killing in Wyoming's Bighorn Mountains.

'Ex-husband,' Nora said aloud, mentally editing the piece as she read. She'd have liked to edit her name out of the story entirely. But there was only one more mention, the obligatory line: *When reached by telephone, Best refused to comment.*

Another feeling welled up, washing away the discomfort at seeing her name in print. Robert Evans had a violent history. He was probably running drugs. Not only was the shooting justified, but Alden was lucky to have escaped alive.

She faced her mother across coffee gone cold.

'He didn't do it!'

Penelope's expression was impossible to read. 'But he did.'

'Yes, yes. He shot him. But he didn't have a choice. He's not what they say he is.'

'Isn't he? Is anyone?'

Penelope followed her question with her tinkling laugh, this time with a bitter undertone that lingered in the air long after she'd taken up her walker and step-thumped her way back to her room, where she closeted herself for the rest of the day.

TWENTY-TWO

1967

I don't care what you say. I'm going anyway.

Grace rehearsed her speech as she marched toward the editor's office at the *Afro*. She was twenty-one, and full of the assurance that comes with working a job where she was no longer beholden to white people. Her boss was black, her colleagues were black, the person who signed her paycheck was black, and the clientele they served were all black – except for the rare white journalist savvy enough to know that reading Baltimore's Afro-American newspaper would give him (almost always a him) insights in segments of his city that may as well have not existed, as far as most white people were concerned.

Grace worked as a clerk, taking messages, making coffee and smothering the occasional trash can fire when one of the cigarettes puffed incessantly by the reporters failed to be completely stubbed out.

But now Bobby was going back to Chateau with a group of students from Morgan State to stage protests of the town's stubborn resistance to integration, and she wanted to cover it.

Cecil, the editor, laughed outright when she suggested it. 'You've never written a newspaper story in your life. And you want to start with this?'

'I write every day. Sir.' Dealing with men, Grace sometimes thought, was not that much different from dealing with the Smythes when she'd worked at Quail House. She spoke softly to Cecil, hands clasped before her, gaze demurely cast down. 'I type up the community columns, the briefs, the church notices, the weddings and engagements.'

'Exactly.' Cecil leaned back in his chair and patted the considerable expanse of his belly. 'You *type*. There's a big difference between typing and writing. I was actually thinking of sending one of the reporters down. Better yet, a columnist. Walter, probably. But you're from there, right? Maybe you could recommend someone who'd put him up while he's there.'

They both knew it was a rare motel on the Eastern Shore that would rent a room to a black person.

Grace forced herself not to turn and look at Walter Call. She didn't need to. He'd be leaning back in his chair, much like Cecil, although Walter's trim frame wouldn't put a strain on even the most delicate chair. The phone would be at his ear, a cigarette dangling from one corner of his mouth, and he'd strolled in that morning in a tan seersucker suit, one of the dozen suits he rotated on workdays. Grace knew, because she'd counted them.

She considered her options. Walter was the *Afro*'s star columnist, taking on malfeasance by white and black politicians alike, amassing heaps of hate mail that it was Grace's job to open, along with the rest of the mail. If Cecil was going to send Walter to Chateau, she didn't stand a chance. But . . .

'Walter's city,' she said.

'Excuse me?'

'They're country in Chateau,' she said. 'Meaning no disrespect – sir – but somebody looking like Walter comes in, people might be, let's say, standoffish. That's why they're sending my brother down to lead the protests. He knows people. They'll trust him. Be less fearful, maybe.'

'Wait.' The front legs of Cecil's chair hit the floor with a thump and a groan. 'Your brother's involved in this? That right there is reason enough why I can't send you. Conflict of interest and all.'

Grace cursed herself for letting that fact slip. She'd been prepared, if Cecil had gone for her proposal, to seek forgiveness later.

'I know that.' She kept her voice smooth, pressing down the vibrating desire to be in the middle of the things happening around the country, to see her name atop a column of print, to never type another engagement announcement again. She dug her fingernails into her palms, stopping just short of splitting skin.

'But I could go along as his assistant, like. Open doors. Introduce him to people. Folks down there are already afraid of what kind of trouble this could bring.' Davita still kept up with friends from Chateau, relaying their concerns to her son, who in turn had told his sister.

'They want to know what will happen when we go back to Baltimore and leave them alone there with a bunch of riled-up white folks,' Bobby had said. 'Not to mention what might happen to me. Mama's afraid I'm going to get myself killed and leave her all alone with you and Kwame and he'll grow up never remembering' – he had paused, fighting for control – 'his big brother.'

He had reached into the playpen and swung Kwame up in his arms, the toddler crowing in delight, then cuddled him close, Kwame's soft plump hands patting Bobby's face.

It was, Grace had to admit, a not unreasonable fear.

Now, she held her breath. Cecil hadn't said anything for a few minutes. He played with a pen on his desk. She felt his eyes on her, looking her up and down, the way he always did when he thought she couldn't tell. She knew he'd hired her on her looks, not much different from the way Philippa Smythe had. Which reminded her. She played her trump card.

'You know, I used to work in the Police Chief's house. No way he'd talk to a reporter from the *Afro*. But he might, if I was there to introduce them. It'd be quite a coup for Walter. Get a window into the mind of a white cop.'

Cecil dropped the pen. 'You've convinced me.' His eyes, only slightly less offensive than his hands would have been, lingered on her breasts, her slender waist, the swell of her hips. 'How about you let me take you to lunch? We can talk strategy.'

Fine, she thought. If that's what it took. Because she had her own strategies – every woman did – for putting off a man with power without enraging him.

She turned and left his office and let him think the swing in her hips was meant for him, rather than the confident sashay of a woman who'd gotten what she wanted.

TWENTY-THREE

Nora laced on her running shoes determined to take advantage of the relief that came with reading the newspaper story, which countered the heavy, ominous feeling that had clung to her since the visit with Grace and the vandalism against Electra.

The night before, she'd even made some progress on her manuscript, enough to justify a reassuring email to her agent, whose voicemails had become increasingly caustic.

So, a celebratory run in what passed for the cool of morning, a way to get the blood moving, clear her head, hit the reset button. She amused herself in the first half-mile by coming up with still more clichés, finally finding the rhythm that emptied her mind of everything but one footfall after the next. Senses expanded – the sun, still slanting low and mellow; the Queen Anne's lace swaying by the side of the road, but, above all, the smell that at first whiff said home – the loamy, skunky mix of contrasts, things growing green and others decomposing, the metallic scent of the river, the dank mud that lined its banks.

She breathed deep and lengthened her stride, despite knowing from previous lapses that she'd pay the next day, waking with muscles kinked and protesting, the lingering bruises – now mostly faded – from her ordeal in Wyoming throbbing anew. She briefly put a hand to her side, touching the scar like a survival talisman. For the moment, the exertion felt good. The back road to town stretched deserted before her, and she luxuriated in the solitude, no need to be alert for Penelope's queries, to tense against the judgment of old acquaintances, to figure out how to respond to new online onslaughts.

Trees lined the road for the next mile, underbrush thick beneath them, no houses in sight, a stretch she'd always known as McKay's Woods, though no sign designated it as such and Nora knew of no McKays in present-day Chateau. But by some obscure edict, no doubt written in feather pen dipped in ink and applied to parchment, the property had been preserved unchanged from colonial times. The woods were thick with whitetail deer and raccoons. Owls and hawks hunched on high branches, waiting to swoop down on prey. Black snakes slithered across the forest floor, vying with the raptors for the same rodents. Nora had always liked its untouched mystery, but especially appreciated it now because of the welcome shade it cast across the road.

A flash of orange caught her eye, bright amid the deep green of leaves, the black of bark. She slowed and peered into the woods. Just a few yards away, a red fox emerged from a mound of earth and perched atop it. She wondered if it was the same one she'd seen the night she drove into town. It yipped at her, flipped its tail and dove back into its den.

Annoyance flashed hot at the sound of a car behind her. She moved farther on to the road's shoulder, slowing to accommodate the uncertain footing there, irritation flaring into anger as she heard the car slow behind her. Anger, and a wriggle of fear. Town lay three miles ahead, the nearest houses not yet in view. She'd been harassed before while running – what woman hadn't? – catcalls and the occasional car crowding close, as this one appeared about to do, and, of course, there were the stories, so many stories, of women abducted, their bodies tossed away like trash, stories she'd determinedly slotted away with statistics about their relative rarity.

Until she herself had been kidnapped, not while on a run, but from the safety of her trailer, and the fact that she'd escaped alive was wholly inadequate to counter the panic now bubbling hard and fast within her, breath coming fast, gaze slewing about, seeking safety, seeing none.

She fumbled with the zipper of her waistpack, feeling for her phone, knowing that in the seconds it took her to extract it, hold down its buttons for the emergency signal, someone could set upon her; that by the time a black-and-white arrived, sirens wailing, she could be far away, screaming uselessly in the trunk of a car, clawing her fingers bloody on its metal surfaces . . .

'Nora. Here you are again.'

Nora fell to her knees by the side of the road, gasping in near sobs, trying to decide whether she wanted to kill Alden Tydings for nearly scaring her to death, or whether his face – as opposed to that of the degenerate she'd expected – was the most beautiful thing she'd ever seen in her life.

First his boat, now his truck.

'Hop in,' he said. 'Wherever you're headed, I'll get you there faster.'

'Like hell.' She backed away. 'The last thing I need is to be seen with you. My picture's already all over the internet. They're making out like I'm your—' She couldn't bring herself to say the words 'side piece,' such a crude characterization of her relationship to the man who so many decades ago had been the love of her life.

He winced. 'I was hoping you hadn't seen that.'

For a moment, she was surprised that he had. But of course the cops would be monitoring every bit of information about the situation.

'I'm sorry. Given everything you've already been through, it seems unfair that your name is out there again. Especially when it's such complete bullshit.'

'Bullshit or not, people believe it.' She jogged in place. 'I'd better get going. Don't want to cramp up.'

She turned away and took a few steps down the road, not bothering to wave.

Sound floated toward her. Madonna?

Sure enough. 'Like a Virgin' – lyrics they'd teased each other with when the words were true.

She laughed and turned back to the truck. Alden raised the radio's volume and crooked a come-hither finger.

'Swear to God I didn't do this on purpose,' he said when she stood again beside the open passenger window. 'It's an oldies station. I turned it down when I spotted you. But then this came on. Talk about memories.'

'No kidding. We used to love this stuff.'

'You used to love it,' he corrected. 'Remember those black fishnet gloves you wore?'

'Noooo,' she groaned. 'Don't remind me.'

'And all those necklaces!'

She blushed, wondering if he was remembering, as she now was, the way he'd remove them one by one, setting them carefully aside so as not to tangle them, before turning his attention to her breasts.

'Not to mention your hair.' He was relentless. She'd applied what probably amounted to gallons of product to her hair during that phase, had scrunched and streaked it, aiming for the supremely tousled look that was supposed to make her look like a contradictory combination of waif and badass but – at least according to Penelope – achieved only an unholy mess.

'I like it better now,' he said.

She touched her hand to it, conscious of the graying roots daily creeping farther into the expertly lightened blond, of its layers long past time for a cut.

Alden reached across the passenger seat and cracked open the door. 'Change your mind? I'll get us some to-go coffee. You can slide down in your seat the way you used to when we'd see your mom's car while were driving around and you were supposed to be at work. We can drink it someplace where nobody'll see us.'

Compared to coffee, Nora's run was fast losing its allure. She got into the truck.

The first houses appeared, a few scattered farms and then a cluster of bungalows that originally allowed their owners to say they'd moved to the country, until the town grew to encompass them.

A soybean field spread out to their left, men moving slowly across its rows, backs bent, staring intently downward. Alden sucked in his breath and touched the brakes. Far ahead, Nora saw the coffee kiosk she'd passed that first night. Realization came slowly. This must be the spot where the shooting occurred. And those men? She looked a question to him.

'They're looking for the gun.' His voice was tight. 'He threw it away. I remember seeing it fly through the air and all I could think was, "Thank God, now he can't shoot me." Didn't even realize I'd already shot him.'

The truck slowed nearly to a stop as a fox dashed out of the field, some prize clenched in its teeth, and across the road. She wondered if it was the same one she'd just seen. 'As much as I want coffee, I've got a better idea,' he said. 'Let's get out of here.'

He steered it through a wide U-turn.

'Where?'

He managed a smile. 'It's a surprise. Close your eyes.'

The truck took a turn and headed east. The rising sun caught her full across the face. She finally obeyed his command to close her eyes. 'Where did you say we were going again?' she murmured.

'I said it was a surprise. Keep your eyes shut. Listen to the music.' And so she did, dozing off in shockingly short order to Pat Benatar reminding her that they belonged together.

Even before she opened her eyes, she knew where they were. Alden lowered the windows so she could feel the air flowing through, lighter and cooler, scented with salt. Gulls screamed overhead.

'The beach!' She sat up, bouncing like a child in her seat. 'You brought me to the beach!' The actual ocean, not the patch along the river where they'd partied as kids.

'Hey.' He raised one hand from the wheel in a half-shrug. 'What else do I have to do with my time?'

She winced at the ugly reminder of his situation, then put it out of her mind as determinedly as he seemed to be barring it from his.

'When was the last time you saw the ocean?' The truck rolled down a wide boulevard, passing old familiar stores advertising saltwater taffy, T-shirts and boogie boards. But a row of tall buildings at the very end of the street blocked the view of the dunes.

'Too long, apparently,' she said. 'What are those?'

He parked the truck in front of one of them. 'Condos. They're all up and down the coast now. A couple of towns have banned them, but most caught on too late to what was happening. Or, more likely, didn't care. You can imagine the kind of money these places bring in.'

He parked in a small lot past the condos and they climbed a set of wooden stairs leading up and over the dunes. Nora stopped on the platform at the top. 'Oh!'

Before her lay a stretch of sand, nearly deserted at this hour. The water beyond it caught and held her eye, stretching endlessly away, sliding toward her and then retreating, inviting her to follow. Decades dropped away as she kicked off her shoes and sprinted for the water, tossing the shoes aside at the last minute, just beyond the reach of the waves, and splashing in up to her ankles, her knees.

She bent and scooped handfuls of it, holding it to her face, breathing in brine, not minding the stickiness it left on her skin. She turned, laughing, to Alden. 'Too long.'

'Come again?'

'You asked me how long it had been. I love the mountains, truly I do. But I'd forgotten about this. It's been way too many years.'

He stood in the shallows, also barefoot, a little unsteady as the water sucked the sand from beneath his feet, then swept in again, darkening the hem of his jeans.

They were still a couple of hours from the arrival of parents burdened by tote bags and umbrellas and low canvas chairs, their kids running ahead, much as Nora had, bright plastic pails swinging from their hands. Now, only a few older people moved along the waterline, studying the sand before them, seeking shells deposited by the retreating tide.

'Look.' Alden pointed. Far beyond the breaking waves, sleek silvery shapes arced from the water, disappeared, curved into the air again. 'Porpoises.'

Nora nodded remembrance. They headed up the coast in the morning and back in the evening, a reminder that the ocean was the aquatic version of McKay's Woods, that wildness lived in its depths. Shoals of stinging jellyfish occasionally floated too close to shore, a misery for swimmers, and the rare shark – more often in recent years – chomped an unfortunate bather.

'Come on.'

'Where?' She turned. Alden stood at the undulating line where damp sand met dry, pulling his T-shirt over his head. He unfastened his belt, unzipped his fly, and began peeling off his pants.

'What are you doing?' She turned away, then back, incapable of not looking.

He stood, one leg in, one leg out of his jeans, boxers blue against bare thigh. 'I'm going in. What about you?'

'Are you crazy? I don't have a suit.'

'So?' He kicked the jeans away. They landed in a heap on the T-shirt. 'What you're wearing is fine. And no one's paying attention anyway. You could go in naked and no one would care.'

'Which I'm not going to do . . . hey!' Water sheeted across her as he ran past, kicking high. 'Knock it off!'

But he'd already dived beneath the foamy curl of a breaking wave, beyond hearing. Nora looked up and down the beach, and calculated the odds of being seen by anyone who might recognize them as approximately nil.

The boardwalk and the main part of town was a few blocks farther up the beach, the shell seekers more numerous there. She and Alden had this stretch mostly to themselves.

'What the hell.' Nora peeled off her tank top and her shorts and flung them behind her on to the sand, glad she'd worn a dark sports bra and underwear, hoping that from a distance it looked like a suit, then – as a wave crested and she gulped air and plunged into the wall of green water – ceasing to care.

She came up, blinking the water from her eyes, to find Alden beside her. 'Quick. Here comes another.' He grabbed her arm and they dove together, emerging and diving through wave after wave, not unlike the porpoises they'd just watched, until they were beyond the breakers, treading water for a few minutes as they caught their breath.

'It's so different,' she said.

He tilted his head. 'The water? I think it's the same. Or do you mean that?' He looked back toward the beach, at the high rises and sprawling vacation homes, built to impress, that had replaced the humble cedar-shake cottages of their youth.

'That, for sure,' she said. 'And the water, too. Not different from the way it was before. Just from what I've been used to these last few years.' She'd grown to love the waters of the West, its narrow rivers winding in oxbows across prairies, its rushing mountain streams, their waters so clear and icy cold. She'd forgotten the ocean's sheer muscularity, the way it grabbed at her and pulled her along in a gentle tug that she knew could turn without warning into a deadly rip tide beyond her capability to fight it.

Alden tilted his head back and let the sun fall on his face. 'This is great,' he said. 'So good to get away from everything for a while.'

Their feet, lazily kicking to keep them afloat, brushed against one another. She dog-paddled a few feet away.

'How much longer do you have to deal with this? When are they going to finish their investigation? I read something in the *Sun* yesterday about Robert Evans . . .' She trailed off, giving him an opening.

Every sentence he'd spoken about the shooting so far had been soaked in remorse. But the story in the *Sun* had painted Robert Evans in such negative terms. If Alden had merely been feigning regret, this was a chance to come clean.

She blinked salt water from her eyes, watching his face for the slightest change in expression. Saw only a pained grimace.

'I read that, too. You know, I've probably spent most of my waking hours going over those few minutes. How I could have handled it differently. What I could have said or done that would have ended up with him still alive.'

The lingering knot of suspicion within her loosened a little more. She swam closer again.

'As to the investigation' – his shoulders rose and fell in a shrug, sending water surging around him – 'who knows? But even when they finish, and I'm exonerated, I don't know that it will matter. I'm always going to be that white cop who killed the black kid, even if it was justified. I'm getting death threats online. I don't mind for my own sake. It's all part of being a cop. We get online abuse no matter what we do. But Kyra and the girls are getting it, too. Even when they clear me, I don't know that I'll be able to stay here. Which might be for the best, anyway.'

The sun shone strong on his face, highlighting the etchings of age. As it also must have her own, Nora thought, wistfully recalling their young, taut flesh, their youthful bodies. Sometimes she thought every encounter of her adult life involved the hope – never realized – of recapturing the aching thrill of those heady months of exploration before they'd finally dared to take that final step. His foot stroked hers again, this time feeling more purposeful than accidental and her breath caught. What had he been saying?

'How could leaving possibly be for the best? That farm – it's been in your family ever since . . . since . . .'

'Since your family got here. First Families, both of us.' They'd joked about it as teens, the utter un-coolness of their parents' pride in being descended from Chateau's first settlers. There was a society, with meticulous genealogical records. Annual events, in which the women laced themselves into tight bodices and voluminous hoop skirts and the men donned knee-length frock coats but disdained the authenticity of powdered wigs, and everybody drank enough rum punch to get past the embarrassment of it all.

'Don't remind me. I think one of the reasons I stayed out West was so I'd never have to go to a Founders' Ball. Do you go?'

'Every year. Kyra insists. She's a double First Family, you know. Both sides.'

Alden sucked in a breath, sank under the water and came up again, shaking his head as though trying to rid himself of something. 'That's another thing I won't miss if I have to leave.'

'Another thing? What else?' The sun was fast drying Nora's hair, but her fingers were beginning to prune, the water leaching warmth from her body.

Alden grimaced. 'Oh, come on. You know how it is. Twenty years married, things get . . . strained. I mean, hell. I know you know. We all know how things went down with you.'

Gratitude briefly warmed Nora at the way he brought it up casually and moved on fast, not a hint of judgment. 'Difference is, we've still got kids at home. We're stuck until they head off to college.

This just makes it harder. Kyra – look, I don't want to badmouth her. She's a great mother. But it was obvious pretty early on that I'd made a mistake. Only problem is, she was pregnant, and . . .'

He went on, but Nora heard little past his admission that he'd made a mistake.

Damn straight he had. And for a few minutes, as the sun danced on the wavelets around them, she entertained a useless series of what-ifs: What if Alden had realized his mistake earlier? Or she hadn't been so quick to throw him over when she'd found out about his fling with Kyra? If she'd never run away West to college, met Joe, married the wrong man, leaving the right one behind?

Alden rolled on to one side and began a lazy sidestroke. Nora did the same, her back to him as she kept pace, trying to talk sense into herself. Because hadn't she heard variations on this before? Colleagues at the university where she'd worked, men at office parties, the former emboldened by familiarity, the latter by alcohol, letting her know in ways subtle or overt that she could feel free to ignore the wedding ring, that they were unhappy and therefore entitled. The presumption of it! Depending on her own level of alcoholic consumption, she'd amused herself by stepping in close, breasts pressing against their chests, her lips to an earlobe, whispering, 'Must be my lucky day. Because I've been looking for a new husband.'

Biting her lips against a smile as the man in question backed away, stammering excuses – but not an apology; no, never – because nothing shriveled lust faster than a suggestion of commitment.

'What you did' – Alden's voice floated across the water to her – 'it took guts. Deciding just to up and leave.'

Had it? It wasn't as though she'd decided anything. She'd acted on raging impulse when she'd caught her husband in flagrante at their own farewell party on the eve of their departure for a cross-country trip in the Airstream. Her rash move had, in a roundabout way, led to Joe's death, the thought of which sent Nora rolling on to her stomach, and digging her arms into the water in a fast crawl that took her out of earshot of the sort of talk that, for the first time in her life, she found enticing.

Shedding her tank top and shorts had felt exuberant, freeing, a throwback to their high school days before they'd bumped up against the limitations of adulthood.

Forcing them back on over damp, salt-sticky skin and underwear felt like reacquiring those burdens, all the disappointments of marriage, the trauma of her kidnapping and, now, the town's suspicions. Her shoes were worse still. The sand she'd been unable to completely clean from her feet chafed and rubbed on the short walk back to the truck, and once inside, after some desultory small talk, she pretended to doze again, gritting her teeth as she imagined facing Penelope, trying to explain her prolonged absence, the sunburn that stung her cheeks and shoulders, her hair disheveled beyond any ability to comb through it with her fingers. Not to mention the fact of arriving in Alden's truck.

'Let me out here,' she said as the truck approached the turnoff to Quail House.

He complied with a sad smile, letting her know he understood.

'It was nice today,' he said. 'Like old times,' and for a moment she thought he might try to kiss her again.

But he didn't, leaving her to wonder for the length of the long, cedar-shaded lane whether she wished he had.

TWENTY-FOUR

1967

Grace had been right about one thing.

People in Chateau, especially her parents' contemporaries, took one look at Walter Call in his seersucker suit – pale-blue stripes this time – his red bow tie, his sheer socks, his thin-soled shoes, and drew back as though they'd come across a copperhead slithering from beneath a carelessly kicked-aside log.

Would they mind giving him just a few minutes of their time to talk about the present situation in Chateau? Why, yes, they would. They would mind very much. Not that their employers, the foremen at the canning plant or the manager at the Wagon Wheel or the white women in their big houses would ever read the *Afro* and see their crab-pickers or dishwashers or maids quoted there. But it would get around that they'd talked to a reporter, and that would be all it would take, for dismissal not just from their present job, but from any future job they might want to have in Chateau. *Nuh-uh, nossir, I do not wish to speak with you. Not on the record or off. Not today, not ever.*

Which is where Grace came in, stepping out from behind Walter, speaking in tones of shy wonder, 'Miss Marie? Is that you?' She'd abandoned her city outfit of kick-pleated pencil skirts and softly draped V-neck blouses and returned to her oldest shirtdresses, deliberately choosing one that – despite being meticulously clean and starched – was just a little faded, fraying about the collar, earning a snort from Walter when they met to begin the day's work.

Let him, she thought. People visibly relaxed before she even opened her mouth for the obligatory five minutes of how's-your-mother and what's-your-daughter-doing-she-was-in-my-class-you-know and yes-life-in-Baltimore-is-surely-different before they'd turn their attention back to Walter, wilting in the sun.

'Yes, he's with me. I work at the *Afro* now. You know, it's hard for someone born and raised in Baltimore to understand what things are like down here. I thought maybe you could help him out. Give him a feel for the way it is.' And that, accompanied by assurances that no names would ever be used, would sometimes bear fruit. More often, the attempt would be in vain, but at least the frostiness would thaw somewhat, the shoulders relax, the pursed lips stretch into a welcoming smile.

On the day of the first action, she stood with Walter across the street from the Wagon Wheel, watching and narrating.

Bobby, as well as her boss, had let it be known that no way could she be part of it, no matter how she longed to join that group of college students, the young men in white shirts and ties, the girls in demure pastel dresses, walking up the steps into the diner. She could see them through the windows as they took their seats in two booths and picked up menus. In other booths, white people leaned toward one another, the urgency of their conversations apparent even from across the street.

'OK, that's Old Miss Reston – she's the owner – standing there at the cash register. That girl next to her, that's her daughter Janet. Guess she's working there now. Look, Miss Reston's called all the waitresses over.'

In the booths, the young people laid down their menus and looked around expectantly.

'Miss Reston is out from behind the cash register. Maybe she's going to talk to them. No, wait. She's going back into the kitchen.' The double doors swung closed behind her.

'What's going to happen now? You think the police will come?' Walter fanned himself with a copy of the *Chateau Crier*, whose headline that morning proclaimed *Outside Agitators Arrive in Chateau.*

'Maybe.'

Grace hugged herself, imagining the bite of cold metal handcuffs into her brother's wrists. She held her breath as white patrons rose to their feet, remembering images from lunch-counter sit-ins in the South, the ketchup bottles emptied on to the heads of black students sitting stoic and silent as white people leaned in close to spit in their food, shower them with jeers and curses.

Inside the diner, Miss Reston emerged from the kitchen and moved among the booths, stopping briefly at each table with white patrons. They rose and followed her and her daughter, scurrying close behind with the waitresses, out the door. A string of black people in grease-splattered aprons, the cooks and dishwashers, emerged from around the back of the building.

'Diner's closed,' Mrs Reston announced to the onlookers. She reached back inside the door, flipped the lights off, and turned the *Open* sign to *Closed*.

'They can sit there until they rot for all I care,' she said.

Walter took a step in her direction, his notebook in one hand, reaching for the pen behind his ear with the other.

'I wouldn't,' Grace said.

'But.' He pointed with the pen to the white reporters clustering around the owner.

'What did you tell me when I wanted to go in there with them?' she reminded him. 'You can't be part of the story.'

'I'm not part of the story. I'm trying to get the story.' He spoke to her as one would to a small and not terribly bright child.

'You walk out there in the midst of all those white people, she's liable to get in your face, or more likely shut you down entirely. Either way, you'll become part of the story. Miss Reston's number is in the book. You go back to the house and give her a call. Tell her you work for a newspaper in Baltimore. She'll think it's the *News-Post*. She doesn't even know the *Afro* exists.'

Walter turned and gave her a long look, absent the disdain of his morning survey.

'Hmph,' was all he said.

It took all Grace had to withhold her triumphant smile until he'd turned away.

TWENTY-FIVE

Nora ducked into Electra after her trip to the beach with Alden. She averted her eyes from the damning graffiti, showered in the trailer's tiny bathroom, and then left for lunch in town, wanting to avoid as long as possible Penelope's honed ability to detect her daughter's emotions via some infinitesimal rearrangement of molecules.

Michael Murphy watched from the stoop, a worthy stand-in for Penelope, somehow managing to project the guilt Nora feared her mother might impose, even though there'd been nothing improper about her morning.

'Shoo.' She flapped her hands at him, but Murph merely lowered his head, adding layers of sadness to his attitude.

Nora headed for the familiarity of the Wagon Wheel, where her family had gone for breakfast every Sunday after church throughout her childhood. The faux railroad dining car stood in the center of town, its shiny aluminum exterior rivaling that of Electra's.

Change assailed her when she stepped inside. Chateau's schools and businesses had been nominally integrated during her childhood, but she remembered the diner's unspoken boundaries. Black people worked there as cooks and dishwashers, out of sight in the kitchen, whites as counter staff and waitresses in the dining room's air-conditioned comfort. Now a black waitress in a white uniform bustled past her, wiping down tables recently occupied and arranging fresh place settings.

At two in the afternoon, the diner's lunch rush was long over, townspeople heading back to their jobs, only a few vacationers lingering over coffee by the time Nora arrived.

'Hey, Nora.' Janet Reston, who'd taken over the diner when her parents retired, sat on a stool behind the counter, working the crossword in the local paper. Her hair, dyed a red so deep it had a purple tinge, was pulled atop her head, although damp strands still clung loosely to her forehead and neck. 'Good to see you back in town. How's your mom doing?'

'A little better every day,' Nora said, wondering even as she spoke if it were true. Beyond the boot on her leg, Penelope seemed unchanging. 'Still going old school on the crossword? Not using that thing?'

Nora pointed to the iPad that had replaced the two-foot-high cash register that sat beside it as a monument to an earlier age; impossibly heavy, covered with intricate brass scrollwork, more buttons than seemed necessary for the simple transactions it recorded, its clanging cash drawer forever silenced.

Janet waggled a pen at her. 'I like not being able to erase my answers. I tried it online. All those prompts and you could erase whatever you put down. Felt like cheating. This way, I've got to get it right on the first try.'

'More power to you, Janet.' The brief exchange of pleasantries, one she could have had ten years ago, or twenty, soothed with its familiar rhythms.

She slid into a booth near the back, against a window, giving her a view of both the street and the rest of the room. The waitress appeared with a glass of water packed with ice cubes that nudged over the rim, the sides already sweating. She wore a green nametag: Virginia. Her glance swept Nora and stopped. She set the glass down so hard some of the water splashed across the table, stared a moment longer at Nora and at the mess she'd made, and hurried away without speaking.

Maybe she'd read the story in the *Afro*. But Nora doubted Virginia could have recognized her from a thirty-three-year-old prom photo. She threw a paper napkin atop the puddle, picked up her glass and held it to her neck, her pulse hot against it, willing her arteries to carry the cool through her veins to the rest of her body, calm the emotions stirred by Alden's revelations about his marriage.

A swish of nylon heralded the waitress's return. But she hustled on past, uniform rustling in her haste, to clear a table that someone had just left.

'Coffee?' Nora called after her. But she gave no sign of having heard. Nora turned, trying to catch her eye. The woman looked tired, shifting from one sneaker-clad foot to the other as she worked. Probably already thinking of going home, shedding the heat-trapping nylon uniform, lying on her bed in her underwear, a washcloth wrung under cold water draped over her eyes, letting the drone of lawn-mowers, the bumblebees humming in the hollyhocks, lull her into something approaching sleep for just a few blessed minutes before it was time for her to rise, to prepare a meal that didn't require an oven, to call the kids in from the street, kiss the husband home from work, all the things that her next shift required.

Nora gave up on coffee and turned her attention to the menu, which served all its selections all day long, offering hungover patrons Salisbury steak for breakfast if they so desired, or omelets for dinner. Nora had thought to order breakfast, but the day was already so warm that the thought of hot food did not appeal.

She eyed the photo of the Waldorf salad, its reds and greens garish on the menu's plastic page, anticipating the dollop of mayo and crunch of apple, the meaty walnuts and the nutritionally bereft iceberg lettuce, and nary a mention of kale.

Virginia swished past again, a tray of dirty coffee mugs in her hands.

'Coffee?' Nora tried again, but she was already gone, disappearing through the swinging doors that led into the kitchen.

The jingling bell on the diner's door announced a new arrival, a black couple about Nora's age. They wore knee-length shorts and roomy T-shirts with images of Ocean City, and Nora took them for tourists, maybe up from Washington, taking a break from a week at the beach to do a little antiquing. Virginia arrived with their water before they'd even slid into the booth, standing there with a glass in each hand until they'd settled themselves, telling them about the blue-crab omelet special. 'Those crabs were pulled from the bay yesterday. You won't get any fresher.'

Nora wondered whether she should switch her order from the salad to the omelet, fresh crabmeat entirely absent during her years in Colorado. She waved, this time calling the woman's name, adding the honorific in hopes of appeasing whatever she'd done to offend her.

'Miss Virginia?'

Yet again, the woman passed her by, this time with a disdainful sniff. At the cash register stand, Janet Reston laid down her pen and pushed the newspaper aside.

The couple who'd just come in pored over the menu with true curiosity, although when Virginia next appeared, the woman turned an anticipatory smile upon her and announced, 'Looks like you've sold us on those omelets.'

'You won't be sorry,' Virginia said. 'And I've taken the liberty of setting aside a couple of slices of peach pie for you. On the house.'

Janet Reston's gaze went back and forth, from the couple enthusing about Virginia's generosity to Nora's table.

'I'd like an omelet, too, please.' Nora raised her menu, pointing to the slip advertising the crab omelet special paper-clipped to the front. 'Maybe you didn't hear me.' Irritation sharpened her words.

Virginia finally turned her way, fixing her with a long, heavy-lidded look.

The couple ceased their desultory conversation, belatedly realizing that something was coiling, rearing up, opening a wide white mouth, exposing the venom-filled fangs.

'No,' Virginia said. 'I did not.'

She turned away, nearly bumping into Janet, who'd come out from behind her stand and waited with hands on hips.

'Virginia,' she said, and despite the ultimatum in her posture, there was pleading in her tone. 'Why don't you bring Nora some coffee? Take her order?'

Virginia's tone was careless, almost bored.

'I ain't bringing her shit. And I sure as hell ain't taking any orders from her.'

'What the . . .?' Nora dropped her menu.

'Virginia! What in the world could you possibly have against Nora?'

Virginia's smile was infinitely worse than her previous impassivity. 'She knows.' She addressed Nora directly for the first time. 'Don't you?'

And, at Nora's look of bewilderment, added, 'Maybe you didn't notice me a couple mornings back, but for sure I noticed you. In that boat. With that cop. The one that shot Robert Evans. Putting this place right back where it was all those years ago, the way I grew up hearing about.'

The woman fishing from the bridge. Who'd clearly recognized Alden. And, even if she hadn't known Nora, had remembered her face.

Janet's hands slid from her hips. She clasped them before her, fingers twining and repositioning themselves, trying to wring hope from a hopeless situation. Because what else could she possibly do?

'You've worked here for how many years now? Ten? Fifteen? Don't throw it all away like this.'

Virginia looked down at the nametag on her chest as though she'd never seen it before. She raised a hand and worked the pin loose. She reached her other hand around her back and untied her apron at the waist, then unfastened the strings around the neck. It slid to the floor. She dropped the nametag atop it and began the long, slow walk toward the door.

The kitchen door swung open, thudding against the wall. The kitchen help – a dishwasher, a busboy, a cook, all of them black – fell in line behind Virginia, the cook reaching reflexively around her to push open the front door, standing aside to let Virginia go first, followed by the busboy and dishwasher, the front of his white uniform one long wet splotch of sudsy water. He started to step through the door himself, then stood aside a final time, holding it wide for the couple who'd come in late, and from far away, but not so far they didn't realize instantly what was happening and opted not to sit idly by.

Unlike Nora.

Who sat frozen watching the exit of every black person in the building, leaving only white people behind, all of them staring, some already reaching for their phones, eager to transmit this latest tidbit about the ongoing scandal that was Nora Best.

TWENTY-SIX

Nora drove home in a hurry, hoping to get to Quail House before the biddies heard what had happened in the Wagon Wheel and took it upon themselves to inform her mother of every delicious detail.

She breathed a sigh of relief upon finding the kitchen dark and deserted, and unplugged the land line there. But Penelope had a bedside phone, too, and – as a lifetime believer in the restorative power of an afternoon nap – was almost certainly lying beside it.

Nora stood outside the closed door of the first-floor suite that had been her grandparents' room and, later, her parents'. She'd taken over their spacious second-floor room with the fireplace and a sitting area, becoming the envy of her friends. She tried to think of a pretext for entering without knocking. The doors in Quail House had latches instead of knobs, heavy wrought-iron affairs that rattled noisily when lifted. Nora put a fingertip to the latch, edging it up by degrees, letting out her breath as the door swung silently open.

Penelope lay within, slight as a child beneath the light summer blanket, white hair in disarray upon the pillow, mouth slack, a slug-trail of spittle from its corner. Nora touched an edge of blanket to it and then smoothed her mother's hair, fingertips recoiling from the pink scalp that was too stark a reminder of the skull beneath. The phone sat atop a rosewood box on the nightstand. She reached behind the nightstand and unplugged it.

Penelope's breath escaped in a low moan. Her lips moved. Nora leaned close. 'What, Mother?'

A puff of air. 'Oh, Grace. You're always here.'

Nora smiled and touched her lips to her mother's forehead, unwilling to disturb her sleep by dragging her back to the present. At least for this little while, Penelope could rest untroubled by her daughter's latest escapades. She straightened and looked with satisfaction toward the silenced phone. A folded newspaper clipping lay beside it.

She glanced again at her mother, waiting for the reassuring rise and fall of the blanket, then reached for the clipping and unfolded it to find the initial story about the shooting: the cop car and the Kia, the photos of Robert Evans and the uncle for whom he was presumably named, Bobby.

Nora refolded the clipping and replaced it. She had a moment's bitter thought to re-attach the phones – if her mother was so damned interested in the case, she'd soon hear more than she ever wanted – and hurried from the room before she could give in to the impulse.

*   *   *

'You don't even know about what happened back then,' Grace had said. 'That's a crime.'

And the waitress, Virginia, in the Wagon Wheel: 'Putting this place right back where it was.'

Not to mention the cryptic comment from the stranger, upon seeing the flyer about the pending march: 'How many times can one town burn?'

'Ask your mother,' Grace had advised. Which she would do. Eventually. But not until she knew as much as possible about what had happened so that Penelope couldn't wriggle away from her questions.

Which brought her back to town, detouring through side streets so as not to pass the Wagon Wheel, heading to the library with something Emily Beattie had said in mind: 'All the newspapers sent reporters, the *Sun*, the *News-Post*, the *Washington Post* and the *Afro*. And, of course, the *Chateau Crier* covered it, too.'

She installed herself in a carrel just off the stacks in the 700 section – plays, poetry, literary criticism; the library's least visited aisle – and set out to educate herself.

There was no internet all those decades ago, nobody posting selfies every other day. The only photo of Bobby Evans accompanying the first newspaper stories about the shooting was the standard high school portrait from his junior year in 1963 that had appeared in the *Crier*. Full Afros, those grand defiant halos, had yet to come into style, but Bobby's photo contained a hint of what was to come, an inch higher than the close-cropped styles of the fifties. It softened an otherwise severe face. Bobby smiling into the camera, facing a future that would end only a few years after that carefully posed photo.

She pushed her chair back from the desk and stared unseeing at the screen, instead conjuring the Chateau of the time. A slow, sultry feel to the images. People sauntering rather than striding briskly. Both women and men dressing up to go downtown, even if downtown consisted of only a few stores on a three-block street just minutes from their own homes. The point was, they would be seen. Roles strictly delineated by age, gender, race. People knew their place, even though black and white, comfortably well-off and poor, were constantly thrown together by sheer proximity, the town too small for physical avoidance that went beyond the smallest of ways, those ways assuming outsize importance as a result. Brown eyes never meeting blue. The sidestep, the bowed head.

What sort of resentment had simmered beneath those soft-spoken 'yessuhs' and 'yes'ms'? Or in the diner's kitchen, as sweat dripped into steaming dishwater, where black hands were allowed to scrape the greasy remnants of food from the plates and wash them clean, but never serve those same plates in the comfort of the dining room? Among the teachers in the 'colored' school on the far end of town, each fall distributing the years-outdated textbooks that were the hand-me-downs from the gleaming new school for white students?

And for Bobby and Grace, what must it have been like to have grown up in that atmosphere and then suddenly be transported to Baltimore, dropped into the middle of an all-black neighborhood, not just a few blocks as in Chateau but acres and acres, no more need for the constant wariness of survival? To lift one's head, laugh loud at jokes, pick up the pace to match the bustle of a big city? For Bobby, heading into college, that pace must have felt like a sprint.

Nora thought of her own introduction to college, the small-town girl thrown into a campus larger than her entire hometown, that early mingled sense of terror and freedom. How much more intense it would have been in her parents' time, the whole country in ferment over race and war and – ever so faintly – the first hints of feminism. Bobby Evans would have been in the thick of it, so flush with hope and purpose that he'd volunteered to go back to Chateau to goose into being the changes that had already come, no matter how reluctantly, to much of the rest of the country.

Nora went back to the screen and clicked around some more, faster now, eyes adjusting to the tiny type, the jumbled layout of those long-ago newspapers.

Bobby had hardly begun his work in Chateau when he'd been killed. The first story about his death, in the hometown paper, was nearly as brief as that about his nephew's.

Negro Found Dead.

Nora supposed that passed for politeness. Earlier she'd scrolled past repeated references to 'colored.'

> The body of Robert Evans, 20, Negro, of Baltimore, was found Sunday morning on the banks of the Lenape River by a passing fisherman.

> Police Chief William Smythe said Evans, a Chateau native who moved with his family to Baltimore, returned recently with a group of Negroes intent on disrupting Chateau's orderly progress of integration. He pointed to recent actions at the town diner and the school administration building as examples.
>
> Smythe speculated that Evans ran afoul of local Negroes resentful of outsiders coming into their community.
>
> 'He came here to stir up trouble,' Smythe said, 'and unfortunately for his family, it looks like he found it.'
>
> Evans leaves behind his parents and two siblings.

End of story. No mention of cause of death, nor even the courtesy of naming the other family members.

She scrolled and scrolled through subsequent weeks. Stories of the unrest that roiled Chateau in the weeks following Bobby's death crowded the front page, accounts of street scuffles and beatings of black residents sharing space with stories about the 4-H fair, the annual chicken fry, the Social Notes.

> Mrs Alexander Massey hosted a flower-arranging workshop, followed by a light repast of chicken salad, iced tea and petit fours. In attendance were Mrs Benjamin Parker, Mrs Gordon Tucker and the young Mrs Andrew Baggs, recently married.

It was a window on to an earlier time, when women had yet to claim their own names. Nora wondered who the young Mrs Andrew Baggs had been before she ceded her name to her husband; wondered what it was like for her to be ushered into the world of matrons. Imagined her hesitating over the bite-sized petit fours, their glazed pastel surfaces topped with tiny sugar flowers, paralyzed over the issue of fingers or fork. Wondered if the new wife was still enveloped in the happy haze of sex, or if the frisson had already faded, leaving her to contemplate the fact that the rest of her life stretched ahead of her in endless rituals of flower arrangements and cake decorating and painting classes – their subjects safe still lifes, heaps of fruit tumbling from copper bowls on to gleaming mahogany tables, or gauzy seascapes, never anything so daring as the human form – nothing to show for it decades later but some inept efforts framed and hung in a guest room and the ability to make her own damn petit fours.

But of Bobby Evans? Nothing more than a single sentence, dropped nearly word for word in every story about escalating unrest: *The problems began after Robert Evans, a Baltimore Negro born in Chateau, was found shot to death.*

Problems. A man dead, a church burned, a family's hearts broken.

And, even though Nora clicked impatiently through the days, still no arrest.

> 'We're investigating the possibility that this might also have been drug-related,' said Chief William Smythe. 'We've seen an uptick in marijuana coming into the county. Drug dealers have discovered our little town. Or it could have been suicide. It wouldn't surprise me that the reaction of the law-abiding Negroes here to his attempts to stir up trouble might have engendered despair. Maybe he was too embarrassed to go back to Baltimore and admit failure.'

Nora turned last to the *Afro-American*, the venerable chronicler of Baltimore's black community, and, when she did, her audible cry prompted several shushes from those working around her in the library.

'Suicide,' his sister told the *Afro*, her bitterness fairly oozing from the word on the page. 'The night before the biggest event of his life.'

The *Afro* had dutifully contacted Chief Smythe and confronted him with Grace Evans's accusations.

> 'These things are naturally hard for a family to accept,' he'd said. 'And I sympathize, believe me, I do. I knew Bobby before he fell in with the wrong crowd up there in Baltimore. He worked in my home, along with his sister. Fine family, not a bit of a problem with any of them. If you ask me the last colored people in Chateau to cause trouble, I'd have said the Evanses. But as I said, that was before they moved away. I tried to explain all this to his sister, what a h--- of a thing it was, but she was having none of it. A shame.'

Nora put a hand to her burning face, mortified at the paternalism of it all. He'd done everything but call them 'my' colored people.

Not so much as an *excuse me, ma'am*, for the mild cursing, unremarkable now, but still impermissible, in that day and age, in the presence of a lady. Of course, Grace would never have been considered a lady. She was a woman, a black woman, and the little courtesies didn't apply, not even to a heartbroken sister.

Her grandfather, Nora thought, would never have ma'amed Grace Evans.

And yet, after her brother was shot, she not only stayed in Chateau but returned to work in Quail House.

'It doesn't make sense,' Nora murmured.

'No, it doesn't,' someone said behind her. 'Not one damn bit of it.'

Nora jerked in her seat, nearly upsetting the go-cup of coffee she'd smuggled into the library, knowing that discovery would have resulted in permanent banishment by Emily Beattie. She turned and stared up into eyes as nearly as green as her own.

The man standing behind her chair wore a linen suit of charcoal gray. It looked hot despite the light fabric. The gray at his temples, the faint etchings at the corners of his eyes and from mouth to chin, those gentle scratches of time destined to become deep gouges, told her they'd been born in the same decade. He apologized in a voice that rumbled at the lower depths of basso, his words so perfunctory that he didn't sound sorry at all.

'Kwame Evans,' he introduced himself.

Maybe, she thought, there was another Kwame Evans. His next words wrecked her foolish fantasy.

'Robert's father. Bobby's and Grace's little brother.'

'Yes,' she said. She could see it now. He had the same broad forehead and wide eyes that gave his face a frank, open look. She remembered her manners.

'Nora Best.' She started to hold out her hand but jerked it back when he didn't respond.

'I know who you are.'

Of course he did. *Killer Cop Has a Side Piece.*

He cut his eyes toward the screen and arched an eyebrow. An accusing headline looked back at both of them.

Community Demands Answers. With a black-bordered photo of his older brother.

Nora felt as though she'd been caught in the act of . . . what, exactly? Whatever it was, there was no hiding it.

'I didn't know about it,' she said. 'Your sister – I've known her ever since I was a little girl. I never knew she'd lost a brother.'

'Lost. That implies she could find him if she just looked hard enough.'

Touché. She nodded acknowledgment and tried again. 'I never knew she'd had a brother who'd been killed. And all the things that happened here, the demonstrations, the riot, the National Guard. And my grandfather – he was right in the middle of all of it. I feel so . . . so . . . stupid.' There was no other word for it.

'You are stupid.'

Nora blinked.

His tone was all equanimity, the smooth pleasant aspect of his face unchanged, not a hint of anger or accusation. Just a statement of fact.

Nora came to her own defense of the charge she'd leveled at herself.

'You could least have allowed as to how I was ignorant, rather than stupid. For one thing, it's true. And for another, that would have been the nice thing to do.' She sucked in her breath, as though she could recall the words. *Good one, Nora. Lecturing a grieving man on manners.*

But he almost smiled.

'You tell me what's nice about this. About any of it. Then or now.'

'You're right. Not a damn thing. Look, I'm sorry. No matter what I say, it's coming out wrong. I'm just trying, at this very late date, to remedy my own ignorance. My *stupidity*. I never even knew about you or your older brother until this happened. Do you mind my asking – what was he like?'

His face softened further still. 'I don't mind. I don't much get a chance to talk about him, especially not about what he was like. All anybody cares about is how he died. But we probably shouldn't talk here. Miss Emily will have our hides.'

Nora glanced toward the front desk and stifled a laugh. 'For someone who didn't grow up here, you've managed to learn one of the most important things. Don't get crosswise with Miss Emily.'

She logged out of the *Afro* and followed Kwame Evans out of the library, pretending not to notice Emily Beattie's quivering attention as they passed.

TWENTY-SEVEN

They settled themselves on a bench beneath a spreading maple tree to one side of the library steps, the shade rendering its broad planks bearable. Just.

A white couple walked past them into the library, the woman twisting as they passed, staring at Nora. Not tourists, Nora decided; they didn't have the sunburnt skin, the salt-stiffened hair, the flagrantly casual clothes – a rip here, a stain there, because *it didn't matter; they were on vacation* – but bore the purposeful look of people running regular errands in town. The hardware store, the supermarket, the library. Indeed, the woman cradled an armful of children's books. Her hair was pulled away from her face into a short ponytail, exposing a large birthmark along her jawline and nearly covering half her neck, like a smear of strawberry jam from a toddler's sticky hand, and Nora gave her credit for not styling her hair so as to hide it.

She leaned close to her husband and whispered something, and he, too, turned to rake his gaze across Nora. One day, Nora thought, she would get used to her own unwelcome notoriety. She just wasn't there yet. She was relieved when Kwame spoke.

'I was only a little boy when Bobby headed back here. I barely remember him. But what I do remember, he was more like a father than a brother, Grace more like a mother; they were both so much older. Our parents, they were really old, at least in my mind. Time I came along, they were past all that child-rearing stuff. So Bobby and Grace mainly took care of me, until Bobby . . .' He briefly closed his eyes.

'Everything changed after that. Grace moved back here. Said she wanted people in town to see her all day, every day, so that nobody could forget Bobby.'

Nobody. An all-encompassing word, but when Grace had returned to Chateau, she'd gone to work for a specific somebody, in the home of the very Police Chief who'd so officiously brushed off her brother's death as either suicide, a drug deal gone awry, or even murder at the hands of the people he'd come to help – and had stayed on there even after Nora's grandfather's death.

'My parents – the life just went out of them after Bobby was killed. It was like being in a house with a couple of ghosts. Kept the shades drawn all day, barely talked, not even between themselves, let alone to me. They sent me down to stay with Grace every summer. I didn't find out until later that she was the one who insisted on getting me out of there. Funny, this being the town where Bobby was killed, but those were some of the best times of my life. I liked it so much that my wife and I sent Robert down here each summer for the same reason. He was on his way to visit Grace when . . .'

He stopped. 'If we'd never sent him down here, he'd still . . .' He stopped again.

Nora fought an impulse to lay a comforting hand on the arm of the man who'd refused to shake her hand.

'For a long time I was almost as ignorant' – he put some English on the word, with a wry smile in her direction – 'as you. It was years before I realized this was where he was killed. Grace kept it from me as long as she could. I think she just wanted to get me out of that sad, dark house. But that's not what she said. Said she was afraid I'd grow up a city boy, not know how to take care of myself. Showed me how to fish, got me a little twenty-two so I could shoot squirrels and rabbits.'

No, thought Nora, Grace wouldn't have brought him into the frosty propriety of Quail House. She'd have kept him as far away as possible, urging him into the woods, down to the river, places where he could skin his knees, dirty up his clothes, come home smiling with leaves in his hair and a string of silvery perch dangling from his hand.

'Fishing, I get,' she said. 'But squirrels?' She made a face. 'I was always told it's a sin to shoot something that you don't intend to eat.' She didn't mention it was a lesson imparted by her grandfather, guessing that a reference to the former Police Chief would be unwelcome.

'Oh, we ate them. She taught me to skin them and dress them and made me help her cook them, too.' He threw back his head and laughed. 'Never did learn to like 'em, though. Well, rabbit. I guess that was OK. It's the one thing that truly does taste like chicken. But not squirrel. And I told her never, ever to think about bringing me no muskrat. Apparently, Bobby was the same way. Never did develop a taste for it.'

'Bobby,' Nora urged. 'What was he like?'

His laughter eased into something soft and fond. 'Big.'

'Big?'

'I was little. To me, he always looked about ten feet tall. He'd ride me around on his shoulders so that my head would bump the ceiling. He named me, you know.'

Of course she didn't know. But she held her tongue as he talked on.

'Way I heard it, he took me right out of my mother's arms and claimed me for his own. I guess I was like a toy to him, or something. Carried me around everywhere and insisted on giving me this name. For years, I thought it was something special in Swahili – you know, like the Brave One, or Wise Child, or something grand. Turns out it means Saturday. The day I was born.'

A laugh boomed out, so deep and easy that Nora was tempted to relax. But how could she, when she knew how the story ended?

He must have been thinking the same thing, because the laugh ended abruptly. 'He was already in college when I was born. Morgan State, so at least he lived at home. I've tried and tried but I can't remember him saying anything in particular about the civil rights stuff he was involved in, but then, why would he have talked about it with me? I was barely more than a baby. It was just . . .'

He stopped. Closed his eyes again.

'He was there one day and then he wasn't. And he never was again.'

'I'm sorry.' The most inadequate phrase ever invented.

He dusted off his immaculate pants and rose to his feet. 'Not as sorry as I am. Thanks for letting me talk about my brother. Sorry I interrupted your research. I noticed you were looking at the old-timey stories. Seen any newer ones?'

Nora shook her head. 'I was just trying to find out what happened back then.'

His lips tightened. 'You might want to pay attention to what's happening now.' He turned to leave, then turned back.

'We're marching today. You ought to come. Might help fix that ignorance.'

TWENTY-EIGHT

1967

The Morgan State students – a dozen of them – boarded with black people all over town.

Despite the Evanses' deep ties in Chateau, it had taken all of Grace and Bobby's powers of persuasion – weeks of visiting, writing follow-up letters and even a few long-distance phone calls from Baltimore – to find enough people willing to take in strangers coming to town for the express purpose of making life difficult.

Because as bad as things were, they could get worse. People could lose their jobs. Their homes – most black people in Chateau rented. Even their lives. Paranoid? Hardly. Nobody had to mention Medgar Evers, shot on his doorstep in Mississippi just a few weeks earlier. Change was coming, yes, but the cost was terrible. Wasn't there the slightest chance that Chateau might follow the rest of the world, years later but at least peacefully?

Grace sat at kitchen tables and drank lemonade in tall, cold glasses set before her by shaking hands; tried to catch downcast gazes, listened hard to whispered excuses. 'I want to, I surely do. But . . .'

'We'll pay our way.' There'd been a collection on campus, funded by students and professors who wished they could take part, but for various reasons – jobs, families and the equally reasonable one of soul-shaking fear – could not. 'It's not much, but it'll cover the cost of food and a little more for your trouble.'

She'd offered once, afraid of how it might be received, and saw those fears realized.

Of course, it had been taken as an insult. The woman had stiffened. Her trembling hands stilled. 'Like I'd take money to do the right thing.'

Grace started to apologize, but the woman spoke over her. 'You send one of those children here. I'll talk to some other people for you.'

For their part, the members of the group respected the danger they'd posed their hosts, slipping in and out of homes via alleys and back doors, heading off to early-morning organizing meetings at AME Zion clutching paper sacks packed with sandwiches wrapped in waxed paper and a piece of fruit picked from a backyard tree, often sent on their way with a hug and a 'God bless.'

Grace had hoped to share a home with Bobby, but the group divvied up the few available rooms by gender, Grace sharing a double bed with a girl named June who snored and kicked her way through each night, giving Grace an excuse to slip out early each morning to stand hidden behind an ancient oak as Bobby emerged from his own lodgings and trail him unobtrusively to the church. Evenings, she followed a similar ritual, lingering outside the white frame church while those inside reviewed the day's events and planned the next day's action, then tiptoeing through yards and ducking behind buildings as she followed him home, her actions an uncomfortable reminder of the way she'd tried to avoid catching the eye of Todd Burris, her high school nemesis.

Then, she'd been trying to protect herself. Now, she was honoring her promise to her mother to protect her brother.

'I won't let anything happen to him. I swear.'

But day after day continued quiet, Chateau doing what Chateau did best, turning its back on unpleasantness, covering its ears, averting its gaze. Wait long enough, and most bad things – everything from inclement weather to a broken heart – resolve on their own.

'It's frustrating,' Bobby told Walter one night. He'd agreed to a series of exclusive interviews that Walter would use as the basis for a special report in the *Afro*: *Inside Civil Disobedience.*

Grace had found some pretext to drop by Miss Lydia's house, where Walter and Bobby were boarding, and sat with them in the kitchen, shades drawn against the possibility of any outside gaze, the room stifling. A plate of Miss Lydia's nut bread sat untouched on the kitchen table. She baked something new each day, tutting and fussing over her charges. Grace took a piece and nibbled at it. It was too hot to eat, but Miss Lydia had gone to the trouble.

'They want to wait us out. Think we'll go away.'

Walter took a handkerchief from his pocket, shook it out and blotted his glistening forehead. 'But you'll have to at some point. People have to get back to their jobs, to school.'

Privately, he'd confessed to Grace that he was about to give up on the idea of a series. It was hard to write about an action when there was no action to speak of. She'd gone cold at the thought. She'd never considered the possibility that Walter might return to Baltimore, expecting her to go with him, forcing her into the awful position of having to choose between going back to her job at the *Afro* or staying to watch over her brother – and kissing her job goodbye.

'But they won't be able to ignore what we're doing next.'

'What's that?' Walter's hand kept straying to his suit jacket, hanging over the back of his chair. Grace knew his cigarettes resided in an inner pocket and knew as well that Miss Lydia forbade smoking in her home. Walter's irritation – at a story falling flat, and at his own urgent need for a smoke – was nearly palpable. Grace edged the plate of nut bread toward him, hoping to distract him.

'A march. Tomorrow's Saturday, when all the town people will be running errands and the country people come in to do their shopping. What they'll see is all our people marching down the middle of Commerce Street.'

Walter snorted, his frustration as clear and pointed as the phrasing in his columns.

'With what – all twelve of you? So the good white people of Chateau can do what they've been doing these last two weeks? Turn their backs and wait until you all have left so everything can go back to the way it's always been?'

'With speakers.' Bobby sliced off a thick piece of nut bread and slathered it with butter slowly melting despite Miss Lydia's placing the crock in a bowl of ice water. 'Miss Lydia,' he called into the parlor where she ostensibly retired each evening to study her Bible but which, of course, enabled her to overhear every word spoken in the kitchen. 'This is the best nut bread I've ever eaten in my life.'

Walter executed an eye roll so prolonged it made Grace think of her mother's admonition whenever she pouted. 'Someday your face gonna freeze like that.'

'Preaching to the choir,' he said. 'What white person is going to come listen to you? Or black people, for that matter? Waste of time.'

Grace kept herself barely awake by imagining Walter living the rest of his life with his eyes rolled up so far in his head that only the whites showed.

His voice jerked her awake.

'You're shittin' me. 'Scuse me, ma'am,' he called into the parlor.

Grace opened her eyes. She'd missed something important. Walter's eyes were right where they belonged in their sockets, alert with the sort of curiosity she hadn't seen from him in days.

'How'd you get him? Last I heard, he was getting so many death threats he's been lying low. For some strange reason, he doesn't trust the FBI to protect him.' Walter and Bobby shared a chuckle, while Grace tried to figure out a way to ask who they were talking about without betraying the fact that she'd dozed off.

'He went to Morgan, at least before he dropped out and joined up with the Panthers.'

The bread fell from Grace's hand, spilling crumbs across the table. Marcus Simmons was coming to Chateau? He'd been briefly jailed a few months earlier after being charged with inciting a riot in Virginia, where he'd given a speech so inflammatory the blacks and whites listening from opposite sides of the street charged one another, breaking through the police lines meant to keep them apart, and tearing into each other with fists and feet, and baseball bats that had been stashed in alleyways for just such an opportunity.

Whenever her brother talked about Simmons, he mentioned his Morgan State connection. He must have worked the college channels to find him and persuade him to come to Chateau.

Walter's whistle was long and low. 'Can't imagine anyone ignoring Marcus. You got a parade permit?'

'Who are you kidding? You think they'd give us one?'

'You prepared to get arrested?'

'Been prepared from the minute we got here.' Which didn't jibe with a single thing he'd told their parents. Grace distinctly remembered a repeated exchange between her mother and Bobby:

'You see cops coming at you, what do you do?'

'Go the other way.'

Walter gave another whistle. 'You think you're ready for jail. After you've been in one, especially one of these little country jails, you give me a call. Collect. Tell me how ready you were.'

Walter had been to jail, swept up during a protest he was covering in Washington, and Grace remembered the tense hours at the *Afro* when the editors had huddled with a lawyer, trying to determine his whereabouts and then working for his release – an incident that, of course, only enhanced his standing.

He'd come through the experience with only minor injuries, if you counted a goose-egg the size of a fist over his right eye and the ruination of one of his beautiful suits. Once back in the newsroom, he'd shrugged off the whole business with a much-remarked-upon nonchalance.

But one day shortly after his return, she made the mistake of walking up silently behind him, not speaking until she was only about a foot away, and his coffee cup had gone flying, its contents besmirching yet another suit, and Grace got stuck with a dry-cleaning bill along with an appreciation of just what a single day in jail could do to a man.

She didn't want to see Bobby become that same sort of jumpy, sideways-glancing man.

'They'll scoop up Marcus before he gets five words out of his mouth.'

Bobby puffed his chest out. 'They'll have to go through us first. There's a whole new contingent from school, bunking with people over in Salisbury. They'll come over just before the march. We'll be five deep around Marcus.'

Walter scribbled some notes on his pad. 'Impressive organizing.'

Grace couldn't help herself. Pride washed through her, briefly sweeping away all her worries on behalf of her brother.

Someone who would muster a second group of students, squirrel them away in a neighboring town so as not to raise suspicions in Chateau, and command the presence of Marcus Simmons wouldn't be so foolish as to risk undermining those accomplishments over something that had happened three years earlier, long enough that whole days went by when Grace didn't think about it.

Nonetheless, when she bade her goodbyes that night, she lingered in the tall rhododendrons in Miss Lydia's back yard until she saw the light in Bobby's window blink off.

TWENTY-NINE

The woman who'd seemed so concerned about the march – 'How many times can one town burn?' – had evoked a restless mob surging through the center of town, shouting for revenge.

Instead, Nora saw a few dozen people, led by Grace, Kwame and a woman – tears drenching her face – who must have been his wife, walking slowly and silently down the middle of the street, the older people wielding cardboard fans against the heat. Several had printed out photos of Robert Evans and fastened them to their shirts or had blown them up and attached them to posters with predictable slogans.

Justice for Robert.

Demand Answers.

Who's Next?

Accompanying the slogans, the image of a gun with a red slash across it.

An image of a police badge with a red slash across it.

An image of Alden's face with a red slash across it.

Nora kept to the sidewalk, ambling a few steps behind the marchers, trying to look as though she just happened to be walking in the same direction on some errand, even though no one else was headed that way. Several people were out and about – it was lunch-time, when lawyers and courthouse clerks and store workers headed to the Wagon Wheel for the daily special. Patrons spilled from the diner's doors to watch the passing parade. People coalesced in groups, black over here and white there, faces stony.

Nora braced herself for more comments of the sort she'd heard from the biddies, but the watchers were wordless as the marchers passed, the heavy silence broken only by the muted thuds of soles against blacktop. The onlookers stared at the marchers, and the marchers stared straight ahead, toward the courthouse that was their destination. Older people led the group, dressed for an occasion, the men like Kwame in suits, the women in flowered dresses and church meeting hats that shielded them from the punishing sun.

Behind them, and in double their numbers, was a contingent of younger people, from their twenties and thirties all the way down to what appeared to be high school and even middle school age, the youngster's faces eager and animated in comparison to the hard stares of their elders, who'd done this before, after all.

Some of the women and a few of the men balanced babies on hips or pushed strollers. The Baltimore contingent was among the younger marchers, Nora guessed, but she couldn't distinguish them from the locals. Years earlier, she'd have been able to tell by how people dressed – city people inevitably decked out in whatever was trendy at the moment – but the internet had made it possible for everybody to keep current.

As they neared it, Nora saw the sort of spectacle she'd initially feared but had begun to think was a product of an overactive imagination. Now, she realized her imagination had been right on target.

A line of people –white people – spread out across the courthouse lawn, blocking the walkway to the steps. They, too, held signs, although their own were nearly identical but for a single word's different: *Blue Lives Matter.* Or *All Lives Matter.*

Parallel rows of police officers lined the final block to the courthouse, in a sort of gauntlet leading toward those waiting on the lawn. Nora scanned the variety of uniforms, picking out the local Chateau police, the county sheriff's deputies and the state police. She tried in vain to make out the features in the shade thrown by peaked caps but realized Alden wouldn't be there. He was on leave and, besides, any Fraternal Order of Police lawyer worth his salt would order him to stay far away from any such gathering.

Together, the cops and counter-protesters far outnumbered the marchers, a fact that registered with an obvious slackening of their already slow pace.

'Aw, shit.' The words floated toward Nora from the middle of the group in the street. Her own thoughts exactly.

Kwame held up his arm and everyone stopped.

'Everybody gather 'round.' His voice boomed over their heads.

Nora edged closer, keeping to the inky pools of shade cast by the maples overarching the sidewalk. As she came even with the group, fast coalescing from a straggling line into a cluster around Kwame, the people at the courthouse glanced at one another, sotto voce comments going up and down the line. The cops, merely alert before, stiffened to full attention.

Nora came nearly even with Kwame and pressed herself into a boxwood hedge, the tiny leaves waxy against her bare arms and legs, their resinous scent strong in her nostrils.

Kwame spoke loud enough so that those waiting on the courthouse lawn could hear.

'They're looking for a confrontation. But that's not what we want. What do we want?'

The response came fast and clear as though they'd rehearsed it.

'Justice for Robert!'

'When do we want it?'

'Now!'

The single syllable hung in the air, dying on a collective expelled breath.

'No, we didn't come here for a fight. And we didn't come simply to honor Robert or to grieve him, although we do both. We honor him deeply, this son and nephew who will never get to be a husband, a father. We mourn the loss of promise, of what he might have become, might have contributed. That grief will never vanish, although we pray it will ease. But in addition to our sorrow, we honor Robert with our anger. Not the sort of raw, destructive anger, the kind that they' – he turned and gestured toward the muttering crowd on the courthouse lawn, the increasingly attentive cops – 'seem to expect, and maybe even want. But we're not going to give it to them. They've already taken too much from us. The life of an innocent boy.'

Was he innocent?

'I had to. He came at me,' Alden had described the heart-stopping moment, lent credence by the account of Robert's violent past.

As much as she leaned toward Alden's version, especially given his consistently voiced regret, what would she prefer? Another black life erased, another layer of indictment for a system that gave tacit permission or even approval, given the despair-inducing repetitiveness of white cops who shot first when confronted by the menace they assigned to black men?

Kwame's fist shot into the air.

'We're going to focus our anger. Use it to get results. Demand an investigation. We've already spoken with the Attorney General's Office. They're sending someone down here.'

A murmur ran through the marchers. Nora hunched farther into her inadequate shelter, lowering her head, turning her face into the shrubbery.

'We're not just going to settle for anyone's word on what happened. We're concentrating our anger, our righteous anger, on demanding the truth. Demanding transparency. We want the recording of the nine-one-one calls, anything that shows what happened that night. We need them to find Robert's phone.'

Nora raised her head. None of the stories she'd read about the shooting had mentioned a phone. She thought of the men she'd seen searching the soybean field for a gun the day she and Alden had gone to the ocean. Maybe they'd find a phone, too.

'And we want it made public, so that everybody knows the *truth*' – another fist punch – 'of what happened that night.'

The truth! Nora's arm nearly jerked in a fist pump of its own. If those few fatal seconds had unfolded as Alden described and were verified by outside investigators, she would no longer have to suppress the twinges of a grownup version of a schoolgirl crush.

Kwame took a breath so deep it was audible even to Nora, half hidden in shrubbery.

'I never thought one family could endure so much pain. First my older brother, the one I barely remember. I was just a little one when he was murdered in this very town, and that murder yet unsolved to this day. Now my one precious son.'

A sob rent the air. The man turned to his wife and held her until her heaves quieted to mere shudders. Grace stared off into the distance, something in her gaze nearly propelling Nora from her green shelter in search of the sun, to warm the blood gone cold in her veins.

'But the abomination surrounding my brother's death will not be repeated. This time, as before, we seek the truth. But this time we shall find it, and when we do, we will shout it to the world that what happened to Robert must never happen again.'

Inarticulate cries rose from the crowd.

An officer broke ranks from the line of the police and, joined by another man, jogged toward them.

Kwame turned to face them. Nora noticed how he held his hands out and down, palms open and empty, in a gesture both practiced and sadly practical. She herself had never thought to take any particular stance when facing a police officer and even had been markedly truculent when confronted with a sheriff's blame-the-victim inclination in Wyoming.

The civilian's white shirt clung damply in large dark patches across his stomach and under his arms. Nora recognized Todd Burris.

'You don't have a permit, Kwame. You need a permit for a parade or gathering.'

Kwame Evans tilted his chin to those at the courthouse. 'They got a permit, Mr Mayor?'

The officer – Nora presumed he was the chief – chimed in.

'They're on public property.'

Kwame's voice dropped a register. 'As are we.'

'But you're in the street. Blocking traffic.'

Kwame stepped to the side of the crowd and made of show of scanning the street behind them, and then turning and looking toward the courthouse, heads turning in sync with his own, everyone seeing a street devoid of moving vehicles, the only cars in sight sitting decorously in parking spaces.

'We're not blocking anything.'

'But it's the law.' Burris's voice rose higher in exact proportion to Kwame's deepening tone. 'You can't walk in the street. You've got to use the sidewalk.'

Kwame nodded, not to the mayor, but to the marchers. 'You heard Mayor Burris,' he said, pointedly using the honorific and last name to the man who'd only addressed him by his first. 'Only allowed to walk on the sidewalk in Chateau.'

The mass of marchers milled together momentarily then split, some going to the sidewalk on one side of the street, others across the way, men helping young mothers lift strollers over the curb, people sighing as they reached the relief of the shade.

The chief spoke up. 'No loitering.'

Some of the marchers stood so close to Nora she could have touched them; indeed, the two young men now hovering impatiently before her cast curious glances over their shoulders at the white woman who'd planted herself inexplicably within the greenery like some sort of ungainly, overgrown wood sprite.

A corner of Kwame Evans's mouth twitched in a not-quite smile. 'Ain't nobody loitering.' His broad casual tone stopped just short of sarcasm. 'These are busy people. Things to do, places to go. Attorney General's coming. Got to be ready for him. Right?'

The crowd murmured something that could have been assent. Mothers performed the ungainly maneuvers necessary to turn around strollers that came equipped with cupholders, baskets for purses and diaper bags, babies a seeming afterthought. Kwame Evans held out his arm and Grace took it. His wife moved to his other side and together, the trio made a retreat that somehow looked like a victory.

At least, it did to Nora.

'This is some bullshit,' one of the young men in front of her muttered.

The other elbowed him. 'Look there. They think it's some bullshit, too.'

The marchers were already vanishing down the side streets. Car doors slammed. Engines turned over. The people on the courthouse lawn milled about, signs drooping. The cops broke their parallel formation and clustered around the chief and the mayor.

'Disappointed, for sure,' one of the young men said. 'Thought they'd get to crack some black heads today.'

They laughed together and then moved away, leaving Nora to extricate herself from the boxwood, brushing leaves from her hair and wondering how long it would take for the leaves' distinctive scent to vanish from her clothing.

The sun hit her full in the face as she emerged. The last of the marchers stood in a small group before her as a few white people lingered across the street, watching them. Nora blinked, half blinded by the sun. A small woman leaning on a cane stood among them, her white head bare, looking for all the world like . . .

But, no. It couldn't be. Penelope was still using her walker. And although she'd hinted she was capable of driving, she'd seemed content to comply with her doctor's advice against it. Anyway, when Nora blinked again, the woman was gone.

THIRTY

1967

It was barely light when Grace slipped out of bed the morning of the march. June still snored lustily on her side of the bed.

Grace paused at the top of the stairs, listening for any sounds from the kitchen. Their host, Miss Theresa, liked to get up early so as to have a full breakfast waiting for them, coffee pale with cream, eggs scrambled with cheese, thick slabs of homemade bread toasted and dripping with butter and jam, and crispy scrapple she'd made herself with the leavings from a friend's hogs. Grace swore her clothes had gotten tighter in just the two weeks she'd stayed with Miss Theresa.

'She's gonna turn you into one of those big-butt farm gals,' Walter had teased, after which Grace had made sure to walk behind him to forestall any more observations about her butt.

She tiptoed in stockinged feet through the dark kitchen, slipping on her shoes only when she'd safely descended the porch steps. She crept warily toward the street where Bobby was staying, keeping to the shadows, mindful as always of rural people's tendency to wake with the dawn.

She'd gotten lucky in one regard. An aging willow anchored the backyard of the Driggs house where Bobby was staying, its branches drooping nearly to the ground, curtaining a shaded spot where old Mr Driggs liked to sit on afternoons in an old kitchen chair smoking his pipe. His chair, curtained from sight within the slender fronds, made the perfect spot for Grace's morning observation, screening her from view, although it did nothing to filter out the scent of the Driggses' breakfast, twin to the one she should have been eating in Miss Theresa's kitchen.

Grace wished she'd thought to grab a piece of bread and butter on her way out the door. Her stomach rumbled so loud she feared it would give her away; indeed, a ragged-eared tomcat creeping across the yard in search of unseen prey stopped suddenly, his head swiveling in her direction.

'Git,' she hissed, and it obliged with a twitch of its moth-eaten tail.

Finally, she saw a shadow at the back door. She started to rise, pins and needles shooting up her leg as she put her weight on her left foot to wake it up. But when the door opened, only Walter emerged. A tiny orange dot glowed at his fingertips, the day's first cigarette. He took a long grateful drag before setting out for the church where the activists met each morning to go over the day's plans.

Grace waited for Bobby. Five minutes, ten. The mosquitoes came to life, whining around her ears, still sleepy enough to be easily brushed away. A garter snake wound through the grass and detoured around the unexpected barrier of her feet.

Finally, keeping to the edges of the yard, she crept toward the house, at the last minute darting toward it in a crouch, raising up by inches until she could peek over the windowsill into the kitchen, praying she wouldn't come eye to eye with Miss Lydia going to fetch another cup of coffee for Bobby.

But the woman had her back to her, clearing the table in an otherwise empty room. She turned toward the window and Grace ducked, but not before she'd seen the single plate in the woman's hand. Maybe Bobby had arisen even earlier, unable to sleep, full of anticipation about the pending events.

Of course he had. Grace cursed her foolishness as she hurried toward the church. Marcus Simmons's presence in Chateau marked a momentous coup for Bobby. He'd want to make sure nothing went wrong.

The voice floating through the open windows in the church hall told her she'd been right. She'd heard it before, tinny through a radio or a black-and-white television barely larger than a toaster, showing Simmons leading marches that filled the broad boulevards of cities whose size made a mockery of a backwater like Chateau; Simmons confronting a row of cops as they struggled – not terribly hard – to hold back German shepherds slavering for his flesh; Simmons, dazed, a hand to his head, blood dripping through his fingers on to his trademark army jacket as the cop beside him holstered his nightstick with a look of satisfaction.

She'd imagined that voice, when she finally heard it in person, would be thunderous, booming a righteous message to the world. But Simmons spoke barely above a whisper, his words nonetheless so insistent, so piercing, that the roomful of just-awakened young people sat at vibrating attention in a silence so absolute that Simmons's message carried through the open windows to Grace, pressed against the wall, listening.

'You all are soldiers, soldiers in the fight of our lives. Fighting to right the grievous wrongs done our parents, our grandparents, our ancestors. Fighting to ensure our children don't suffer those same wrongs. When we march today, we march for them. And we don't march alone. Our ancestors are beside us. Our children are just out of sight, in the future. We march toward them, through any obstacles in our way. Maybe because this town is small, out of the way, it doesn't seem as if our cause here carries the same weight as it does elsewhere, in bigger places that get more attention. But that's what makes this so important. Because the battle is not won until it's won everywhere. Look at Ole Miss, integrated last year. Mississippi! And here you are, practically in the North, and white only going to school with white, black only with black.

'I thank you all for bringing me here to help you change this. It was an honor to receive the invitation from Bobby Evans, and if he were here right now, standing beside me, I'd thank him in person – again.'

What?

Grace came away from the wall. She stood on tiptoe, but the church windows were too high off the ground. She ran around to the door at the back of the church hall and cracked it, peering in. Walter was there, off to one side, scribbling away in his notebook as Simmons spoke.

But no Bobby. Which couldn't be right. She looked again, checking the corners of the room. She looked low – what if, for some reason, Bobby had seated himself on the floor, largely out of sight? He hadn't.

She let go of the door, not caring that it banged shut, and sprinted back to the Driggs home, not bothering with alleys this time, not caring who saw a black woman in a Sunday dress running down the middle of the street, full skirt flaring as it caught the breeze, white patent-leather shoes tapping a terrified beat on the pavement.

She reached the house and ran up the front steps, pressing one hand to the pain knifing through her side and pounding the door with the other. 'Miss Lydia! Miss Lydia!'

She nearly fell through the door as Miss Lydia flung it open.

'Child, what in the world—'

'My brother,' she gasped. 'Is he here?'

Miss Lydia turned her head so slowly from side to side that Grace wanted to shake her. 'He sure isn't. Left first thing this morning, must have. Gone before I could make him breakfast.'

'Are you sure?' Grace looked past her, willing Bobby to materialize from the small parlor, or bound down the narrow stairwell, taking the steps two at a time, laughing at her near hysteria. But no shadows wavered in the parlor. The stairwell remained stubbornly deserted.

'Maybe he's in his room. Let me just check.' Grace pushed her way past Miss Lydia, even as the woman shook her head again, and ran up the stairs. The first bedroom was obviously the Driggses', a double bed with a wedding band quilt in soft, faded colors bespeaking the fabric's previous use as clothing. She pushed open the next door. Two single beds greeted her, one unmade, with a mess of skinny reporter's notebooks on the nightstand and a pair of black wingtips to go with the gray and blue suits – Walter had been wearing a beige-striped suit with his brown shoes in the church – beneath the bed.

The covers on the other bed stretched so tightly across it Grace could have bounced pennies off its surface. She looked at it and her heart broke. Both she and her mother, with their years of experience getting paid to make other people's beds, had tried to teach Bobby how to make his own bed neatly, if at all, but he'd mocked their house-proud ways. 'What's the use if I'm just going to get back in it and mess it up again?'

No matter what Miss Lydia thought and Grace devoutly wished, Bobby Evans had not slept in that bed the previous night.

THIRTY-ONE

'Whenever I'm with you, it feels like we're in some sort of time warp.'

Alden and Nora lounged at Electra's dinette, drinking beer from bottles.

She'd been taking a stab at her book – circling ever closer to the moment when she'd have to write about the kidnapping itself – when a tap at the door rescued her.

'Hey.' Alden stood nearly invisible in the dusk. 'I was on the river. Saw your light. Took a chance. OK if I come in?'

'More than OK.' She shut the laptop with relief.

Now, she clinked her bottle against his. 'Here's to time warps.'

It was, she told herself, time for a break – a break from the book, a break from her lingering questions about the shootings of Robert and Bobby, a break from her vow to push back against the unspoken rule about avoiding unpleasantness, a rule for which she increasingly felt nudges of sympathy. It was exhausting to hold people accountable and more exhausting still to turn that same uncompromising gaze upon oneself. For at least this moment in time, she was content to kick back over beers with an old friend.

They swapped only the most innocuous shared memories, of the year Alden's steer won a blue ribbon at the state fair and he took Nora for a ride on the Ferris wheel to celebrate, whereupon she'd discovered her fear of heights. She'd screamed so that the operator was forced to stop the ride to let her off and then had to restrain Alden from punching the man who'd called her a chickenshit.

'My hero.' She laughed at the recollection.

'First time I realized you might be scared of anything. Remember that time . . .'

With each tilt of the bottle, they strenuously ignored the fact that they couldn't risk anything as innocent as a chance meeting on the street, or another coffee-shop conversation with the entire clientele reading God knows what into every innocuous word, snapping surreptitious photos with their cellphones and posting them seconds later with lurid captions.

But even as the beer relaxed Nora, it emboldened her, too. For all that she'd granted herself a break, a particular bit of unpleasantness had nagged at her ever since their dip in the ocean.

'Where does Kyra think you are?' She held her breath, awaiting the answer.

'Probably down at the Beach. A few of us at the department would head there after we finished up back when I worked night shift. Safer drinking there than at a bar where everyone would be up in our business. And sometimes I row down there at night just to build a little fire and sit and think. These days, it's the only way to get away from everything.'

'She doesn't mind?' Not what she really wanted to know. But she got the answer she sought anyway.

'Are you kidding? She and the elementary school principal have been going at it for years. It's why she's the PTA queen. Gives her the perfect excuse to be over at the school damn near twenty-four/seven. Word is they've done it in every nook and cranny in the whole school; that the reason the principal's desk has such a nice high gloss is from Kyra's back rubbing all over it.'

Nora felt a stab of envy even as she laughed beneath her breath. At least Kyra and her principal had a way to be together in the open.

'Everybody in town knows about it and everybody pretends not to because of the girls.' Alden peered into the neck of his bottle as though seeking something within.

'We'd already started the paperwork for the divorce, given that the twins will be heading off to college in just a few more weeks. But the lawyer said we can't do it now; that it'll look bad in the midst of all this. We have to' – his fingers wiggled air quotes – '"present a united front."'

Nora held her breath.

'But when all this is over . . .' He spoke so softly that she had to lean in to hear him. 'Nora, I made a mistake all those years ago. She threw herself at me, and kept coming at me, even though I told her no. And you were away . . . and then I slipped, and I knew I could never face you again, that you'd take one look at me and just *know*. I'm so sorry. I know I can never make up for it. But I do know one thing.'

Nora's heart jackhammered.

'What's that?' she finally managed.

'I didn't wait for you back then. And I have no right to ask anything of you. So I won't. I'll just tell you that I hope you'll be waiting for me on the other side of this. I surely do.'

She didn't make any promises. Didn't throw herself into his arms and weep in gratitude. Or even the converse – allow herself to luxuriate in the icy, bitter vindication of his admission of that long-ago mistake. But a few minutes later, when he handed her his empty bottle with a rueful shrug and closed the trailer door behind him, she watched from the window as he crossed the lawn, only pulling the shade down after he stepped into the boat.

She wondered if he'd go to the Beach, as he said he sometimes liked to do. She left the trailer and returned to a darkened Quail House. Michael Murphy lay on his bed in a corner of the kitchen. He lifted his head, ascertained that she was safely inside, then rose groaning to his feet and headed down the hall to Penelope's room.

Nora stood a moment at the base of the stairs, listening for the tense silence that would indicate her mother lay awake on the other side of her bedroom door, likewise listening. But the house had the deep, peaceful stillness of slumber.

She climbed the stairs and fell into her own bed. But sleep remained elusive, her mind humming with unexpected possibilities. Could she and Alden really find a way forward again? Silly to hold on to the pain of abandonment after all these years – decades! – but with the recent anguish of Joe's betrayal still scouring her psyche, it seemed just as silly to ignore it.

She remembered the promise she'd made the night she'd driven into Chateau, moments before Alden shot Robert Evans: that she was done running. But was ignoring the possibility of a future with Alden just another form of running, or – just as bad – of staying curled into the emotional fetal position she'd assumed when she'd left Joe?

What if, instead of running away, she ran *toward*, and damn the rest of the world and its judgment? Alden would be exonerated soon, and then . . .

Then . . .

A thought that propelled Nora Best out of bed and into her clothes and down the stairs and across the lawn at a dead run to the dock, where she untied the ancient rowboat and pushed off into the river, praying it hadn't developed any leaks over the years, and if it had, that at least it wouldn't sink before she got to the Beach.

THIRTY-TWO

1967

This march was different.

For one thing, it was bigger. The students staying in Salisbury had driven over before dawn, black marchers packed into cars driven by their white sympathizers, sardining themselves on to floorboards as the vehicles approached Chateau so as not to alert anyone to their presence.

And, of course, there was Marcus Simmons, his name known even – and especially – to white people. No preacher-dark suit for Simmons, no polite-but-firm discourse, no meeting people halfway, taking things slow. When the evening news showed him in his Army jacket and black beret and played sound bites from his fiery speeches, so full of words like 'revolution' and 'burn' and 'power,' white sphincters around the country clamped shut.

Somehow, despite all the precautions, word had gotten out. A provocateur, Grace thought. They'd infiltrated most civil rights groups around the country, often coerced into their roles with threats of outsize penalties for real or imagined crimes, and so when the demonstrators poured from the church hall on to the street, an exuberant party feel to those first few blocks as they quick-stepped with Simmons at the fore, a triple line of police in full riot gear awaited them.

Any minute, Grace had told herself as she trailed behind them, Bobby would emerge from an alley and join them – whether with good reason or stupid excuse for his whereabouts, she didn't care. Then she saw the cops and hoped that wherever he was, he'd stay put.

The cops stood shoulder to shoulder across Commerce Street. At a signal from Simmons, the marchers lined up in similar formation. The cops had guns but the marchers had numbers, and Grace watched the two groups – only about fifty feet apart – size each other up and calculate the odds.

The few white people who'd been on the street, getting an early start on their weekend errands, vanished into stores and other businesses, standing among the mannequins in the windows of La Mode Better Dresses, putting down their silverware in the Wagon Wheel as their untouched coffee cooled.

Chief Smythe and Simmons each took a few steps forward.

The Chief's voice held the same low menace Grace heard on the day he fired Bobby. 'We don't need any trouble here in Chateau. Haven't had any yet, nothing serious, and we aren't about to let it start now. You aren't from here. Go on back where you came from.'

'No trouble.' As in the church, Simmons spoke quietly. Grace, even wrapped as she was in worry about Bobby, leaned in to listen. Across the street, she saw Walter doing the same, just a few feet away from a contingent of white reporters and photographers. Someone must have tipped them off, too.

'No trouble,' Simmons repeated. 'When a man was lynched the next county over not ten years ago. When there's not a single black face on your force, nor behind the counters in your banks and stores. When the only jobs for black people are picking crabs or picking crops.' His voice rose steadily.

'You say you don't want trouble? You already got trouble. And you're about to get more because we are here to Burn. This. System. Down!'

A full-throated cry burst from the crowd behind him at those last words, an inarticulate roar that coalesced into a chant. 'Burn it down!'

The crowd surged forward.

The police raised their shields.

Simmons raised his hand.

But Chief Smythe had one more thing to say.

'You're the ones who've got trouble,' he said. 'You've already lost one of your own.'

The shouting subsided into a puzzled murmur. Even Marcus Simmons looked baffled.

Graze puzzled over the expression on the Chief's face. Try as she might, she could only attribute it to a simple, searing emotion: satisfaction.

He puffed his chest out and raised his voice so that everyone on the street – the marchers, the cops, the press and the onlookers, now opening store doors, ready to slam them shut and throw deadbolts into place at the first sign of trouble – could hear.

'We fished Bobby Evans out of the Lenape River first thing this morning. He'd been shot dead.'

THIRTY-THREE

The rowing soothed Nora – the rhythmic dip and splash, propelling the boat at barely beyond the speed of the current, following the dancing moonlit path toward the Beach. A breeze lifted her hair, wafting away the occasional keening mosquito.

She didn't know what she was going to say to Alden. Maybe they didn't need words. She could just sit with him, gaze into the fire, its glowing coals a symbol of the love that had burned quietly through the long years and the wrong marriages, needing only a puff of air to burst into the flame it was always meant to be.

He'd said he and Kyra were postponing their divorce to lend the appearance of a united front during the investigation into Robert Evans's death. Fine. Let Kyra do her fake-supportive act, even as Alden drew strength from the fact that she, Nora, would be waiting for him, as he phrased it, on the other side.

She caught an acrid whiff of smoke and smiled. The Beach was just ahead. He'd already built the fire she'd imagined.

But when the boat rounded the bend, she saw not the single flicker she'd expected but a roaring bonfire with at least a half-dozen people around it. Nora dug an oar into the water and the boat shot out of the klieg light laid down by the moon and into the shadows along the shore.

Alden must have gone home after all.

Nora tried to shrug away the thud of disappointment, telling herself the exertion of rowing back against the current would at least tire her to the point of easy sleep when she returned to bed. The boat bobbed aimlessly for a moment. She took up the oars again. At least the breeze would be with her on the way back. It carried the words of the partyers on the Beach, male voices, some inarticulate guffaws and curses, and then one raised above the rest.

'Got her right where I want her.'

Which is when Nora realized Alden had gone to the Beach after all.

The Beach was the only spot of bare land along the riverbank until the Lenape reached the bay, and so Nora stayed in the boat, clutching at reeds uncertainly anchored in quaking marsh mud, hoping they wouldn't pull loose and send the boat shooting into the middle of the river where Alden and all the other cops would be able to see her.

The combined glare of firelight and full moon revealed Brittingham, along with Lewis, the cop who'd been there when they'd shown her the photo lineup, while the others had the swaggery stance she associated with people equipped with guns and the power of arrest. They all held cans and, as the fire leapt higher, showering sparks, she saw cases of beer stacked to one side of the gathering.

'Did you tell her you *looooooved* her?' one asked now, drawing out the word in a falsetto. 'That always gets them.'

'Hell, no. These things, they take finesse – not something you'd know anything about.' Alden again. He made a cranking motion with one arm. 'I'm reeling her in slow.'

'Hell.' Brittingham's partner, Lewis. 'You got to take it slow with her. Woman's thick as a plank. Took forever to get the photo ID from her.'

'Yeah, but we finally got it.' Brittingham, not nearly as drunk as the rest. 'Between that and the story we fed the *Sun* reporter, things are looking pretty good for you.'

'Got to hand it to you. That was a genius move, getting the dirt on that kid out in public.' Alden lifted his beer can in a toast.

'Had to, after the way Nelson went blabbing to the *Afro*.'

Nelson. Nora puzzled for a moment, then remembered the black cop stationed at the police department's entrance.

'Black bastard's gonna spend the rest of his life pushing paper in Records after that little stunt,' Brittingham said. 'But things are working out just fine. Few more weeks, this'll all be behind you.'

'Here's to that,' someone shouted. Beers were lifted, drained, cans tossed away, new ones retrieved.

'Hey, Alden. I'd say the worst is still ahead of you,' Lewis offered.

'How's that?'

''Cause at some point you're going to have to get loose of her.'

'The sooner the better. Been playing her like a fiddle so long my arm is tired.' Alden tossed his can into the fire. It hissed and popped. Someone passed him a flask. He took a long pull, gave it back and swiped the back of his hand across his mouth. 'That's more like it. Swear to God, if I have to say one more time how sorry I am that I shot that motherfucker . . . Give me that back.' He reached for the flask again.

The light of the fire played across his face, highlighting cheekbones and jutting jaw, throwing his eyes into deep shadow. For the first time since she'd been back, Nora saw him as the stranger he'd become.

'Better watch yourself,' someone else said. 'She went after that guy in Montana, Wyoming, wherever the hell it was, with an ax. Guy almost lost his arm. You're likely to lose your pecker.'

Just a few moments earlier, Nora had thought of warm coals, steady, comforting. Sustaining. Now she knew her reunion with Alden to have been fueled by sentiment, a conflagration rooted in memory, a willful turning away from the reality blazing bright before her.

The laughter stayed with Nora the whole way back to Quail House, long after it had actually died away.

THIRTY-FOUR

1967

People would say later that Grace's scream touched everything off, her anguished 'No!' ringing out like a cry to battle, echoed by a hundred voices in a roar that ripped the lid from Chateau's determined tranquility, setting loose two centuries of suppressed rage.

A brick, snatched from the construction site next to the ball field where the new bank was going in, flew toward the cops. They rushed the protesters, who in turn grabbed more bricks as they fled, hurling them through the plate-glass display windows of the

Commerce Street businesses. Befrocked mannequins toppled in La Mode. The projectiles took out both of the two-foot-tall antique glass vials in the window of Slocum's Pharmacy, one displaying a mysterious red liquid, the other green, the resulting spray soaking the greeting-card display and puddling like liquid Christmas on the floor.

The floor-to-ceiling windows of Burris's car dealership attracted a whole hail of bricks that landed on the Chrysler Newport convertible, next year's model that had arrived that very week, caving in the hood, ruining the Seafoam Turquoise Metallic paint job and gouging the creamy leather seats.

The cops halted their headlong, baton-swinging charge at the protesters and milled about, uncertain of their mission. Detain the protesters? Or protect their neighbors' property?

'Here!' the Chief called. Rallying them, getting them focused. 'Leave off those folks. Get him!' He pointed to Simmons, who'd hopped into the bed of a pickup parked along the street and was yelling at the top of his lungs.

'Burn it! Burn it all down!'

The cops advanced on the truck but not before some of the demonstrators saw what was going on and surrounded it, and in the pitched battle that ensued, the cops cracking heads right and left until they finally were able to pull Simmons from the truck into a forest of swinging nightsticks, nobody noticed at first the young men who'd climbed through the pharmacy's open windows, helped themselves to cigarette lighters and cans of hair spray, and were going from store to store, methodically spraying their makeshift flamethrowers at whatever would catch fire.

Soon, white men would come running with shotguns, sending the protesters scattering for good. Marcus Simmons would be hauled to a hospital and shackled to a bed for treatment of a shattered forearm, several broken ribs – the jagged end of one just barely missing his heart – and bruises swelling his face into unrecognizability in the subsequent mug shot. Chateau's volunteer fire department would muster too late to prevent the severe damage to the stores already afire, but sprayed down adjoining buildings to keep the whole block from going up. Later that night, when someone emptied gallons of gasoline around the perimeter of the AME Zion church and tossed a match on to the reeking stream, the fire chief refused to send a truck, citing fears of violence.

Just as no one came to the aid of a lone young black woman, her fists bloodied from pounding them on the sidewalk as she screamed herself silent, when she rose stone-faced and walked like an automaton through the burning town and beyond, her fury propelling her along the dusty country road that led toward Quail House.

THIRTY-FIVE

Nora sat in the boat for a long time after tying up at the dock, clambering out only after realizing that at some point Alden inevitably would row past and she would . . . what?

Go upside his head with an oar?

Scream at him?

Run for her truck and flee yet again? Which, frankly, was her first impulse. But how many times could one woman run?

How smug she'd been for her half-assed efforts to face things head-on! And how eagerly she now dropped them, embracing the Chateau way, pretending none of it had ever existed – not the shooting, nor the outing of her relationship with Alden, and especially not the damning information she'd just learned.

She'd have to deal with all of those things, and figure out the rest of her life, at some point. For now, she would stay in Chateau just long enough to make sure her mother was healed, holing up in her trailer and finishing the goddamn book in the process.

Which was why, when her phone rang a few hours later and her agent's number showed on the screen, she finally answered, secure in the knowledge that she could honestly say she was making progress.

But Lilith cut her off before she could say as much.

'What the hell, Nora? What for the love of Christ is going on with you?'

Murph, sitting at what should have been a safe distance, whined as the piercing tone registered.

'I'm almost done.' Every writer's lie. 'Truly. You should have a first draft in' – Nora thought of a realistic time and halved it – 'six weeks.'

Lilith forged on as though Nora hadn't spoken.

'What the hell do you think you're doing, carrying on with some married cop who shot a black kid? Are you out of your fucking mind?'

If, to use Grace's word, Nora was radioactive in Chateau, the *Justice for Robert* Facebook page had sent her to some level of galactic destruction in the publishing world.

'Did you not read your fucking contract? The part that says you won't engage in publicly condemned behavior? And even if you didn't, have you not read a single news story in the last few months? Writers aren't allowed to fuck up anymore. It's not colorful now. It's just plain racist – which is what it's always been, except that before we all just looked the other way.'

Nora finally managed to get a word in edgewise. 'But I didn't do anything. For God's sake, Lilith, it's not like I slept with him.' And now she never would. In fact, if the universe ever dealt her a break, she'd never see Alden Tydings again.

'Doesn't matter.' Lilith's tone was as emphatic as a slammed book. 'Perception is everything. You of all people know that. The publisher is canceling your contract. I think I can work it so that you don't have to pay back your advance. You can thank me anytime.'

'Thank you. But—'

Lilith cut her off. 'And, Nora, this officially ends our partnership. I can't afford to represent a client with this hanging over her.' She hung up in the midst of Nora's goodbye.

'Wait—'

Nora looked at the dog. The cat had joined him, sitting a few feet away, lifting a paw and licking it, ignoring them both.

'What about you two? Are you ditching me as well?'

Murph's tail pounded the ground in an affirmation of unending loyalty. Thank God.

She looked to Mooch, now slinking away by infinitesimal degrees across the lawn, belly low to the ground, tail twitching in anticipation. A grasshopper was about to meet its demise.

Never mind. She wasn't so far gone as to need reassurance from a cat.

But she was pretty far gone.

A long time ago, she'd left this place, trying to outrun heartbreak, eventually pronouncing herself older and wiser – until history kicked her in the ass by repeating itself.

'It's not fair.' A child's phrase.

But it *wasn't* fair. Nothing people thought they knew was true.

She knew that she could say that until she was blue in the face, could plaster it on big billboards leading into Chateau, could proclaim it to the world on every social media site she knew, and it wouldn't matter a damn.

How many clients had she lectured with the very phrase Lilith had just turned on her? Perception is reality. 'If you want to change your reality,' she'd tell them, 'you've got to put a different image out there, starting about five minutes ago. Let's get to work.'

She slammed her laptop shut.

Alden, *that fucker*, had bragged about playing her like a fiddle.

Nora drummed her fingers on the table, a tune of her own beginning to take shape in her mind.

She opened the laptop and typed *Robert Evans* and *Chateau* into a search engine. She'd read something, early on – 'Yes!'

Kwame Evans had said the family was calling on the Attorney General to conduct an independent investigation.

A few clicks led to a phone number for the Attorney General's Office in Baltimore, and a few numbers punched into an automated voicemail system finally led to a recording that invited her to leave a message. Which she did, after spelling out her name and repeating her cellphone number twice.

'Please call me as soon as possible,' she said. 'I have some information about Robert Evans's killing.'

THIRTY-SIX

1967

The sounds of the melee faded as Grace walked toward Quail House and were gone entirely by the time she entered the deep shade of McKay's Woods. Tree limbs stretched out over the road, and deep underbrush formed a seemingly impenetrable screen.

Grace fought an impulse to push through it, to flee deep into the forest, foraging for the plentiful food found in it and in the river, existing among the animals, whose lives were so much simpler than those of humans, their sole task finding enough to eat without getting eaten themselves. No constant tension of how to hold your body, direct your gaze, control your words, so as to avoid giving offense or attracting attention in any way. Because that attention could be fatal. As it had been with—

She forced back the sob in her throat. Now was not the time. Mosquitoes found her, coalescing by the hundreds into a hovering dark cloud that moved along with her, needling her neck, her ears, the soft flesh of her inner arms. She welcomed the physical pain, a balancing counterpart to the unbearable anguish within. When they crowded her face to the point where it was hard to see, feasting at the damp corners of her eyes and mouth, clustering at her nostrils, she wiped away their engorged bodies, leaving hands and face alike streaked with her own blood.

She watched her feet moving forward, seemingly of their own accord, her low-heeled white patent-leather pumps grimed with road dust, her hose laddered from her fall to the sidewalk. Her dress dampened under the arms. The cotton stuck to her back. She'd chosen pale green, an unforgiving color that would quickly darken with telltale circles of sweat. She didn't care. Let them see what grief – the grief they caused – does to a person.

She emerged from the woods, briefly blinded by the full sun. Ahead, off to the left, the twin rows of cedars curved away toward Quail House. She could admit to herself now, with a flash of bitter inner laughter, that yes, it had once been a thrill to walk up this grand approach, catch her breath as she rounded that last curve, designed for exactly that effect as the vista opened up to perfectly frame the grandeur of Quail House.

A charnel house, more like it, she thought now, rattling with the bones of dead dreams and a dead young man.

Fished from the river, the Chief had said. Shot dead. Had the bullet found him in the back? His heart? Or had it made a ruin of his beautiful face?

The dog, the same one they'd had when she'd worked there,

trotted around the corner of the house, hackles raised. She stopped, sniffed the air and bounded joyfully toward Grace. She'd liked the dog. No more.

'Git,' she said, and Kathleen Mavourneen stopped again, eyes puzzled, tail wagging uncertainly.

Grace brushed past her and walked right up to the front door, grabbed the brass pineapple knocker – how many times had she polished it? – and banged five times in quick succession.

'Open up! I know you're in there! Get on out here before I bust a window and let myself in!'

She stepped back. Listened hard. Thought she heard a voice.

She went at the door again, both fists now, words inarticulate, some strangled version of 'no-no-no-no-no' when the door swung open and she nearly fell in.

'Gracious.' Philippa Smythe stood in the foyer, the wide staircase that Grace had mopped so many times rising behind her into the gloomy interior. 'Such a racket. And' – her gaze raked Grace, taking in the tattered hose, the filthy shoes, the blood-streaked skin, hair standing out in wild hanks – 'you're in such a state. Why don't you come around the back door and we can discuss whatever has you so upset?' Her old commanding tone, but Grace heard the quiver in it, saw the fingers knotted together, the calves tensed and poised to flee.

'I ain't going around to no back door to talk about my dead brother.' For so long, she'd acted her most proper around the Smythes. No more.

Philippa's hand flew to her mouth. 'That nice young man who used to do our yard work? Oh, my dear, I'm so sorry. What happened?'

'Don't be slinging your bullshit all over me. Where is she?'

She made as though to push past Philippa, but suddenly the dog was between them, tail stiff and still, lips curled away from teeth.

'Where is who, my dear?'

She had to give it to Philippa. Backbone of steel, not like her cowardly daughter.

'That bitch you raised. Where she at?'

Philippa stiffened. 'Language.' At least she'd dropped that 'my dear' shit. 'If you mean my daughter, Penelope and Hiram are out of town at the moment.'

'Like hell they are.' But she couldn't help herself. Her glance flicked to the long, low shed where the family parked their cars and, indeed, the only ones there were Philippa's black Lincoln and the old Army Jeep the Chief used on hunting forays in the fields and marsh.

'Perhaps you'd like to come back another time.'

'Where the Chief?'

Even though she knew full well.

'He's . . . busy. At work.'

'Then I'll just wait until he comes back.'

Grace turned her back on Philippa, folded herself down on to the top step, and propped her elbows on her knees and her chin on her hands.

'You can't do that. It's private property.' Philippa finally sounded rattled. 'I'll call the police.'

'Go 'head and call the police.' Grace didn't turn around. 'But don't hold your breath. They're a little busy right now.'

The Chief didn't get home until the sun had set and fireflies spangled the air above the lawn. The mosquitoes' assault increased in ferocity after sunset, waning only when the temperature finally dropped a few degrees.

Grace's skin was a mass of bites gone lumpy where she'd scratched. She was hungry and thirsty and had left her perch only twice, to pee in the shrubbery, squatting over Philippa's herb garden, taking grim pleasure in the thought of Philippa plucking mint leaves to put in her tea the next day.

She was half asleep when the headlights brushed her face. She shielded her eyes and squinted into the glare. Chief Smythe pulled up directly in front of her and let the engine idle a few moments before he cut it, so she was good and blind when he stepped out of the car.

'Grace. My wife said you were here.'

She stood, trying to hide the wobble in her knees.

'What happened to my brother? Do my mama and daddy know?'

Her sight returned slowly, the Chief merely a tall shadow before her. 'We contacted the Baltimore police. They sent somebody over.'

Grace could see it, the white police officer standing tense and resentful at being assigned the unwelcome duty, the rote words, her parents' anguish intensified because the thing they'd most feared had come to pass.

Her throat felt as though someone had taken sandpaper to her vocal cords. Somehow, words emerged.

'What happened?'

'That's what we're working on, Grace. It looks as though he was shot and dumped – left – at the Beach. Under the circumstances, we don't have much to go on. No murder weapon, no witnesses.'

'Where was *she*?'

The Chief's voice took on an edge. 'I'm sure I don't know what you're talking about.'

'I'm sure you do.' No wobble in her knees now, nor her voice. 'I need to know who killed my brother.'

The Chief shook his head. 'It could be a long investigation. You go on home to your family. They'll need you.'

'I ain't going nowhere. Not till I find out what happened. Although . . .' She thought a minute. Made her voice as hard as his. 'You know I work for the *Afro* now.'

'The *Afro*?'

'The *Baltimore Afro-American*. It's a newspaper. They're down here covering this, just like the white papers. Looking for a story those papers won't have. Something nobody else has.'

Putting it out there, letting it hang in the air between them.

'I'm staying here,' she said before he could reply. 'Until I find out what happened to my brother, I'll be on this doorstep every damn day.'

The Chief shifted. 'Well, now. That would make things difficult for everyone.'

'Difficult? My brother lying somewhere shot dead and you talking difficult?'

'Quite right.'

She stiffened. What was he up to?

'So you're staying in Chateau,' he mused.

'Yes, I am.' She'd figure out the details later.

But he got to them now. 'How are you going to live? Where are you going to work?'

She had a little money saved. It wouldn't last long. He didn't need to know that.

He took a step toward her. 'I could help you with that.'

She started at his silky, confiding tone, on full alert now. She'd made a demand. He was making an offer. What could it possibly be? Whatever it was, she straightened, her rage distilling into something cold, purposeful.

She had power – not the sexual power that every woman possessed and, no matter her best intentions, sometimes found wielding it the easier path. This sort of power was different. Grace rolled it around like an unexpected delicacy, tasting it, savoring its bitter tang.

'What you got in mind?'

'You've announced your intention to stay in Chateau.'

Lord help her if he didn't sound just like his wife then, same prissy phrasing, using a whole mouthful of words when two – 'You're staying?' – would do.

Maybe he was going to try to talk her out of it.

'Yes, I'm staying.'

The Chief rubbed his long jaw. 'We haven't had good household help since you left.'

Grace's mouth dropped open. He couldn't possibly be saying what she thought he was.

The sinewy clout she'd felt just seconds earlier dissolved into a furious sort of despair. Sooner or later – and it was almost always sooner – white people got around to insulting you, even – and especially – when it was in the guise of offering help.

He hurried on before she could speak. 'Of course, things have changed.'

Damn straight they have. My brother's dead.

'Wages have gone up. The canning factory barely turns a profit. Look at me, with a town job.'

Grace gaped at him. What was he talking about? All the First Families in Chateau had town jobs, either on the town council or the police force or some make-work city job. It's how they made sure everything worked to their advantage. 'This whole town is nothing but one big plantation,' her mother had complained more than once. 'All they did was plant flowers on top of the manure pile. They breathe perfume and leave us the stink.'

'We'd offer you double what you made before.'

She blinked at him, desperately willing her voice to work.

'You . . . you want me to come work in this house. After you killed my brother.'

He relaxed so visibly it startled her.

'I didn't kill your brother, Grace.'

Oh, he had the upper hand again, and he knew it, that paternal, condescending tone.

But someone in this house knows. With the thought, an idea. She tasted it again, stronger now, astringent, bracing.

'I been . . .' She stopped and started again. 'I've been making Baltimore wages these past years. Good money. Saving for college.' He didn't need to know that at the rate she was saving she'd be in her thirties before she had enough money.

She looked him right in the eye and was gratified beyond all measure when his gaze slid away.

His lips tightened. 'Triple. Couple of years making that kind of money and you could pay tuition at Harvard. It's the least we can do for your family under these tragic circumstances.'

How stupid did he think she was? Harvard didn't accept women, and she'd never heard of a black man studying there. And his reference to a couple of years – he probably thought that by then all the fuss would've died down. They'd do their investigation, turn up nothing, and Bobby would still be dead.

Unless somebody else turned up something. Somebody watching them every day. Waiting for the inevitable slip.

'Triple, you say.'

She nodded, calculations ticking in her brain. Triple her old pay; a yearly amount more than anything she could ever hope to earn even with a college degree. She wondered if, with this offer, his entire salary as Chief would be going to her family. Then she reconsidered: People who lived in places like Quail House probably had all sorts of money stashed away. Must be nice.

He withdrew a money clip from his pocket and counted out four fifties. 'With a bonus.' He held out the bills.

Grace snatched them away.

'So we'll see you tomorrow.'

'You'll see me after the funeral.'

She stalked away.

Smoke from the burning buildings in town rose high, turning the sky the angry red of her own emotions.

With each step, the money rustled in the pocket of her shirtwaist, and a plan took shape.

THIRTY-SEVEN

A black sedan with the white tags of a government vehicle awaited Nora in the circular driveway of Quail House when she returned from her morning run.

She stopped a few feet away. Two people got out of the car, one a tall, slender woman in a white shirt so beautifully smooth Nora could only imagine that she existed within an air-conditioned cocoon, slipping so quickly from house to car, from car to office, and so on throughout her day that the relentless humidity had no time to seep into the cotton fibers and wilt them into wrinkles against which even generous applications of starch were no defense. She'd twisted skinny dreadlocks away from her face into a knot so tight it tugged at the skin around her eyes.

The white man with her was dressed identically in white shirt and dark pants. They could have been a pair of Mormon missionaries, although something about their bearing, a certain set to the jaw, an unbending rigidity, screamed cop.

Close.

'George Satterline.' He introduced himself first. Establishing dominance? Although, thought Nora, the woman with him didn't look as if she let anyone or anything dominate. 'This is Brenda Holiday. We're from the Attorney General's Office.'

She'd waited a whole day for a return call to her voicemail. It never came, and by day's end, she'd decided it was just as well. She'd brought trouble enough on herself. Maybe best to just leave. (And go where? Do what? Thoughts she resolutely pushed away for about the fiftieth time.)

'Do you have some kind of identification?' It just slipped out. Something about them, their officious air, their presumption that they could pull into the driveway in their ostentatiously clean government car and stand before her in their formal clothes as she shifted from one foot to another, sweaty and disheveled from her run.

'Of course.' The woman's voice was low, soothing. 'You're smart to ask. We were just sitting here a moment admiring your beautiful home.'

Trying to disarm her with reassurance and a compliment, Nora thought. Not to mention angling for an invitation inside. Which they weren't going to get.

Satterline and Holiday exchanged glances. They were about the same age; in their forties, Nora guessed. Old enough to have graduated from law school, worked their way through various prosecutors' offices in the smaller counties and up to the big time in a place like Baltimore or Montgomery County, before making the jump to state government.

Smart of the AG's office to send a black woman and a white man to look into something like this, she thought. The cops would talk to him, black people to her. Maybe.

'You told the Chateau police you saw it. Now tell us.'

'I didn't exactly see *it*.'

Nora fought an impulse to invite them in after all. She could make herself coffee, think straighter, give herself something to do with her hands, which kept creeping toward each other, as Satterline and Holiday stared in heavy-lidded expectation, waiting for her to elaborate. Nora knew this part. They'd stand silent until she offered up something.

'I drove past a car that had been pulled over. I didn't see much. It was almost dark.'

'What time was it?' Satterline. He had small eyes in a large blank face. Nora wondered if they taught them that utter lack of emotion in whatever academy they went to.

'A little before eight.' She remembered the dashboard clock glowing its green warning that it was far too late for coffee. 'I passed the coffee kiosk outside town at seven forty-seven. I looked at the time because I wanted coffee, but figured if I got some, I'd be awake all night. So it would have been maybe a mile after that.'

Dammit. It had worked, their silence, had set her to babbling like an idiot. On the other hand, her answer had been as innocuous as his question.

Holiday had her phone out, typing into it with great concentration. She stopped, nodded at whatever was on the screen and looked up.

'Sunset isn't until about eight fifteen. So it wouldn't have been dark then.'

'It *felt* dark.'

So much for the straight faces. Holiday arched a precisely plucked eyebrow. Satterline pursed his lips.

Nora fumbled for a recovery. 'I'd been driving for a long time, going on four days. I was really tired. Hence, wanting that coffee.'

'Do you typically suffer from impaired vision when you're tired? And drive anyway?' Holiday's expression was all professional concern.

'My vision wasn't impaired. It was late in the evening, starting to feel dark. You know how it does?'

No, their faces suggested. They did not. Nora was almost glad when Satterline blinked his little eyes and refocused on the matter at hand. 'Can you please describe exactly what you saw?'

Nora shrugged. 'I saw the lights first – a cop car. Then, when I drove by, a cop standing next to the car he'd pulled over.'

'What kind of car?'

'A green Kia.'

'You sure about that? Given your tired eyes?' Holiday this time.

Oh, give it a rest, Nora wanted to say, but limited her answer to, 'Yes, I'm sure.'

'The car that nearly forced you off the road.'

'That's a bit of an exaggeration. I swerved.'

'Do you always exaggerate?'

'No.' Nora folded her arms across her chest. She, too, could play the waiting game.

'But you told the Chateau police you feared for your life. Described it as road rage.'

'Their words, not mine.'

'And what would your words be' – a beat – 'now?'

'He passed me. Hit his horn and cut around me so close he almost clipped me. Startled me.'

'Startled is a long way from scared for your life.'

'Yes.'

'And yet you didn't contradict their account.'

'I am now.'

Satterline blinked again, slow, reptilian.

'And his attitude?'

She shrugged and smiled, imitating Robert Evans's own gesture. 'Like that.'

'I can see why you'd be scared for your life.' Holiday didn't bother to hide the sarcasm.

'I just said those were their words.'

'And the ID in the photo lineup? Was that theirs, too?'

In a way it was. The way they'd directed her to Number Four. Another way she'd let herself be played.

'I told them I wasn't sure. I made that clear.'

'And yet you initialed it.'

'I said it could have been him.'

'And then you signed off on it.'

I just wanted to get out of that room. A realization nudged her: *Running away again. How's that working out for you, Nora?*

She rubbed at her forehead, wiping away sweat and introspection.

'Yes.'

Their eyes flicked toward each other.

'When you saw the car again, what was happening?'

'Nothing. The car was stopped, the cop standing by it. I passed by it in the blink of an eye.' She braced herself for another comment from Holiday about her tired and presumably unreliable eyes. But Holiday merely shut the leather folder that enclosed her phone.

'And your relationship with Alden Tydings?'

'You've read the papers. We dated in high school.'

'And now?'

'Nothing.' Which, as of a few hours earlier, was true.

She and Satterline held out business cards. 'If you think of anything else, anything helpful.'

She wasn't imagining the emphasis Holiday put on *helpful*.

She climbed the stoop as they drove away. The front door was cracked open a few inches. She must not have pulled it closed when she'd left on her run. She pushed through it and leapt backward in surprise, nearly tumbling from the stoop.

'Mother!'

Penelope stood just inside, nearly invisible in the shadows.

'What are you doing here?'

'Nora, who were those people?' Penelope's voice quavered.

'They were from the Attorney General's Office. They're investigating the shooting.'

'But you already talked to the police. Why did they come here?'

Because I no longer trust the police. But that would trigger a raft of questions that would make Satterline and Holiday look like amateurs.

'Because I called them.'

Penelope's hands left the walker and flew to her face. Nora put out a hand to steady her. Penelope trembled beneath her touch.

'Oh, Nora,' she managed. 'What have you done?'

THIRTY-EIGHT

1967

Grace walked past tanks – tanks! – on her way to work every morning.

At that hour they sat silent, but by the time she trudged home in the evening, they'd be clanking into action, their turrets swerving toward the crowds of young people that seemed to grow larger every night, black people streaming in from cities up and down the East Coast – Philadelphia, Wilmington, Baltimore, Washington – and even some of the smaller towns – Dover, Salisbury, Chestertown – places like Chateau, where hope had been crushed so many decades ago that an opportunity to grasp at it was not to be missed.

To Grace, hope tasted like the ashes stirred up by the determined efforts of white business owners to rebuild the business district under the protective eye of the National Guard. But every afternoon the young people marched, timing their actions – under the direction of the seasoned organizers who hurried in from those larger cities after Bobby's death and Simmons's beating – to ensure footage on the evening news. They held news conferences for the gaggle of reporters, wrote op-eds for newspapers both black and white, and harangued the U.S. Justice Department to open a federal investigation. Above all, they demanded an arrest in Bobby's killing.

'Wasting your time,' Grace muttered as she stalked past.

Her first day back at work, she surveyed Quail House with a

sinking feeling. So many rooms. So many things with drawers – dressers and secretaries and highboys and the hulking rolltop desk in the room the Chief used as an office – to search. So many blanket chests, closets, storerooms. The pantry and every container in it. The kitchen alone – all those canisters and little-used pots. The root cellar, with its damp dirt floor that turned to mud when water bubbled up from below during heavy rainstorms. The outbuildings. And who knew what lay beneath the birdbaths and benches in the gardens?

It didn't matter, she told herself. *I've got months. Years, if need be.* To hell with her job at the *Afro*. To hell with college. She'd find out what happened to Bobby if it took the rest of her life.

THIRTY-NINE

What had she done?

Nothing, apparently. Nora waited for a follow-up call from investigators in the Attorney General's Office. An email, or even a letter, something with the state's seal stamped atop the paper, informing her that . . . what?

That she'd helped prove Alden guilty? Or, even not guilty, which, while it wouldn't satisfy the small, mean desire to see him punished for his perfidy, at least would let her put the whole mess behind her.

Robert Evans's parents continued to push for answers, giving interviews to every reporter who would talk to them, although the number dwindled as the days passed, the stories moving from the front page of the newspapers to deep within, or down toward the bottom of webpages.

'Find the phone,' Kwame told the *Sun*. 'He was like every other young person alive, face in his phone every waking minute. Where is it?'

Brittingham had a ready answer when the reporter called him for a response.

'It's common practice for drug dealers to either use burner phones or switch out their regular phones. For all we know, that phone is sitting at the bottom of the Inner Harbor in Baltimore. If he was smart, he ditched it before he headed down here.'

The reporter hadn't gone back to Kwame for a response to Brittingham's explanation, but Kwame had seen it and exploded in anger in an exclusive interview with the *Afro*. He was not, he proclaimed, talking to the big dailies anymore, 'not after that trash they printed.'

'My son was not a drug dealer. They never found drugs in his car, or in his dorm room or even here in our home. Lucky our lawyer just happened to be here when they showed up with a search warrant; otherwise, I wouldn't have put it past them to plant something. Robert did not have a mess of burner phones. His one phone, his only phone, was a graduation present from us, one of those iPhones he'd been begging us for. If it's at the bottom of the Inner Harbor, it's because some damn crooked cop dropped it there.'

Words not inclined to endear him to the police but maybe it didn't matter, Nora thought. After her own encounter with them, and given what she'd seen at the Beach, she was inclined to sympathize with Kwame.

She'd awoken early each morning since, watching from her bedroom window as the dark form of Alden's boat coasted toward her dock, bobbed beside it for long minutes, then continued on its lonely journey toward the bay, a scenario repeated a half-hour later as he rowed back to his home.

Her days stretched long and silent. Penelope had refused to explain her outburst after Satterline and Holiday's departure, and generally kept to her bedroom during the day, pleading headaches from the heat, emerging to pick at her dinner and talk of inconsequential things and return immediately afterward to her room. Nora's phone lay lonely on her bedside table. She'd let the battery run down after her interview with Satterline and Holiday so as to avoid an inbox filled with texts and voicemails from Alden and the occasional reporter. There was no need to use her laptop, now that her book deal was dead.

Mornings, she ran, keeping to the back roads; evenings, before it got too dark, she worked at removing the graffiti from Electra, pouring rubbing alcohol on to a sponge and dabbing at the paint, removing a few inches each day. At this rate, she thought, it would only take her about six months to return Electra to her former glory.

Headlights swept Electra's surface one evening as she was putting away her sponge and rags. She spun around to see Emerson Crothers pulling up in a Porsche Boxster. He cut the engine, unfolded himself from a front seat just inches above the ground and ambled over.

She greeted him without preamble. 'Em, I have to ask . . .'

He stopped a few feet away and hooked his fingers in his belt loops. 'Shoot.'

'Why'd a big guy like you get himself such a tiny little car?'

He turned and studied the car as though he hadn't seen it before.

'When you put it that way, I suppose it wasn't the best idea. You really want to know?'

Not really. 'Sure.' It was the polite thing.

He went back to the car and held open the passenger door. 'Come on. I'll show you.'

She hung back. Alden had urged her into his truck and look how that had turned out. On the other hand, her only substantive conversations recently had been with Satterline, Holiday and reporters, and the latter hadn't been conversations at all, unless you counted as meaningful discussion her clicking off the phone the minute someone announced an affiliation with a news organization. She'd started talking to the dog and the cat. Murph fawned delightedly at the attention but the cat puffed out its fur and hissed at her, apparently annoyed at any interruption to a mission that resulted in a small gray carcass just outside her bedroom door nearly every morning.

She got in the car.

A half-hour later, it was fully dark and they were deep in the county on a back road without so much as the light from a single farmhouse visible.

'Where are we?'

'The old nine-foot road. Don't you remember?'

Heaven help her, she did. The long, straight stretch drew so little traffic that the county had paved only one side of it, leaving the other dirt or, depending on the season, mud. Motorists drove on the paved section, and when approaching one another counted on the town-bound driver to pull off on to the dirt. The set-up invited games of chicken that inevitably resulted in sideswipes and full-on crashes, one of which killed a young mother and her baby, prompting the county to finally – reluctantly – cough up the money to pave the other half. People still called it the nine-foot road, though, and it remained a favored drag-racing spot for high schoolers fueled by hard liquor and testosterone.

The blue glow from the dashboard lit Em's grin. 'Ready?'

'For what?'

'Hang on!'

And before she could ask what he meant, he jammed the accelerator to the floor. The car leapt forward, her back slamming into the seat as the sedately purring engine came to life with a joyous roar.

The odometer quivered past 160 kilometers per hour, Nora screaming with the exhilaration of speed, of being with someone who asked nothing of her, heading nowhere that mattered.

The wind whipped the sound away and tugged tears from her eyes. Her hair lashed her face, everything but Em beside her and the road ahead a blur.

It was over too soon, her hair settling slowly back around her shoulders as Em eased up on the accelerator and the car coasted toward a normal speed, then nearly to a stop as he swung the wheel in a U-turn and headed back toward Chateau.

He glanced toward her. 'Fun?'

'So much fun!'

'I read the papers, you know. Figured you could use some fun. Ever gone that fast before?'

She nodded, enjoying his startled look. 'Once. In Wyoming. A road as empty as this one. In the daytime, though. And in my truck. It took a little longer – a lot longer – to get up to speed.'

She waited for him to ask her about Wyoming, but he didn't; at least, not in the way she expected.

'You sorry about your husband?'

She combed the tangles from her hair with her fingers.

'Yes and no. I'll never again say I wish somebody dead. It's such a lighthearted saying, until it happens. But do I miss him?'

Something about the darkness, the deserted road, led her to say the impermissible aloud.

'No, not really. I found out our marriage had been over for a lot longer than I'd realized. Pretty embarrassing. Pretty infuriating. It sure shortens the grieving process, though.' She waited for more questions. None came. Em hummed a little, tuneless but relaxed.

'What about you? Ever marry?' He didn't wear a ring.

'Came close a couple of times. Played the field for a long while first. You'd be surprised how many women want to sleep with someone they think will sell their house without taking a commission. At night I'd hear how great I was, and the minute I opened my eyes in the morning they'd be telling me how great their house was. I learned to mention, when things looked as though they were about to take a certain turn, that it's unethical to sleep with a client.' He laughed. 'For a nerd like me, it was fun for a while, though.'

Nora offered the obligatory demurral. 'You were never a nerd.'

'I was totally a nerd. Took me a while to realize there was more to life than basketball. By the time I was done fooling around and ready to settle down, I'd missed all my good chances. Serves me right, I guess.'

'And you stayed here. Ever tempted to leave?'

The lights of Chateau glimmered in the distance. The ribbon of river unspooled beside the road. Lightning bugs winked in the fields, a mirror image of the stars.

'I love it here,' he said simply and unembarrassed. 'I guess I don't have your adventurous spirit.'

Nora didn't tell him she'd had enough adventure to last a lifetime; that boredom dangled before her, maddeningly just out of reach, as the most desirable of states.

They rode in silence until he pulled up at Quail House. His headlights shone on the graffiti defiling Electra, most of it still there, despite her efforts.

'Burris's body shop could take care of that.'

'I know. But the thought of towing it through town the way it is now – everybody seeing it – I just can't bring myself to do it.'

They sat and contemplated the trailer.

'I've got an idea,' Em said. 'You around tomorrow morning?'

'Tomorrow and every morning.' Which sounded like an invitation. Too late, though.

He went through the maneuvers required to extricate himself from the car and came around to her door. Nora wondered if he'd try to kiss her, or ask himself in. Their encounter hadn't had that vibe, but with men, you never knew. But he merely held open her door with a bit of a flourish.

'I'll be by around nine. See you then.'

He showed up the next morning with a tarp rolled up and belted like a companion into the passenger seat, and a small ladder sticking out of the narrow space behind the two seats.

'I looked up the measurements for your trailer last night. This should do the trick. It'll cover the graffiti so no one will see it when you tow it in.'

She hurried to help him unroll it. 'This looks brand-new. You have to let me pay you for it.'

'Not a chance. I'm forever working on my house. Just bring it by when you're done with it. I can always use another tarp. I'm going to climb up on the ladder and pull it over the top. Would you please hang on to your end so it doesn't slide all the way over?'

She liked the way he asked, even though her task was obvious, not barking orders the way Joe would have. Together they tugged at the tarp until it covered the damning letters.

'Now for the fun part.' He climbed down the ladder and retrieved a bundle of bungee cords from the car. Once again, she held one end as he slithered beneath the trailer and fastened the other, and then repeated the exercise until a veritable spiderweb of elastic cords wrapped Electra's underside.

Em emerged and stood, dusting his pants. 'You could drive that thing through a hurricane and that tarp wouldn't come off. Need any help hitching it up?'

She did but hadn't wanted to ask. 'If you could just direct me while I back it up . . .'

She'd become adept at hitching and unhitching, but without a second person to guide her as she edged truck toward trailer, she was apt to waste time with near misses. With Em's help, she maneuvered the truck into place on the first try.

'Anything else?' He reached for the safety chains. She waved him away.

'Thanks, but I've got my own system. I'm not comfortable unless I've gone through everything on my checklist and then gone over it again.'

'Like a pilot. Speaking of which, what's with the airplane decal?'

'It's a Lockheed Electra. Amelia Earhart's airplane. The whole idea was that we – Joe and I – would have great adventures in this thing. I know, I know.' She held up a hand to forestall the obvious. 'Things didn't end well for her and they sure didn't for me, either. But at least I've still got Electra. That's what I call her.' She patted the trailer's tarp-wrapped side and sought a way to change the subject.

'Hey, Em.'

'What?'

'All those things that happened back in the day. Bobby Evans getting shot. The riot. Did you know anything about it?'

He shook his head. 'Nothing. Or almost nothing. Maybe bits and pieces, but never enough to really catch my attention. When I look back on growing up here, it seems idyllic. But I guess for a lot of people, it wasn't.'

She thought of her conversation with Kwame, his memories of summers in Chateau, fishing and shooting varmints. That part, at least, had been idyllic for him, too. Things didn't turn sour until black people and white came into one another's orbits, apparently.

Nora remembered her manners. 'You want coffee? Or tea? Mother always has a pot on, but I can make coffee.'

'Thanks, but I've got a full day.'

He turned and surveyed Quail House, the gardens and outbuildings, the sweep of lawn to the river, and she could almost see the dollar signs blinking in his brain. She'd seen men look at women with less obvious lust. 'You sure you and your mother don't want to sell? I know she drew up that trust for you, but we could always change it. Place needs work, but it's still mostly cosmetic. That's not always the case in these old houses. The upkeep is so expensive and people let it go until things are past the point of no return.'

Nora thought Penelope would rather lose a limb than see Quail House pass out of the family and said as much.

Disappointment leaked from his words. 'And you're happy to take it over?'

'That was the plan. Until all of this happened. Now, I don't know what I'm going to do.' She hoped he hadn't heard the wobble in her voice.

'Give it a while,' he said. 'You know this place. Everything gets swept under the rug eventually. Look how neither of us ever heard about what had happened before. Six months from now, it'll be like none of this ever happened. And you'll still be here and so will I.'

Nora shook her head as he drove away. If that had been Em's idea of a come-on, no wonder he'd done so poorly with women for so long.

She surveyed the checklist she'd printed up back when she and Joe had first bought the trailer, when their plan had been to travel around the country with the goal of a book about midlife marital bliss. At least the trailer had survived the wreckage of that particular dream. She was no longer so sure about herself.

She laid the list on the ground beside her as she lowered the trailer hitch on to the truck's ball, attached the safety chains and the breakaway cord, raised the stabilizers and kicked the chocks from beneath the wheels. She tucked the steps under the trailer bed, then she made a slow circuit of Electra, double-checking everything she'd already done, tugging at the safety chains and breakaway cord, peering beneath it to make sure she hadn't left anything there, or that nothing had rolled under it. The grass was bare, except for a snoozing ball of orange fur.

'Mooch!' She clapped her hands. 'Get out from there, unless you want to be turned into a flat cat instead of a fat cat.'

The cat opened one disdainful eye, then rose to his feet in slow motion with an extravagant yawn and stretch, ambling away toward the house, where he no doubt hoped to con Penelope into giving him scraps from her breakfast.

Nora followed him with a warning. 'Don't even think about it. I've got my eye on you.'

Her mother was at the table, a cup of tea steaming beside her. If she'd eaten breakfast at all, she'd long since washed the dishes and put them away. The cat assessed the situation and turned away with a last, baleful look in Nora's direction.

'Why don't you drink iced tea in this weather? I can pick some mint and have it ready in just a few minutes,' Nora offered. 'All I did was hitch up the trailer and I'm already sweating. I feel the same way about iced coffee that you do about iced tea, but that's what I'm having this morning.'

She filled a mug with ice and set it on the counter, next to the trailer-hitching checklist.

'Iced tea is an abomination,' Penelope said, as Nora had known she would. 'But you could do me a favor.'

Nora scooped more ice from the freezer into a glass, filled it with tap water and drank deep while she waited for her coffee to brew. She held up the glass to her mother in a sort of toast. 'Plain ice water. Not an abomination. What can I do for you?'

'Could you please run into town and pick up my prescription? The pharmacy just called and said it was finally ready. Just in time. I took my last pill yesterday. I'm sorry to be such a bother.'

'No bother at all. I'm heading into town anyway to drop the trailer off. I'll have to spend some time at Burris's, but I can get it afterward. I should be home in an hour or two.'

'That long?' Penelope lifted her cup and directed a dainty breath across the surface of the tea. 'Oh, dear. I'm afraid that won't do. You see, I have to take these pills at exactly the same time every day. The doctor was very specific.'

She picked her napkin up and dabbed delicately at the sweat glistening at her hairline, her throat. 'I know! Why don't you take my car? It's air-conditioned.' Spoken as one who'd never ceased to marvel at the comfort of an air-cooled vehicle.

'Sure. I can bring the trailer in later.' The thing she'd been trying to avoid, but the concession seemed the least she could do for her mother.

'I'm so sorry to make you take two trips.'

'Stop apologizing and give me your keys.' Nora kissed her mother's cheek. 'It's not as though I've got anything else to do, anyway.'

Nora made it in and out of Chateau without seeing anyone she knew. She wondered if her luck would hold on her second trip, to Burris's.

As she drove up the lane toward the house, she saw her mother moving slowly through the pools of shade beneath the cedars, planting her walker firmly with each step. Nora pulled up beside her and rolled down the window.

'Ahhh.' Penelope closed her eyes in pleasure and leaned into the stream of cool air rushing from the car. 'That's delicious.'

'What are you doing out here?'

'Finally following up on my doctor's orders to walk every day. I've been waiting for this heat to break, but it appears I'll be old as Methuselah before that happens. If I do well enough, on my next visit I'll graduate to a cane. Whoever thought I'd look forward to being an old lady with a cane?'

Nora held up the white bag from the pharmacy. 'Do you want to take this now? I've got a water bottle with me.'

Penelope brandished her walker with grim determination. 'No, thank you. I'll take them when I get home. It'll be a good incentive for me to hurry. "Hurry," of course, being a relative term.'

'Do you want me to walk with you? I can come back and get the car later.'

Penelope's chuckle was breathless, forced, her making-the-best-of-it-aren't-I-brave laugh.

'Heavens, no. You run along. I'm almost there. We can sit down and have tea when I get back.'

Nora pulled the Lincoln into the shed, setting the parking brake as her mother always directed, even though the ground was perfectly level, and left the bag with the prescription on the kitchen counter along with a note for her mother. 'Rain check on the tea?'

She wanted to get the trailer to Burris's before any more time elapsed, and the likelihood of seeing someone she knew increased exponentially.

Penelope was just emerging from the cedars as Nora's truck approached, trailer in tow. She stopped and turned as though to retrace her steps, then edged to the side of the lane where it broadened as it made its final turn.

Nora steered truck and trailer as far as she dared to the other side of the lane to give her mother plenty of room.

The trailer lurched behind her. She must have hit a pothole. She gave the truck a little gas to get past it, speeding up with an apologetic wave, glancing in the side mirror to make sure her mother had seen, and watching instead as the trailer separated from the hitch and careened backward toward Penelope who was frozen in shock at the sight of a mountain of metal tilting her way in slow motion.

Electra teetered on two wheels and crashed on to her side.

Nora's scream caught in her throat.

'Oh, no, no,' she whimpered as she half fell from the truck in her haste. She ran on legs gone leaden, wanting to get to her mother as fast as possible, terrified of what she'd find, her mind doing split-second calculations of the effect of more than three and a half tons of grinding metal on one hundred and ten pounds of brittle-boned septuagenarian.

She wrenched her gaze from the trailer lying on its side, still rocking as its weight settled into place, to a few feet away, where her mother struggled to sit up.

'Mother!'

If Nora had taken yet another precious second to think back over the fifty years of her life, she would not have been able to remember a single time Penelope lost her composure. Now she stretched trembling hands toward her daughter, face gone pale as putty, green eyes black with terror. Her mouth opened and closed soundlessly

Nora stooped beside her. 'It's all right, Mother. I'm here. Are you hurt?'

She took it as a good sign that Penelope had been able to sit up. No spinal injuries, then. 'Can you stand?' She looked around. 'Where's your walker?'

Penelope raised an arm again. Pointed. Managed a single word. 'Under.'

The trailer emitted a final metallic groan. Its rocking stilled.

'I jumped.' A whisper, barely audible.

'My God.' On a broken ankle, barely able to walk, let alone leap. 'On second thought, don't move. I'm going to call an ambulance.'

She hated to leave her mother, even for the few moments it took to rush back to the truck to retrieve her phone. She dialed 911 as she jogged back to Penelope, and somehow managed to give the dispatcher the necessary details before starting to cry.

The EMT explained a final time to Nora that she couldn't ride in the ambulance with her mother. He signaled to the driver and closed the doors.

Nora watched it vanish beneath the cedars.

She turned to the cop. Brittingham knelt behind her truck, examining the trailer hitch.

'Do we have to do this now? I need to be with my mother.'

'You have time.' He spoke without turning around. 'They'll need to get her checked in, take her vitals, probably X-ray that leg again. My guess is, beyond being a little banged up, she's fine. She's lucky. And so are you.'

'Excuse me?' Nora jogged in place, impatient to be off. 'What do you need to know? Can we do this at the hospital?'

Brittingham put a hand to the ground and pushed himself up. The concerned, paternal manner of his previous visit had fled. Anger flamed in his eyes.

'I wish you'd had enough concern for your mother to properly hitch this trailer. If she hadn't jumped in time, you could have found yourself facing a negligent manslaughter charge.'

Nora gaped. 'What are you talking about?'

'Look at this.'

She took a few reluctant steps toward him.

He nudged the ground with the toe of his mirror-polished shoe, now filmed with dust, drawing her attention to the trailer's safety chains lying in the dust, along with the emergency brake cable.

'You said you drove across the country with this thing. Given your carelessness, it's a wonder you made it alive – or didn't kill someone else on the way. You damn near killed your mother today.'

Nora stared at the chains. 'I don't understand.'

'Not much to understand. If you'd hooked it up properly, it'd already be sitting in Burris's body shop. What would it have taken you, an extra five minutes' worth of effort? But you couldn't be bothered.'

'No! I hitched it just this morning. I crossed the chains and fastened them, and the breakaway cable. I have a checklist that I follow. It's in the house. I can show you.'

Brittingham's face was brutal in its skepticism.

Nora stammered on. 'I drew it up just so I'd never forget anything, no matter how tired I am when I hitch and unhitch it. And when I'm done, I go back and check everything twice. Officer Brittingham, I hooked those chains myself, screwed the fastener on breakaway cable tight. Plugged in the brake lights, pushed the latch down on the ball and fastened it. The only way this came undone is if someone undid it.'

His lips twisted as though in an effort to hold back words. A single one escaped.

'Who?'

'I have no idea. There's no one here but me and my mother. Well, Em Crothers came by this morning with the tarp for the trailer, but he left before I did. I hitched the trailer up, but then Mother needed her medicine right away, so I took her car into town and came back for the trailer. I was taking it into Burris's to finally get the paint removed. Somebody must have unfastened the chains while I was gone.'

'Who?' The man was relentless.

'I have no idea. We could ask Mother. Maybe she heard something.'

'I will.' He looked at Michael Murphy, standing at quivering attention in the middle of the lane, gazing after his departed mistress.

'What about you, boy? Did you hear anything?' Murph glanced at him and looked away without so much as a single wag of his tail. 'When your mother's able to talk, I'll ask if he barked at anyone. He's a pretty decent watchdog. Gave me the impression he wanted to take my head off when I was here before.'

'About that. Somebody already took the trouble to vandalize my trailer. Is it so farfetched to think the same person might have done this, too?'

'But why?'

Isn't that what you're supposed to find out? Nora had regained enough composure not to respond aloud. She crossed her arms and waited.

'Go see your mother. Tell her I'll be around to speak with her.' He started for his car and stopped. 'You going to be here all by yourself?'

'Yes. Well, me and Murph.' The dog chanced another quick backward glance at the sound of his name. 'And there's a cat around here somewhere.'

'If' – Brittingham stressed the word in a way that let her know he thought it was a pretty big *if* – 'someone did sabotage your trailer, you want to be careful. You've obviously pissed off the black crowd.'

Crowd. As though they were nameless and faceless.

'And talking with the Attorney General's Office hasn't won you any friends in the police department.'

'How did you . . .'

Of course he knew. If Satterline and Holiday were worth their salt, they'd have run her version of the police interview past the cops in Chateau. Which meant that Alden knew she'd gone to the Attorney General's Office. And even though nothing she'd told them implicated him in any way, it didn't help him, either.

'You're not afraid, staying all the way out here in this big house alone? Under the circumstances.'

His tone suggested she should be very much afraid.

'Of course not,' she snapped. 'You know what scares me?'

'I'd love to hear it.'

'Mother's condition. I really need to go see her. Now.'

Thing is, she thought as he finally drove away, it wasn't just bravado.

She knew that he was right; that given a second attack on her trailer, one that had very nearly killed her mother, or could have killed someone, she should be panicked.

But all she could see was her mother's chalky face, eyes wide with terror.

She could worry about her own safety later. First, she had to reassure herself of her mother's.

FORTY

1967

After her first week back at work at Quail House, Grace was too tired to take the long way home, going blocks out of her way around the tanks and National Guard troops on Commerce Street.

She trudged past them, stopping when she glimpsed the light glimmering between the cracks in the plywood over the pharmacy's broken-out windows. She looked one of the soldiers in the eye, an impermissible bit of defiance unthinkable just weeks earlier. But that was before Bobby. Nothing scared her now.

She jutted her chin toward the pharmacy. 'They open?'

'What's it to you?'

'I want to buy something in there.'

He was shorter by half a head, the kind of stocky that would turn fat in just a few more years, his pale skin blotchy with freckles, sweat sliding down his cheeks from beneath his helmet. His jaw muscles popped as they worked a wad of gum.

'Ain't much left in there after what you all done. Go on now.'

You all.

Grace stretched herself to her full height, looking down on him. 'I want to go in there.'

He snapped the gum. 'Then you got to have an escort.' He raised his gun and stood aside to let her pass, then followed so close behind the barrel of the gun nudged her back. She stiffened. Had the person who shot Bobby put the gun to his body? Looked him in the eye and pulled the trigger? Or – as would happen to her if her escort as much as stumbled – shot him in the back? Or had the bullet that robbed her of her brother come from a great distance, someone lying in wait?

She tapped at the boarded-up door. Heard footsteps, then a feminine gasp. 'Oh, Myron. They're back. I thought the Guard was supposed to be protecting us.'

Grace rapped harder. 'Miss Slocum? It's me, Grace Evans. I need to buy something.' She waited. The street was utterly silent except for a crow soaring overhead, diving low for a look, cawing as it swooped away.

'One of those soldiers is here with me.'

The door cracked an inch. Verna Slocum peered out, saw the Guardsman and opened the door a bit wider. Her husband stood behind her in his white pharmacist's coat, a baseball bat in his hand.

'I just want to buy a notebook. Anything left in stationery?'

'That's about all they left.' Grace knew she was included in that damning *they*. 'And now here you come, wanting to buy something instead of just taking it. If that isn't just rich. Hold on.'

Her husband's knuckles whitened around the bat. Grace had known him since she was a little girl, and she'd stopped in regularly when she'd worked at Quail House before to pick up the Smythes' prescriptions. Now he refused to look at her, not deigning to offer so much as a 'Sorry about your brother' or even a simple 'hello.'

His wife returned and flung something through the door. A notebook, its black-and-white marbled cardboard cover smeared with greasy soot, landed at Grace's feet.

'There. You happy?' She slammed the door.

The Guardsman smirked at her. 'You got what you came for. And for free, too. That lady's a lot nicer than I would've been.'

'Go fuck yourself,' Grace said, counting on the shock and embarrassment of hearing such language from a woman's mouth to stop him from coming after her – or, worse yet, siccing his fellow Guardsmen on her.

She strode away quickly, tensed for the sound of booted feet, shouts, magazines clicking into place, but heard nothing except her own footsteps as she walked through the wreckage of Chateau.

FORTY-ONE

Penelope was barely a bump beneath the white blanket stretched across the high, narrow bed in Chateau Community Medical Center.

Nora pulled up a chair beside the bed and watched her mother breathe. After what she had feared as Electra tilted toward Penelope, it was enough.

A young black woman clopped quietly into the room on those white rubber-soled clogs all the staff seemed to wear. 'I'm Dr Abell. They told me family was here.'

'I'm her daughter. Is she all right?'

Tape fastened an IV needle to the back of Penelope's hand, her papery skin bruised blue and angry around it. Lines ran from beneath the blanket to beeping machines.

'We gave her something to help her sleep. She's got some pretty large contusions up and down her left side. Don't be startled when you see them. They'll be sore for a long time, but they're not serious. Remarkably, she didn't reinjure her leg. In fact, it's practically healed. She's a long way past needing the walker, although she may want to use it again, given how banged up she is.'

Nora recalled the pretzeled bit of metal peeping from beneath Electra and made a mental note to ask Slocum's Pharmacy to order a new one.

'Our more serious concern is that she's got a couple of broken ribs. She needs rest to heal but if she lies still too long, fluid could collect in her lungs and lead to pneumonia. But if she moves around too much, a rib could pierce her lungs. We've taped her chest, but that's all we can do.'

Pneumonia. A pierced lung. The doctor was still talking but Nora heard nothing past those words. 'Excuse me?'

'I said we're going to keep her for a couple of days for observation. Don't worry. We'll take good care of her. You're family, so you can visit at any time. I'd discourage other visitors, though.'

The doctor's words were perfunctory, clipped. Nora had seen the way the doctor's gaze swept her up and down, the start of recognition as she came into the room. Judgment hung heavy in the air. Nora wanted to apologize but didn't know what for. Wanted to say, 'You've got it all wrong,' the protest of any accused person, no matter how accurate the charge.

She settled for 'I appreciate everything you're doing for her,' and endured an incredulous snort as the doctor left the room.

Penelope's eyes moved beneath her closed lids.

'Mother? Are you awake?' She bent close to hear words barely more than a breath.

'Of course I am.'

'Did you hear what she said? You have two broken ribs. You'll be here for a couple of days. They're being very careful. Mother, I'm so sorry.'

Penelope's eyes flew open, her stare surprisingly bright. 'What happened?'

'Somebody unhitched my trailer – not quite all the way, just enough so that it would come loose while I was driving it. It's a miracle you weren't killed. I'm so sorry.'

Penelope's eyes slid shut. A long moan escaped.

'Mother!' Nora was on her feet. 'Are you in pain? Do you want me to call a nurse?'

Penelope started to lift the hand with the IV, grimaced and waved her other one. 'No. I'm fine. Your trailer . . .'

'I called a tow truck. It's at Burris's. And the police are looking into it.'

Penelope's head moved on the flat pillow. 'They're after me.'

'What? Who?' Nora bent over the bed. 'Mother, who's after you?'

Penelope started to raise her hand in a trembling version of her old imperious wave, wincing at the tug of the IV. 'You. I meant you. I told you before, and I really mean it. You need to go. I can't bear the thought of someone trying to hurt you.'

She closed her eyes against Nora's protestations and, when Nora persisted, pressed the call button for a nurse. 'I'm in so much pain. Can't you give me something for it?'

The nurse procured two fat pills and a tiny paper cup of water. 'You'll be asleep in no time. You'll be out for a couple of hours. No reason for anyone to stay.'

Nora, knowing herself defeated, left without saying goodbye.

She wanted to go home but feared police would still be on the scene, doing whatever it was they did after such an occurrence. Brittingham had been busy putting small orange plastic markers at various places on the lane as she'd left.

Instead, she sought reliable refuge at the library, with its carrels tucked in out-of-the-way places where she was unlikely to encounter anyone but the most determined browser or student with a particularly challenging assignment.

But when she sat down at the computer, she didn't even know what to search. 'They're after me,' her mother had said, only to follow it with a demurral that, to Nora's ears, rang false.

But why would anyone be after her mother? As far as she knew, her mother's life after her father's death had continued much the same: endless rounds of luncheons and genteel good works and community involvement – the gardening club, the historical society – the sort of small, neat existence that Nora had once envisioned for herself. Thanks to Alden's early betrayal, she had instead catapulted herself into a world of academic and career achievements. It occurred to her – why only now, after all these years? – that maybe Alden had done her a favor.

The blank search field mocked her. She typed in her mother's maiden name and the town, Chateau, and saw evidence of exactly the kind of life she'd remembered, short one- or two-paragraph notices of this function or that. A photo of Penelope at the Founders' Ball, resplendent in hoopskirt and tight bodice that showed what was, to a daughter's eye, a daring amount of décolletage. Nora's father's obituary: Hiram Best, born in North Troy, Vermont. Met his bride at a dance held by their respective boarding schools in Massachusetts. Served as a manager at Smythe's Backfin Crabs until his untimely demise. Survived by his loving wife, Penelope, and daughter, Nora.

And, scrolling back farther still, the briefest notices of Nora's birth and her parents' wedding. *Hiram Best and Penelope Smythe* . . .

Nora sat up straight. Weddings in Chateau, especially when involving a First Family, were lavish affairs, with receptions featuring long linen-draped tables sagging beneath the weight of glistening pink hams, pyramids of beaten biscuits, and pats of butter with leafy designs pressed into them.

The description of the gown alone could run on for paragraphs, detailing type of lace, bodice, sleeve and train, the hundreds of beads, the satin-covered buttons – all that before the writer turned attention to the veil and bouquet. Yet for Hiram and Penelope, just a few short paragraphs:

> Penelope Emmaline Smythe, daughter of Philippa and Geoffrey Smythe of Chateau, was joined in holy matrimony to Hiram Charles Best, son of Nathaniel and Louisa Best, in Newport, Vermont, on June 12, 1966. The groom will work as a manager at Smythe's Backfin Crab. The bride recently graduated from Miss Phipps's Academy and will be a homemaker . . .

No mention of a church, which meant they'd been married in a courthouse. That, and the lack of even a photo, led Nora Best at the age of fifty to the first-time realization that her parents had eloped.

She closed her eyes and thought hard. She must have asked her mother about her wedding. Hadn't she, in the throes of first love with Alden, imagined herself in a dress of Alençon lace sweeping down the aisle as the music swelled? And, wrapping herself in shimmering fantasies, asked her mother about her own wedding? A memory, wispy as the fingertip veil she'd eventually worn when she and Joe married in a ceremony as briskly managed as the faculty meetings over which Nora by then presided, teased at her.

'Mother, what if I wear your gown? You'd like that, wouldn't you?' A teenager's clumsy attempt to finally view the dress she'd never seen.

Penelope's laugh chimed. 'Oh, I gave that away years ago, once I realized it would be too short for you.' Nora had inherited her father's height, towering nearly eight inches above her tiny mother.

At the time, it had seemed a reasonable explanation. Now she wondered. Women in Chateau preserved their wedding gowns like precious heirlooms, sending them to dry cleaners who handled the fragile lace with white cotton gloves before sealing them in airtight containers, which then were stored in cool, dark closets and never, ever the heat of an attic. A thought struck her and she scrolled back to the perfunctory announcement, sighing in relief at the date. Her own birth was a respectable two years later.

So why elope? Beyond the utter foreignness of his New England background, her father was a perfectly acceptable husband, his private school background easing his way in status-conscious Chateau. Having spent many a fall weekend in Vermont's deer camps, he took to hunting ducks and geese with alacrity – 'a lot easier to carry a bird home than a deer' – and switched from Scotch to bourbon with what Nora would belatedly realize was far too much genteel enthusiasm.

Her eyes burned. She logged off the computer and sat a moment, not ready yet to return to Quail House, its empty echoing rooms a reminder that, had the trailer detached just a split second earlier, might have become its permanent state. She stepped out of the stacks and scanned the library's main room to make sure she didn't see anyone she knew, then headed across its expanse to the distraction of the reference room, where decades of Chateau High School's yearbooks marched in gilt-lettered rows down the shelves. She started to pull her own from the shelf, then replaced it. She wasn't sure she could handle all of those old photos of herself and Alden at the prom, sitting side by side in candid classroom shots, of Alden holding an ice-cream cone toward her at a senior social.

She ran her fingers along their spines until she came to her mother's graduation year. The books were skinnier then, the photos faded, the crewcut boys in the geeky horn-rimmed glasses now favored by hipsters, the girls in pearls and lofty bouffant hairstyles that bespoke considerable time and effort with hairspray and a rattail comb.

She flipped through the seniors once, then twice, before laughing at her mistake. Penelope hadn't graduated from Chateau High. She'd gone off to Miss Phipps's Academy for her final two years. She selected a book from three years earlier, paging through to the sophomores, checking the S's twice, but failed to see Penelope. Maybe she'd gotten the year wrong. She grabbed the previous year's book and there was Penelope as a sophomore – the date on the wedding announcement must have been a typo – hair still falling loose around her shoulders rather than tortured into a tower atop her head, eyes wide and bright and expectant. Nora's heart lurched.

What had her mother so looked forward to? Women's lives were so prescribed then, especially in a place like Chateau. There was a template: Finish high school or, in a few rare cases, secretarial or nursing school, and immediately marry a local boy, preferably from another First Family and never mind the dwindling gene pool, produce between two and four children, spend the rest of your life doing socially acceptable works – yes to the Dahlia Club and under no circumstances a nascent civil rights group.

To her credit, Penelope had briefly broken the mold when she'd gone off to Miss Phipps's and eloped with an outsider. But then, after those two brief but significant rebellions, she returned to Chateau and lived exactly the life expected of her.

Nora shook her head. The library lights blinked, Emily Beattie's decades-old signal that closing time approached. The police would be long done with their investigation. It was safe to leave. Nora headed back to Quail House, with nothing to show for her hours of screen time but more questions.

FORTY-TWO

1967

Grace wiped her new notebook clean with a handkerchief. Then she put pencil to paper, listing every room in Quail House and noting the pieces of furniture in each, stopping every few minutes to sharpen the pencil with a paring knife. She aimed to check each piece and each room off after she'd searched it.

The library would pose her biggest challenge. She'd examine every book, flip through its pages, hold it open and shake it just in case. Who knows what bit of evidence the Chief might have hidden, and where he might have put it? She'd put off the library and start with his den, the big desk there, moving on to the bedroom he shared with his wife.

Then she'd tackle Penelope's bedroom upstairs, now shared by her new husband, a taciturn New Englander only beginning to understand – as Grace surmised from the puzzled, hurt expression she so often glimpsed in his eyes – that the exquisite politesse of Southerners masked a rapier viciousness dripping honey until it drew blood. The only custom he'd apparently acquired since his arrival had been a taste for the bourbon she detected as she rinsed out his coffee cup, his toothbrush mug, the glass of iced tea that Penelope so disdained. Every time she looked at him, she wondered what he knew.

He tried to talk with her, in the clumsy way well-meaning white people had when they wanted to establish themselves as not like the rest. 'I hope you understand,' he said one day, 'that not all of us feel the same way.'

But you married her, she thought. Some warning must have flashed in her eyes, for he backed away hurriedly, mumbling something about having to get down to the plant, the scent of bourbon and regret lingering long moments after his departure.

Penelope and her husband stayed away from Chateau for two weeks after Bobby's death.

They'd been visiting his relatives in Vermont, the Chief explained, as though Grace gave a damn. The husband disappeared into the processing plant as soon as they returned, leaving for work before Grace arrived in the morning and returning home long after she'd prepared dinner and left it for Philippa to serve. Which was fine with Grace. She didn't care about the husband. She cared very much about Penelope.

Penelope remained a ghost, returning to her teenage habits of sleeping until noon, the now-marital-bedroom door firmly shut against any possible intrusions, emerging at the last possible minute to drive into town with her mother for errands and social occasions. If she stepped to the top of the stairs only to find Grace polishing a balustrade, she hurried to take the back stairs down to the kitchen. When she and her mother returned from town, she avoided the enticing display of a tea tray set with two cups and melt-in-your-mouth divinity, snatching a piece from the plate and taking it and a cup of tea back to her bedroom. And once, when Grace rose up from her knees where she'd been working unseen in the herb garden, screened by a riotous Bluebeard shrub, Penelope leapt from the chaise where she'd settled herself with a magazine and ran across the lawn to the dock, declaring to no one in particular her intention to row all the way to the bay.

One morning, though, well into autumn, her bedroom door stood uncharacteristically open. Grace peeped in, expecting to see Penelope at her vanity, or maybe on the phone. The room looked much as it did before the husband's arrival, only now Penelope's chaos was confined to one side, shoes lying wherever she'd kicked them off in contrast to the husband's neat lineup beneath his side of the bed, clothing in a heap in insulting proximity to the hamper, a jumble of hairbrushes and makeup on the dressing table. But no Penelope.

Grace glanced across the hall. Quail House was built long before indoor plumbing, and even when it arrived, it preceded en suite bathrooms.

Grace crept to the bathroom door. Heard water running. Which failed to mask the sound of uncontrollable retching and the reek of vomit. She flung open the door.

A half-naked Penelope knelt on the black and white octagonal tiles, bent over the toilet, shoulders heaving.

'Aw, hell, no!' Grace lunged for her, grabbed a skinny shoulder and wrenched her away from the toilet.

Penelope collapsed on to the floor, wrapping her arms around herself in an inadequate effort to hide breasts markedly plump and shiny in contrast to her ribby torso. 'No, Grace,' she whimpered. Vomit streaked her face and clung to her stringy, unwashed hair.

'Tell me you're not. That you've just got the flu or some shit.'

Penelope's head bobbed weakly.

'The flu. I've got the flu.'

Grace bent and slapped her.

'Maybe something I ate.'

Grace slapped her again.

Penelope started to cry, ugly, strangled sobs. Her nose ran.

'I'm sorry,' she blubbered through strings of snot. 'I'm so sorry.'

'Not as sorry as you're about to be.'

'Grace, no!' Penelope scrabbled on the floor, grabbing at Grace's ankles. 'Stop. What are you going to do?'

But it was too late. Grace was already gone.

* * *

Problem was, Grace didn't know what she was going to do. She was in the kitchen, still scrubbing her hands although they'd long since been cleaned of the residue from Penelope's befouled face, when the front door slammed and, moments later, the Chief burst into the kitchen, breathing hard.

Penelope must have called him from the princess phone in her room as soon as Grace's foot had hit the top step.

The Chief stopped and made a visible attempt to compose himself. 'Ah, Grace, there you are. I understand you and Penelope had a . . . conversation.'

Grace turned off the water and examined her hands, red and raw from her prolonged scouring. She dried them on a towel, deliberately taking her time, and turned to face the Chief, who now stood so close he loomed over her. The sink's porcelain rim pressed into the small of her back.

'We've been very generous with you, Grace.'

Generous to yourselves, more like. Paying to cover your own asses.

She squared her shoulders and stared into his cold gray eyes.

'Be a shame to see that end.'

Hell with it. We don't need your damn money.

'I know you're helping to support your parents. I thought they might use the money to move into a safer neighborhood. That part of Baltimore's getting rougher by the day. Drugs, gangs, drive-bys – people getting shot right on the street in broad daylight. Kids. Even little kids. Kids as young as your brother Kwame.'

Motherfucker. Was he actually saying what she thought he was?

The words boiled up in her, dangerously close to the surface. She took a breath and clamped her lips shut.

'My daughter is having my grandchild. The baby who will carry on the Smythe line. If anything, *anything* were to happen—'

Grace lost her internal battle.

'Your grandchild? Your grandchild? Let's tell the world just how much you care about your grandchild.'

The Chief's hand strayed toward his waist. Grace's gaze followed it as his fingertips caressed the service weapon there.

She actually smiled. 'You wouldn't dare. One Evans shot – you've gotten away with that. A second? I don't think so.'

The hand on the gun trembled. Rage? Or fear? It didn't matter. Now she knew what she was going to do.

'Here's what's going to happen. Not one goddamn thing. I'm going to stay here in your house. You're going to keep paying me, and I'm going to pay for Kwame's college, and things are going to go along exactly as they've been.' She stopped, but her thoughts ran on:

Until the day comes, when I find out what I need, and then I'm going to tell the world and take every last one of you, including that baby percolating in your daughter's belly, straight to hell.

FORTY-THREE

At two in the morning, Nora kicked away the sweat-soaked sheets, headed into the kitchen and poured a glass of ice water.

She started back up the stairs but hesitated at the thought of returning to her room, which had yet to lose the heat of the day. Instead, she headed outdoors, trailed by the dog and cat, to the dock, secure in the knowledge that at this hour she could sit by the river untroubled by either insects or the possibility of Alden rowing past.

She dangled her feet in the water, and held the glass to her neck, willing her body temperature a couple of degrees lower. A flash caught her eye, far away, over the bay. Heat lightning, that cruel tease. She longed for the real thing, the blinding jagged line across a darkening sky, the subsequent crash and roar of thunder, the drenching downpour like a benediction.

She slid from the dock into the water, seeking the cool of its depths. The bottom dropped steeply away from the bank, her toes barely brushing it. She stroked toward the middle of the river, angling against the current, wary of the effort of her return should she let it carry her too far downstream.

Her nightgown clung to her skin, so light it was little impediment to her progress. She rolled on to her back and frog-kicked in the general direction of the dock. A mighty splash interrupted her languid progress. She gulped air and sank deep into the river, an instinctive urge to hide from whatever was that large, even as she reached for reasonable explanations. A deer? They sometimes swam the river. A muskrat of freakish proportions? A goose performing the clumsiest landing of all time? She crouched on the river bottom, buffeted by the current, praying that whatever had entered the water with her was anything but human.

But when her bursting lungs forced her to surface, Murph's dripping face met her gaze as he churned toward her, huffing with exertion and delight at finally having a companion in his favorite activity. Nora grabbed him as he approached.

'Tow me back to the dock, old man. After that heart attack you nearly gave me, I'm not sure I've got the strength to swim.'

She managed to get him turned around and, with one hand clutching his furry back, kicked alongside him toward the dock, where the cat paced in high feline dudgeon at their antics. Nora pulled herself from the water and fell on to the boards, now grateful for their lingering warmth. The time in the water, and the flash of fear, had finally cooled her.

She turned her head toward the hulking black mass of Quail House.

Hers. And yet her mother was urging her away.

But she couldn't leave, not with her mother lying bruised and broken in the hospital.

She thought again of the yearbook photo, the look of barely concealed expectation on Penelope's face. What had driven her away from the gentle lowlands and marshes and soft, humid air of the Eastern Shore to a school in New England's hardwood forests, with their jagged rocky outcroppings? And why had she denied her parents the bragging rights of a lavish wedding, without the excuse of pregnancy? And even that mattered little; Nora had seen more than one Chateau bride pace demurely down the aisle in a flowing gown of purest white organza with a disguising Empire waist.

She wondered what her mother had worn in that brief ceremony. The announcement had omitted even that detail. Somehow she couldn't imagine Penelope, even in her moment of rebellion, in a peasant skirt with rings on her sandaled toes and daisies in her waist-length hair. Had flower power reached Vermont in 1966?

She sat up so abruptly the cat hissed at her.

'No. It can't be.'

Murph cocked his head and lifted his ears.

She sat a few moments more, water falling in slow droplets from her sopping nightgown on to the dock. She ran across the lawn and into the house, flipping the light switches as she made her way from room to room, the animals at her heels, excited and puzzled by this middle-of-the-night activity. She flung open the library's double doors and turned on more lights, heedless of the trail of wet footprints across the carpet's faded flowers.

'Where is it, where is it?' She searched the shelves, impatient. So many books! When was the last time anyone had read any of them? 'There!'

She pulled from a shelf the same slender, gilt-lettered volume she'd scanned in the library the previous afternoon. *The Chateau Osprey*, with a drawing of the school's mascot covering the yearbook's cover.

She flipped fast to the sophomores and there was her mother again, beaming bright-eyed from the page. In 1963. Three years before her mother's wedding in 1966, right after her graduation from Miss Phipps's Academy. She'd attributed the date in the wedding announcement to a typo, but that was crazy. She'd been looking through 1966 copies of the *Crier*. By the time she turned to the yearbooks in the library, not finding her mother where she expected, the mistake she'd attributed to a typo more likely had been due to fatigue.

Now, she counted on her fingers, trying to make the math come out right. If her mother graduated from Miss Phipps's in 1966, she should have been a sophomore in 1964.

She sank on to the rug, the yearbook's slick pages slowly wrinkling as she riffled them in her damp hands. Just as there was only one reason for an elopement in Chateau, there was only one – the same reason – for a girl to disappear for a year in the middle of high school.

But Nora was an only child.

Or so she'd always thought.

Hours later found her in her grandfather's study, sitting on the floor, surrounded by files and a litter of papers that stretched nearly to the door. Her nightgown had long since dried into a wrinkled horror.

She'd started with the obvious – Penelope's bedroom – but other than the clipping about the shooting on her nightstand, she'd found nothing of consequence, beyond learning that even at her advanced age, Penelope favored wispy scraps of silk and lace underwear, flirty things that put Nora's sturdy Jockeys to shame.

At some point, she'd made a pot of coffee and then another and fed the animals, who sprawled bored into somnolence in the lone corner not covered with paper. Nora wasn't exactly sure what she was looking for. A birth certificate? A doctor's outsize bill, with a reference to an insignificant gynecological procedure? If, by some miracle, the Smythes had managed to procure an abortion for their daughter in those pre-*Roe* years, she couldn't imagine they'd have gone the back-alley route. But the only thing she'd discovered, after hours of searching, was that William Smythe never threw away a piece of paper in his life.

There were medical bills aplenty, not only for the care he received in his own decline, but also her father's, who'd not so much died as faded away over the course of the years it took for the twin scourges of cancer and alcoholism to work their final victory. But nothing for Penelope beyond routine yearly checkups, teeth cleaning and – when she was in middle school – braces; as well as for Nora's own safely legitimate birth. So many receipts – not just for doctors' bills, but for garden tools, roof maintenance, a new dishwasher, dry-cleaning bills for his police uniforms. By contrast, Nora's parents' paperwork filled a single tall file cabinet to her grandfather's half-dozen. But, beyond discovering that Smythe's Best Backfin had been hemorrhaging money before her mother wisely sold it after her father's death, she found little of interest.

Her eyes stung from half a night's and the whole morning's unproductive reading. Her butt hurt from sitting on the floor. She stood and stretched, then bent and tried to touch her toes. The cartilage in her knees crackled a protest. Her stomach rumbled.

Food, maybe. A break, so that she could come back to her task with her mind refreshed, and maybe having figured out a better way to tackle it. At some point, she'd need to visit Penelope, but she didn't want to face her mother until she had an answer to her urgent question. Penelope, even doped up on painkillers, had an unerring sense of something amiss, and would question her mercilessly. And, without some sort of proof, Nora could not imagine asking her mother, 'Did you have another baby before me?' and 'Who was the father?' And, most urgently, 'If you had the baby, where is my sibling now?'

She had a pretty good idea about at least one answer. Hadn't Todd Burris stood on a sidewalk with the midday sun glinting off his silver mane and told her he'd courted Penelope in high school, before she'd disappeared to New England. Why hadn't they just got married?

Even when Nora was in high school, with birth control and abortions readily available, there'd been a handful of young marriages. And the Burrises were a First Family, something that would have papered over the smear of scandal. But for whatever reason, Penelope hadn't gone that route. Maybe, once installed at Miss Phipps's after the necessary year's disappearance, she'd simply met Nora's father in one of the usual ways and fallen in love with someone wonderfully new and different and wholly lacking in the baggage she'd shed when she left Chateau – the explanation Nora preferred.

Because, even though Penelope had probably been as young and foolish and swayed by a handsome face as any other dizzy fifteen-year-old, Nora couldn't imagine her mother truly in love with someone like Todd Burris.

FORTY-FOUR

1968

When, nearly a year after Bobby's murder, the *Chateau Crier* trumpeted the Chief's announcement of Todd Burris's alibi to the world, Grace almost gave up.

Because, what was the point? Wasn't she the one who'd told Bobby over and over again that nothing would ever change in Chateau? What had ever made her think that even if Todd Burris made a full confession, signed it in blood and took a lie detector test for good measure, he'd ever be held accountable for killing her brother?

The Chief had made a point of leaving the newspaper spread out on the kitchen table that morning. As if she hadn't already heard. As if every black person in Chateau, along with all of Bobby's friends from Morgan State and the people who'd come in from Baltimore and Washington and Philadelphia, hadn't heard.

'All these months, waiting on nothing,' Davita Evans had said when Grace made the collect call from a Quail House phone to Baltimore, trying to get ahead of the grapevine. Turned out one of Baltimore's finest had already delivered the news.

'Stood on my doorstep like he owned it and told me what I already knew. That nobody was ever going to face judgment for killing my son.'

The bitterness in her mother's voice seeped across the ninety-mile distance. Grace switched the receiver from one hand to the other, almost as though it had become too hot to grasp. Kwame babbled in the background – *Vroom, Vroom* – followed by small crashing sounds. She imagined a tiny demolition derby with his Matchbox cars.

'Took them all this time to get up the nerve to tell me.' Davita's voice turned peevish. 'Kwame. Hush that noise.'

A fretful wail arose.

'Mama. How about I come up next weekend and bring Kwame back here with me for a while?'

Grief lay heavy on her parents, but they'd had a lifetime of practice in dealing with disappointments both small and life-shattering. But a child deserved smiles and sunshine, the boisterous high spirits that had permeated the rowhouse when Bobby and Grace still lived there. Grace wondered if Kwame connected Bobby's abrupt disappearance to the home's transformation into a sort of crypt, within which her parents only went through the motions of living.

'Oh, Grace. You don't have to do that.' The deep weariness in her mother's obligatory protest told her exactly how badly she needed to.

'It's no trouble.'

Even though it was. She'd have to find someone to watch Kwame while she worked at Quail House. No way she was going to take him from one poisoned atmosphere into another. Maybe she'd quit her job there. But she'd been putting part of her generous paycheck aside each week into the college fund she'd started for Kwame.

She'd be lucky to make half as much anywhere else in Chateau. Maybe, instead of bringing Kwame back to Chateau with her, she'd try to get her old job at the *Afro* back. Live with her parents again, try to bring some sort of normalcy back into the house in Baltimore.

Because even if her methodical search of Quail House unexpectedly yielded fruit, even if she found hard evidence, the Chief would find a way to negate it. It served his purposes to have Bobby dead and, as he'd proven by accepting Todd's bullshit alibi, he intended to sweep the whole troublesome mess under the rug and leave it moldering there for eternity.

Whatever had made her think she could prevail against the most powerful forces in Chateau?

She hung up the phone and sagged against the wall. To hell with it. To hell with it all.

'Grace?'

She hardly recognized Penelope's voice. She'd barely seen her in the months following their confrontation in the bathroom. Now she stood in the doorway's shadows, her hugely pregnant belly an unspeakable affront.

'Grace?' Penelope moved into the bright light of the kitchen. It was noon but she was still in her nightgown, stretched tight across her stomach. She hitched it up, away from the liquid pooling at her feet.

'I think the baby's coming.'

The tense apprehension that had permeated Quail House after Bobby's killing and the subsequent riot and demonstrations vanished with the arrival of baby Nora.

Elaborately wrapped gifts arrived daily – tiny, hand-embroidered dresses, a whole family of winsome Steiff teddy bears, mobiles and quilts and knitted socks and caps and toys and more toys, enough to stock a store. A diaper service weekly delivered stacks of snowy cloth, whisking away the dirty ones in their malodorous pail.

Whatever wisps of suspicion clung to Penelope due to her departure to New England and hasty marriage evaporated with the addition to the next generation of First Families.

The Chief was besotted. Baby Nora rested in his arms from the moment he came home from work until her bedtime, unless, of course, she grew fussy, and then he handed her off to her mother or grandmother or even her father.

But never to Grace. She washed clothes stiff with spit-up, sterilized bottles and cooked the protein-rich meals deemed necessary to rebuild Penelope's depleted strength, but the entire family, including Penelope's husband, seemed locked in an unspoken conspiracy to bar her access to the baby.

And with good reason, she thought one morning several weeks later. The Chief and Hiram Best were at their respective jobs, and Philippa's black Lincoln had disappeared down the lane toward an errand in town, Philippa apparently not realizing her daughter had stepped into the shower, leaving the baby alone.

Grace checked the window to make sure the car was gone. She tiptoed upstairs and listened outside the bathroom to ensure the shower was running.

Then she slipped into the baby's room.

Nora slept in the most ridiculous contraption Grace had ever seen – a four-poster crib with a sheer canopy, a dainty, white-painted replica of the hulking bed in her parents' room. A cushioned rocking chair sat in one corner. A vase of fresh flowers – she herself had arranged them in the kitchen that morning – sat on a low table beside it, along with a stack of the fashion magazines Penelope skimmed as she rocked the baby to sleep. Stuffed animals populated a shelf, staring beady-eyed at Grace.

She thought about the day Kwame had arrived, how her father had hauled down the old crib from the attic and wedged it into a corner of her parents' tiny bedroom. She and Bobby had unearthed some childhood toys, worse for wear, and Davita crocheted a pale-blue blanket of whisper-soft yarn, Kwame's one luxury.

Baby Nora slept on her back, on soft flannel sheets printed with smiling pastel ducks, pink fists curled beside her round pink face. Her eyes fluttered beneath their lids.

Grace held her breath and listened. Yes, the shower still ran. One of the few times Grace had seen the Chief raise his voice to his daughter concerned the length of her showers, and the lack of hot water for hours afterward.

There was no pillow in the crib. Grace had overheard long conversations about the dangers of accidental suffocation.

She looked around the room and caught the glassy gaze of one of the Steiff bears. She reached for it, squeezing to make sure. Yes, it was just soft enough.

She held the bear near the baby's face, edging it toward her soft cheeks, her nose and mouth mere inches away.

Nora opened her eyes.

Like those of all babies, they were blue at first, but now were fast going green. They fixed on Grace with somber regard. A corner of her mouth twitched. She broke into an enormous, toothless grin, waving her little fists and crowing in delight.

Grace stepped back, shaking. The bear fell from her hand. She fled.

FORTY-FIVE

When Nora ushered a stiff and bruised but on-the-mend Penelope back into Quail House, she led her straight to the kitchen, where she'd laid an array of photographs across the long table.

Baby Nora in her christening gown.

A formal family portrait, her father standing behind a seated Penelope, holding the baby on her lap.

Toddler Nora using Murph's predecessor, Kathleen Mavourneen, as a pillow.

Nora on her first day of school – a photo every year for twelve years straight.

Nora in her graduation gown. (She'd deliberately omitted photos from the prom she attended with Alden.)

Nora on a snowy Colorado mountain, learning to ski during her sophomore year in college.

Nora in a business suit with grotesquely padded shoulders, a black grosgrain ribbon tied in a coy bow at her collar, her hair permed into unrecognizability as the eighties version of a successful career woman in her first public relations job.

And so on.

Penelope clapped her hands in delight, then winced.

'Oh, I shouldn't have done that. But, Nora, what a wonderful surprise! How beautiful.'

Nora, who'd prepped the sterling teapot with hot water before she'd left for the hospital, emptied it, measured in tea leaves, and filled it with water just off the boil. The aroma of bergamot wafted from the pot.

She popped two pieces of bread into the toaster, poured milk into a pitcher and sat it and the sugar bowl in front of Penelope.

'Let's have some tea and toast first.'

By the time she'd smeared butter across the toast and sprinkled it with cinnamon and sugar, the tea was ready. 'You always made me cinnamon toast when I was sick. Now it's my turn to look after you.'

Penelope took a long, appreciative sip of her tea. 'Oh, my. You wouldn't believe what passed for tea in the hospital. Dreadful Lipton, and always lukewarm.' She shuddered. 'Thank you for this. And the cinnamon toast – and all of these photos. Such good memories! What's the occasion?'

'Isn't your homecoming occasion enough? Even the animals are celebrating.'

Murph leaned against Penelope's chair while Mooch crouched on the floor, ready to race him to any stray crumb that might fall.

'Wherever did you find all of these photos?'

'All the albums are in the library.' Nora thought of the many photos she'd paged through in order to gather the collection. Photos of her father with a shotgun over one arm and a brace of fat mallards in his hand, Kathleen Mavourneen's tail a blur as she stood beside him. Of her grandparents, beaming upon their beautiful daughter as she leaned from her pony's saddle to present them with the blue ribbon she'd just won.

She thought also of all the photos that weren't there – the missing years of Penelope's time in New England, but for a single group shot of Penelope posed with her classmates before a brick building thick with the requisite ivy. It was as though Penelope had transitioned from high school sophomore to young matron with a baby in the blink of an eye, a gap papered over as just one more uncomfortable reality to be ignored by the good people of Chateau, just as one ignored everything from intestinal discomfort to the long-ago and still-unsolved murder of a black man.

And one other subject was missing from the row of family albums, labeled in precise copperplate by generations of Smythe women. Nora waited until Penelope finished her first cup of tea – she didn't want to risk another broken cup – and broached it.

'I went through all of the albums, Mother – at least, all of those from the last fifty years, and a few before that – but I couldn't find a single photo of my sibling.'

Give Penelope credit. She didn't so much as flinch. Nora wondered how long she'd been waiting for this moment. Preparing for it. Penelope reached for the pot and poured another cup of tea. A few drops spilled on to the saucer, the only betrayal of her inner tension.

Nora bluffed. 'Mother, I know about it. I ran into Todd Burris downtown. Mother, why didn't you two just get married? Was it because . . . oh, no.' A thought had just occurred to her, one she struggled to put into words. Would Penelope even recognize the term 'date rape'?

'Did he . . . did he hurt you?'

Penelope buried her face in her hands. When she raised it, the brief strain had drained from her features, leaving them unnervingly serene.

'No, Nora. Nothing like that. I didn't marry Todd because I didn't love him.'

Which opened up another possibility nearly as unnerving as an assault – that, as a teenager, Penelope had been comfortable with the idea, sacrilege at the time, that sex in no way needed to be connected to love and marriage. Nora's face grew hot, embarrassment overcoming her attempts at tact as she blurted her next question.

'But isn't it awkward living in the same town as him?'

Penelope waved her hand. 'It's not discussed.'

Of course not. But there was one more thing Nora needed to discuss.

'What happened to the baby?'

A last chance for Penelope to deny a baby ever existed. Nora wondered who had the more pressing need for denial – herself or her mother?

'Adopted.'

Which, given that she answered the question at all, is what Nora had expected her to say. If Penelope had had an abortion, would she even admit it? She pushed harder.

'Boy or girl?'

Penelope's composure cracked so briefly that Nora wasn't sure she'd seen it, eyes widening, a wild despair within.

'Boy.'

'I have a brother?'

Penelope lifted her chin and there it was, the iron control that told Nora she'd learned all she would.

'No. Some other family has a lovely son. And' – on the offensive now – 'don't go looking for him. Adoption records were sealed then, and for good reason. Some secrets are best kept.'

FORTY-SIX

Then, fifty years after that fraught moment beside the baby's crib and nearly thirty years after Grace had last seen her, Nora was back.

The fact barely registered at first in the plunge back into despair, somehow so much worse in its very familiarity, after Robert's killing. It was all Grace could do to hold it together for the sake of Kwame and Dorothy, whose stunned silence and slow, shaky movements, recalled her parents in the days following Bobby's shooting.

And her own grief, then and now?

A clawing, private thing, descending at night, even as she buried her face in her pillow and screamed for it to be gone.

She couldn't remember when it dawned on her that Nora had returned to Chateau. She'd heard about her over the years, of course. Grace had cut back her time at Quail House to three times weekly, then once a week, but despite her best efforts to avoid Penelope, she occasionally ran into her. After years of a tense, guarded silence in Grace's presence, Penelope became voluble after Nora's departure for college, following her around as she worked, regaling her with bits of gossip and the occasional tidbits about Nora – her job, her marriage – in the inexplicable assumption that Grace cared.

At first, Grace fumed, fighting an impulse to backhand her across her lipsticked mouth to shut her up. Then she forced herself to listen in the hope that, after all this time, Penelope might drop some tidbit.

Because even if she'd apparently forgotten – or, more likely, had successfully suppressed – the most consequential event of her lifetime, Grace had not.

She had, however, made her peace with the fact that she might never get at the truth of things; that it was enough that she hadn't given up. Or so she'd told herself until Chateau's lone black cop – oh, they'd known whom to send – showed up at her door on a soupy August night and told her that one of his colleagues had shot her beloved nephew.

She'd caught a glimpse of Nora at the demonstration and had gone through the mental gymnastics to link the grown woman to the shy, skinny child who'd never divined the simmering rage that lay beneath Grace's stony façade. And, having placed her, and felt the stab of fury that any member of the Smythe family provoked, willed her focus back to Kwame and Dorothy.

But then Nora had shown up on her doorstep, with a peach cake in her hand and the gall to ask about Bobby.

Grace was tempted, then, to tell her. But that would have let Penelope off the hook, and if anyone deserved to be held to account, like an insect writhing on a collector's pin before the chloroformed bit of cotton descended, it was Penelope.

'Talk to your mother,' she'd said. She wondered if Nora had.

Nora had given the police some cockamamie story about Robert and road rage. Then she'd been caught gallivanting with Alden. Worse than Penelope. Well, maybe not worse. But just as bad. 'Blood tells,' Grace muttered.

Maybe it was time for her to tell.

FORTY-SEVEN

She had a brother.

Nora started her run without stretching, not even a slow warm-up jog, pounding down the lane toward the main road as though trying to outrun the questions in her head.

Where was he? What did he look like? Did he have his father's luxuriant hair, his stocky build? Her mother's green eyes and discerning sensibilities? If she saw him in a crowd, would she do a double take, divining some resemblance, some indefinable emotional affinity? Was he liberal or conservative, professional or blue-collar, city sophisticate or contented suburbanite?

Did he have children of his own? Did she have nieces and nephews? She'd never had, nor particularly wanted, children of her own, but enjoyed friends' children and had often rued the lack of younger family members to spoil with gifts and play dates.

She hit the main road, sprinting for McKay's Woods, then slowed to savor the shade. Sweat dripped in her eyes. The fox emerged from its den, an orange blur. She swiped a hand across her face and it came into focus, swishing its bottle-brush tail and regarding her with a tilt-headed, bright-eyed stare.

It had something in his mouth, something shiny. It looked like . . .

'Hey!' She yelled and waved her hands. The fox dropped it and ducked back down into the den.

She looked up and down the road – no cars – then picked her way across the ditch and toward the mound where the fox made its home, stepping carefully around the shiny green patches of poison ivy.

The smell hit her, the fox's own musky scent plus a whiff of decomposition, the entrance to the den a litter of small bones. Nora peered into the darkness, half expecting to see a pair of eyes shining back. But the fox had retreated deep within. Its treasures lay scattered about. Some golf balls. A leather glove, well chewed. A Croc, likewise shredded into near-unrecognizability. And there, so recently acquired as to have suffered little damage, a cellphone. She grabbed it and ran.

The phone could have been anyone's.

But she remembered the fox darting across the road moments before the shooting. Kwame Evans's quote in the *Afro*: 'Where's his damn phone?'

The phone in her hand could have served as an advertisement for the impermeability of its case. Other than being crusted with dirt and ineffectually scratched by small sharp teeth, it was unscathed. Nora hadn't seen rain since her return to Chateau, but mornings had been heavy with dew. Back at Quail House, she unearthed a box of white rice from deep within the pantry, dumped its contents into a bowl, buried the phone within it, and, for good measure, took it to her room against the possibility that Penelope might discover it.

More than ever, she missed Electra, her own safe hideaway that she could lock against intruders. At least she'd have it back in a couple of days, according to a phone call from Todd Burris.

She'd recognized the dealership's number and let the call go to voicemail, sure that somehow in a conversation he'd divine that she'd discovered he was her half-brother's father. 'It's not discussed,' Penelope had said. As though it were the easiest thing in the world.

She tried to imagine the years of encounters they must have had, at Founders' Balls with their respective spouses, in the grocery store, at parades. Her mother would have attended events with Todd's wife. Had her father ever gone duck-hunting with Todd? Did her father know about that previous baby?

Given her mother's chilly dismissal – 'I didn't love him' – Nora wondered whether she'd loved the man she'd married, either. It had been a smart move to wed someone from far away, who wouldn't have heard the inevitable speculative whispers about Penelope's disappearance from Chateau, her delayed graduation date; who wouldn't have known to question her about those things before rushing into a courthouse ceremony.

She wondered if he'd heard them later, as he was slowly drawn into Chateau's social life, where the matrons held doctorates in the art of sly insinuation. She could just imagine someone like Miss Alice clasping her father's hands in welcome, holding them a little too long, as she looked meaningfully into his eyes. 'Now we know why our dear Penelope was in such a hurry to run away up North. We were all so curious when she left us, but here you are!'

Leaving him, probably, to linger over the words 'run away' and 'curious.' What was so curious about a girl going away to school?

Had he ever figured it out? Or at least had his suspicions? It would explain his slide into cocktails after work, wine with dinner and bourbon by the fire afterward, the resulting mental blur masking his awareness of the signs of cancer until far too late.

The phone proved a welcome distraction from those needling questions. She knew she should call the Attorney General's Office about her find. It probably wasn't even Robert's. The AG would be able to figure it out. And she *would* call . . . as soon as she'd examined the phone for herself. She no longer trusted anyone around her to give her a straight answer about anything.

She was supposed to leave the phone in the rice for at least twenty-four hours. She managed sixteen.

At eleven at night, with Penelope presumably deep in sleep, and even the animals slumbering, Nora sat up in bed, dug the phone out of the rice in the bowl on her nightstand, and plugged it into her charger, giving thanks that it, like hers, was an iPhone.

She closed her eyes, said a prayer to the gods of technology and, like a new millennium miracle, felt an answering vibration in her hand. She looked down. A red bar glowed back at her. The phone would need to recharge before she could proceed.

Beside her, the cat opened one brilliant green eye, and closed it again.

'Go back to sleep. Nothing's going to happen for a while.'

She tried to take her own advice, forcing her eyes closed, only opening them every five minutes to check. The phone signaled green in a gratifyingly short time. But it also demanded a passcode. Shit.

She tried variations of the obvious Hail Mary – Pass1234 – only to see them rejected. She wondered how many tries she'd get before the phone shut down again.

What did she know about Robert Evans? Not nearly enough. His age, nineteen, but not his birthday. She'd look it up, maybe paying for access to one of those stalker websites, if other options failed.

He attended Morgan State. She checked a few things on her own phone and typed in 'Bears,' the school's mascot. No dice.

But . . . he'd been wearing a Baltimore Ravens jersey the night he was shot. She typed in Ravens, then Baltimore Ravens. Nothing.

She returned to her own phone. A few clicks told her it was a Jacoby Jones jersey.

J-o-n-e-s. Nothing.

J-a-c-o-b-y-J-o-n-e-s. Nada.

J-a-c-o-b-y-J-o-n-e-s-R-a-v-e-n-s. Zip.

She tried various combinations of capital and small letters until she threw the phone down in defeat. She returned to her own phone to check one last thing.

Then typed: J-o-n-e-s-1-2. The number on his jersey.

The phone opened like a flower, showing a photo of – her heart lurched – Robert's Uncle Bobby. A man he'd never met, but whose fate pursued the family through the decades, catching up with Robert on a country road just a few miles away from where his uncle had been murdered.

Nora took a few deep breaths and then got down to business.

First, Robert's texts. She scrolled back through several days' worth of nearly incomprehensible messages comprising acronyms and emojis before giving up and turning to his photos, swiping back a few days from the final image and scrutinizing them in reverse order.

Selfies, mostly, several taken with friends, including a number of pretty girls, though not enough of any one girl to suggest someone steady. Robert at backyard barbecues. Robert, sweaty and grinning, after winning a race. Robert holding up a textbook and making a sad face – paired with his beaming visage beside a test displaying an A+ scrawled in red. 'Winning!'

Robert in a suit and tie between an equally formally dressed Kwame and Dorothy. Robert, in the same suit, next to Grace – some sort of family event, apparently. In nearly all, the same wide smile that pushed his cheeks high, crinkling his eyes – the grin he'd flashed as an apology when he'd passed her on the road that night.

The final image, on the day of the shooting, was a brown blur, so dark she almost missed the arrow signaling a video. She tapped it.

It didn't show anything at first, just the same dark smear, although now she heard music. She held the phone close to her face, ducked beneath the covers, and raised the volume. A hip-hop beat sounded and, over it, shouting.

'I said, turn off that goddamn music and step out of the fucking vehicle *now*.'

Even distorted by the music and the phone's tinny quality, she recognized Alden's voice. A minute later, the image swerved past a dashboard and steering wheel and toward an open car window. Alden's face loomed on the tiny screen.

Another voice, disembodied, slow and even, but with an edge.

'And I said, do you have a warrant? You haven't even told me why you're stopping me. For sure I wasn't speeding. I've been coming down here for years. I know all about this speed trap.'

'Your taillight's out. *Step out of the car*.'

'My taillight is not out.'

Alden's face disappeared. Nora heard a crunch, and the video wavered as though something had struck the car. Alden's face reappeared.

'It is now. Don't make me tell you again.'

'You know I got that on video. Well, audio . . . *Whoa*.'

A gun barrel filled the screen.

'I'm getting out.' Robert's voice shook. 'Put that thing down. I'm getting out now.'

'Too late, motherfucker.'

The images jerked and wavered, views of car and sky and the briefest flash of Robert's wide-eyed face, and a last terrified plea – 'Hey, wait! I'm doing what you say' – as Alden snarled, 'Give me that fucking phone' before the image soared high, sky and field alternating, only the sound of a single shot before everything went black.

FORTY-EIGHT

Robert hadn't had a gun.

He hadn't lunged for Alden's weapon.

He'd just been a terrified kid, responding reasonably to an unreasonable request and paying for it with his life.

Nora huddled under the covers, shaking. The cat paced the bed, meowing anxiously, stopping to knead at her with his paws. Murph laid his head on the bed with a soft thump and whined.

The phone glowed beside her. She shoved it away with an index finger. She wished she'd left it with the fox. Because what did it really show?

There'd been no question that Alden shot Robert. Yes, he'd claimed self-defense, but did it really matter? Robert was still dead, and Alden suspended. The suspension might be lifted, but he himself acknowledged the impossibility of ever returning to work in Chateau, even if a significant portion of the population – the white residents, anyway – supported him.

Only hours earlier, she'd disdained her mother's words: 'Some secrets are best kept.'

Revelations about the phone would only stir things up again – for everyone, not just her. Kwame and Dorothy and Grace had already been through so much. Why tear at their wounds anew?

Because.

No. Nora shoved the phone farther away.

You know why.

She pulled the pillow over her head, unable to blot out the argument within.

The cops think their son was a drug dealer.

So? This doesn't prove differently.

That he was violent. See: road rage. But he wasn't. That shrug . . .

Maybe I saw it wrong.

You know you didn't. Who are you trying to protect, Nora?

His family.

Bullshit.

Alden. If I turn this in, it'll look like I'm just being vindictive. Besides, my mother's been through enough.

So he evades true justice just so you and your mother can escape the judgment of the good people of Chateau?

She moaned aloud, swatting at the covers as though somehow that would quiet her conscience.

That's what's most important? Covering your own cowardly ass? You've got a brother out there you'll never see just because of crap like this.

Nora's fingers scrabbled for her own phone. Scrolled through the contacts. Tapped a number.

The voice on the other end had that peculiar combination of sleep and instantaneous adrenaline prompted by a midnight call.

'Brenda Holiday.'

'This is Nora Best. I found Robert Evans's phone.'

She clicked off. The phone burned in her hand. She held it another long moment, trying to figure out how to word her message in a way that removed her own involvement, before dialing another number.

'Miss Grace? It's Nora Best. I'm sorry to wake you at this hour. I wanted you to be the first to know. The AG's got Robert's phone. There's a video. It wasn't self-defense.'

The silence went on forever, so long Nora took the phone away from her ear and checked the screen to make sure the call was still connected. Grace's voice shot from it, wide awake and hard as a slap.

'Didn't need a video to figure that out. You called me in the middle of the night to tell me what I already knew?'

The phone went dark.

Things weren't as bad as she thought they might be.

They were worse.

Two identical black sedans pulled up in front of Quail House at seven a.m., setting up a great outcry from Murph and a dash for cover by the cat. The staccato raps of the brass door knocker made no allowances for the possibility that anyone might still be sleeping.

Nora, of course, wasn't. She opened the door to Holiday. Beyond, George Satterline sat behind the wheel of the second car. She wordlessly handed Holiday the phone, now encased in a Ziploc bag.

Holiday pinched the bag between two fingers. 'Is this to make me believe you haven't looked at it?'

'I've looked. I figured out his password. It's Jones-twelve. For Jacoby Jones and the number on his jersey.' She hoped that her complete honesty in this regard would help Holiday believe the preposterous answer to her logical next question.

'I know who Jacoby Jones is. 2013. The Miracle at Mile High. Where did you get this?'

'A fox had it.'

The look on Holiday's face. Nora almost felt sorry for her. 'Would you like some coffee?'

Holiday's voice dripped icicles. 'No. I would not like coffee. I would like you to immediately drive to Baltimore to answer some questions. You can follow me. Satterline will drive behind.'

'Am I under arrest?'

'No,' said Holiday. But her voice said, 'Not yet.'

FORTY-NINE

She wasn't arrested. But Alden was, charged with involuntary manslaughter, which set off a whole new round of outrage and protests.

'Is that what we're calling murder these days?' Kwame said to the *Afro*, declining to speak to the *Sun* at all.

The governor sent the state police to buttress Chateau's force. Downtown businesses closed, and some even boarded up their windows, in preparation for violence that never erupted, the renewed protests as sad and somber as the first. With no excitement downtown, a parade of reporters made their way to Quail House, even though Nora's role had not been publicly revealed. Robert's cellphone, according to a terse news release from the AG's office, had been found by 'a citizen' in a field some distance from the shooting site, near a fox's den.

Whether the reporters had been tipped off about her role in finding the phone or pursued her only because of her earlier involvement with Alden, Nora didn't know and didn't care.

She locked the doors, pinned the drapes closed, unplugged the landline, shut down her phone and computer, and barely resisted the idea of drugging the dog so that he wouldn't drive them crazy with his barking every time another reporter knocked at the door.

Other approaches weren't as easy to ignore.

Dear Penelope, read a note that arrived on engraved stationery with a pleasurably tactile high rag content.

> Under the circumstances, we think it best that you not attend the Beautification Society meeting this month until this unfortunate situation has been resolved. We know you understand. Best wishes to you in this difficult time. Regards.

Best wishes. Regards.

Penelope received a half-dozen such notes in the following days. The Neighborhood Association. The Soroptimists. The Hospital Committee. And – probably the one that truly stung – the Founders' Ball Committee.

She and Nora moved around the darkened house, existing within a subdued formality, their platitudes belying the betrayal smoldering in Penelope's eyes.

'If only you'd left . . .' she began once.

'Well, I didn't.' Nora didn't add the obvious. Where would she have gone? At some point, she'd have to talk to Penelope about Quail House. Her misty imaginings of settling into some sort of leisurely early retirement, sheltered in the place where she'd grown up – a life of limitations, yes, but also one blissfully free of risk, dissolved in the harsh light of reality.

Her mother had managed to overcome a scandal and return to Chateau with her head held high, but Nora knew she didn't have that sort of intestinal fortitude. Anyway, having a baby out of wedlock was one thing. The shame was personal, and people could congratulate themselves on their own magnanimity for overlooking it. But exposing one of their own to the world as a racist killer? Nora had brought shame upon the entire town – the white residents, anyway – and that was unacceptable.

She could call Emerson, have him negate the agreement leaving Quail House to her in trust. But then what? Penelope would never consent to sell the place. Wait until her mother died, and then sell it herself? But then she'd have to return to Chateau to deal with the paperwork. In the meantime – circling back to the original issue – where would she go?

She distracted herself by retreating to her grandfather's office, intent upon reordering the ankle-deep litter of files she'd left strewn across the floor in her futile search for information about her sibling, a task she hoped would require just enough concentration to quiet the bubbling stew of doubt and guilt.

It worked; if not entirely erasing her emotions, at least quieting them to a simmer. The file drawers, standing open and empty, began to fill. The floor reappeared. She granted herself a lunch break, returning to the office with a ham sandwich and a glass of milk, paging idly through one of the remaining files, labeled *Business Checking Account*, as she ate.

She'd scrutinized its pages and pages of statements with more care than some of the other documents. If she'd learned nothing in her years of public relations, finances tripped people up more than anything else, even illicit affairs or public misbehavior.

She ate listlessly, despite her hunger. The air, even indoors, hung thick and heavy. Sunlight poured a gap in the drapes. It had a glazed quality, portending a change in the weather. As far as she was concerned, the sooner the better.

She spread the bank statements across the desk, their rows of names and numbers almost soothing, looking again for something out of the ordinary, different from the payments for power, telephone and insurance, the quarterly property tax bill. A five-hundred-dollar monthly payment to Advance Bank, whatever that was. All the family accounts were at the First National Bank of Chateau. She'd noted it before and figured – well, she couldn't remember what she'd thought in her haste that day. She took another bite and glared at the pages and, for lack of anything else to do, tapped Advance Bank into her phone.

Advance had a Baltimore address. Five hundred dollars was a considerable sum back in – she checked the date – 1963. A mortgage payment? Perhaps her father had invested in property in Baltimore. Smythe's Best Backfin was trucked to restaurants throughout the city. Maybe her grandfather had thought to open a satellite plant in the Inner Harbor, an industrial area that, decades later, after the factories closed, would rise phoenix-like as a tourism mecca of museums, restaurants and condos with shocking price tags in the old warehouses.

She sat her half-eaten sandwich on its plate and went to one of the cabinets, retrieving some of the files she'd just replaced, turning in time to see the dog and cat edging toward the remains of her sandwich, the cat atop the table, the dog on a chair.

She threw the statements at them, sending papers, cat, dog and sandwich remnants flying.

'That was my lunch!'

Even as she spoke, Murph and Mooch came slinking back, side-eying her as they vied for bits of meat and crust.

'You'll be sorry when you don't get dinner tonight.'

She turned her attention back to the bank statements, trying to assemble them in some sort of order. But no matter what year she held in her hand – 1967, when the monthly amount tripled, all the way to 1985, when they abruptly ended – the deposits to Advance were there.

She fetched her laptop and opened her browser, searching property records in Baltimore. Nothing for a Smythe's Best Backfin, or William Smythe or Penelope Smythe. She clicked on Advance Bank's website, thinking to find a phone number and call them, ask for information, knowing even as she did that no reputable bank would tell her anything.

She clicked away from the bank's page, scrolling through sites that mentioned Advance, until a bit of information caught her eye.

Advance Bank, one of Baltimore's oldest black-owned banks . . .

'What the . . .?'

Her thoughts ping-ponged among the possibilities, returning relentlessly to one.

She slammed the laptop shut and swept the papers from the table, sending Mooch and Murph scrambling anew to avoid the cascade.

She found her phone and brought up Grace's number.

She was beginning to figure out what had happened to her brother.

FIFTY

Grace clicked out of the call, laid the phone down and sat open-mouthed.

Kwame looked at the phone, and then at her. 'You OK?'

She nodded, afraid to speak. Who knew what might come out?

'Who was that?'

She freed a hand and reached for her lemonade. She'd made it the way he liked it, just enough sugar to keep your mouth from puckering, and tangy with crushed mint. It steadied her.

'That was Nora Best.'

His face clouded. 'What's she want now?'

'Says she wants to see me.'

Kwame brought his fist down on the table. Lemonade sloshed from their glasses. 'What for? To try and sell you on that crazy story about a fox finding the phone?' Brenda Holiday had filled them in just before the AG's office, trying to forestall an avalanche of public records requests, released the video to the media.

It went viral within moments, somehow more chilling because of Robert's disembodied voice, verging from irritable calm to terror, and its final kaleidoscope of earth and sky and the single piercing sound of the shot.

It had taken the combined strength of Kwame and Grace to hold Dorothy as she screamed and sobbed anew upon hearing her son's final moments, to keep her from tearing at her clothing, her hair, her face. Only later would they hold each other, weeping quietly together after the departure of Grace's longtime doctor, hastily summoned to administer Dorothy a sedative.

'She didn't say. Just said it was urgent and that she had to see me in person.'

'Then why doesn't she get her ass over here instead of making you haul all the way out there?'

After Holiday's call, Grace had wondered if she'd ever smile again. Now she found out she could, although this was a new, foreign sort of smile, coldly satisfied.

'Probably because the last time she was here, I threw her off my damn porch.'

'Good for you. You're not going, are you?'

Grace considered the various reasons Nora might now demand her presence. One rose to the surface.

'You know, I just might.'

'No.'

She gave him The Look, the one she'd used on him his whole life whenever he'd dared to cross her.

His shoulders sagged. 'All right, then. But if you go, I'm coming with you.'

She started to object, then thought better of it. She'd sheltered him his whole life, and what good had it done?

A breeze stirred the kitchen curtains, not the hot breath of the past weeks, but cool, nearly as refreshing as the lemonade.

Grace lifted her head and breathed deep. 'If we're going, we'd better go now. Storm's coming.'

At first, Nora thought the Subaru in the driveway might be delivering another reporter. It pulled up next to Electra, returned just that morning from the body shop, restored to her gleaming glory.

Nora backed away from the window beside the door, hoping the car's occupants hadn't already glimpsed her. Then Kwame emerged and held the passenger door open for Grace.

In all the years Grace had worked at Quail House, she'd always arrived by foot. Until this moment, Nora had never considered the three-mile walk – each way – that entailed. Decades after the fact, she was finally beginning to understand the contempt that lurked just behind Grace's bland gaze.

She'd installed her mother at the kitchen table, with her usual hot tea, and glasses of iced tea for herself and Grace. Now she hurried to pour another for Kwame, falling back on propriety on this most infelicitous of occasions.

'What's this about?'

'Yes, Nora. We're all so curious.'

Nora wasn't sure whose voice held more frost, Grace's or Penelope's.

'Sit down. Please. This won't take long.'

Kwame looked at Grace. She nodded, once, permission reluctantly dispensed. They both sat, Grace glaring at Nora and Penelope in turn. Penelope stared down at the table; Kwame, at the stack of files in front of Nora.

She caught his gaze and nodded. 'Yes,' she said. She opened one of the files and withdrew a piece of paper, dense with printed numbers, and spoke first to Penelope.

'Mother, when I realized you must have had another child, I started looking for evidence. I never found it, but you were good enough to finally tell me yourself – at least, once I asked you directly.'

The color drained from Penelope's face. She gripped the table as though afraid if she let go, she'd slide straight to the floor.

'But you wouldn't tell me where he was. I think I have an idea, though. Or, at least, I think maybe Grace knows.'

An odd half-smile crossed Grace's face. 'Let's hear it.'

'This didn't jump out at me the first time I looked. Maybe I'd just seen too many documents that day. But I came across it again and saw all these payments to Advance Bank. In Baltimore.'

Penelope's head jerked. 'What are you talking about? I never sent any money to a bank in Baltimore.'

'Granddaddy did, starting not long after you went away to New England. Five hundred dollars a month for the first few years. Then fifteen hundred, coming out of the business account. When you sold the processing plant, it was this far' – she held her thumb and forefinger a millimeter apart – 'from bankruptcy. But he supported that child, didn't he, Miss Grace?'

Grace nodded slowly. 'Yes, he did.'

Penelope made a strangled sound.

'The money went to you.'

Grace nodded again. 'Yes, it did.'

'For his care.'

'Yes.'

Wind gusted through the screened window, so hard it toppled a vase on the counter.

Nora and Kwame jumped. The dog yelped. The cat darted beneath the sideboard.

Grace and Penelope sat still as death.

'You know where he is.'

'Yes.'

Nora spoke in a rush, eager for the information she so longed to discover. 'You were the go-between, right? Granddaddy sent you the money, and you gave it to the family who took care of him.'

Grace sat serene as a saint. Penelope's face went from gray to white.

Nora hurried on.

'Granddaddy supported him until he was twenty-one. So you knew where he was right into adulthood. Do you know where he is now?'

Grace dipped her head.

'Could you help me find him? Do you think he'd mind?' She turned to her mother, giddy with her own daring. 'I'm sorry, Mother. I know this is probably painful to you. But all these secrets, all these years. The hell with them. Let's wipe the slate clean, start again. Who cares what people in Chateau think?'

It took her a moment to recognize the sound Grace made as a chuckle.

'Could you contact him, ask if he'd like to meet us?'

Clouds swept in, black and heavy, defeating the sun that had held triumphant sway for so many weeks. They sat in near darkness, the silence in the room absolute. The wind, as though respecting the gravity of the moment, stopped abruptly. The curtains sighed back into place.

Even in the dim light, Nora saw the long look that passed between her mother and Grace.

'No,' said Grace. 'I won't ask him. But maybe your mother would.'

Nora's and Kwame's heads swiveled in unison toward Penelope, then toward each other. Kwame shrugged, signaling his bewilderment.

Nora voiced her own. 'But she doesn't know where he is.'

Lightning ran across the sky, the flash illuminating the moisture on Penelope's face. She held out her hands, imploring. 'Grace, please.'

Grace looked as though she had plenty to say in response, practically vibrating with the effort of holding it back. Still, she maintained her silence.

'Please, please, don't do this.' Openly weeping now.

Thunder cracked, underscoring Grace's command. 'Tell her.'

The hand Penelope lifted danced with nerves. She tucked three fingers against her palm, folding her thumb across it. She grasped her wrist with her other hand, steadying it so her index finger finally stilled in an implacable point. 'I–I . . .' She sobbed too hard for speech.

Grace helped her out.

'Nora Best, meet your brother. Kwame, meet your mother.'

FIFTY-ONE

Grace figured Nora hoped for some kind of big kumbaya moment – Kwame wrapping Penelope in a hug, crying, 'Mama, mama!'

And then turning to Nora, opening his arms wide. 'Lil Sis!'

Guess what didn't happen?

She almost felt bad. Because it was one thing letting it go all this time without confronting Penelope. But she wanted to protect Kwame. Far as she was concerned, he could have lived the rest of his life thinking Bobby was his big brother, not his father. Although there was a special sort of satisfaction in having Penelope's daughter figure it out – even if she got the father part wrong.

But Kwame's face. All this time he'd believed her mother – her gentle, brokenhearted mother, who thought he walked on water and would have done anything for him, even though she was too old to be the fun kind of mother most kids wanted – was his own.

Now he just sat there and stared at this shriveled-up old white lady, crying and shaking and unable to get herself under control enough to blubber anything but, 'I'm sorry. I'm sorry.'

'Grace?' he said, his voice as high and uncertain as a child's.

She battled the temptation to go easy, soften the blow. Even though there was no way to pretty-up such news. Case in point:

Nora and her mother, looking like the damn world had come to an end. Even though, given Quail House's age, it probably wasn't the first time those walls had seen a black child from a white parent.

'Grace?' This time it was Nora. When Grace didn't answer, Nora turned to Kwame, each of them registering the other's green eyes, the same gaze they'd seen in the mirror over the years, something passing between them – not the sort of thing that led to hugs and tears – but a wary acknowledgment and, much stronger, curiosity.

Grace interrupted the moment.

'Here's all you need to know about your new big brother. Someone killed his daddy. And *your* daddy' – she shot a look across the table at the weeping Penelope – 'covered it up. Best I can figure, he found the gun that killed him and threw it so far away nobody'll ever see it again. Now his son's been shot dead and' – she swung back toward Nora – 'you helped cover *that* up. So you'll have to excuse him if he's not jumping into the arms of his new-found family. Because if it hadn't been for you people, he'd still have his own family. My mother was all the mother he ever needed. She wanted him. Not like this one, who threw him away like trash and danced through the rest of her life like none of it had ever happened. Well? Well?'

Penelope's mouth opened and closed like that of a fish suddenly finding itself on dry land, unable to dart and twist away. Tears cut tracks through the layer of powder on her face.

'Oh, Grace,' she whispered. 'You've ruined us all.'

For just a moment there, Grace almost felt sorry for her. But she saw the word 'ruined' land like a slap across Kwame's face.

'You can thank your daughter for that. If she hadn't figured it out, you'd still be getting away with everything, the way you have your whole life. But she looked at the money.'

Nora had been staring at Kwame as if she wanted to memorize every line and mole on his face. Her eyes never left it as she spoke, almost absently. 'Yes. That's right. The money.'

Kwame's lips barely moved. 'The money?'

If the unthinkable had been possible all those years ago, if Nora and Kwame had grown up together like the brother and sister they were, would they have echoed each other's words like this?

'The five hundred dollars each month,' Nora said. 'Fifteen hundred after a few years.'

It came to Kwame so slowly that Grace could almost see the words forming before he spoke them. 'My college. That's what paid for it.'

What was there to lose by telling him? 'Yes.'

'Tuition at Gilman?'

'Yes.'

'Moving Daddy and Mama' – he threw a glance at Penelope; for the rest of his life, *Mama* would now come with an asterisk – 'out of the city.'

'Yes.'

The next question came slowly.

'What'd he get for his money?'

The answer came from Penelope, the quaver suddenly gone from her voice.

'She kept her mouth shut, that's what. My father thought he was buying protection for me, so that nobody would ever know. But there's more to it than that, isn't there, Grace?'

She was a mess, hair coming out of its bun and hanging white and stringy around her face, mouth long since chewed free of lipstick. But spite firmed up her features, and Grace registered the malicious enjoyment she took in her next words.

'Hard for your brother to be the great black martyr when he sneaked away from the cause every chance he got to be with a white girl.'

FIFTY-TWO

Penelope knew that the First Families of Chateau would have viewed it as some sort of Mandingo scenario, she and Bobby lust-crazed by the mere proximity of flesh of a different hue. It wasn't like that.

She was an only child. Not even a sister, let alone a brother, so boys were alien. And the boys in school were hardly the best introduction, sworn enemies for the first few years, then all of a sudden the girls were supposed to turn around and like them, those same smelly creatures who had pulled their hair, called them names and punched their arms as they sprinted past. Then, seemingly a minute later, they were ogling the girls' chests, snapping bra straps and trying to grind up against them at school dances. And the girls were meant to enjoy that?

Bobby was different.

Penelope, thrown off her stride by the unfamiliar presence of a black boy her own age – how in the world was she supposed to act around him? – was relieved when he didn't even talk to her for the longest time. At most, he'd nod from his perch on the ladder when she went down to the river for a dip off the dock. The couple of times she'd gone to pool parties in town, the boys wolf-whistled at the sight of her in her new two-piece, but Bobby just went back to sliding his squeegee down a pane, flicking the excess water away at the last minute.

When he finally did talk to her, that day she came into the kitchen as Grace was murdering the dough for beaten biscuits, he teased her, but in a gentle way that was new to her, one that made her want to tease him back, just to see that slow smile spread across his face.

And that's all it was. She'd join him and Grace when they took their breaks, the three of them sitting sideways in the patio chairs, legs dangling over the wrought-iron arms, sucking on cherries and tossing the pits at each other. Even Grace would unbend a little, although she always played the big-sister role, treating Penelope and Bobby like troublesome younger siblings.

It could have gone on like that forever, except for the day Todd came by to take Penelope to Ocean City. She wasn't wild about Todd, but the other girls oohed and aahed over him as if he was God's gift to the distaff side of Chateau High. He was handsome in an almost-cartoonish way, all blond hair and jutting jaw, and shoulders that made you wonder why he chose baseball over football. The fact that he was a senior and Penelope was only a sophomore gave things even more cachet, despite the fact that he was dumber than the proverbial box of rocks.

Still, she had a boyfriend, something that seemed to be required in high school. A friend just laughed after Penelope told her about the time Todd offered her a ride home from school but pulled on to the marsh road to the Beach instead, stopping the car and turning to her all unzipped and a smile on his face as though the pale stalk emerging from his pants were a precious gift. 'They all do that,' her friend said.

Penelope slapped him that day and he promised never again, which is why she agreed to the Ocean City outing a few weeks later. But something happened before she and Todd left. She, Grace and Bobby were taking one of their breaks when Todd arrived. Penelope went upstairs to get ready, and when she came back down, their glasses lay in shards, glittering against the green of the patio's mossy bricks.

Grace looked at her wild-eyed, as though she hardly recognized her. Bobby's hands were clenched. His chest heaved. Kathleen Mavourneen paced a few yards away, whining softly, tail low, sure signs of agitation. Only Todd seemed unchanged. 'Let's go,' he said, grabbing Penelope's arm and steering her through the house and into his car before she could object, waving off her questions by accusing her of having an overactive imagination.

She didn't wait for the traditional mid-morning break the next day but confronted Grace in the kitchen as soon as she was sure her parents were gone. Grace was making beaten biscuits again, and this time there'd be no need for Bobby to urge more force. She walloped that dough so hard the whole counter shook. Penelope had to yell to make herself heard. 'Grace. Grace!'

She whirled to face Penelope with the rolling pin raised high. 'What you want?'

Penelope jumped back. She waited until Grace lowered her arm.

'I just wondered what happened yesterday.'

Grace's free hand strayed to her chest. 'Nothing.'

'On the patio. Something happened out there.'

'Oh, that. I dropped the tray.' She turned back to the dough.

'No. Something else. While I was upstairs.'

Grace dealt the dough a blow so vicious the rolling pin splintered, one end flying across the kitchen. She shoved the other, jagged-tipped, in Penelope's direction.

'Now look what you made me do. How am I going to finish these biscuits? Get out of my kitchen.'

Penelope got out.

For once, Bobby was not washing windows, though the ladder leaned against the wall at one of the guest rooms just past Penelope's bedroom. She wondered why he even bothered. Nobody ever stayed in those rooms, which dated to the days of horse and carriage, when previous Smythes threw fancy dress balls and the guests stayed over for days, the men hunting ducks at dawn, the ladies rowing sedately on the river at midday.

Of course, Bobby had no way of knowing that. His instructions were to wash windows and so he did, creating sparkling new views for Quail House's residents and visitors alike. Penelope checked the sheds, but they stood musty and empty. She did a slow circuit around the house, thinking to find him weeding one of the flowerbeds. But the peonies bobbed heavy-headed, undisturbed by anything but a breeze just strong enough to discourage all but the most bloodthirsty greenheads. She flicked a couple from the tender skin inside her elbow and continued her search.

She found him up on a stepstool, going after the boxwood with the hedge clippers, branches flying high from his energetic slashes, landing in heaps at his feet. Mindful of how Grace had turned on her with the rolling pin, she called out in plenty of time. 'Hey, Bobby.'

Even so, she found herself staring at the pointy ends of those blades, their gleaming surfaces smeared waxy green with vanquished leaves. He saw her looking and snapped them shut. He stepped down from the stool and set them aside.

'Hey, Penelope.' He wiped his brow. She wished she'd brought him something to drink.

'What happened here yesterday?'

'Here?' He looked around at the surrounding hedges, taller than their heads. 'These things grew another two inches, seems like.'

Penelope was tired of being treated as if she was stupid and said as much.

'Something happened out on the patio. When I was upstairs. And don't tell me it was nothing, the way your sister and Todd did.'

'Todd told you nothing happened? Yeah, I'll bet he did.'

She folded her arms and waited.

He sighed and looked away. 'Look. I honestly don't know. But something happened between Todd and Grace.'

'What do you think it was?'

'I think he put some kind of a move on her.'

'So?' She thought of Todd that day in the car, the way he grabbed her hand and tried to put it on him. She'd slapped him so hard it left a mark on his face and told him never to try anything like that again. And he hadn't.

'All she had to do was tell him to knock it off.'

He bestowed a look upon her, a hurtful mixture of pity and contempt. 'That might be all *you* have to do. But it's different for Grace.'

Even as he spoke, her mind went elsewhere. She should have been more upset at the thought of Todd going after Grace. But she wasn't, not at all. A twinge of relief shot through her at Bobby's words. She finally had an excuse to break up with Todd. It would be tricky to explain at school. But all she'd have to do is say, 'He'd rather be with another girl,' which would set off the sort of feeding frenzy that would sweep away any further questions.

She jerked her attention back to Bobby. 'What do you mean, it's different for Grace?'

Contempt overtook pity. 'She's supposed to tell a white boy to knock it off?'

Penelope's hands went to her hips.

'Yes. Because things are different now.'

'What if I made a move on you? You think I'd get away with you just telling me to knock it off?'

Their eyes locked. Penelope's hands fell to her side.

'I wouldn't tell you to knock it off.'

As soon as Penelope said it, she knew the truth of it. She saw the surprise and doubt in Bobby's eyes.

His kiss started angry, plenty of 'Oh, yeah?' in it, and then turned soft and sweet, and went on and on, her arms sliding around him and his around her, and that's how it began.

FIFTY-THREE

The keys lay in the middle of the table where Kwame had thrown them.

'I need some air. I'm gonna walk home. Grace, you can take the car.'

He crashed out of the house before any of them could stop him.

Penelope's lips thinned and stretched in a smile. 'Happy now, Grace?'

Grace sat so still Nora wondered if she was even breathing.

Penelope patted her hair back into some semblance of order.

'Mother, Grace, please. Can't we leave the past behind? It was all so long ago. I've just found out I have a brother. All I want to do is get to know him better.'

If Nora had thought to placate her mother and Grace – who was what, exactly, to her now? If Kwame was her brother, did that make Grace a sort of aunt? – she'd thought wrong.

'Why would he want to get to know you? You covered up for the cop who killed his son.'

'I turned in the phone as soon as I found it!'

Grace snorted.

Nora's next protest lacked the vigor of the first.

'And Alden's been charged. It's not at all like that other case.' Too late, she realized she'd tossed the focus back on her mother.

'You're right,' Grace said. 'Bobby's killer was never found. But he could be. Your mother knows what happened that night. Don't you?'

Penelope lifted her hands, palms up. 'No one knows what happened that night.'

The wind rose again, the window screens no impediment as it swept through the room, the temperature dropping by the moment. Rain chased it, fat drops splashing through the screens on to the counter.

'That's not true. The person who shot him knows. And your father knew. He protected him, didn't he? That's why Todd Burris – excuse me, *Mayor* Burris – is walking around owning the biggest car dealership in the county instead of rotting in a prison cell.'

'Todd didn't do it.' Penelope spoke with such finality that Grace blinked.

'If he didn't, who did?'

Penelope shook her head, silently underscoring the fact that she had no intention of telling.

Nora rose to close the windows, happy for something to do, anywhere to look other than at those two faces, one serene, the other contorted in fury.

'What's the point in holding back now? Did your father kill him? Find out that you'd taken up with him when he came back, no way to send you away and hide another black baby if you got pregnant again?'

'My father didn't kill anyone!'

Rain lashed the windows with a volley of sharp retorts.

Grace's voice dropped nearly to a whisper, so loaded with menace that Nora shivered.

'If he didn't, then who did?'

Nora knew her mother well enough to see her hastily restored façade cracking, lips quivering, fingers knitted tight together.

'*Who did?*'

Grace was on her feet and at Penelope's throat so quickly Nora didn't have time to stop her.

She lunged across the table, grabbing at Grace, surprised at the strength in the elderly woman's arms, ropy muscles gone taut beneath loose skin. She was screaming and Penelope was screaming and Grace was, too. 'Tell me! Tell me!'

The dog scrambled to his feet, nails scratching and sliding on the floor. The cat fled for safety, leaping to the sideboard, colliding with the silver tea service. The coffeepot crashed to the floor, its lid popping open, something falling out with a clatter.

All three women froze, Grace with her hands still at Penelope's throat, Nora clinging to Grace's arm, Penelope's eyes wide, fastened in terror and resignation on the small pistol spinning across the kitchen floor.

Nora knew right away.

All those years ago. She'd been, what? Ten, twelve, maybe. Down near the river with her grandfather, squinting at the Mason jar atop a hay bale. Her grandfather's gentle, patient instructions.

'You never take off the safety until you're ready. Ready? Good. Wrap your hand around the slide and pull it back. Hold it with both hands when you aim it. Line up your target with that little sight on the end of the barrel. Breathe in. Breathe out. Don't jerk the trigger, just a steady pull . . . now.'

Nora squeezed. Nothing happened. She squeezed harder. Still nothing. She yanked. The gun bucked in her hands, the movement startling her more than its retort, and she tumbled backward, her shot going wild, leaving the Mason jar unscathed but scaring the hell out of an audience of jeering crows.

She blinked tears from her eyes as the crows soared and wheeled, returning to the trees with a final volley of aggrieved squawks.

'It gets easier. Your mother picked it up pretty quickly. Come back to the house. I'll show you something. I got it for your mother when she turned twelve.'

Nora had expected something small and elegant, pearl-handled with some decorative engraving, the kind of thing a woman might hitch up her skirt, pull from a garter and smile as she saw the realization spreading slowly across a bad guy's face.

The velvet-lined rosewood case her grandfather set before her only strengthened her anticipation. But there was nothing beautiful about the thing that lay inside, unless deadly efficiency counted as beauty. It was black and stubby, so small it nearly disappeared within her grandfather's knobbed hand as he offered it to her. She took it cautiously, careful to point it away from either of them, surprised at the solid weight warming against her palm.

'It's a Baby Browning.'

'What's it for? It's so tiny.'

'That it is. It'll fit inside a handbag, or a coat pocket. Self-defense, mostly, and it's not even very good for that. You have to be close, almost too close, and shoot straight. Here's the thing about a gun. Sometimes, just the sight of one is enough to stop somebody. And that's what you want. You don't ever want to shoot unless you absolutely have to. You kill someone, even someone who's trying to kill you, it stays with you the rest of your life.'

Had he been speaking from experience? If her grandfather had shot someone while on duty, she'd have heard about it. But what about when he was off duty? At night, in a secluded spot along the river?

She saw the same thought come to Grace.

'This is it, isn't it? The gun that killed him? The one they said they never found. It's been here all these years?'

Penelope nodded.

'And your father killed him?'

The storm lashed the house with increasing fury, rain drumming so loud Grace had to raise her voice.

Nora strained to hear Penelope's answer.
Her mother's lips pursed, forming the single syllable.
'No.'

FIFTY-FOUR

1967

They were so young. So stupid.

Truly, though, is any stupidity more blissful than first love? Don't people spend the rest of their lives willing to trade every single thing away for just a few more moments of that same unthinking stupidity?

Because that's what Penelope did when she heard Bobby Evans was back in Chateau.

Her parents must have known. The *Chateau Crier* disappeared from the house. 'Their circulation department is having some sort of problem. It should start up again in a few days,' her mother said, when she looked for it one morning to read the comics.

Rather than tuning in to a station that featured news and weather on the half-hour, her mother switched to one that played classical music all day and night. When Penelope accused her of trying to drive her crazy, her mother retorted that it was never too late for Penelope to improve her mind.

And, where her parents always watched the local news and Walter Cronkite at night, they found a sudden enthusiasm for bridge after dinner, rushing through the meal and setting up in the library, where there was no television to tempt everyone. Penelope's husband gamely went along, doing his best to adjust to yet another bewildering circumstance foisted upon him in this new place.

Hiram was a good man, and Penelope loved him in the grateful way you love someone who pulls you from quicksand, oblivious to the fact that some indefinable part of you remained trapped just below that heaving, sucking surface. That part of her might have stayed submerged forever and she might even, over time, have fallen truly and deeply in love with Hiram or at least settled into the sort of bland contentment expected of her, but for a surprise visit from Jayne and Alice, two former schoolmates at Chateau High and, like her, newly married.

At least, they billed it as a surprise. In retrospect, it occurred to Penelope that they cooked it up as an antidote to their own bland, contented lives.

In high school they'd been part of a group of older girls whose circle had widened to include Penelope by dint of her relationship with Todd, admittance abruptly withdrawn as soon as she and Todd broke up. She didn't care, of course, so deeply immersed she was by then in the fizzy Champagne haze of love and sex.

Now, even though they were well past the intrigues and rigid judgments of high school and into their new lives as young matrons, the old insecurities rose up as Penelope led them to the patio, carrying a tray of coffee and lemonade to accompany the meringue kisses that were Jayne's ostensible reason for stopping by.

'I picked up Alice on the way and said, "You know what? It's just been ages since we've seen Penelope." You two can be my test subjects,' she simpered. 'I want to include these meringues in the Newcomers Club baskets. How are they? Too dry? Too sticky?'

Perfection, Penelope assured her, even as she surreptitiously tried with her tongue to dislodge stray bits from her molars, where they'd settled like glue.

Alice gazed toward the river. 'It's so peaceful out here, Penelope. You're lucky to be far away from everything that's going on in town.'

Penelope shoved her tongue hard against a tooth, popping the meringue loose, and swallowed quickly. 'What's happening in town?'

They turned to her, eyes large and round and innocent. Which should have been her clue.

'Don't you know?' A look passed between them. Penelope quickly flicked the remaining meringue on her plate into the boxwood, praying the blue jay swooping toward it wouldn't drag it back into view.

'Mother and I were supposed to run some errands yesterday, but she wasn't feeling well and Father insisted upon doing them for her, so I just stayed home. What did I miss?'

'Well!' They leaned forward with the avid, hungry expressions the meringues should have provoked. 'The whole town is full of colored people down from Baltimore. They're doing those civil rights marches, trying to make out Chateau is some place like Alabama or Mississippi. Can you imagine?'

At one time, Penelope couldn't have. But she'd paid the price, hustled out of town to the home of a relative she'd never heard of – in Arkansas, of all places – and then to private school in New England; the idea that black flesh had touched hers, not just touched but entered it and left a black baby inside her white body, apparently so abhorrent that nothing but banishment sufficed, leaving her to figure out for herself that childless and married was the only safe way to return.

So she offered an all-purpose 'Mmm' and forced herself to reach for another awful meringue.

'And you won't believe what else! The person who's stirring up all the trouble? Someone who's from here. Bobby Evans. Do you remember him? Didn't he used to work for your family?'

And there it was, the thing she'd been expecting ever since she'd come home, a knife slipped between her ribs so skillfully she didn't feel it until it was already carving into her heart.

She looked into their hard, bright eyes and wondered how long they'd waited for this chance; how they'd put it together. Although it didn't take a genius. A white girl leaves town the same time as the black family whose children – one of them a boy her own age – had worked in her home. *Something* had happened, and it didn't take too much imagination to guess what. Which didn't stop them from trying to shake the truth loose with a swift and efficient thuggery barely masked by careful makeup and flowered summer dresses.

Penelope scrunched up her face as though she were thinking. 'Has to be the same guy. Grace had a brother who did some yard work for us. But they moved away a long time ago.'

Jayne's turn. 'I guess she's back, too. Both of them, right in the thick of it. Nobody feels safe going downtown. That's why we came out here today. So happy to find you at home.'

Her eyes fastened on Penelope's face, a cat ready to pounce at the slightest sign of a twitch. 'Sure you don't remember him? We saw him – Alice thinks he's really handsome. Says if I hadn't been there to hold her back, she might've thrown herself at him.'

'Jayne!' Alice shrieked and batted at her. 'I would never!'

'You sure? What about you, Penelope? Would you throw yourself at a colored boy?'

Two could play this game – especially when one's future depended upon it.

'Why, Jayne. You're talking crazy. Did you sneak something into the lemonade? Alice, check her purse. Dollars to doughnuts there's a flask in there.'

Alice hacked up a dutiful laugh and made a halfhearted reach for Jayne's bag. The moment passed. But Penelope felt Jayne's eyes on her for the rest of the too-long visit. Cold. Assessing. And – almost – knowing.

Getting downtown alone was almost impossible. Her father and Hiram went to work every day, of course, but her mother found excuses not to go to any of her lunches or clubs, and took to popping in on Penelope at odd moments – when she was getting dressed, or eating lunch on the patio, or even taking a swim in the river – as though to reassure herself Penelope hadn't somehow slipped away.

She escaped in the most cartoonish way, wandering downstairs to breakfast one morning after her father and Hiram had already left, and flinching away from her mother's offer of tea and French toast. 'I don't feel well. My stomach's really upset. I'm going to go back to bed and try and sleep it off.'

She caught the flash of delight across her mother's face before she turned and made her way upstairs, to the bed she'd convincingly – she hoped – stuffed with clothes in the approximate shape of her slumbering form. Her mother probably thought she was pregnant again, the best insurance policy against the possibility of more foolish, reputation-destroying behavior. The speed with which Philippa left the house told Penelope she was as sick of watching her daughter as Penelope was of being watched. Penelope gave her a fifteen-minute head start, then pedaled to town on her childhood bicycle, praying the tires she'd hastily pumped full of air wouldn't go flat again before she got there.

She wasn't sure what to expect. Shouting crowds? Snarling police dogs struggling to pull free of thick leather leashes? Broken windows?

A small crowd clogged the sidewalk, but nobody was shouting. She sidled through them until she had a view of Commerce Street and the row of black people, five across, walking up the middle. The row in front held a wide banner that rippled with their steps, the words briefly obscured and then unfurling: *End Segregation Now*.

A lone voice rose: 'What do we want?'

Dozens replied: 'Equal treatment!'

'When do we want it?'

'Now!'

Somewhere sniggered deep within the group of white onlookers: 'What do we want?'

The answer came sotto voce: 'A rope and a tree.'

'When do we want it?'

'As fast as can be.'

But she barely heard the vile words. It had been four years. She'd birthed a brown baby boy she'd clutched to her chest for only a few moments before he was wrested away by a nurse who didn't even bother to hide her disgust. Married a man by convincing him that eloping would be a grand adventure. Returned to Chateau with her head held high, daring anybody to make anything of it. Nineteen years old and she thought she was steel amid marshmallows, tempered by more trouble than some people saw in a lifetime. She didn't even know exactly what she wanted when she pedaled to town that day. Some sort of closure, a word that had yet to come into vogue, but that made sense in retrospect.

But as soon as she saw Bobby, she knew. She wanted *him*.

He marched in the front row, leading the chant, punctuating each 'Now!' with a jubilant raised fist, a broad smile on his face and a bounce in his step, looking as happy as she'd ever seen him. Her heart cracked. He'd *moved on*, as they say now. Found his life's work. The young women marching with him, features alight – had he found a new love with one of them?

'Goodbye, Bobby,' she whispered. She rubbed tears from her eyes. Took one last look.

His gaze caught hers. His eyes widened. He stumbled. Shook his head in response to something the person next to him said, and then looked her way again. Mouthed two words. Then another.

Her knees buckled.

Someone nearby caught her. Voices came from far away.

'Miss. Are you all right?'

'She fainted.'

'No wonder. She shouldn't have to see something like this.'

She struggled to free herself, desperate to nod toward Bobby before he passed.

'I'm fine,' she said, 'It's just the heat. I'm fine.'

'You should go home,' someone said. 'This is no place for a young lady.'

'You're right. I'm going.'

But she turned for a last look, the marchers moving away, and as she pedaled home, she punched the air with the same sense of anticipatory triumph they'd displayed, the silent words Bobby had directed her way like a shout in her heart:

'The Beach. Tonight.'

FIFTY-FIVE

The gun spun in ever-slower revolutions, coming to a stop in the middle of the kitchen.

'That's it.' Grace looked at Penelope. 'Isn't it?'

All those years. All those places she'd looked. Inside every single book in the library fat enough to have concealed even a gun as little as this one, expecting with every new volume to find it hollowed out inside to conceal the weapon that killed her brother.

Every dresser and nightstand and desk and file drawer. Cupboards, closets, crawlspaces, the inner recesses of the grandfather clock. She'd dipped her hand into bins of flour and sugar and birdseed, removed the lids from toilet tanks, even slit a seam of Kathleen Mavourneen's dog bed and felt amid the stuffing for a hard metallic object. And spent far too many moments at the end of the dock, staring at the hypnotic current, imagining the soft muck beneath where she figured the gun almost certainly lay, sinking incrementally deeper year by year, snails and other bottom-dwelling creatures attaching themselves to it as they would any innocuous rock or bit of jetsam.

But the one place she'd never looked was the goddamned silver tea service and its never-used coffeepot, so foolishly proud she was of her refusal to polish it.

Penelope took a step toward the gun. Grace hustled past her, but Nora was quicker, kicking it away and then leaping upon it, snatching it up and backing away, breathing heavily.

No one spoke or moved. The rain slackened, the storm's fury abating, the sky slowly lightening. Just moments earlier, it had been so dark Grace would not have been surprised to hear the grandfather clock chime midnight.

'That's mine.' She held out her hand, mentally compelling Nora to deliver it.

'Actually, it's mine.' Penelope's voice held both command and rebuke.

'It's evidence. Nora, give me the gun.'

'I'll turn it over to the Attorney General's Office. Just like I did with the phone.'

Penelope gasped. 'But Nora!'

Nora gripped the gun tight in both hands, holding it away from her as though afraid it might somehow go off and destroy yet another member of this strange, knit-together family. The dog stood stiff-legged beside her, a low growl starting.

'The phone, that was different. Your mother knows why. Don't you, Penelope.' Grace didn't make it a question. She didn't need to. Penelope knew.

'Nora.' Pleading now.

'What is it, Mother?'

Fifty years since her brother's murder. Grace was out of patience.

'That gun in your hand? It's what'll let the whole town know your grandfather shot my brother in cold blood. Isn't that right, Penelope?'

She'd denied it before. She didn't this time. Just lifted her chin and stared off into space as though facing some long-awaited reckoning and spoke.

FIFTY-SIX

1967

Penelope was in a state the rest of the day after seeing Bobby at the march.

She managed to get home before her mother returned,

shedding her clothes and climbing back into her nightgown so as to maintain her fiction of illness. Not a moment too soon – she heard her mother's car pull up as she finished changing. She kicked her clothes under the bed and climbed in. A few minutes later, her mother stood framed within the bedroom door.

'You're awake.'

She took a couple of steps into the room, then came closer still. She brushed the hair away from Penelope's face and laid her wrist against her forehead.

'You're flushed. But you don't seem to have a fever. Is . . . your stomach still upset?'

Penelope noticed the hesitation. Her mother would have thought it crass to come right out and ask if she was pregnant.

'I'm fine.' Stronger and sharper than it should have been. Penelope slumped on the pillows and made her voice small. 'Sleep will help.' She closed her eyes in dismissal.

But of course she couldn't sleep. No wonder she was flushed. She was in a fever all day. Her brain buzzed with questions. The Beach – that same night. But what time? Midnight? Two a.m.? What if Todd and his friends were partying there? Then what? And how in the world was she going to creep out of bed without waking Hiram?

She could barely bring herself to be civil to him when he came home and rushed upstairs, radiating concern, stretching beside her on the bed despite her protestations that he might catch whatever had laid her low.

'I don't care, Bunny.' A nickname for her that, until that very moment, she'd found endearing and suddenly despised – almost as much as she despised herself for how she was about to betray him. 'I just want you to feel better.'

She spoke into his chest. 'Maybe it's best you sleep in the guest room tonight. I'd feel terrible if you were to get sick, too.' Oh, how easily the lies came back, honed those years earlier during her too-brief time with Bobby. Was it so wrong to want to steal just a few more hours?

Still, she feared facing her father. She pressed her ear to a floor grate when he came home and was relieved to hear her mother dissuade him from checking on her. 'Poor thing. Let her rest. I don't want to speak too soon, but it looks as though we might be grandparents!'

A long pause, both of them obviously considering the incongruity of her words – and all too aware of Hiram's presence.

'That will be lovely,' he said finally.

But then after an entire day on high alert, nerves twanging almost audibly, her body aflame with anticipation, Penelope actually dozed off as the house fell silent, her parents gone to bed and Hiram retreating to the guest room after tiptoeing in to retrieve his pillow and pajamas.

She awoke with a hand over her mouth and a voice in her ear.

'Don't say a word. Or they'll kill us both.'

'Bobby!'

His hand went back over her mouth. She nodded understanding and tried again. 'Bobby,' she breathed, his name sweet on her lips. 'What are you doing here? How did you get in?'

His shoulders shook with laughter. 'How many weeks did I spend up on a ladder at all of these windows?'

She went shivery as his lips moved at her ear. 'I started to go to the Beach, but there were cars on the marsh road. So I came here. Was afraid you'd already be in the boat. So glad to find you here—'

She cut him off. 'Not as glad as I am,' and those were the last words they spoke for quite a while.

Later, they lay whispering, something she'd always loved, their conversations about anything and everything, falling back into the old easy habits. Even so, her voice shook as she finally asked the question she'd buried for all those years. 'How is . . .?'

'Beautiful. Smart and strong and funny. You'd be so proud. Hey. Hey. Are you crying?'

She was, her tears a hot, bittersweet mixture of joy and regret. He kissed them away, covering her cheeks, and then his lips found hers again. Earlier they'd fallen on each other with the famished, pent-up passion of four years, but this was slow, unbearably sweet. They teased each other, murmured words of love, lost themselves in one another, single-mindedly pushing reality away.

Bobby called it back.

'We can do this, you know.'

'Yes, we can.' Penelope stretched and smiled, luxuriating in the mischief of even mildly naughty wordplay, something she was sure would have shocked her staid husband. 'We're pretty good at it.'

'Yes, we are. But that's not what I meant.'

She'd been drifting toward sleep – dangerous, she knew, but irresistible. 'What did you mean?' she mumbled, her words barely intelligible even to herself.

'We can be together now. Things are changing.'

Her eyes flew open. She stared into the room's blackness. 'What do you mean, be together?' She took a hopeful guess. 'How long are you going to be in town? Can we be together again?'

'A few more days. And yes, we can be together again. But not just while I'm in town. Forever.'

She sat up. 'Forever?'

His hand again, over her mouth. 'The world's changed. It'll still be hard, for both of us. My family won't like it any more than yours. But we can leave. Get out of this little slice of Dixie and go someplace like New York, where nobody knows us and nobody cares. Take him with us. Be a real family.'

He was the Bobby she remembered, spinning dreams out of whole cloth, no more realistic now than they were when they were first together.

'Our families won't just dislike it. Don't you remember how they were before?' Her father's white-lipped fury, the humiliation and fear on Gerald Evans's face when her father summoned him to Quail House to spell out exactly what was going to happen, and the fate that would befall the entire Evans family if even a whisper got around.

'We were kids then. We can make our own decisions now. They don't have any legal say over us anymore.'

He was serious. He was *serious*.

The good feeling leached from her body, chased by self-pity. Couldn't they have had this one wonderful night? Why did he have to go and ruin things?

'Speaking of legal – have you forgotten I'm married?'

He actually laughed, that silent shoulder-shake again, flash of teeth in the moonlight. 'Have you forgotten divorce is legal? Look, I know it'll take a while to get everything straightened out. But I'll be waiting for you. And so will our son.'

She spoke very slowly and carefully.

'Bobby. I can't get divorced.'

His voice lost some of his lightness. 'Wait – are you Catholic?

Somehow I always thought you were Methodist, like everybody else around here. I guess we'll just have to live in sin.' Struggling now to fend off reality, just as she had been a few moments earlier.

Before, their parents had torn them apart. Now she had to do it herself. And she had to do it fast. How long had he been in her room? Not just *her* room – the room that on every other night she shared with her husband.

'No. I can't do it because . . . because I just can't. Also, it's getting late.' She shifted on the bed, hoping to stir him into movement.

He didn't take the hint.

'You just . . . can't.' His mimicry like a slap.

She tried for the right mix of sorrow and decisiveness. 'No. I can't.'

'Why, Penelope? Why can't you?' He wasn't going to let her off the hook.

'Bobby, you of all people know why.' She put her arms around him but he shook her off.

'I, of all people,' he mused. 'You're right. I do know why. But I'm willing to brave it. I thought you were, too.'

She didn't know she was crying until the tears pattered against the sheets. 'I'm not brave like you.'

'Oh, yes, you are.'

She raised her head, hopeful. He was going to make it easy, after all.

'Big, brave white girl. Not scared to sleep with the black boy. As long as nobody – 'specially nobody white – never, ever finds out about it. Fuck him and then kick him to the curb and go on her merry way.'

'Stop it! It's not like that.'

He wouldn't stop. 'It's not? Prove it.'

He was on his feet and so was she. They faced each other across the expanse of the rumpled bed.

'I just did.' She gestured toward the bed. 'What we have – it's special.'

'So special it's a secret best kept.'

She leapt at the lifeline he'd thrown her. 'Yes! Yes!'

He hissed his reply. 'Well, I'm done keeping secrets. From your people and from mine. You think it'll be any easier on me than it will on you? But I'm willing to stand up for us. Shout it to the world. Trust me, Penelope – it'll be such a relief once it's out there.'

Was it a plea or a threat? Or the bravado of a young man who'd spent the last week fighting for a universal cause and was now prepared to take the battle on behalf of his own personal cause?

She had to be sure.

'Shout it to the world? It's just an expression, right?' She attempted a laugh.

'Watch me! I'll lead the march tomorrow.' He struck a pose. 'What do I want? Penelope! When do I want her? Now!'

The words ominous when spoken in a whisper.

He came around the end of the bed and took her in his arms. 'It'll be all right. You'll see.'

'No. It won't. You can't do this.'

His arms tightened. 'Watch me.'

She wrestled free. 'Don't.'

His arms fell to his side. He backed away, toward the window.

'We have a son, Penelope. We have a son.'

'Don't leave like this.' She'd raised her voice.

Down the hall, a door banged. A voice called her name. Hiram.

'Bobby! Hurry. You've got to get out of here.'

But he didn't move. 'Is that your husband? Good. We can settle this now.'

Footsteps, approaching. 'Penelope? Penelope? Are you all right?'

'Bobby.' She willed him out the window. Instead, he reached for the light. Switched it on. Stood shirtless in the middle of the room, eyes shining as he faced the door with the mixture of resolve and anticipation she'd seen when he marched up Commerce Street in the middle of the day to the jeers and disdain of dozens of white people.

Hiram's footsteps halted outside the door. 'Penelope?' Courteous as always, not barging in the way anyone else would have.

It was too late.

Bobby opened his mouth to speak.

She flipped up the lid of the rosewood box on her nightstand, movements automatic.

Ease down the safety.

Rack the slide.

Squeeze.

FIFTY-SEVEN

'Come. I'll show you.'

Penelope's command dragged Nora from the dark place into which she'd fallen as her mother spoke, a slow-motion tumble past images her mind refused to accept. Her mother, a gun in her hand. A man collapsing even as another burst into the room.

'We told him it was a burglary,' Penelope said as Nora and Grace, stunned and silent, followed her up the stairs. 'My parents, of course, understood what was going on. My father was able to convince Hiram that it would be better for all concerned if it was kept quiet – which, as Chief of Police, he was able to do. "Chateau is already a tinderbox," Father said. "What with everything happening in town, we'd set off a panic if people knew a black man had broken into a white woman's bedroom."'

'The town blew up anyway,' Grace reminded her.

Penelope looked over her shoulder. 'Yes, it did.' As calmly as if she'd said, 'Yes, it's raining.'

She pushed open the bedroom door – the room where Nora had slept nearly every night since her arrival – and, again, Nora saw the scene play out in her mind. Grace must have had the same thoughts.

'Where?' she asked.

Penelope flipped back a corner of the rug with her toe to reveal the damning stain beneath, dark and irregular, spreading across the wide floorboards as it must have that night when Bobby's lifeblood leaked away.

'We scrubbed and scrubbed but couldn't get it out. Father even refinished the floor, but he couldn't sand it away. It had sunk in too deep, and, of course, we didn't dare call someone to replace the floor.'

'Of course not.'

Nora wondered if Grace's dry responses were a way of keeping the horror at bay. But Grace's next utterance indicated she had every intention of drawing it nearer still.

'Where was the gun?'

'Why, in its box on my nightstand, where it always was. I still have it. Would you like to see it?' You'd have thought she was a tour guide in a museum.

'Yes. I would.'

Nora didn't want to see it. Didn't want to see or hear anything else that made it more impossible by the moment to deny the fact that her mother had killed a man. And not in self-defense, a burglar perhaps intent upon a far more heinous crime, as her father had been led to believe, but because he was about to *embarrass* her.

She bent double, gagging, and straightened to see Grace's eyes upon her, cold and steady. *If I can take it, so can you*, they said.

Back down the stairs, the dog trailing, the cat disappeared to who knows where.

Penelope opened her bedroom door and stood aside. Nora followed Grace halfway into the room, watching as she lifted the lid to the box by the bed. A litter of jewelry lay within, earrings, a tangle of necklaces, a few bracelets, costume pieces that she wore for daytime.

'I looked in there.' Grace's voice had lost its hard edge, rising in protest. 'But I looked there!'

'Look again.'

Grace started to lift out the jewelry piece by piece, then upended the box, its contents scattering across the table and on to the floor. She turned it so that Nora could see the gun-shaped recess within. 'Useless,' she snapped. 'It wouldn't have been proof, not without the gun.'

'Which was in the coffeepot.' A look of sly satisfaction crossed Penelope's face. 'You never touched the tea service. And we certainly never used the coffeepot. Not even Nora.' A bit of bewilderment in those last words, incomprehension that someone would scorn the extra moments of preparation to pour their coffee from the elegant silver vessel with the swooping Smythe monogram, rather than a pedestrian glass pot.

Grace ran her fingers around the worn velvet depression inside the box, evidently reconsidering. 'Maybe not completely useless. It would have shown a gun was missing from this house. Maybe even the type of gun. I would have known.'

'You would have guessed,' Penelope corrected her.

'I would have guessed right.'

'Yes.'

The gun in question hung in Nora's hand. It was so small, yet so heavy.

Grace held the box out to Nora. 'Here. You can put it back where it belongs. Hand it over to the police in a nice, pretty package.'

Nora took it and backed away. It was one thing to give up her grandfather, a man long dead, as Bobby's killer. But her mother?

'She could end up in prison. The press will crucify her,' she protested.

'She should. And they should.'

And still Penelope gazed off into the distance, as though politely waiting for Grace and Nora to finish a discussion about the weather.

'She's seventy years old!'

'That's about fifty more years than my brother got.'

Nora imagined Grace speaking those same words before judge and jury. The effect they would have.

She tried again. 'She's had to live every one of those years knowing what she did.'

Grace gave a long, ostentatious look around the room, its four-poster bed and crocheted canopy, the skirted vanity with its crystal perfume bottles and monogrammed silver-backed brushes, the brocade fainting couch across the room, the bathroom door open just enough to reveal the marble tub, the separate shower, the toilet and exotic bidet.

'I'm just guessing,' she drawled, 'that a cell is about the size of that bathroom there. She should feel right at home. You just hang on to that gun. I'm calling the Attorney General's Office first thing in the morning. Gun or no gun, they'll want to talk with you. And with her.' She lifted her chin toward Penelope.

Nora made a final supplication.

'Grace, please. You know what happened now. Isn't that enough?'

Grace opened her mouth to reply, but Penelope answered the question first.

'No. It's not.'

Grace left without the gun, wheeling on her heel and slamming the heavy front door – the one she'd only used once before – so hard the frame shook.

'I told you that you should have left.'

Nora and Penelope stood in the hallway, watching Grace drive away, the view warped by the thick, wavy glass in the long windows beside the door.

'The rain's stopped,' Nora said pointlessly. As she spoke, sunlight poured through a break in the clouds, spilling across the lawn toward Electra, setting her aluminum surface agleam.

'The body shop did a good job.' She couldn't seem to stop talking about meaningless things.

Penelope turned back toward the kitchen.

'Yes, he did. After all the work I put into it.'

'What?' Nora hurried to catch up with her.

'Sit,' Penelope commanded. 'I'll get you a sweater.'

Nora sat, shivering. The storm had dropped the temperature a good ten degrees, maybe even twenty. With the heat finally broken, Nora found herself wishing its return, missing the way the syrupy humidity slowed things down, softened them. Now everything seemed hard and cold.

Penelope returned with a light mohair sweater, draping it around Nora's shoulders. She put water on to boil and retrieved the silver teapot, stepping around the companion coffeepot on the floor, untouched since it had given up the gun that effectively indicted her.

'What do you mean,' Nora asked, 'about all the work you put into it?'

Penelope studied the tins of tea on a narrow shelf beside the stove. 'Herbal, I think. We could all stand to calm down.' Even though there were only two of them now.

She measured leaves into the pot. Nora smelled mint, an old childhood remedy when her stomach was upset. Penelope turned to her.

'I painted it.'

Nora shook her head. She'd heard one too many unbelievable things on this day. 'Painted what?'

A watercolor, she willed Penelope to say. An old chair that needed brightening. An accent wall in the bathroom.

'Your trailer, of course. I thought it might convince you to leave.'

Left unspoken. *And if you had, none of this would have happened.*

Nora tried to imagine her tiny mother, clumsy in her boot, clambering on to a stepladder, a bucket and brush in one hand, to splash the scarlet words across Electra's pristine surface.

'When?'

'That part was easy.' Penelope poured the tea in cups and limped to the table. 'You were always running off to town. I had plenty of time.'

The day she'd delivered the cake to Grace. Plenty of time, indeed.

Nora sipped her tea, nearly choking on a sudden thought. 'Mother!' She took what she'd hoped would be a steadying gulp of her tea, instead succeeded in burning her mouth. She touched her tongue to her lower lip. 'The day the trailer came loose. You didn't – of course you didn't. You couldn't possibly.'

Penelope's lips quirked. 'Oh, couldn't I?'

When Nora gaped, she explained. 'You left your checklist on the kitchen counter. It was so easy. I just followed the instructions in reverse. It wasn't that hard – although those safety chains were terribly heavy. I unhooked them and looped them back into place so they still looked as though they were fastened. The same with that skinny wire.'

'The breakaway cord.'

'Is that what it's called? And I took out the pin in the hitch.'

'My God, Mother. You almost got yourself killed. And even if it hadn't come off when it did, it could have killed someone else.'

Penelope poured more tea. 'That wasn't part of the plan. I thought it would come off somewhere toward the end of the lane. If I'd known you were heading to town so soon, I'd have postponed my walk. I thought if the graffiti didn't scare you away from here, this surely would.'

She took her daughter's hand in her thin, age-spotted ones. For the first time that day, tears shone in her eyes.

'Oh, Nora. Why did you have to ask so many questions?'

FIFTY-EIGHT

Nora slept in Electra that night.

She couldn't imagine ever sleeping in her childhood bedroom again, although Electra left her nearly as uneasy as she lay there imagining her mother stroking a red-dipped paintbrush down its side or fumbling to unhitch it.

The gun slept beside her, nestled in the soft velvet embrace of its case, rather than the cold interior of the sterling coffeepot.

She could throw it away. Open the box, lift it from within, follow the path of moonlight across the lawn and on to the dock, row the boat downriver toward the Beach and let it fall into the water somewhere along the way. Why on earth hadn't her grandfather or even her mother done that? If Penelope was capable of unhitching a trailer, lobbing a gun into the river's depths would have been the easiest thing in the world.

She hadn't told Nora and Grace what happened after the shooting, but it was easy enough to conjecture. Her grandfather, maybe with her father's help, had carried Bobby's body from the house to the boat, and then dumped it at the Beach, where it would give a terrible fright to a man just hoping to pull a couple of perch from the river before breakfast, bring them home to his wife to clean and dredge in cornmeal and fry next to his eggs. Instead, he was met with Bobby's lifeless, accusing gaze, his body half in, half out of the water, head nodding gently with the current, the hole in his forehead washed neat and clean.

And then they all – her grandfather and grandmother, her father and, most of all, her mother – had gone about their lives without ever mentioning it again. Her grandfather had spent the next hellish weeks immersed in working with the National Guard to control the riots that followed Bobby's killing, and to keep the town from erupting again once the protesters' initial fury had abated.

Her grandmother would have slipped back into her First Families social set when Chateau finally returned to stultifying rhythms, the events of past weeks discussed only in the vaguest generalities, with a combined sense of dismay and airy relief that things were back to normal.

Her father would have gotten up the next morning and gone to his job as plant manager at Smythe's Best Backfin, and every weekday morning thereafter, his drinking steadily increasing over the years until his liver became a scarred, petrified thing and his skin and eyes turned yellow, his stomach and ankles swelling to grotesquerie, and he died as quietly as he had lived.

And her mother? Nora wondered at the iron strength of will that enabled her to trip gaily through the rest of her life, sharing her husband's bed – Nora herself the proof of that – even as every single day she came face to face with the woman who knew, or at least suspected, what she'd done.

Nora imagined the two of them, Grace and Penelope, locked in a sort of silent, mortal, decades-long combat, the unspoken subtext that ran between each sentence exchanged between them.

And now Grace was going to call the Attorney General's Office. Who, without the gun, would have only circumstantial evidence. Grace was right – the press would swarm yet again. Grace would probably make sure of that.

But lacking the hard evidence of a murder weapon, Grace's accusation could be framed as the rantings of a woman unhinged when her little brother lost his only son. Because as far as the wider world knew, Kwame remained Grace's brother, not her nephew. White Chateau would be only too pleased to imagine Grace as a vengeful villain.

But then, who wouldn't be vengeful? Nora thought that, for the rest of her life, she'd see Robert Evans's face, the sheepish smile, the apologetic shrug, just minutes before his death. She'd done the right thing by Robert – albeit belatedly – turning in the phone when she'd found it. Wasn't it enough to see Alden punished?

Did Bobby's face rise before her mother whenever she closed her eyes? Had her mother ever been tempted to do the right thing, after she'd done the very worst thing? She had to have known, when she'd taken Nora and Grace into the very room where she'd shot him, showed them where his blood had darkened the floor, that Grace would demand justice. But did justice have to come at the hands of her own daughter?

Nora took the gun from its case.

Walked it across the lawn.

Sat down on the dock and let her feet dangle in the water, just as she had that first time when Alden had rowed around the bend and pulled her into a legacy she hadn't realized was her own.

She watched the sun rise on a world washed clean by the previous night's rain, chevrons of geese honking overhead, the year-round flocks seeing their numbers grow daily as their cousins from Canada arrived.

Murph found her there, her joints gone stiff as his own during her long hours on the dock's unforgiving boards. He shoved his face against hers, giving her cheek a swipe with his tongue for good measure. She sent a couple of texts, put a hand on the dog's warm broad back and pushed herself to her feet and walked weeping back to her trailer.

Grace arrived well before Holiday and Satterline.

She and Nora sat on opposite sides of the front step, Nora in jeans – it was finally cool enough to wear them – and a T-shirt, Grace proper in a blue pin-tucked blouse, navy skirt, hose and pumps, the rosewood box in her lap, hands wrapped protectively around it. Could nothing crack the woman's composure?

'I want to let her sleep as long as possible. I'll wake her when I hear their car turn into the lane.'

Grace gave a brief nod, permitting this last bit of mercy.

Nora wondered if they'd arrest her mother on the spot. She tried to recall the legal details of her own brush with the law. Surely there'd be an investigation first? There'd be the indignity of the initial booking, the mug shot. Some hearings, maybe – red meat for the press. Bail, at some point. She'd have to put up Quail House as a guarantee. Unless, of course, a judge could be convinced that an elderly woman posed no threat to society and could be counted on to show up for all her court appearances.

Which is how it almost certainly would have gone years earlier. But now, Nora could imagine the justifiable outrage such a decision would provoke – a wealthy white woman given the kind of consideration never, ever shown to black murder suspects and precious few white ones. A few minutes' extra sleep seemed the least she could do.

Murph paced, whining. He'd been like that ever since she emerged from the trailer, where a shower and clean clothes had failed to restore her spirits. Every few minutes he climbed partway up the stairs, laid his head on her knee and stared urgently before resuming his pacing. The cat, who'd started all the trouble, was nowhere to be seen.

The minutes oozed past.

'Probably ran into traffic on Fifty,' Nora said. Anything to break the silence.

'In the middle of the week?'

Grace had a point. Beach traffic clogged the road on weekends, but most days it stretched straight and empty, an irresistible temptation to speeders.

A greenhead or two buzzed around them but bumbled away, as though knowing fall lurked. The sun rose higher, a friend after weeks of blazing enmity, lulling Nora – her nerves scraped raw after the events of the previous day and the sleepless night on the dock – into a half-doze.

Then, the car.

She jolted upright. Surely it was too soon.

Grace stood in a single fluid motion, the box now clutched to her chest. 'Get her.'

'Grace . . .'

There was still time. Grace was an elderly woman. She could snatch the box away, race to the river, do what she should have done the previous night.

The black car came into view.

Grace's words hit like hard-flung stones. 'Do you want them to take her away in her nightclothes?'

Nora pushed open the front door. Her steps echoed in the hallway, past the parlor, the kitchen, the dining room, the library and to her mother's bedroom at the back of the house, Murph shoving past her, leading the way, trotting now, casting anxious glances over his shoulder.

She stopped outside the bedroom. 'Mother?'

She tapped on the door. 'Mother?'

Murph gave her a disgusted look and nosed it open.

Penelope lay on her side, her back to Nora, a bony bare shoulder peeking from beneath the sheet. Nora tiptoed over, pulled up the shoulder strap of her mother's nightgown, and shook her gently. 'Mother. Wake up. There's something I need to tell you.'

Penelope fell over on to her back. Her eyes stared sightless at the ceiling.

Nora backed away. Her breath came harsh, drowning out the sound of three pairs of feet moving deliberately toward the room. Bodies moved like shadows around and past her, hovering over the bed.

A scream gouged the air, Grace's composure finally cracking with a long, drawn-out 'Noooooooo' that carried fifty years of pain and frustration and thwarted judgment.

FIFTY-NINE

Nora parked truck and trailer at the far end of Commerce Street, where there was space enough to accommodate them.

She lowered the truck's windows a few inches to give Murph some air and told Mooch, caterwauling in his plastic carrier, to knock it off. 'We've got a lot of miles ahead. You're just going to have to get used to it.'

She walked the few blocks to the coffee shop, back stiffened against the curious stares of passers-by.

Grace had been wrong in thinking Penelope had cheated everyone by checking out – even though Brittingham had assured Nora that the coroner would almost certainly rule the death as accidental.

'It's pretty clear that her heart just stopped,' he said. 'Given her age and everything she's been through recently, I'm not surprised. There's no note. I don't see any need for an autopsy.'

A few days after her death, Nora, Grace and Kwame all received registered letters from George Hathaway, the Smythe family attorney. Enclosed in each was another letter, sealed.

'Mrs Best wrote these letters some years ago and asked that they be delivered to you upon her passing along with a separate letter that she asked me to mail to the Attorney General's Office,' Hathaway wrote.

Nora's letter detailed an abbreviated version of the account she'd given Grace and Nora of Bobby's death. She also penned an apology to Grace and a longer one to Kwame, as she wrote in her letter to Nora.

I don't expect either of them to forgive me, or you either, for that matter. I only ask that you live your life unafraid, as I wish I had done.

The Attorney General's Office had released a short statement, to the effect that one Penelope Emmaline Smythe Best had confessed to the 1967 killing of Robert Gerald Evans, and that ballistics tests on a recently discovered Baby Browning gun bore out her account. Case closed.

Chateau, black and white alike, would feast for years on the story.

Nora would forever be the child of a murderer. But, unless the Evans family chose to reveal it, Bobby's liaison with a white girl, and Kwame's parentage, would remain a secret best kept.

Which is what Nora told her brother over coffee that morning.

'If you choose to tell, I'll corroborate it. And I'll add that, no matter how you feel about it, I'm happy to have a brother. Whether you want to see me again, or have anything to do with me at all, it's up to you. But you're the only family I've got now.'

She held her coffee cup in front of her face as she spoke, the steam rising between them, obscuring Kwame's face. She put it down, reminding herself one last time of the vow she'd made as she'd driven into Chateau the night Robert was killed. She was done running, done hiding from things.

She'd failed, badly, on that promise. But she could try again. Hence, her call to Grace, asking her to pass along a message to Kwame requesting this meeting. She'd been surprised when Grace agreed, more surprised still when he showed up.

'I don't know about us seeing each other again,' Kwame said. 'Might take me a while. A long while.'

She held the cup so tightly she was afraid it might crack within her grip. She let go of it and flexed her fingers. 'That's fair.'

'Our mother,' he said, as though testing out the notion.

'She kept a picture of you, you know. From the newspaper. I found it on her nightstand. I thought she'd just forgotten to throw away that day's paper. But there were photos of both you and your father with that story. And then, the day of the march in town, she was there. I thought I spotted her and told myself I was seeing things. But she'd said something to me about being able to drive, even with the boot on her leg. Now I realize she didn't want to miss a chance to see you in person.'

He lifted his own coffee cup and stared into it as though expecting answers to emerge.

'I don't mind telling you that I'm having a hard time dealing with all of this.' He set it down without drinking.

'Me, too.'

They shared a brief, rueful smile.

'I have something for you.' She put a fat envelope in front of him.

He regarded it as one might eyeball a snake charmer's basket, waiting for the cobra to raise its head, spread its hood, hiss a warning.

'What is it?'

'A deed to the house. It's in both your name and Grace's. I worked it out with Emerson Crothers and Mr Hathaway to make sure there won't be a tax penalty.'

He reared back as though a snake indeed had slithered from the envelope.

'I don't want it.'

She nudged it toward him. 'I don't blame you. Everything needs fixing. The bricks need pointing, the floors refinishing, and the rugs are worn through. Now that I'm taking the cat away, it'll probably be overrun with mice again within the week. Oh, and the river is eroding the bank, taking a little more of the lawn every year. At some point, it'll be lapping at the back patio.'

'When you put it that way, I can't imagine why you want to get rid of it.'

She guffawed and was gratified when, after a moment, he joined in. For a split second, they were two siblings, enjoying a laugh at their own expense.

'Mother would spin in her grave. Maybe. On the other hand, you're family. Better you than strangers. That said, you can always sell it. Em assures me he's got half a dozen clients in Washington who'll fight each other to pay way more than it's worth.'

'White people.' Kwame shook his head.

'Rich people,' she said.

'Same thing, usually.'

They sipped their coffee in silent contemplation of the gulf between them.

'Couldn't you just keep it and rent it out to those same rich people?' he asked after a time.

'Sure. But I'm never coming back here. That saying – "You can't go home again." I had to find out the hard way that it's true. It would have been, even if all this hadn't happened.'

But it was more than that, more even than the fact that a young man had bled out as her mother stood over him, gun in hand.

For her whole life, she'd listened to her mother spin fantasies about the women who'd once populated Quail House. It had never occurred to her that many of those women must have been slaves, washing and scrubbing and polishing the pretty things handed down through the generations, the things Penelope so cherished. The house and everything in it felt tainted.

After Penelope's body had been taken away, and Satterline and Holiday and the local police and coroner and even Grace had left, she'd wandered the rooms in the echoing silence, fingering the heavy, dusty drapes at the windows, the acres of book in the library, and wondered what it might be like to touch a match – several matches – to such ready fuel. Wasn't that how great houses that shield corruption are supposed to meet their end? Manderley ablaze; the madwoman on the ramparts of Thornfield, backlit by dancing flames.

Instead, she grabbed a few keepsakes – framed photos of her parents and grandparents and, after a moment's hesitation, the tea service – and fled to the safety of Electra before temptation could get the upper hand.

Kwame fingered the envelope. 'Where are you headed?'

I don't know.

She'd thought herself done running when she arrived in Chateau, returning to a ready-made home, taking the easy way out of her dilemma. Wherever she landed next, she'd have to make her own home.

'For now, I'm going back to Colorado. I got a call yesterday. They caught the woman who killed my ex. Her husband nearly killed me. There'll be a trial. They want me there for the court hearings.'

She'd imagined going through a similar scenario with her mother, with Grace and Kwame sitting in the courtroom, the judgment in their eyes far exceeding anything the legal system might administer.

Now she'd be the one demanding justice. She wondered if the woman – a longtime grifter who'd been calling herself Miranda Gardner when Nora met her – had a family who would come to her court appearances, let her know she wasn't alone in the world, that no matter how much damage she'd done on the worst day of her life, someone still loved her.

She rose from the table. 'Please tell Grace I said goodbye.'

That wry smile again. 'She'd probably say good riddance.'

Nora smiled back. 'She probably would.'

Kwame started to say something, then stopped.

'What is it?'

'She's got your cell number, right?'

Nora's heart leapt. 'Yes. But I can give it to you just in case.'

'I'd like that.'

She tiptoed out on to a limb.

'If you give me yours, I'll text it to you.'

She held her breath.

He recited a string of numbers. She punched them into her phone.

'Just in case we ever need to be in touch,' he said. 'About the house, or something.'

Or all the things our families never talked about.

They looked into each other's eyes. Penelope's eyes.

Maybe they'd see each other again someday. Maybe, on that day, she and her brother would hug.

On this day, Nora was just grateful for the handshake he offered.

Murphy's nose poked through the lowered window as she approached the truck. Right on cue, Mooch resumed yowling.

Driving the truck on its own, the trip to Denver would take a full three days. Hauling the trailer – and without the frantic, sleepless energy that had propelled her return to Chateau – it would take considerably longer.

She felt a moment's pang as she steered the truck past the outskirts of town, on to the highway, the cornfields spooling past, the arches of the Bay Bridge rising before her, leading her up and out of the Eastern Shore, back on to the mainland and west toward the unknown. Again.

Which, given what now constituted her known world, was newly attractive.

There'd been a second letter – just a note, really. It fell to her lap when she lowered the truck's sun visor on her first drive to town after Penelope's death. She imagined her mother on that last endless night sitting at her dressing table, writing the few lines, folding the paper in triplicate, slipping it into the envelope. Puzzling over where to leave it. Not the coffee canister – Nora would dip into that as soon as she awoke; might find her too soon. Not beneath Nora's pillow in the upstairs bedroom. She had to know Nora would never sleep there again.

So, the truck, probably holding her breath as she crept past the trailer, hoping the sound of the truck's door opening and closing wouldn't wake Nora, sleeping – maybe – in the trailer just a few feet away. A smile of satisfaction at this final small feat. Then, hurrying back to the house and preparing a last cup of tea, swallowing a pill between each sip.

I won't ask your forgiveness for the unforgivable, Penelope wrote.

> My cowardice deprived you of a brother and him of a mother – and, worst of all, of a father. All because I didn't want people to think poorly of me. Now they will think the worst, and rightfully so. I hope you will leave Chateau and the rot within it behind. Just know that the same danger lurks in every town. In these past weeks, you've shown me that you're braver than I. I love you and, even more than that, I'm proud of you.

A greenhead fly flew through the open window, landed on her neck and helped itself to a great, bloodthirsty chomp. Nora smashed it against her skin, flung its carcass away and drove on.

ACKNOWLEDGMENTS

Eternal gratitude to my agent, Richard Curtis. Respect and a healthy serving of amazement to editor Carl Smith, who guided a manuscript written in the midst of the pandemic into coherence. Deep thanks to the rest of the Severn House team – Kate Lyall Grant, Natasha Bell, Katherine Laidler, Jem Butcher, Michelle Duff and Kathryn Blair. J.J. Hensley provided key gun-related phrasing. When I sought information about Porsches, Beth Major reminded me that Dennis Major (license plate: No Decaf) would have recommended a Boxster. Apologies to my parents for the heresy of giving the names of our beloved black Labradors, Kathleen Mavourneen and Michael Murphy, to Chesapeake Bay retrievers. In memory of Nell, who slept across my feet, effectively keeping me in my chair as I wrote. And, always, love to Scott for his unwavering support for this crazy writing life.